KRISTA HALL

BROKEN PLACES

For Mom,
With love

PROLOGUE

Sunday, February 16

LOLA SANCHEZ LEANED over the open trunk as she pulled the last hundred-dollar bill from her waistband and crammed it into a slit along the rim of the spare tire. Then she tugged her shirt—really more of a stretchy floral tent—over the bulk of her belly and tried to close her jacket against the frigid air of the dimly lit parking garage.

It was hardly worth the effort. At eight months pregnant, there was little difference in her girth now than when the money had been stuffed down the front of her maternity pants, and the edges of her jacket still wouldn't meet. Spring was only a few weeks away, though, so soon it wouldn't matter. With a sigh of impatience, she flipped the tire to hide the slit.

The spare was heavier, but not noticeably so. Ten thousand dollars—one hundred worn, green bills—didn't weigh much. Lola secured the tire in the wheel well and shut the trunk of the dull orange BMW. The sound echoed in the deserted parking garage beneath the New Hope Community Center on the eastern edge of the District of Columbia. At ten minutes past eight, she was alone. Her money was safe.

Eager to be on her way before the security guard's routine after-hours sweep of the parking garage, Lola fingered the key on the long pink velvet ribbon she wore around her neck. She slipped the makeshift necklace over her head and unlocked the driver side door of the old coupe. Her back ached. Her toes were little blocks of ice in her fake leather shoes. She longed to be in her room, snuggled under the covers of the bed she shared with her sister. Warm and safe.

But not yet. Bandit would be waiting at the side door of the community center. She was already late, and if she didn't show up soon, he might come looking for her. That would be almost as bad as getting caught by the center's rent-a-cops. She had to hurry.

She ducked her head through the loop of velvet and settled the cold key between her heavy breasts. Lola tugged the driver's seat forward so she could lean into the back and reach underneath it with the flat of her hand. Her fingers closed on the cold s-shaped curves of exposed springs, but that was all she felt.

Where is it? An icy trickle of unease slithered down her spine. She couldn't let Bandit go to Razor empty-handed.

The harsh squeak of brakes, echoing in the dead air of the parking garage, startled her. She pushed the seat back into place as quickly as she could, but was still wedged in the open doorway when a black sedan glided to a stop behind the BMW, blocking her in.

The passenger side window lowered with a hushed hum of sound. "Looking for something?" The rough voice brushed over Lola, raising tiny goose bumps on her arms.

The ominous click of the car door opening sent Lola scrambling out of the old clunker as fast as her bulk would allow. *Don't panic*, she told herself, straightening to her not very impressive height of five feet. A stranger wouldn't know that this wasn't her car. A stranger wouldn't know she was a thief and a liar.

Lola pasted a smile on her face. Everyone wanted to help a pregnant woman, especially one who was barely seventeen. She pushed her dark hair out of her eyes.

"Everything's fine," she said, willing the stranger to stay in his car and drive away. Pronto. There was still that rent-a-cop to worry about. And Bandit. *Go away, go away*, she silently chanted as if repeating the words over and over might give them power.

She heard the soft scrape of shoes against the concrete floor.

"Everything is not fine," the stranger said as he circled the front of his car and walked toward her, slow but steady. The hood of his gray parka was pulled low over his face, and his hands were gloved. Everything about him spoke of menace. "Did you think I wouldn't notice?"

She took one step back and then another.

"Do I know you?" She tried to make out his features, but they were hidden in shadow. *Run.* The thought came from somewhere deep inside her. It was the same instinct that had cautioned her not to tell anyone, not even Bandit, about her secret stash. She swiveled her head, searching for an escape route.

The elevator and stairs were a hundred yards behind her. Clutching her swollen belly, she made a sudden lunge forward, knocking the stranger off balance with her shoulder. Then she pivoted on her heels, her long hair fanning out like a banner. She raced toward the stairs.

"*Mierda*," she heard him grunt as he came rushing after her.

Her fear gave her speed, but he was faster. The sound of his rapid footsteps pounding against the concrete floor was her only warning before he grabbed her by the hair, the sting of pain bringing tears to her eyes.

With a feral sound of desperation, she jerked her head forward, leaving a hank of long black hair hanging from his tightly fisted hand. Ignoring the tearing pain, she ran faster, straining against the solid weight of the baby that slowed her down.

A few more steps. The door to the stairs was almost within reach. *Keep going. Don't stop now.* If she could just get to the fire alarm on the other side of the door, she could set it off and then the security guard who patrolled the community center would head down to the garage to investigate. Breathing hard, she gripped the cold metal door handle with both hands and pulled with all her might.

It was locked.

She only had an instant to feel the sickening slide of fear, and then the stranger was on her, trapping her against the door, smashing the tight melon of her belly against the unyielding metal. She couldn't think, couldn't move, couldn't breathe.

His gloved fingers brushed against her throat as he grabbed the key on the pink ribbon she wore around her neck, and lightly scraped its serrated edge against the flesh of her cheek. A promise of pain.

"Where's the money?"

Shock held her silent.

"Tell me, *puta*." The quick tap of metal against her temple was the only warning before he slashed the sharp point of the key across her forehead, leaving jagged cuts.

She bit down on the cry that swelled in her throat along with the temptation to give him what he wanted. She couldn't let him take her baby's money. She had worked too hard for it, risked too much.

"Where?"

Warm trails of blood snaked down her face. The ribbon tightened, and black spots crowded the edge of her vision.

The low rumble of the elevator as it descended from the main floor of the New Hope Community Center saved her from answering. The security guard was on his way at last. Her attacker heard it too. The ribbon eased. Inhaling in harsh, heavy sobs, Lola sagged against the door. He would run now.

Heat poured off him, burning her back where he pressed against her. He leaned his head closer to hers, tightening the ribbon again, choking her. She tried to free her hands, but he was still holding her against the door.

"I'll get it back," he whispered in Lola's ear.

The elevator groaned to a halt. Soon the double doors would slide open. Why wasn't he letting her go? His warm breath brushed against her face. Did he want to get caught?

Fueled by desperation, she turned her head in an attempt to loosen his grip. Her lips slid along the hard edge of his jacket zipper and caught on a scratchy square of Velcro. If she could figure out who he was, maybe she'd know how to get him to leave her alone. She raised her eyes and met his gaze.

Then he jerked the ribbon tighter.

ONE

Sunday, February 16

"*¡CHINGAZOS LOCOS!*" THE muffled cry from the hallway filtered into the overheated classroom in the New Hope Community Center, drowning out the quiet squeak of marker against whiteboard. Trevy Barlow turned, marker in hand, as more sounds bombarded the room—running feet and the crackle of a police radio. Ten pairs of eyes darted to the window set in the closed door at the back of the room.

"Wait here," Trevy said, forcing herself to sound calmer than she was. "I'll find out what's going on."

On her way to the back of the room, Trevy smiled reassuringly at the teenage girls an instant before the door swung open and a dark-haired teenage boy careened into her. She fell back against an empty desk as a District of Columbia policeman barreled into the room after him, gun drawn.

"Hey! There's no need for that," Trevy protested, her heart firmly lodged in her throat. "This is a classroom."

"*¿Dónde está?*" the teen demanded, his dark eyes searching the faces of the girls, who had all risen from their chairs by now. Their alarmed chatter filled the room. Trevy realized that she recognized him. He was the boyfriend of one of her no-show students, Lola Sanchez.

"*¿Bandit, qué pasa?*" one of the girls called out to him.

He ignored her and fixed his gaze on Trevy. "*¿Dónde está Lola?*"

Trevy slowly backed away from the teenager, who looked wild-eyed with panic. One of the girls in the room said in rapid-fire Spanish, "Lola didn't come tonight. We thought she was with you."

"*Sí, sí*," a chorus of agreement sounded behind Trevy.

"I was supposed to meet her before class, but I was late," Bandit answered in Spanish. He grabbed Trevy's arm. "*¿Dónde está?*" Where is she?

Before she could reply, the policeman yanked Bandit away. Trevy was relieved to see he had holstered his gun. Relieved, that is, until he pushed Bandit face first into the wall. Hard.

"Careful," Trevy said. "Don't hurt him."

"Hold still," the policeman grunted, ignoring her. He handcuffed Bandit's wrists with a plastic restraint. Then he keyed his radio. "Runner secured. He entered the building through a propped-open fire door on the east side. I'm on the main level. Third room on the left."

"Hey! *¡Páralo!*" Stop it, the girls protested. They crowded in behind Trevy.

The policeman glanced over his shoulder at them, his face a hard, pale oval beneath his hat.

"Quiet," he snapped, his mouth set in a line. He shoved Bandit into a chair. "Sit." He keyed his radio again. "I got ten teenage girls here, and a woman—" he paused to assess Trevy "—late twenties, early thirties. They know the gangbanger."

"Take names and hold 'em till Larsen gets there," came the static-filled reply. "He'll want to talk to them."

"Ten-four." He cut his eyes to Trevy. "You in charge?" His hand rested on the holster of his gun, an unspoken threat.

"What has he done?" Trevy cast a worried glance at the teenager who sat slumped on a metal chair, his face turned away from her, all of the fight drained out of him. Her eyes caught on the tattoo of a clenched fist, dark against the smooth skin of his neck. The gang symbol of Chingazos Locos. The girls shifted restlessly behind her. She could feel their fear pulsing against her like a living thing.

"Just answer the question," the policeman said. "Are you in

charge?"

"Yes. Trevania Barlow. I teach a literacy class for high school dropouts," she said, carefully neglecting to mention the girls' gang affiliation with Chingazos Locos. "The community center lets me use this classroom on Sunday evenings."

"I'll need to see some identification."

Dropping her gaze to the nameplate pinned on his dark blue jacket opposite the gold badge with the Metropolitan Police Department logo, she said, "My driver's license is in my bag, Officer Janklow." Then she pointed toward a large leather satchel in the corner near the whiteboard.

"Get it," he said, before shifting his glance to the nervous herd of teenagers standing behind her. "The rest of you, back to your desks."

The girls ignored him and followed Trevy to the front of the classroom.

"Wait here," she told them before returning to the policeman and handing him her license.

Officer Janklow jotted down her contact information in a small notebook he pulled from his jacket pocket. "How about him," he said, jerking his chin toward Bandit. "What's his name?"

"Bandit."

"His real name."

Trevy studied the officer for a moment, debating how forthcoming she should be. She shrugged. "Ask him."

Janklow's mouth tightened. "You don't know his real name?"

"There's no reason I would, Officer," she said, sidestepping the question. "He's just the boyfriend of one of my students."

The officer gave a small snort of disbelief and rubbed a hand across his forehead. "All right, Ms. Barlow. Let's move on to the girls. You must know their names."

The girls tittered nervously. She could sense one or two of them were ready to bolt from the room. They were afraid. In their world, the police were the enemy.

"Why do you need their names?"

"Let's start with her."

He pointed directly at Rosa. Of course he would choose one of the girls who was undocumented. And on the verge of panicking—Trevy could tell from the way she had sidled away from the others to better position herself for escape.

"I don't remember," Trevy said, lying without hesitation. She wasn't sure she trusted Officer Janklow not to detain Rosa, even though it was unlikely the teen was mixed up in the trouble Bandit had been running from.

"You don't remember!" Officer Janklow slammed a fist on the table. He stalked across the room. "What's your name?"

"*No hablo inglés,*" Rosa said in a quavering voice.

"I don't believe this." He jammed a hand on his hip. "How about you?" He looked at Angel, who stood next to Rosa.

Angel shrugged and raised her eyebrows in a parody of confusion. "*¿Qué?*"

"I've had enough of this bull." Janklow unsnapped his holster and fingered the handle of his gun.

It was an empty threat, Trevy told herself. But her heart rate increased just the same, fear settling in her stomach like a lump of ice.

"Each and every one of you is going to tell me your name and address."

"Why do you need that information?" Trevy asked again. "We haven't done anything wrong."

"If you don't cooperate, then we'll have to go down to the police station to straighten this out."

As if it had been choreographed, the girls all raced for the door at the same time.

Officer Janklow swore under his breath and drew his gun. "Nobody move!"

"Put your gun away," Trevy shouted over the din. She positioned herself between the officer and the stampeding girls. "Can't you see you've frightened them?"

On the verge of losing control, he waved his gun at her midsection. "Get out of my way!"

"Put the gun away, and they won't try to run," Trevy said even though she knew the gun hadn't fazed them. His threat of a visit to the police station had done that. Still, they'd all be a lot safer once Officer Janklow holstered his weapon.

The girls already had the door open, Rosa in the lead, when they suddenly pulled back. Another frightened murmur rippled through the group. They huddled closer together, giving Trevy an unobstructed view of the doorway. And of the man who stood there, filling the space with his powerful presence.

One glance explained why her students had frozen in place. It wasn't just his height or the breadth of his shoulders that made him so intimidating, but the tightly leashed energy that seemed to hum just beneath the surface of his skin. His black hair was a touch too long and a couple of days of stubble shadowed his hard jaw. Even the herringbone sport coat he was wearing—a half-hearted stab at respectability?—did little to soften the effect of his black T-shirt, faded jeans, and take-no-prisoners stare.

"Going somewhere, ladies?" His voice was deceptively soft, but it had more power to sway than the other man's gun.

Only Officer Janklow seemed immune. "About time you got here, Larsen. Things are going to hell."

Larsen's sharp gaze took in the room, a quick survey that seemed to miss nothing. "Put the gun away," he said with a quiet menace that was impossible to ignore.

Janklow scowled, but did as he was told. "If you can believe it, nobody in this room appears to speak English. Except for Ms. Barlow." He stabbed a finger in her direction. "And so far, she doesn't seem to know anyone's name except for her own. Oh, and his."

"Really." Larsen raised a dark brow. "Well, that's something, isn't it?" he said. Trevy thought she could detect the trace of a West Texas drawl. "What's his name?"

"Bandit."

"Bandit?"

"That's *all* Ms. Barlow can recall." Janklow's voice was heavy with sarcasm.

Trevy ignored Officer Janklow and moved closer to this man

called Larsen. He outranked the patrolman, that much was obvious. She didn't know whether that was good or bad. The new guy seemed like a hard-ass, but at least he wasn't waving a gun around like a lunatic. She and the girls had done nothing wrong, so they didn't deserve to be treated like criminals. Her glance cut from Bandit to the girls, who had regrouped by the whiteboard.

Larsen held his ground in the open doorway, effectively blocking the girls' escape route. His measuring gaze touched on Bandit before settling on Trevy. She opened her mouth to complain about Officer Janklow's outrageous behavior, but couldn't find the words. She was thrown off by his narrowed eyes. They were the color of pale green jade, cold and intense, all the more startling in contrast to the straight black brows that were arrowing downward in disapproval.

"Ms. Barlow?" he asked.

"Yes, Trevania Barlow. Who are you?"

His impenetrable façade slipped for an instant, his eyes showing a quick flash of surprise. And then, just as quickly, his shuttered expression was firmly back in place.

"Special Agent Larsen, ma'am." He pulled identification out of his jacket pocket and handed it to her.

"Diego Cruz Larsen," she read aloud for the benefit of the girls, who were watching her from the front of the room with a mixture of hope and fear in their eyes. They were counting on her to protect them. "FBI."

Interesting name, she couldn't help but think as she handed back his badge. Of course, the blending of cultures was as American as apple pie, baseball, and fireworks on the Fourth of July. She wondered what had brought an FBI agent to the community center on Sunday night. His unshaven face and casual attire spoke volumes. He hadn't planned on working this evening.

With a careless motion, doubtless one he'd made a thousand times before, he clipped his ID on the pocket of his jacket. "I'm with the Metro Area Gang Task Force," he said in a low voice, taking Trevy's arm and moving her out into the deserted hallway. "I'd appreciate your cooperation in this matter."

"Ms. Barlow doesn't know the meaning of the word cooperation," Janklow muttered under his breath as he took over Agent Larsen's position in the open doorway.

"I don't cooperate with gun-toting lunatics," Trevy retorted.

The tightening of his fingers on her arm was the only indication that Agent Larsen was annoyed by their sparring. His voice was deceptively calm when he said to Janklow, "It's Doctor Barlow."

"What?" Janklow replied, voicing the same one-word question that was bouncing around in Trevy's head.

"Dr. Trevania Barlow is a sociology professor at George Washington University. An expert on Latino gangs."

So, Agent Larsen was familiar with her work? He probably had no idea how much that meant to her. It was rare for her to get any acknowledgment outside of academic circles. Even rarer for someone in law enforcement to know her by reputation.

"You teach at GW?" Janklow asked her as if Agent Larsen might be trying to trick him.

"That's right."

"She also studies gangs in their natural habitats," Agent Larsen said, turning to Janklow, "and then writes books with weighty titles like *The Influence of Cultural Roots on Gang Formation*. The chapter on Latino gang symbols is a must-read." He glanced at her. "Are you here for more research, Dr. Barlow?"

"Research?" She tugged her arm free of his grasp, stung by the implication that she was using her students to further her academic career.

"This class is not about research," she said through clenched teeth. "These young women want to improve their reading skills and prepare for the GED. The school system has failed them. Miserably. I couldn't stand by without trying to do something about it."

"And then you'll write a book about it," he said, unconvinced. "A memoir if you're aiming for the bestseller lists."

"Pretty hard to pass the GED if you don't know English," Officer Janklow smirked.

"It's offered in Spanish," Trevy said, hands fisted on her hips.

She turned her glare to Janklow. And then Larsen. "What's wrong with you? We haven't broken any laws. Why are you harassing us?"

The patrolman stared straight ahead, conveniently deaf and dumb.

"Coward," Trevy muttered under her breath.

"Shut the door, Janklow." Agent Larsen waited until the door clicked into place, then he turned to Trevy. "There's a dead girl in the parking garage."

TWO

"LOLA SANCHEZ. THAT'S the name on her photo ID," Agent Larsen said, pinning Trevy in place with his hard green gaze. "Ever heard of *her*?"

The sarcasm was not lost on Trevy, but she was too shocked to care.

"I know her." The tremor in her voice made it impossible for her to continue without taking a deep breath first. "She comes here every Sunday with the rest of the girls. She was making such great progress. She wanted to be able to read to her baby." She slumped against the wall for support and looked up at Agent Larsen. "Lola was pregnant. Eight months. Did her baby survive?"

Agent Larsen shook his head, his mouth tightening. Black hair fell across his forehead and he brushed it back with an impatient hand.

"What happened? Was it an accident?" she asked, ignoring the sharp twist in her gut.

"No," he said in a voice so devoid of emotion that she mentally braced herself for the words that would surely follow. "She was murdered."

"How?" she managed to ask. She almost envied his self-control. She tried to swallow her grief, but it churned in her gut like nitroglycerin.

"That information isn't being released to the public."

Public? She wasn't the public. She was Lola's teacher. And friend. She folded her arms across her chest and looked away from him before he did or said anything to detonate the unstable mix of hot, messy emotions that felt too strong for her skin to contain. The last thing she wanted to do was to lose control around this man. She pushed away from the wall, moving to peer into the classroom through the window set in the top half of the door. Officer Janklow was still standing near the back of the room, guarding the door from any further escape attempts. Her gaze slid to Bandit. Hands cuffed behind him, he was slumped over in the metal chair, staring straight ahead without making eye contact with anyone.

A terrible conviction took hold of her.

"Lola's boyfriend, did he—? Do you think he—?" She couldn't finish. She felt shaky, hot and cold at the same time. Lola was dead. Her baby too. If she repeated the words enough times in her head, maybe she would start to believe them. The girls would be devastated when they found out. "Is that why Officer Janklow cuffed him?"

"He's cuffed because he ran away when Officer Janklow tried to question him."

"But he came into the classroom looking for Lola," Trevy said, turning her eyes toward the FBI agent. "And don't you need a better reason to detain someone? Probable cause, perhaps?"

Agent Larsen inhaled audibly. At the same time, the faint lines bracketing his mouth deepened for an instant. "Save the lecture on the Bill of Rights for your students. I'm more interested in learning why Bandit is hanging around the community center while his girlfriend is lying dead in the parking garage. Any thoughts, Professor Barlow?"

"Then he's not a suspect?"

"I didn't say that." He shifted, sticking a hand in the front pocket of his jeans. Trevy heard the jingle of change. "Now if you're done asking me questions, I have a few more for you."

"And if I don't cooperate, will your buddy cuff me too?"

Instead of answering, Agent Larsen opted for selective deafness. But the tightness in his jaw told her that he was hanging onto his calm, cool, and collected façade with both hands. "You said Lola came here every Sunday. Weren't you worried when she didn't show tonight?"

Trevy forced herself to focus on Agent Larsen's question. He was just trying to do his job, after all. And talking with him was easier than thinking about what had happened to Lola. "She's not very punctual."

"Is that why the fire door at the end of the hall was propped open?"

"I didn't know it was. The security guard in the lobby has a list of the girls in the class, so he would have let Lola in through the front doors."

"Then who would have propped open the side entrance to the building?"

"No idea. It's usually kept locked. Is that where Bandit was hanging out?"

Agent Larsen shook his head. Apparently resigned to the fact that he wasn't going to be the only one asking questions, he said, "Bandit was walking down the ramp to the garage. He took off when he spotted the first responders, and Janklow chased him into the community center. Through a door that should have been locked. Why would he go that way unless he knew it would be propped open?"

"That's a bit of a stretch," she suggested, but he shrugged off her doubt.

"You have a different explanation, Dr. Barlow?"

"I don't," she said, flinging up her hand. "None of this makes sense. Why was Lola in the parking garage in the first place? I don't think she even knows—*knew* how to drive."

"Maybe she was meeting Bandit. Or maybe someone drove her there. Someone she didn't want Bandit to know about."

"And Bandit was spying on her?"

"At this stage in the investigation guessing is a waste of time." He folded his arms across his chest. "Let's stick to what you know. When did you arrive at New Hope? And how'd you get inside the building?"

Trevy bristled at the implication that she'd been wasting his time, but the sooner she answered all his questions, the sooner she'd be free to talk with the girls. How was she going to find the strength to tell them about Lola? "I was running a little late, so I didn't get here until around 7:50," she told Larsen. "I parked in the garage and took the elevator to the lobby. After signing in at the security desk, I headed to this classroom."

"Anyone else in the garage? Anything strike you as off?" She started to shake her head, but he held up a hand. "Take a minute. Close your eyes and visualize it. Sometimes that helps."

She did as he asked, but nothing surfaced. "I drove into the garage. Security hadn't closed the entrance yet, which is normal. The guards usually wait until after I leave. I wasn't exactly looking, but I didn't notice any other cars. And I didn't see anyone until I got to the lobby. From there, I went straight to the classroom. The girls were already in here."

"Except for Lola?"

She snapped her eyes open and met Agent Larsen's intense gaze.

"Yes." The word left a bitter tang in her mouth. Had Lola been hiding somewhere in the garage? If only she'd paid more attention on the short walk from her car to the elevator. She might have seen her—

"And that wasn't unusual?"

"That Lola was late? No. Like I said, that happened a lot." Agent Larsen's question cut off her useless self-recriminations, an unintentional kindness that left her lightheaded with gratitude.

Until he shifted his gaze to the classroom door.

"I'm going to have to question them," he said. "Wait here. Don't leave."

As if she would go anywhere without talking to them first. Trevy set her hand on the doorknob as she peered through the inset window. The girls were doing their best to be invisible. Except for Angel, who was leaning against the wall and batting her kohl-lined eyes at Officer Janklow—typical behavior for her. A frisson of alarm slid through Trevy when the patrolman angled his head to get a closer look at the cleavage spilling from the neckline of the girl's tight blouse. When had he moved away from the door? Trevy turned the knob and pushed. "First let me tell them about Lola."

The FBI agent's eyes locked on her. "No," he said, moving into the open doorway to block her way.

"It would be kinder to let me—"

"Dr. Barlow, we're running an investigation here."

"Yo, Larsen"—a plainclothes officer with an MPD badge clipped to his jacket called from down the hallway—"I got something."

"I need a minute with Detective Alvarado," Agent Larsen told her and turned to greet the detective with a fist bump.

Trevy nodded and returned her attention to the girls. Officer Janklow was still leering at Angel. Determined to put a stop to that, she took a step toward the open doorway.

"Don't move," Agent Larsen snapped before she could cross the threshold. "And don't talk," he added when she opened her mouth to protest. He pointed to the wall opposite the classroom door. "Stand over there."

Clearly, he didn't trust her to obey. He and the detective huddled together just outside the open doorway, blocking her path into the room. She glared at the agent's broad back before leaning to one side to keep an eye on the teens. And Officer Janklow.

Then Trevy realized that standing on her toes gave her a clear view of Detective Alvarado's face. She strained to hear the detective, but he was speaking too softly.

Too bad for Agent Larsen, but she was fairly good at reading lips.

PG Police…Metro station…stolen black Camry. Trevy tried to make sense of his words. Alvarado's thick black mustache made the task more challenging. PG or Prince George's County, Maryland, was just across the DC line, less than a mile away. What did the Metro station and a stolen Camry have to do with Lola's murder? She tried to remember if she'd seen a black car in the garage, but she'd been in such a rush…

"Janklow, a word please," Agent Larsen called out, startling Trevy off her tiptoes. "That is, if you're not too busy." From her position in the hallway, she watched with interest as Officer Janklow tore his eyes from Angel's cleavage and slowly crossed the room, deliberately taking his time. He clearly didn't like following orders, and everything about his posture and expression broadcast that fact.

For an instant, Agent Larsen's gaze swiveled to Trevy. *Don't talk. Don't move,* his eyes telegraphed. Her breath stalling in her throat, she looked in the opposite direction and studied the closed doors lining the hallway.

From the corner of her eye, she saw Larsen turn to the policemen, and only then did she remember to exhale. Relieved that Janklow's attention had been diverted from Angel, Trevy hopped back on her toes, hoping for more lip-reading. Janklow stood in profile, so she couldn't see his mouth. But it didn't matter. He wasn't making much of an effort to speak softly. "What makes you think there's a connection?" Trevy heard him ask.

Agent Larsen's voice was a low, even rumble, betraying no hint of irritation. But his broad shoulders stiffened just the tiniest bit, Trevy noticed. Detective Alvarado frowned and cut his eyes toward Janklow as he brought the uniformed officer up to speed on the stolen Camry. In the second telling, Trevy filled in a few of the missing pieces: The stolen car had been found at the West Hyattsville Metro Station, just a five-minute drive from the community center.

When the detective added, "LDR was scratched on the hood," Trevy felt a cold weight settle on her chest. She dropped the pretense of disinterest and took a small step closer to the men. LDR—Los Diablos Rojos—was a rival gang. This was not good.

"Shit. Another turf war between the Diablos and the Chingazos?" Janklow said loudly.

"For Christ's sake, Janklow, keep it down," Detective Alvarado said, his gaze flicking to her before zeroing in on the patrolman. Disapproval deepened the downward vee of his dark mustache. "Janklow, I want you to follow up with PG—"

"The Diablos wouldn't attack the Chingazos," Trevy said, stepping toward the men. She couldn't stand the thought of Lola's death stirring up old, simmering resentments between the two gangs.

The trio of law enforcement officers turned to look at her with varying degrees of surprise. Except for Agent Larsen. Trevy watched as irritation and interest did battle across his features before his cop face dropped back into place. He motioned her closer and Trevy reluctantly obeyed.

"Eavesdropping, Dr. Barlow." It wasn't a question. Larsen pinned her with a gaze that almost made her sorry she had spoken up. He rubbed his temple as if warding off a headache. Then he asked, "Why rule out LDR?"

What kind of game was Agent Larsen playing? This shouldn't be news to him. Wasn't it the Gang Task Force's job to track this kind of activity? His cool green gaze drilled into her. Fighting the urge to increase the distance between them, she shifted her eyes to the MPD officers.

"The rivalry between the Diablos and the Chingazos died down last year when the Chingazos abandoned their territory in Southeast for turf in the Northeastern quadrant of the city."

"Then why'd some dirtbag carved *CL Puta* across the victim's forehead?" Janklow asked with a gotcha gleam in his eyes.

"No," Trevy said. She reached for the wall as her stomach performed a slow, grinding flip. Oh God, she was going to be sick. Using one hand to steady herself, she pressed the other to her lips and inhaled through her nose as a fresh wave of grief and horror threatened to swamp her.

"Zip it, Janklow," Agent Larsen said.

Trevy shifted her eyes from Officer Janklow's smirking face to the FBI agent's unreadable green gaze. She didn't want to believe the rivalry was heating up again, but what other explanation was there? "Let the girls go. I'll tell you what I can."

"After I question them," he said without apology, then turned to the detective. "Alvarado, follow up on the stolen Camry."

"I'm on it," Alvarado said. "Officer Janklow can guard the door. Nobody leaves or enters without Special Agent Larsen's say-so."

When Janklow opened his mouth to protest, the detective cut him off with a slash of his hand. "And I want your crime scene report on my desk by eight a.m. tomorrow. No excuses. Eight a.m."

"I wasn't exaggerating earlier when I said most of the girls don't speak much English," Trevy told Agent Larsen after the detective strode down the hall.

His lips quirked upward. "*Por suerte, yo hablo español.*" Luckily, I speak Spanish.

"Yes, lucky us," Trevy mumbled under her breath, following on Agent Larsen's heels as he entered the room and walked over to the girls. He introduced himself in fluent Spanish and was surprisingly gentle when he broke the news about Lola.

Momentarily robbed of speech, the girls turned pleading eyes on Trevy, as if beseeching her to tell them it wasn't true. Then Bandit surged to his feet. "No! Not Lola. Please, not Lola." His cry cut through the shocked silence, releasing the girls from their state of suspended animation. Moments later, the noisy outpouring of their grief mixed in with Bandit's loud sobs.

Unmoved by the raw anguish all around him, Officer Janklow shoved Bandit back into his seat with a clipped, "Shut up."

Trevy blinked back tears and shot a prodding glance at Agent Larsen, hoping to shame him into reprimanding the patrolman. But the FBI agent had his back to her and was busy dragging two chairs into the hallway. When he returned to the room, he allowed the teenagers a moment to exchange hugs and then assigned them to desks that would keep them separated until he could interview each of them. Numb with disbelief, the girls quietly obeyed. Even Bandit's wild sobbing settled into loud sniffles, though his grief was still painful to witness.

Officer Janklow resumed his post by the door, but his attention was on the private interviews in the hallway. Trevy positioned herself behind him so that she could keep a watchful eye on him and Agent Larsen.

The FBI agent maintained a non-threatening demeanor as he interviewed each girl. He listened intently, taking notes on a small spiral pad before calling for his next interviewee. Seated at the desk farthest from the door, Rosa was the last to be questioned.

"*¿Cual es su nombre?*" Agent Larsen said, his voice low and unintimidating. Trevy watched the teen squirm in her seat and then glance back at Angel, who still lingered near the open doorway, and Officer Janklow.

Uh-oh, Trevy thought, her chest tightening. Rosa was going to lie.

"Jennifer Lopez," she finally answered.

Trevy stifled a groan of dismay. Jennifer Lopez? Couldn't Rosa have come up with a better alias on the fly?

From his post at the door, Janklow snorted in disbelief. "She's lying, Larsen."

Rosa's pleading eyes locked onto Trevy. *Help me.* But before Trevy could intervene, Agent Larsen continued with his questions, ignoring the patrolman's comment. "*¿Dónde vive?*"

"Stupid *cholo*," Janklow muttered under his breath and the insult drained the blood from Trevy's face. Angel made a strangled sound of disbelief.

"You say something, Officer Janklow?" Agent Larsen looked dangerous, capable of anything, but his voice was quiet as his eyes zeroed in on the MPD officer. Trevy couldn't help but admire his self-control.

"J Lo? Come on. You know she's lying because she's illegal. But you're not going to do anything about it, are you?" Janklow's voice was a tight, angry slap. An accusation of unethical behavior.

Rosa started sobbing in earnest until Angel left the doorway to hiss something into her ear that made her stop.

So afraid for her student that she could barely breathe, Trevy tried to interpret the taut expression on Agent Larsen's face. What would he do next? Would he let Officer Janklow goad him into questioning Rosa about her papers? He was a federal agent, so he didn't have to follow the MPD's non-enforcement policies on civil immigration laws. Did he?

In answer, Agent Larsen stood and walked over to the MPD officer. "Do you need to reacquaint yourself with your department's policies?" When Janklow didn't reply, he said, "Good. Take Bandit to the station. I'll question him there."

If he was angered by the patrolman's insolence and bigotry,

Agent Larsen didn't let it show. He waited by the door until Janklow left with Bandit, and then returned to the empty chair in the hallway to continue questioning Rosa. As he sat down, he tossed a glance over his shoulder at Trevy and Angel. "The two of you, wait in the room. Away from the door."

Minutes later, Rosa slunk back into the classroom, Agent Larsen on her heels. He thanked the girls for their cooperation, and then passed out business cards. He saved the last one for Trevy, their fingers meeting for a heartbeat as she took it from his outstretched hand. "Dr. Barlow, I'll be in touch."

A promise or a threat?

As she searched for the answer in his hard green gaze, the girls crowded around her, talking and crying in a discordant chorus. Trevy watched the FBI agent leave the room. At the same time, she unearthed a small package of tissues from her purse and passed them out, giving each girl a hug and few words of comfort before sending them home.

It was nearly ten-thirty when Trevy turned her car onto the small side street near the C&O Canal where her Georgetown apartment was located. Fingers trembling, she keyed in the security code to enter the building's garage. The metal door rolled up and she drove her orange BMW down the ramp, keeping her eyes glued to the rearview mirror as the large door slid shut behind her. After tonight, the last place in the world she wanted to be was alone in another dimly lit garage.

She pulled into her spot and cut the lights. As she opened the door, she heard the beep of a car lock. So she wasn't alone after all. Relief washed over her as two men dressed in evening clothes strolled into her field of vision, heading for the elevator. The man in the lead tossed his keys into the air before pocketing them and then glanced over his shoulder and said something that made the other man laugh.

Rafael Montoyez, the Spanish diplomat who lived in the penthouse suite. And, if she wasn't mistaken, he was accompanied by the U.S. Trade Rep.

Trevy loosened her death grip on the steering wheel. Rafael was her brother JC's friend. If she hurried, maybe she could catch up to the duo.

In her haste to climb out of the car, she dropped her keys down by the brake pedal. By the time she retrieved them, the men were already in the elevator that would take them up to the lobby. There they would have to switch to the elevator that serviced the private apartments on the floors above. She flung up an arm. "Rafael, wait."

He was deep in conversation with the Trade Rep and didn't hear her until it was too late. Their eyes met for a split-second as the doors slid shut. All Rafael could do was send her a silent apology.

Defeated, Trevy let her arm fall. The loud clank of her keys banging against the side of her leg sent a fresh wave of anxiety surging through her. *Don't be such a scared little mouse.* She pushed away from the car. Her hearing on high alert, she swiveled her head from left to right as she speed-walked across the garage.

Perhaps it was better for her to be alone. *In a perfectly safe garage*, she added in an attempt to calm her racing heart, which lurched with each strike of her boot heels against the concrete floor. It wouldn't have taken much prodding on Rafael's part for all the horrible events of the night to come spewing out of her mouth in an unstoppable geyser. Memories of Lola surfaced in her mind. Bright eyes, a contagious laugh, and a steely determination to make a better life for herself and her unborn child.

Trevy stopped in front of the elevator door and pressed the call button. She desperately wanted to believe that teaching these at-risk teenage girls English language skills and helping them complete their GEDs would change their lives for the better. But that was so much harder to believe now.

Maybe she should cancel the Sunday evening classes.

Cold air stung her nose and tears pricked at the back of Trevy's eyes. What was taking so long? The lobby was only two levels up. She jabbed the call button until the deep thrum of the elevator motor signaled its descent. *Calm down, Trevy.* Soon she'd be in the brightly lit lobby where a security guard was stationed to keep non-residents away from the private floors of the building. The tightness in her chest loosened.

She took her first easy breath since leaving her car. Then the stairwell door banged open and every muscle in her body jumped in alarm. Her bag slid from her shoulder, scattering pens and papers across the floor, as she spun away from the elevator, ready to sprint across the garage.

"Dr. Barlow, is everything all right?"

"Joe?" She stopped mid-stride and pressed a hand to her hammering heart. It was the security guard from the lobby. Although concern had added a few more wrinkles to the aging guard's normally placid face, he was about as threatening as Mr. Rogers.

"Mr. Montoyez sent me down." The fluorescent lights gleamed off his bald spot when he squatted to collect her scattered belongings. "He didn't think you should be alone in the garage so late at night."

The guard straightened and held out her satchel.

"Thanks, Joe," Trevy said, forcing a smile. Taking a deep breath in an attempt to stop her body from trembling, she settled the strap on her shoulder and stiffened her spine. Time to stop acting like a scared fool.

Ten girls needed her now more than ever.

THREE

CRUZ LARSEN SLOUCHED behind the wheel of a piece-of-shit stakeout car at six a.m. on Tuesday. The sky was still dark, and a thick layer of low-hanging clouds promised rain. The government-owned sedan smelled like the inside of a chain-smoker's ashtray. Nursing a cup of overpriced coffee that had gone from extra-hot to cold in the hour he'd been waiting, he stared at the apartment building across the street. Dr. Trevania Barlow lived on the sixth floor.

Most stakeouts were dead boring. And this one was no exception. If Trevania Barlow had returned any one of the dozen or so urgent messages he'd left on her voice mail yesterday, he wouldn't have been reduced to skulking around her building at the crack of dawn like a damned stalker.

His eyelids felt like sandpaper, but at least they were still propped open. Even cold, the coffee was doing the trick. The interviews with the community center security guards and Dr. Do-Good's students hadn't yielded much new information. None of them had admitted to propping the fire door open or knowing anything about why Lola Sanchez might have been in the garage. Bandit probably could have shed a little light on the situation, but he'd refused to talk to anyone. Except Dr. Barlow. And then he'd gone to ground. Maybe permanently.

After the gang task force meeting, Cruz had spent the rest of Monday tracking down known members of Los Diablo Rojos and the Chingazos Locos. He'd even made a wasted trip to Dr. Barlow's building last night, but he hadn't been able to get past the security guard, not without the good doctor's permission. And there'd been no answer when the guard called her apartment to get the go-ahead.

No big surprise. He got it. She was avoiding him. Since she wasn't a suspect or even a person of interest in his investigation, he had let it slide for the moment and headed back to the Northeastern quadrant of the city to help his task force partner MPD Detective Lou Alvarado canvass the neighbors and interview more gang members. Well past midnight, he had gone home for a couple hours of shut-eye before returning to Dr. Barlow's building for this morning's stakeout. One way or another, he and the good doctor were going to have a long chat today.

In the distance he could hear the hum of cars and trucks on M Street as rush hour traffic began to build on one of Georgetown's major thoroughfares. Taking another sip of coffee, he scowled. Just how long would he have to wait before Dr. Do-Good decided to venture out into the great wide world?

Possibly hours. Academics weren't known for their nine-to-five schedules.

He sighed as he kept his eyes locked on the seven-story brick building. A quick Google search of the address on the professor's driver's license had revealed that the building was home to several diplomats and foreign policy gadflies, no doubt for its proximity to Foggy Bottom and the State Department. Dr. Barlow lived well for an untenured assistant professor. His gaze touched upon the fluted pilasters framing the glass-and-steel front entrance and then shifted to the elaborate frieze decorating the metal door of the underground parking garage. In a section of the city notorious for its lack of available street parking, she didn't even have to worry about finding a parking space for her 1970 BMW 2002, a vintage coupe that was still sporty despite its faded orange exterior. The royalties from her book sales must be keeping pace with the escalating gang violence claiming the blocks along the city's eastern border. Abandoned buildings, rundown housing projects, failing schools. *Broken places*, he thought, making a mental note to do a more thorough background check on her.

The wind off the river buffeted the car, seeping into every possible crack until the no-frills interior was no warmer than the outside air. Cruz pulled up the collar of his battered leather jacket. Just thinking about Trevania Barlow stirred up uncomfortable feelings. Jesus, the way she'd stood up to Janklow when he drew his gun. It would be a long time before he forgot his bone-deep horror at the sight of the MPD officer on the verge of losing control, Dr. Do-Good volunteering to be his target. Her determination to protect those girls went beyond reckless. It was stupid. And dangerous.

But he couldn't help admiring her just the tiniest bit. She was brave as hell. A real surprise that threatened to shake loose some of his notions about professional do-gooders.

And damn it, mixed in with that reluctant admiration for Trevania Barlow was a big hunk of resentment for her role in unearthing feelings that were best left buried. Not one do-gooder in his sorry excuse for a childhood had ever been brave enough to stand up for him the way Dr. Barlow had stood up for her students.

But he didn't like feeling sorry for himself any more than he liked thinking about a past he couldn't change, so he forced his thoughts back to the investigation. Trevania Barlow was a valuable asset: a person with boots on the ground Sunday night who might be able to help him nail the murderer before he hurt anyone else or caused an all-out gang war.

Shifting restlessly, he flexed his fingers to keep them warm. His breath fogged the air just as the front door of the apartment building swung open, emitting a woman dressed in running clothes —leg-hugging black pants and a slim red jacket. Hmmm. Nice. Very nice. Momentarily distracted, Cruz watched the swing of her excellent ass as she ran up the block toward M Street.

The day was improving by leaps and bounds. Right up to the moment when he realized that the babe in the tight running clothes was none other than Dr. Do-Good. With her hair covered by a red fleece hat, except for the caramel-colored braid swinging between her shoulders, she was well disguised.

Shit. He climbed out of the car and took off after her. At least he was wearing running shoes. And his jeans were old and flexible. But he sure as hell wished he had gloves.

When she headed west on M Street, he settled into an easy jog, allowing the distance between them to open up a bit more. He didn't want to stop her here. The narrow brick sidewalks were lined with stores and restaurants and, even this early, enough pedestrian traffic to make it difficult to have a private conversation. Feet pounding against the uneven bricks, he followed her when she crossed with the light and ran up Thirty-First Street, where the storefronts gave way to townhouses. She turned right on R Street, passing the gated entrance to the Dumbarton Oaks estate, and then entered Montrose Park.

An icy drizzle began to fall as Dr. Do-Good turned down a wide gravel path, taking her deeper into the wooded parkland that connected Georgetown to the Rock Creek Park trails. Icy droplets clung to his face and seeped into his clothes like the brush of clammy fingers. Oh, yeah, Cruz definitely hated stakeouts in the Capital City.

Rock Creek Park was an eight-mile strip of woodland dividing the city into east and west. Seen through the screen of barren trees, cars zoomed along a winding parkway already congested with commuter traffic from Maryland. The way his luck was going, he'd waste the entire morning following Trevania Barlow from Georgetown all the way to the city limits and back again with nothing to show for it except aching feet and a bad head cold.

Time for a new plan. The park trail was practically deserted. Only the hardy—or the fanatic—were out today. Cruz waited until a man in all-weather running gear trotted past Trevania Barlow before closing the distance that separated them. She heard him coming and glanced over her shoulder. She apparently didn't like what she saw, because she picked up her pace to a sprint.

Shit. It was an unfortunate fact of the city that lone women were vulnerable to attack in the more isolated parts of the running paths. It was little wonder that she was wary of being chased by a large guy in street clothes. He accelerated.

And so did she. She was much faster than he'd expected. It was just more bad luck that Dr. Do-Good was a champion sprinter. As he settled in for the long haul, his mood darkening with every wet slap of his running shoes, he considered letting her go. But she'd proved too adept at avoidance for him to waste this opportunity.

Carpe fucking Diem. The first seventy-two hours of an investigation were crucial. He let the rhythm of his arms and legs take over until his only thought was keeping Trevania Barlow's red jacket in view. She couldn't keep up this world-record-setting pace forever. And then the advantage would be his.

After another couple of minutes of misery—all uphill—her pace finally slowed. She swiveled her head from side to side in search of escape. Or help. Neither option presented itself.

"Dr. Barlow," Cruz called out, wanting to ease her panic and end this ridiculous race.

But she didn't stop.

Probably couldn't hear him over the pounding of her heart as adrenaline flooded her system. He knew that feeling well. The difference was that he was used to it and could control it. He felt a moment of regret—should he really be involving this woman in his case, drawing her into the ugliness and danger of his world?—but he ruthlessly pushed it away. He had a job to do. There was more at stake here than Trevania Barlow's sensibilities.

She tripped on a tree root in the path and went down hard. A cry of surprise and pain ripped from her throat. Hands angled in front of her body, she slid across dirt and gravel.

"Stay away!" She scrambled to her feet and began to run again.

But it was too late. Cruz was on her in a flash. He grabbed her arm and spun her into his body, holding her locked against him as she struggled.

"Easy," he said, moving them both to the edge of the path. "I'm not going to hurt you, Dr. Barlow."

At the sound of her name, she stopped thrashing about like a trapped rabbit and looked up at him. He could feel the trembling of her body. Then sudden recognition flared in her eyes. Eyes that were not plain brown as he'd first thought, but an unusual mix of brown and green and gold. Woodland fairy eyes. Easy to miss at first glance.

"Agent Larsen?" she asked in a breathless contralto that warmed him even in the freezing drizzle. She shoved against him with her scraped hands. This time he let her move away. "You scared me. I thought you were a—"

"Rapist? Murderer?"

"I was going to say a mugger. You were following me."

"Yes," he said, unrepentant. "We need to talk."

"Here? Now? Why couldn't you just call me to set up an appointment like a normal person?" She studied her palms for a minute before blowing on them.

Cruz clenched his teeth. A mixture of rain and sweat trickled down the back of his neck in a steady drip, soaking his shirt collar and heading south toward his shoulder blades.

"If you'd returned even one of my messages *like a normal person*, we could have arranged to meet somewhere dry. And warm." He grabbed her hands. She was wearing gloves, but the fabric was torn and dirty. He could see shallow cuts along the outside edge of one palm. "You'll live," he said.

Even gloved, her fingers heated his skin.

"I appreciate the sympathy," she said tartly, tugging her hands free, taking away her warmth. A shiver chased down his spine. "I would have called you today."

He arched an eyebrow in disbelief.

"I don't suppose you have any Band-Aids tucked away in your pockets," he said, letting his gaze travel over her. Did her form-fitting pants even have pockets?

"No," she said, not amused by his insinuation, "running isn't usually a dangerous sport."

"Except in an effing ice storm," he grumbled before he cut himself off. He had alienated her enough for one day. All he wanted to do was ask her a few questions. And get out of the damned freezing rain.

"Hardly an ice storm." Trevy shrugged. "A little rain never hurt anyone. What do you want, Agent Larsen?"

"I want to talk to you about Lola Sanchez."

"Me? All I do is research and write books, remember?"

He should have kept his thoughts to himself when he questioned her on Sunday. Now he was going to have to eat those words. And possibly more. He cleared his throat. "That's exactly why your cooperation is crucial. You've been studying the Chingazos Locos gang. You know the key players."

When she didn't reply—just stared at him as if he'd been speaking in some dead language—he shifted uncomfortably and added, "They trust you. They'll talk to you."

"Isn't that your job, Agent Larsen? To get them to talk to you?"

Bull's-eye, Dr. Barlow. Hell yeah, it was his job. But that would take time. Time he didn't have. Not when every known gang member in the eastern quadrants of the city, including the teens in Trevy Barlow's literacy class, had sealed their lips with Super Glue.

Except for Hector Bonilla, aka Bandit.

"Bandit's the only Chingazo who'll talk to me. But only if you're there."

"Is he under arrest?"

Larsen spread his arms wide. "No reason to hold him. A mile-long rap sheet of petty crimes and proximity to a murder aren't enough for a prolonged stay in the city jail."

"But he's still a suspect?"

"Everyone without a rock-solid alibi is a suspect. Bandit is the Chingazos' most prolific tagger, right?"

"Yes, but what does that have to do with the investigation?"

"A twelve-year-old kid on his way home last Sunday saw someone in an alley near New Hope spray-painting a message on the brick wall at around seven-thirty."

That got Dr. Do-Good's attention. She took a step toward him, and for a moment he thought she was going to reach out and touch his arm. But then she checked herself and let her hand drop to her side, her mouth flattening as she clamped down on whatever she'd been about to say. He tried to ignore the instant spurt of disappointment he felt even as he wondered why she'd changed her mind. And how he was going to drag it out of her anyway.

Then she surprised him, her curiosity apparently overriding her distrust. "Did this kid recognize the writer?"

Interest glittered in her pretty hazel eyes. He thought he saw concern there too.

"You mean the guy defacing private property?" he asked, unwilling to acknowledge the tagger as anything more than a common vandal.

A terse nod was her only response.

"Nope, the kid didn't recognize the guy hitting up the wall. A man in a dark parka with the hood up. That's all I've got. Sound like anyone you know? "

Dr. Barlow's expression of disbelief was almost comical. If a thought bubble had appeared over her head, it would have said, *Get real, Agent Dumb Shit.*

"At least half the city's male population fits that description, Agent Larsen, as I'm sure you know. I doubt it was Bandit, if that's what you're thinking. I've never seen him in anything other than an Oakland Raiders jacket."

Cruz didn't think Bandit had hit up the wall. But he had a hunch that the gangbanger had been involved in something on Sunday. Something illegal. Maybe even big enough to get Lola Sanchez killed. And Cruz wanted to know what it was. The success or failure of this investigation might depend on that missing piece.

Keeping that thought to himself, he said, "Bandit might be able to give us a lead on the tagger."

"I suppose," she shrugged. "What did your mystery man in the dark parka write?"

Damn, now she was mocking him. He felt a small, inappropriate grin tugging at one corner of his mouth. He couldn't help it. He liked a woman who wasn't afraid to take a verbal pot shot now and then. Especially a woman as buttoned-up as Dr. Trevania Barlow. It made him wonder what else she was hiding underneath her do-good exterior. Everyone had secrets.

"I don't know," he admitted. "Between Sunday evening and Monday, when I went to look at the wall, someone had covered the message with a layer of spray paint."

If that meant anything to Dr. Do-Good, she wasn't sharing.

She just tapped a finger against her plump lips and said, "Hmmm." As she processed the information, her shoulders visibly relaxed. She leaned closer.

Cruz tore his gaze from her rain-dampened mouth. Ogling Dr. Do-Good wasn't going to get his job done. He had a homicide to solve, he reminded himself.

"Does the writer in the dark parka have anything to do with the stolen car found at the West Hyattsville Metro station? The one with the LDR markings?" she asked, not bothering to pretend she hadn't been eavesdropping that night in the community center.

She knew about the Camry, but that didn't mean he was under any obligation to confirm her guess about the driver's identity. Surveillance video had captured the image of a person in a dark parka with the hood pulled up driving into the commuter lot at West Hyattsville about fifteen minutes after the New Hope security guard found Lola Sanchez with a pink velvet ribbon wrapped around her neck like a tourniquet.

But that was proprietary information, so Cruz just shrugged. He watched the expression in Trevania Barlow's eyes flatten before she turned her head to look at the trail leading back to Georgetown. She was ready to *adios*.

"Agent Larsen, I don't know who your tagger is, but I'll talk to Bandit. Tell me when and where."

Securing her cooperation should have felt more like a victory, but it was a hollow one. Cruz still had one more obstacle to overcome. And it was a gamestopper. "When was the last time you saw Bandit?"

"Sunday. At the community center." She stared at him for a moment, then comprehension sparked in her eyes. "You don't know where he is."

"Haven't seen him since he left the Fifth District Station. His mother said he hasn't been home since Sunday morning. Any ideas?" And Christ, it stung to admit that to her.

She was shaking her head before he even finished the question.

"The girls in your literacy class might know where he's hiding."

"Forget it, Agent Larsen," she said, each word a terse, sharp-edged slap of sound. Dr. Do-Good knew exactly where this discussion was heading.

"Why don't you want to talk to me? Have you been threatened by someone?"

"How long do you think the girls will continue to trust me if I let you use my relationship with them to pin the murder on Bandit?" She folded her arms across her chest. He thought she was finished speaking, but then she added, "Whether he's guilty or not."

"Why would I do that?"

"Isn't the boyfriend or the husband always the first person you look at when a woman is murdered?"

A tight jerk of his head was all Cruz could manage. So she thought he was looking for an easy target to blame for Lola's death. Well, it wouldn't be the first time someone had thought the worst of him. He was surprised by how much it stung.

"Bandit's the easy answer," she said, unfolding one arm and holding up her hand. She began listing the reasons one finger at time. "He's the boyfriend. He was seen running from the scene of the crime. And a quick arrest gets the mayor off your back. She doesn't want gang violence marring her cross-border crime initiative."

"As head of the gang task force I'm going to do whatever it takes to keep the violence from escalating," he said through clenched teeth. "And the best way to do that is to arrest Lola Sanchez's killer. The *real* one."

"Because you care so much about the mayor's initiative?"

"I don't give a damn about the mayor's initiative." His jaw had tightened to the breaking point.

"Really?" She took a step back, increasing the distance between them. "The New Hope Community Center is the crown jewel of the initiative. Seems to me that the mayor has good reason to be concerned, especially if she hopes to defeat her challenger in the April primary. Didn't she promise the citizens of DC that the annual murder rate would decrease during her administration, especially along the border with Prince George's County? I haven't noticed much improvement, even with the mayor's cross-border crime initiative."

"Then help us, Dr. Barlow," he said, putting his simmering indignation on hold to seize the opening she'd inadvertently given him. "Help us keep a lid on it. That part of the city could explode. Christ, this is the capital of the United States and yet there are neighborhoods here that even I'm afraid to go into unarmed. What's the average citizen supposed to do? What about those girls you're trying to help? You don't want more of them to end up like Lola, do you?"

A cheap shot, even for him. But he was feeling mean.

She took another step back, her eyes dropping to her bloodied hands.

He was not going to apologize for being an asshole. Not when so much was riding on her cooperation. He studied her downcast eyes. Her wet lashes were rich, dark crescents against her damp skin. Despite everything she'd said, despite her low opinion of him, his fingers twitched with the urge to touch her. He shook it off, forcing himself to concentrate on the real reason he was out here in the cold.

For a long moment she didn't speak. When she finally raised her gaze to meet his, outrage burned in her eyes. Good. He wanted her angry. So fucking mad she'd rip off those rose-colored glasses and take a good hard look at the real world. Then maybe she'd see what he saw. Violence didn't care about good or bad, innocent or depraved, right or wrong.

"I can't help you find Bandit," she said, breaking the silence between them. *Can't.* He hated that word. It meant failure and delay. His hands tightened into fists. What would it take to convince her? "Why aren't you talking to the Diablos?"

"I am." He blinked away the icy rain that dripped into his eyes to better read her expression. "They all have alibis. They were hanging out in an apartment in Southeast."

"They could be lying."

"Everyone lies to law enforcement, Dr. Barlow. Some out of guilt. Others out of embarrassment or the desire to protect someone." He paused to let Dr. Do-Good digest that little tidbit.

"If this homicide isn't solved quickly, more innocent people are going to get hurt. Can you live with that?"

Didn't she understand that the only way to stop the senseless bloodshed was to work with him?

"Can you?" he demanded.

"Tell me how Lola died." A note of pleading entered her voice.

"No" he said, even though the answer was burning a hole on his tongue. He wanted to tell her. Maybe it would get her to cooperate. Nothing less than unconditional surrender was going to get the job done. "Tell me what she was doing in that parking garage."

"I don't know." This time there was little force behind her refusal. Her resistance was crumbling.

"Talk to the girls. See if they know why Lola was there. Or where Bandit is hiding." When she didn't answer, he pushed harder. "I'm not the enemy."

The minute he'd spoken, he wanted to call back those last four words. He should never have framed the allegiances in this case so starkly—us against them. It was the wrong tack to take with someone who lived in the gray areas of a black-and-white world.

Sure enough, she raised her chin, a don't-fuck-with-me expression on her face. "You're not a friend, either. Call me when you find Bandit." She walked around him, back to the dirt trail.

Cruz didn't try to stop her when she broke into a run. He just clenched his hands into tight fists and watched her get away.

FOUR

THE CITY WAS never completely dark. Not even at ten minutes till ten on a Wednesday evening. The street lamps lit the way for Bandit. He tried to keep his pace unhurried—purposeless—when he left the low-rent motel where he'd been hiding out and walked three blocks to the New Hope Community Center. His baggy clothes hid the cans of spray paint that clanked against one another with every step he took. He'd stashed a few in the large front pocket of his hoodie and was carrying the rest in the pockets of the Oakland Raiders jacket he wore over his sweatshirt.

Lo-la, Lo-la, her name echoed in his head, pulsed through his blood with every footfall until he could think of nothing else. A black rage howled through him like a hot El Niño wind. *Lo-la*. He had loved her. He still did and didn't know how to stop. Even now when it was hopeless. Razor and the others would laugh at him if they knew. "Be a man," they'd tell him. "Strike back, then move on."

But he didn't want to strike back. All he wanted was his girl. He turned the corner and walked north, keeping to the shadows as much as possible. There wasn't a lot of traffic on the streets, but that didn't mean a car full of Los Diablos Rojos wouldn't come ripping around the corner, looking to kick ass. One lone Chingazo would be dead meat.

A block away from the community center, Bandit ducked into an alley. He felt a little safer until he noticed the shapeless stain on the brick wall. What the fuck? It looked like someone had started to paint the entire wall black before giving up, leaving an ugly mess.

His fingers slid against the cold surface of one of his spray cans. Maybe he could even out the edges and spray CL in white block letters—

What was he thinking? He shook off his stupid urge to reclaim the wall for the Chingazos. Flattening himself against the paint-stained bricks, he glanced back over his shoulder, a nervous habit he couldn't shake. Not a soul in sight. Only *vatos locos* were out on night like this. Although the rain had stopped, it was still cold. Not good for what he had in mind. But he didn't give a shit. He had a job to do.

Her name drummed in his ears—*Lo-la, Lo-la*—as he followed the alley to the end of the block. Up ahead, the New Hope Community Center gleamed—clean, unbroken, and shiny as a rich *chica* slumming with homeboys for thrills. He wanted to break all the windows. Fill the empty rooms with gasoline and light a match. Strap dynamite to his chest like a suicide bomber and blow the place to bits.

But he was chickenshit.

The only sound in the night was the rattle of the paint cans in his pockets. His weapon of choice. He poured on speed, his boots pounding against the wet asphalt, setting off icy sprays of water that soaked the bottoms of his baggy jeans. The rough scrape of the brick against his Raiders jacket set his teeth on edge as he slid along the back wall of the community center. Moving into the shadows, he let out a swift breath of relief. Time to get to work. He reached into his pockets for the spray paint.

Dark shapes came at him from the shadows. Bandit fell back and raised his fists, letting the paint cans crash to the ground and roll between his feet. The slow, steady thud of anger in his heart was replaced by the more rapid beat of fear. It was too late to run.

Razor, the leader of the Chingazos Locos, stepped out of the shadows and grabbed him by the front of his jacket. "*Hola*, Bandit. *¿Qué pasa?*" He kicked at one of the cans of spray paint and waited for an answer.

Bandit dropped his fists. "The wall of the community center," he said, each word pulled from him against his will. He didn't want

Razor messing with his tribute. "I was going to paint it for Lola." He bent down and gathered the loose cans.

"I got a better plan." Razor shoved him toward the black Lincoln Navigator that was parked nearby. "Get in."

GQ turned from the passenger seat to smile back at Bandit. His gold-capped front teeth glinted in the overhead light that cut through the darkness when Razor opened the front door to climb behind the wheel.

"Bandit," GQ said, "you're gonna like this. Guaranteed. For Lola."

A cold ball of ice formed in Bandit's stomach. He doubted he was going to like what Razor had in mind. But protest wasn't an option. Razor was the boss.

As they traveled south, away from the New Hope Community Center, his survival instinct kicked into high gear. The fact that Razor was driving through the quiet streets like a model citizen only increased his alarm. Even the car speakers, which were blasting tracks from Daddy Yankee's *Barrio Fino en Directo* album, were pitched several decibels below earsplitting. Whatever he had planned, Razor didn't want to draw attention to himself.

Yet.

GQ leaned across the seat and handed Bandit a 9mm semi-automatic. "For Lola, eh?"

"For Lola," Bandit echoed. Now he understood. Revenge would be Lola's tribute, not a stupid tag painted by some *pendejo* who thought he was Pablo-fucking-Picasso. *This is the way it should be*, he told himself fiercely. Someone deserved to die. Someone deserved to feel the same pain. His hand shook as he looked down at the gun and tried to man up for the task ahead.

The car slowed. They must be getting close now. They rolled past the 7-Eleven on the corner. Bandit glanced out the window. Nothing promising. A couple of girls climbed out of a car and hurried inside.

They drove several blocks south, passing a squat brick apartment building in Diablos territory. More nothing. Razor kept going, a shark trolling for prey.

The third time they passed the apartment building, a group of four people spilled into the rectangle of light cast by the open door.

"Now," Razor shouted without looking back. He pressed the buttons on his door panel and the windows on the passenger side of the car slid down.

"*¡Chingazos Locos!*" GQ yelled.

Bandit pointed the gun out the window.

Somebody cranked the volume on the radio.

The aggressive bass beat of "Gangsta Zone" filled Bandit's head, pushing away the sound of his blood pounding in his veins, pushing away all restraint. He closed his eyes and squeezed the trigger until nothing was left but empty clicks.

Shouts from outside the car.

A stray bullet nicked the side mirror with a high whining ping.

GQ shouted, "*¡Vámonos!*" Go!

The roar of sudden acceleration. The scream of tires as Razor took a turn too fast.

Chaos vibrated through Bandit as he clutched the gun like it was the only thing keeping him from flying into a million pieces.

"Beginner's luck," GQ said with an excited laugh. He grabbed the 9mm from Bandit. "I counted two down."

Bandit forced his eyes open. He had honored Lola by taking down a couple of Diablos. The enemy. Shouldn't he feel better? He tried to churn up some of the anger he'd felt before. He had done it for her. *Lo-la, Lo-la*, her name was a hollowed-out beat deep inside him.

Minutes later, Razor parked the car so that the headlights spotlit the wall of a run-down brick building deep in Diablos territory. The windows were broken and the front door was boarded up. Razor climbed out of the car. "This is where you paint your RIP," he told Bandit.

The wall was covered in LDR graffiti. Bandit stared at it until the images blurred together. He had shot two people. Maybe even killed them. Until now, he had believed God would forgive him for all the petty crimes, the screw-ups. But there would be no forgiveness for this sin. He was going to hell and nothing he could do would change that. The thought paralyzed him and he couldn't find the strength to open the car door.

Razor yanked it open for him. Tossing a sharp knife from hand to hand, he glared at Bandit. "Do it now, *vato*."

Reluctantly, Bandit left the warmth of the car. He pulled a headlamp from his pocket and slid it on his head. Clicked it on. A circle of light chased across the graffiti-covered wall as he stooped to carefully line up the cans of spray paint on the sidewalk near his feet. Without checking the color, he grabbed the closest can and sprayed. An outline of a fist bloomed on the wall. Blood red.

He worked for nearly an hour, pausing only to switch an empty can for a full one or one color for another. Every now and then, Razor interrupted with demands of his own. "No *placas*," he ordered when Bandit started on the signatures. "First letters only." Spraying medium-sized round letters, he wrote: *Somos* B, R, G. He finished his tribute with praying hands and the interlocking C and L tag that he had designed. *For Lola*, he thought.

But Razor wasn't finished. He wanted Bandit to add *ratos* to the LDR tags that hadn't already been painted over by his tribute to Lola. Then he tapped the wall below the signature letters. "Add *trece*."

Retreating into a zombie-like state that kept him from thinking about what he'd done, Bandit followed Razor's order. There was just enough paint left to form the number thirteen. Bandit let the empty can fall from his numb fingers. It rolled off the curb.

GQ kicked it as he walked over to the storm drain, then tossed the gun in after it. "Let's go," he said to Razor. "I'm freezing my ass off."

"Not yet." Razor shoved Bandit against the wall and used one hand to press his knife to his throat, the other to thrust his phone in Bandit's face. There was a picture on the screen. "Look at it."

At first Bandit didn't understand. He squinted to get a better view of the screen without leaning into the sharp edge of the blade at his throat. It looked like a picture of the brick wall in the alley by the community center. *But that can't be right*, he thought, remembering the dark stain that now covered most of the wall. The words, which had been sprayed on the wall in uneven white lines, were hard to read on the small phone screen. "What does it say? Did LD Ratos hit up our wall?" Bandit asked, referring to Los Diablos Rojos as devil rats.

"It's a *trucha*." A warning. Razor held out the phone to GQ. "Read it to the *idiota*."

Bandit took shallow breaths while GQ squinted at the screen. In halting English that was simple enough for even an *idiota* like him to understand, GQ read, "CL *Puta* stole $10K, give it back or die, *soy trece*."

Soy trece. I am thirteen. Bandit's insides turned to water.

"What ten K, Bandit?" Razor wanted to know. "You been stealing money?"

Lola had been so certain no one would notice a few thousand dollars missing from *El Trece's* profits. And now she was dead. His gut churned. He hadn't honored Lola. He'd shot at people who had nothing to do with her. *Nada*. How was he going to live with that?

Razor pressed the sharp edge into Bandit's skin until a trickle of blood ran down his throat and then jerked the knife away. "Where's the money?" he said, his flat inflection cutting into Bandit's thoughts. It was hard to believe, but his problems had suddenly become worse. Ten thousand times worse.

"I don't know. Lola—"

Razor shook him. His head banged against the wall. Tiny spots of white light danced in the dark. "Don't hide behind a dead *puta*. Where is it?"

"I'm being straight with you. Lola took the money. Not me." He hadn't known Lola was a thief until last month when he'd caught her stuffing hundred-dollar bills from *El Trece's* payoff into her pockets. A thousand dollars at most, not ten thousand. She had sworn it was the first time. Just enough to help with the hospital bills for the baby.

And he had shit for brains. How else could he explain why he'd believed her?

Ten thousand dollars. Lola must have begun stealing money a few months after their first trip to New York City in the U-Haul truck filled with contraband cigarettes. She was a thief. And a liar.

"Swear to God, Razor, I don't know where she hid it."

"You got Lola's key, right?" Razor asked, getting up in Bandit's face.

"Yeah, I got it," Bandit lied. Lola had always worn the key to the old BMW on a pink ribbon around her neck, which meant the police had it now. But he knew she had another copy; it had been his idea to get the spare made. "Do you still want me to move the next shipment?"

Bandit didn't know if their cargo was stolen or counterfeit. He didn't give a shit. All he knew was it was illegal to haul thousands of cigarette cartons from DC to New York City. Even someone with shit for brains could figure out that there was money to be made in smuggling cheap cigarettes north.

And it was safer than selling pot or cocaine.

Chingazos were the middlemen and raked in a three percent cut of the profits with every successful delivery. *El Trece* got the rest. Easy money that made life on the streets pretty good—even if Razor kept the biggest share of their take for his fancy car and roving lifestyle, while providing for the gang by doling out weapons and walking-around money. And buying extra protection from the MS-13 clique in nearby Prince George's County didn't come cheap. Lola's medical bills hadn't been a gang priority.

Razor grunted and shoved him away. "Yeah, I want you to drive. You know the route."

"Like the back of my hand." The knot of fear in Bandit's chest eased. Lola had always gone with him when he drove the shipments north, but he could do the drive by himself, easy.

Then a new worry flashed through Bandit's overheated brain.

How was he going to get the delivery instructions from *El Trece*? That had been Lola's job. And while he wasn't about to admit it to the others, he had no idea where Lola kept the extra BMW key. His eyes caught on Razor's flat black gaze. Was he off the hook for the money? Hopeful, Bandit said, "I'll get some black paint to cross out the *trucha*."

Razor bared his teeth in the snarl that had earned him his street name. Light from Bandit's headlamp caught on the razor-sharp points of his broken front teeth. He grabbed the front of Bandit's jacket and said, "GQ took care of it."

Understanding bloomed in Bandit's brain. The ugly black paint on the alley wall near the community center was covering *El Trece*'s warning. A simple crossing out wouldn't have been nearly enough to satisfy Razor. All he had was his pride, and he would protect it all costs.

"Next Sunday," Razor said, "bring the ten thousand dollars so we can give it back to *El Trece*. Ain't no way it's coming out of my cut. It's all on you, Bandit. However you can get it."

Then just for the hell of it, Razor backhanded him, and Bandit's mouth filled with blood. "And don't even think of running," he warned.

Razor and GQ drove off, leaving Bandit deep in enemy territory. Bile rose up in his throat, mixing with the bitter taste of blood. He fell to his knees, puked out his guts.

At that moment, he didn't know who he hated more. Razor. Or Lola, for getting him into this mess.

He wiped his hand across his bruised mouth. Instinct had him pushing to his feet and moving deeper into the shadows. The only way to get to Northeast safely was to become invisible.

Along the way, he had to figure out where Lola had hidden the key to the BMW.

And find ten thousand dollars.

FIVE

THE SOFT GLOW of the computer was the only light in his loft apartment. Cruz sat hunched over it, his eyes moving rapidly across the screen as he scrolled down pages with a few flicks of his finger across the touchpad.

The Chingazos Locos would not let Lola's death go unavenged. Cruz knew that like he knew his own name. And thanks to one of the first responders at the crime scene—Officer Janklow, perhaps—word had leaked out about the getaway car with LDR scratched across the hood. With the rumor on the street that Diablos were responsible for Lola Sanchez's death, the feud between the rival gangs was bound to heat up again.

But he could stop all that if he could get his hands on Bandit. He was convinced the gangbanger knew something about his girlfriend's murder. Something that would give him a solid lead to make an arrest.

Something Bandit would only tell Dr. Barlow.

Without a doubt, Trevania Barlow had lied to Officer Janklow Sunday night at the community center when she'd claimed not to know her students' names. He'd written that off as a misguided effort to protect them. But had she lied again yesterday when she said she didn't know where Bandit was hiding out?

Cruz logged into another public database. He wanted to know everything there was to know about Trevania Barlow. Maybe then he could figure out a way to gain her trust. With the mayor riding his ass to make some arrests and the magic seventy-two-hour window closing fast, Dr. Do-Good was his best lead. She could secure insider information from the girls that he wouldn't be able to get from days of questioning.

By midnight, he had a pretty thorough timeline of the major events in the sociology professor's life—places she'd lived, her alma maters, and high-profile social shindigs she'd attended. Even a six-month oops of a marriage a decade ago at age twenty-two, followed by a quick divorce and grad school.

She'd been born with a silver spoon in her mouth and a big, fat trust fund with her name on it. All he'd been born with were his wits and his fists. No wonder he'd failed to enlist her cooperation. A reformed thug like him had little hope of getting through to a do-gooder debutante who thought she could change the world with hand wringing and sympathy. A swift kick in the pants was what he'd needed to pull himself together. And the military had given him just that, with an assist from his former platoon sergeant and current task force partner: Lou Alvarado.

Maybe Alvarado could get through to her. Cruz pulled his phone from his pants pocket and called the detective. It was late, but Lou might still be awake.

Or not.

The call went to voice mail. "Call me," Cruz said, then hung up.

He and Alvarado had always been a good team, yet Cruz felt oddly deflated by his decision to hand off the sociology professor —a feeling that was not lessened by its irrationality. He closed his eyes for a minute, but instead of blank darkness, he conjured up Trevania Barlow's face. Her eyes were so serious. Camouflage eyes, the color of leaves and moss. You had to look closely or you might overlook their beauty.

Scrubbing a hand over his face, he shifted his shoulders to ease the sudden tension in his back. What was up with him? It was completely irrelevant that she had pretty eyes and hair the color of his favorite caramel candies. She was a source, pure and simple, even if she did move him in a way that a woman hadn't in longer than he cared to think about. He shut down his computer. Time to get some badly needed sleep. And maybe let his subconscious work on the more important problem of who had killed Lola Sanchez.

He climbed the stairs to the loft and toed off his running shoes before sinking down onto the king-size bed—his one luxury in an otherwise Spartan existence. As he leaned back against the headboard, his phone vibrated. His mind still stuck on the intractable sociology professor, he fished it out of his pocket. Good, it was Alvarado.

"Lou, I need you to work on Trevania Barlow," he said, getting straight to the point. "I just piss her off every time I open my mouth. We're oil and water. Dr. Do-Good's a freaking heiress with a French socialite for a mother. Her father's a career ambassador and her brother's a State Department public affairs officer, all currently posted overseas. How am I supposed to—"

Alvarado cut him off with a snort. "Dr. Do-Good? Real smooth, Larsen. Thought I taught you some manners when you were a noog. Guess it didn't take."

"I don't call her that to her face," Cruz said, feeling a little more defensive than the comment warranted.

"Yeah, well, I think she heard you anyway," Alvarado commented dryly before shifting back to the reason for the late night call. "There's been a drive-by shooting."

Cruz sat up abruptly, his fatigue dropping away. "Where? In Southeast?"

"You guessed it. Along the border. A thirteen-year-old girl is dead. Gunshot wound to the chest."

Shit. Diablo territory. The Chingazos had retaliated just like Cruz had guessed they would. "Suspects?"

"You're gonna want to come out here. We found a tag spray-painted on an abandoned building a couple of blocks from the crime scene. Praying hands with the letters CL and Lola's name."

"On my way." Already standing, he shoved his feet back into his running shoes. "What else have you got?"

"Not much. The victim was walking out the front door of a housing complex with her older brother and his friends when shots were fired from a black SUV. The brother was hit in the shoulder."

"Gang members?"

"The brother claims he and his sister aren't part of any gang."

"And the friends?"

"Only one was still on the scene when the first responders arrived. A member of LDR. He was trying to keep the girl alive. Her name was Samantha. Samantha Vega."

"You'd better give me directions." Cruz listened while he opened the wall safe in his closet where he kept his gun. He recognized the sinking feeling in the pit of his stomach. Failure. He hadn't wrapped up the Sanchez homicide quickly enough and now another girl was dead. "I'll be there in ten."

With the ease of familiarity, he loaded his gun and holstered it, then grabbed his leather jacket from the closet. Swearing softly, he ran down the stairs, scooped up his keys from the kitchen counter where he had tossed them earlier, and headed for the door. It was going to be another long night.

By the time Cruz got to the housing complex in the Southeast section of Washington, the crime scene unit was wrapping up. Alvarado saw Cruz and walked toward him.

"We got nothing," he said, anticipating Cruz's questions. "A couple of spent bullets. That's all. Like I said, she was just thirteen." He spat on the ground and then wiped his mouth with the back of his hand. "My daughter's thirteen. Holy Jesus, it'd rip the heart out of me."

Cruz nodded. "Anything useful from the eyewitnesses?"

"Not really. Black SUV. Dirty license plates. No make or model." Alvarado pulled a small notebook from his pocket and flipped through it. "A woman living in the apartment building claims she saw return fire. Her window's right up there, on the front corner. Said she looked out when she heard the shots. Saw someone firing back."

"She heard gunshots and went to the window?"

Alvarado laughed, a short bark of sound. "Yeah, I asked her about that too. She told me that at eighty-seven not much scares her anymore. She's a pretty tough old lady."

She'd have to be to survive here. "How's her eyesight?"

"Coke-bottle lenses in her glasses."

So much for the eyewitness. "Any leads on the second shooter? The brother?"

"No, he denied it."

"Do you believe him?"

Alvarado shrugged. "No gun on him."

"What about the friends? The Diablos?"

"No."

"The brother could have ditched the weapon before the police arrived."

"I don't think so," Alvarado said. "Between the wound in his shoulder and his sister bleeding out next to him, Charlie Vega was in rough shape. My theory's that the second shooter ran when he heard the sirens. There was a lot of confusion and none of the witnesses are sure whether they saw one or two friends with the Vega kids."

"Where's the Chingazos hit up?"

"About five blocks east. I'll send you the pictures of the graffiti as soon as they're downloaded."

"Good. I'd still like to eyeball it myself. We can take my car."

Alvarado sat in the passenger seat and directed Cruz to an abandoned building, not far from the railroad tracks. Before leaving the car, Cruz pulled a flashlight out of the glove compartment. He could hear the steady rumble of a freight train passing nearby as he walked toward the poorly lit building. It was nearing one in the morning, and the place was deserted. Cruz swung the beam of light across the boarded-up door and the crumbling brick wall.

"Dr. Barlow would have a field day here," he mumbled under his breath. The red outlines of a fist and praying hands caught his attention. He redirected the beam and moved closer. "Chingazos Locos. Lola," he read aloud. He touched the paint. It was dry. "Doesn't leave much to the imagination, does it?"

"Nope," said Alvarado.

"Pretty ballsy." He swept the flashlight beam along the ground, searching. For what, he didn't know, but it was his habit to be thorough. "No crime scene tape. Why?"

"Impossible to keep the scene intact without assigning a unit to patrol the site. The city doesn't have the resources for that. We took pictures and searched the area. Nothing turned up."

Cruz walked along the curb, moving away from the front of the building. Trash littered the street. He kicked an empty beer bottle with his foot and watched it roll away. It slowly picked up speed as it spiraled down the street and then suddenly disappeared. What the hell? Cruz jogged over to the place where the bottle had vanished. Crouching, he trained his light on the curb.

A storm drain.

The street had crumbled away from the rectangular mouth of the drain in uneven chunks, turning it into a gaping hole. With his flashlight, he could just make out the beer bottle in the murky darkness about six feet down. Christ, it stunk down there. He moved the light. It reflected off the eyes of an animal. A rat? There was a loud clank as it pushed off the bottle to scurry away. Cruz shifted the beam slightly, following the sound. The bright letters of a spray paint can glowed faintly in the dark. Shit, he was going to have to climb down there. He snapped on a pair of latex gloves.

"Alvarado, I found something," he said, already lowering himself through the crumbling maw. He dropped down and landed in a couple of inches of foul-smelling water and trash. "Christ, another pair of perfectly good running shoes ruined," he grumbled. "Fourth pair this year."

Alvarado poked his head into the narrow opening, adding the beam of his flashlight to that of Cruz's. "Better you than me," he said with a laugh.

"Ha-ha. Get me an evidence bag."

Still laughing, Alvarado disappeared and returned a moment later with the plastic bag. "Jesus, you're going to stink when you get out of there. Good thing we came in your car." Almost as an afterthought, he added, "What'd you find?"

"Spray paint can. I thought you said this place had been thoroughly searched."

Alvarado's laughter stopped abruptly when Cruz handed the bagged evidence up to him. "Son of a bitch. Red fingerprints.

Someone with paint on his hands handled this can. If we're lucky, we'll get a match."

The water underfoot was murky brown, almost impossible to see through, even with the aid of a flashlight. Cruz kicked his feet through it, searching by feel.

"Having fun down there?" Alvarado said.

"Bite me," Cruz growled. His foot his snagged on something and he trained the light on it. A small branch protruded from the water. Cruz picked it up and used it to stir through the debris. Was there anything more to find here? Another spray paint can, maybe?

Alvarado was growing impatient. "I'd like to get this back to the crime scene unit. Maybe rub their noses in it a little. Jesus, how could they have missed it?"

"It's pretty hard to see much of anything down here," Cruz had to concede. Garbage stew. He threw down the stick, tucked his flashlight in his waistband, and stripped off the latex gloves. "I'm coming up." He shoved the gloves in his back pocket as he waded through the water and trash.

The street was at eye level. It was going to take one hell of a push up to get himself out. He kicked at the wall, looking for a toehold. Finding one halfway up the crumbling cement, he started to lever himself out of the storm sewer. The cement gave way beneath his weight and his hands lost their purchase on the rough asphalt. He careened backward, his feet splashing water everywhere as he struggled to maintain his balance. His foot caught on the branch he'd thrown down earlier and he lost his balance, landing with a thud in the water.

"Whoa, you fighting with a rat down there?" Alvarado poked his head through the opening and shined his flashlight in Cruz's face.

"You're blinding me with that goddamn thing." Cruz shielded his eyes with one dripping hand. His palm stung like it had been peeled with a cheese grater. God only knew what nasty bugs he was likely to pick up down here. Ignoring the pain, he reached down to push himself to his feet. His fingers closed over something that felt an awful lot like a gun. Shit. He pulled it out of the water and looked at it in the dim light cast by Alvarado's flashlight.

A 9mm semiautomatic.

"That's a gun," Alvarado said, his voice filled with disbelief.

"No shit, Sherlock." Cruz handed it up to him. "You'd better bag it. Maybe we'll get a print off the trigger."

"Maybe." Alvarado's voice was doubtful. Just the same, he pulled another evidence bag from his pocket and slid it over the gun. "Want me to radio the fire department to come get your ass out of there?"

"Practicing your stand-up comedy routine?" Cruz set his hands on the uneven ledge of the storm drain. "Don't quit your day job," he grunted, ignoring the pain that shot through his right palm as he levered himself upward until he was half in and half out of the storm sewer. Alvarado pulled him the rest of the way out. Stinking, soaking wet, aching from what felt like a thousand stinging cuts on his hand, Cruz lay on the street for a moment.

"God, I love this job," he said.

"You are one crazy son of a bitch," Alvarado said.

There was admiration in his voice.

SIX

"TREVY," A FAMILIAR voice called out as she entered the lobby of her apartment building after her early morning run—a futile effort to outrun the troubles that clung to her like shadows. Lola's death. The threat of more violence. Hardly daring to believe her ears, Trevy looked up as a tall man rose from one of the overstuffed chairs lining the foyer.

"JC!" The shadows momentarily pushed aside by a spurt of joy, she launched herself into the arms of her baby brother. Not much of a baby anymore. Three years her junior, he towered over her. He had inherited her father's height and her mother's tawny beauty. "What are you doing here? Were you waiting long? How long can you stay?"

JC laughed. "Have mercy, T. Coffee first. Then I'll answer your questions."

"I'm going to hold you to that," she said, linking her arm with his and leading him toward the elevator.

"Why do I feel like I volunteered to be first in line for the Spanish Inquisition?"

"Very funny." Trevy lightly slugged her brother's shoulder and rolled her eyes when he fell theatrically against the wood-paneled interior of the elevator.

When they reached the sixth floor, they disembarked and Trevy unlocked the apartment. The smell of freshly brewed coffee wafted from the kitchen. JC paused in the doorway and inhaled in noisy appreciation. "You're terrifyingly efficient, T."

"Setting a timer on a coffeemaker hardly qualifies as terrifying." Trevy followed him into the kitchen and swept past him to pull a couple of mugs from a cabinet. Setting them on the counter, she turned in time to catch the slight curve of amusement on her brother's lips before it faded away. No one knew how to push her buttons like JC. She watched him hook a tall kitchen stool with his foot to pull it toward him before settling on the cushioned seat. He planted an elbow on the marble countertop and studied Trevy.

"You look tired," he told her, and Trevy felt a faint sting of irritation. Instead of waiting for the coffee to finish brewing, she yanked the carafe from the machine and filled JC's mug.

"This is *my* inquisition, Jean-Claude. Here's your coffee." Trevy set the full mug on the counter in front of him. "What brings you to D.C.? Why no advance notice?" She poured coffee into a mug for herself. "And no holding back. A promise is a promise."

Before JC could form an answer—or, more likely, an evasion—the phone rang.

"I'll let it go to voice mail," Trevy said, glancing at the cordless phone mounted on the wall. "I can check my messages later."

"Go ahead, get it. Then I'll have more time to drink my coffee before the inquisition commences."

"Don't think you're getting off the hook that easily," she warned him. With a mock scowl still on her face, she answered the phone. She recognized the impatient voice even before he finished saying, "It's Cruz Larsen."

Crazy thoughts chased through her brain, leaving her breathless. Had he found Bandit? Or had someone else been hurt? Rosa? Maybe even Angel, who wasn't nearly as invincible as she'd like the world to believe. She could feel the heat of anxiety rising in her cheeks. Her brother touched her arm, reminding her that he was watching the distress unfold on her face.

"Yes?" Trevy deliberately forced a light, friendly note into the question and JC, apparently reassured, let his hand drop. He returned to his seat at the counter and lifted his coffee mug for another sip. Good. She didn't want to spend the rest of his visit defending her work.

"Meet me in the lobby in fifteen minutes," Agent Larsen said, drawing her attention back to the phone receiver pressed against her ear.

"I'm afraid today's impossible." Mindful that JC was still watching her from his nearby perch, she muted the phone and said, "I'll be right back, JC," then left the kitchen.

"Did you find Bandit?" she asked Agent Larsen in a low voice as she neared the privacy of the extra bedroom that she used as an office.

"Not yet."

"Then there's no need—"

"I need an hour of your time, Dr. Barlow. Meet me in the lobby, or I'll come knocking at your door."

"You won't get past the front desk."

His scornful laughter had Trevy clenching her teeth. Agent Larsen was as arrogant as he was unreasonable. At least he hadn't chased her down a running path this time, scaring her half to death in the process. Today, he'd settled for threatening her.

"You'd be surprised how accommodating people are when they see an FBI badge."

"My brother's visiting. I don't want him to know about the murder. He'll worry."

There was a long beat of silence. Just when Trevy began to wonder if he had severed the connection, she heard him sigh. "Meet me at Montrose Park in fifteen minutes. By the sundial," he ordered. Her irritation ratcheted up a notch when he added, "You know where it is, don't you?"

"Of course." The large brass armillary sundial was the centerpiece of a half-moon brick terrace near the entrance to the park. She passed it every morning as she headed toward the Rock Creek trails for her daily run. "But I won't be able to meet you today. My brother and I have plans. And I have two classes plus afternoon office hours."

"The park or your apartment, Dr. Barlow. Your choice. You have fifteen minutes to decide. Bring your camera. You'll want it." He hung up, cutting off any further discussion.

Her temperature now perilously close to the boiling point, Trevy's fingers shook as she set the portable phone receiver on her desk. What did Agent Larsen mean by that last crack? She glanced up to see JC in the doorway, one broad shoulder propped against the jamb.

Without giving away his thoughts, he took a sip of his coffee, then said, "Book troubles?" His gaze swept over her, taking in her flushed face and tensed shoulders. She forced her lips into a rueful smile.

"Yes," she said and her temperature elevated yet another notch. Now she was lying and it was all Special Agent Cruz Larsen's fault. Damn him. But telling JC the truth was out of the question. Her family was every bit as disapproving of her profession as Cruz Larsen was. Only they were nicer about it.

And the working draft of her next book was an EF-5 disaster. That part wasn't a lie. But she didn't want to think about that unfinished project right now. Not when JC was standing in front of her and Agent Larsen would be knocking on her door in fifteen minutes if she didn't act quickly enough to head him off.

"In all the excitement of seeing you, I completely forgot that I'm expected at the university in a few minutes. For a meeting." Trevy glanced at her watch. The clock was ticking. "I'll be late if I don't leave now."

Fifteen minutes to walk to the park. Two minutes to make it clear to that hardheaded, unreasonable federal agent that she was a dead-end for his investigation unless he located Bandit. Another fifteen to get back to her apartment. "It shouldn't take too long. An hour, maybe less."

Her brother nodded. "My day's free until three. Rafael Montoyez invited me to the Spanish Embassy to meet the new ambassador."

She could feel the weight of his gaze as she grabbed her camera from the shelf behind her desk. He was studying her much too closely. Trevy could tell he was trying to figure out what was going on with her. But like the rest of the family, he was too much of a diplomat to just come out and ask her.

"I know you didn't come all the way from Moscow just to meet the Spanish ambassador. What's the real reason you're in town?" Trevy asked, trying to distract him while she stuffed her camera into her satchel. "And why didn't you call me?"

"I've been reassigned." He settled onto the daybed across from the desk. "I'll be back in D.C. by the end of April."

"Working at Foggy Bottom?" Trevy asked, referring to the State Department. She couldn't keep the grin off her face. "That's great news. I'll start looking for a new place so you can have your apartment back."

"Stay put, T. You'll save me the trouble of having to find a new tenant when I leave in three months. I'll find a temporary rental."

"What happens after three months?"

"I'm going to Tegucigalpa."

"Honduras." Her smile flatlined. "That sounds dangerous, Jean-Claude."

That Central American country held the dubious honor of being the murder capital of the world. With miles of undeveloped coastline, an unstable government, and an influx of gang members deported from the United States, Honduras had become a violent haven for Colombian drug cartels trafficking cocaine north and for Mexican cartels fleeing the government crackdown in their own country.

JC raised an eyebrow. "Hello, pot, I'm kettle."

Trevy ignored his poor attempt at humor. She knew from experience that nothing she said would change his mind. A quick glance at her watch confirmed she had less than fifteen minutes before Cruz Larsen would come knocking on her door. And diplomat or not, her brother would want to know why an FBI agent had come to call. She settled the strap of her satchel on her shoulder.

"It's the U.S. Embassy, Trev," JC said. "Not a consulate or a military base. I'll be well protected. Besides, you live in D.C. You know as well as I do that there are no guarantees—9/11 ripped away that illusion."

Trevy didn't want to think about that either. JC followed her out of the room without uttering another word. But she knew her brother well enough not to be fooled by his silence. More than likely, he was scheming to accompany her. The very fact that he hadn't asked why she needed her camera had her worried. Time to head him off with another question. "How long will you be in town this time?"

"Long enough to find a place to live."

"A week?" Trevy guessed. She grabbed her keys off the small table near the front door.

"Almost. I have a flight back to Moscow next Wednesday."

"Oh, JC, that's not much time. I wish I didn't have to go to this —this—" Damn, what had she told JC? "—this appointment," she finished lamely. She paused in the open doorway to look back at him. Really look at him. His eyes were shadowed and faint lines bracketed his mouth. Maybe she wasn't the only one keeping secrets. "I won't be long."

"Don't rush, Trevy," he said, his dark blue eyes inscrutable. "It was a long flight from Moscow. I'm going to crash on the daybed in your office. When you get back, I'll take you to lunch. You can even come with me to meet the ambassador."

"Deal," said Trevy, "except I can't go to the embassy afterward. I have afternoon classes. You can use my car." The fact that he hadn't thrown up any additional roadblocks worried her more than the wariness of his expression.

"Don't you mean my car?" he said, reminding her that the vintage BMW 2002 was still his baby and she was just the caretaker.

"Get a country desk job in Foggy Bottom. I'd be more than happy to hand over the car keys. Maybe then you'll find time to get it a new paint job." Why had he accepted such a dangerous post? As a public affairs officer, he wouldn't be spending all of his time behind the protected walls of the U.S. Embassy.

"Some day," he promised vaguely. And that was going to have to do for now. Her fifteen minutes were almost up.

The instant Trevy closed the apartment door, JC dashed into the kitchen. Trevy kept an extra apartment key on a magnetic hook on the refrigerator. He pocketed it and grabbed a baseball cap from the carry-on bag he'd left in the hall, slapping it on his head as he rushed out the door after her. Trevy was hiding something from him and he intended to find out what.

Taking the stairs two steps at a time, he beat the elevator to the lobby. Slightly out of breath, he cracked the stairwell door open in time to watch her leave through the lobby door, which had to mean she was walking to her "appointment." It was a lucky break. Following her would be a simple matter.

Her behavior had set off instant alarm bells in his head. It didn't make sense that she would go to a meeting without first changing out of her running clothes. Add in the stormy look on her face and the lame excuse of the forgotten appointment, and his senses were all on red alert. Besides, if she were meeting someone at the university, why would she have taken her camera?

Because she was putting herself in danger with the research for another one of her damned books. She was probably off to meet some gangbanger. What did she hope to accomplish, trying to understand people like that? Dangerous people who wouldn't think twice about hurting her, killing her?

Trevy and her damn social conscience. He picked up his pace when she turned left on M Street. Now her lie was confirmed. The university was in the opposite direction. And she was in a hurry, he noted, annoyed that he had to practically run to keep her in sight. Hardly the best way to look inconspicuous. But then Trevy wasn't the suspicious type. It would never occur to her that someone might be following her. She was too damned trusting for her own good.

When Trevy walked up to a dark-haired guy sitting on a park bench near the large sundial, JC almost forgot to stay out of sight in the narrow alley across the street. Big sis was blowing him off for this guy? Not a gangbanger, at least. Upscale Montrose Park wasn't a hotbed of gang activity. What then? A boyfriend?

Even from across the street he sensed the tension between the two of them. Suppressed desire? Eagerness? Something wasn't adding up, but he couldn't quite nail down what it was. The guy stood up and moved down the street without waiting to see if Trevy would follow. What was that all about? Dude had the social graces of a caveman. Was that what Trevy was into these days? Cro-Magnon man?

And why the secret meeting?

JC followed them. Cro-Magnon was tall, so it was easy to keep sight of him over the roof of the parked cars. He moved with a well-coordinated grace that JC recognized immediately. Former military. Wasn't practically everybody in this town? If he was her boyfriend, he could understand why she had lied. He wouldn't have wanted to introduce this guy to a family member either.

It was all JC could do to hold himself back when Cro-Magnon climbed into a well-used sedan in just about the ugliest shade of beige JC had ever seen, and didn't bother to open the door for his sister. "You can do better, Trev," he muttered under his breath.

The car pulled out. JC memorized the license plate as he watched them drive away. He didn't know whether to be relieved or concerned, but he decided he was going to find out who the caveman was and pay him a little visit while he was in town. Nothing Trevy needed to know about. Not yet, anyway.

"It's a wall of respect. A memorial to fallen gang members," Trevy said, her eyes glued to the graffiti covering the brick wall of the abandoned building. Her fingers brushed over the crudely painted outlines of the tombstones, names, dates. RIP. Rest in peace.

"Yeah, Doc, tell me something I don't already know."

She gave him a sideways glance—one dismissive flick of the eyes—before pointing to the red devil heads and tridents. "It's also a celebration of LDR's courage, a tribute to their gang pride. Why are we here, Agent Larsen?"

"What about this?" Cruz stepped back to let Trevy see the part of the wall he'd been blocking with his body. He watched for how she would react to her first glimpse of the large red fist.

Her gaze collided with his, the sharp interest in her eyes darkening to horror. "What happened? Tell me."

"How do you know something happened?"

"So many things. The fist is the Chingazos gang's emblem. That it's crushing the devil suggests dominance over the Diablos. The disrespect of painting over LDR graffiti. The single line insult: LD Ratos. It's an unusual combination of a crossing out and a RIP."

"What do you mean?"

"Well, this piece of work has all the typical elements of crossing-out graffiti. The paint lines drawn through the LDR names and symbols. The derogatory nickname for the gang—the use of Ratos instead of Rojos. But it also appears to be a tribute for Lola, a RIP. See how her name was written in Old English Block letters underneath Chingazos Locos."

"Yeah." Cruz eyed the red letters outlined in black. "The colors are all wrong though. Red? Aren't most Chingazos hit-ups predominantly yellow?"

Trevy nodded, then pulled out her camera and started to take pictures of the wall.

"The colors suggest to me that this crossing out might not have been planned," she said while she worked. "Usually the gang name is the largest element and the gang members' names are spray-painted in descending size in direct proportion to their importance. That's not the case here."

"I guess the tagger must have been off his game."

"I think it's significant." Trevy shifted her gaze from the camera to him. The heat in her eyes told him she didn't like his read on the situation. "Lola's death is not an individual loss, but a collective injury. In a gang, individuals aren't important. It's the group. Everything is for the gang. It's a form of social control that replaces the usual norms of family, school, and community."

"Spare me the lecture, Doc."

She fastened the cover on the zoom lens of her camera and stuffed it back into her bag with short, jerky motions that betrayed her rising temper. "Don't you see, if you'd only take the time to understand how these children fall victim to gangs—"

"I know more about it than you ever could," he said, revealing more than he'd intended. But the good doctor was too wrapped up in her thoughts to notice. "To you, everyone's a victim. Christ, I'm sick of that mentality."

"They *are* victims," Trevy said, her hands forming tight little fists at her sides. She looked furious enough to hit him, but her voice was remarkably calm. "These children are living on the margin, between two cultures, if you will. Do you know what kind of extreme talent and resolve it takes for even one of them to climb the economic ladder out of poverty?"

"These *children* are killing each other." Cruz turned his back on her. He didn't like the look of the group of teenage boys across the street. They all seemed to have shopped at the same store with the same shopping list. Red sports jerseys, baggy jeans tucked into high-top sneakers, red bandanas in back pockets. LDRs or LDR wannabes, thugs in the making. He cut a warning glance at them and then stepped nearer to Trevy, blocking her from view.

Trevy paused a moment to glare at him before pulling out a notebook and tape measure from her satchel. Tools of her trade, Cruz noted as she began measuring the images on the wall and jotting down notes. "Do you have a heart?" she asked, as if picking up the thread of a dropped conversation.

"Excuse me, Dr. Barlow, if I don't feel like joining your pity party for a bunch of street thugs who are intent on turning this part of the city into a war zone," he said, leaning close enough to smell her shampoo. The scent—light and clean, with a floral note—only made him angrier. "Two girls are dead. Save your pity for them."

Her head turned so quickly he didn't have time to move away. Her warm breath feathered across his skin. Her pupils were large dark circles surrounded by green-gold. For a moment, he couldn't move. Then she said, "Two?" and he jerked his head back and straightened to his full height.

"Lola Sanchez and, last night, a thirteen-year-old girl. Witnesses saw a black SUV leaving the scene of the crime. Sound familiar?"

Trevy nodded. He watched her throat convulse as she swallowed back her reaction.

"Razor has a black SUV," she volunteered after a moment. "But there are a lot of black SUVs in this city. Did anyone see the plates?"

"No," Cruz said.

"Tell me what happened."

Cruz blew out a breath of air to calm himself and tamp down his own disgust. How much violence could a man witness without darkness taking up permanent residence in his soul?

"The girl's name was Samantha Vega. She walked out her front door with her brother Charlie and some friends. Charlie was the lucky one. The bullet struck the meaty part of his shoulder. Samantha, not so much. A direct hit to the chest nicked an artery, and she bled out before the paramedics could get there. *She's* the real victim here. *She's* the one who deserves justice. How many dead girls is it going to take before you'll work with me, Dr. Barlow?"

Her body stiffened as if absorbing a punch. She stepped away from him.

He pulled her back from the edge of the curb. "This is Bandit's artwork, isn't it?"

"Yes." Trevy shook off his hand and moved closer to the wall. Cruz followed, using his body to shield her from the kids who were still watching from across the street.

"You're sure?" he asked, thinking about the parka-wearing tagger who had been seen near the community center around the time of Lola Sanchez's murder. He reached past her to tap the signature lines done in large round letters—*Somos B, R, G, 13*—with his finger. "No names."

She turned her head, her gaze following his fingers to the wall and then back to his face.

"A crossing-out tag is risky business," she said. Her knuckles turned white as she tightened her grip on her notebook, but her voice was still composed. "You're in enemy territory and you're publicly disrespecting a rival gang. The writer needs to be quick to avoid detection. And if the writer makes a mistake, everyone will see it. Whoever did this was very skilled. The lettering style is elaborate and symmetrical. Bandit has the ability and the speed. I've seen him paint with a spray can in each hand. See the distinctive interlocking C and L letters ringing the index fingers of the praying hands? It's his design. And then there's the B in the signature. Usually the writer's name goes first."

"That means he's probably involved in the drive-by shooting. The graffiti puts him in the area." Dr. Do-Good's expert testimony that Hector Bonilla aka Bandit had painted praying hands with a distinctive yellow CL would help him build a case against the gangbanger. But would it be enough to convince the assistant U.S. attorney to take the case to a grand jury?

"This is unusual," Trevy said, recapturing his attention. He watched her trace the number thirteen with the tip of her finger. "I haven't seen it before in CL hit-ups. *Trece*, thirteen, is typical of the multivocality of many gang symbols. In this instance, it could represent Southern California where the Chingazos have roots. Or *sur*, south in Spanish. Those letters also stand for *Surenos Unidos Raza*—United People of the South. The Diablos Rojos have roots in Northern California. "

"Yeah, yeah, I know about the layered meanings of *trece*. Don't you think it's a warning to the Diablos that CL buys protection from MS-13?"

"That makes sense." She looked at him with hope shining in her eyes. "Maybe it'll be enough to keep the Diablos from retaliating."

"Not a chance. The Diablos will strike back. The only question is when."

"The MS-13 group in Langley Park is twice the size of the Diablos and the Chingazos combined."

"And ten times as vicious. The Diablos won't care. It's a matter of pride. You know that, Doc. I'm going to ask you again: Do you have any idea where Bandit is hiding out?"

Even if Bandit wasn't the shooter, he very likely knew who killed Samantha Vega. And maybe a quick arrest would be enough to keep the Diablos from retaliating.

"No idea," she said, then sighed. "Poor Bandit."

"Poor Bandit? What about poor Samantha? Poor Lola? Save your sympathy for someone who deserves it."

"And you're the one who's going to decide who deserves it and who doesn't? Bandit is as much a victim as they—"

"Bandit had a choice. Did Lola Sanchez? Did Samantha Vega?"

"Maybe, maybe not. It's not that simple. But don't misinterpret what I'm saying. If Bandit was involved in Samantha Vega's murder, he should be punished."

"I'm amazed to hear you say that, Doc."

Instead of firing back a scathing retort, she turned away. But not before their gazes caught. In that instant, the sharp edges of her emotions spanned the distance between them and sliced into him. Shock. Sorrow. Regret. Her distress seemed genuine. As if the violence of the last four days had been a personal affront. A personal failure. He wished then that he'd kept his mouth shut.

She wasn't lying to him. The certainty washed over him, impossible to ignore. To protect those girls in her class, she'd offer Bandit to him on a silver platter. Hell, he owed her an apology. Probably more than one. And she'd never cooperate with him if all they did was trade insults.

"That doesn't mean Bandit wasn't a victim," she said before he could decide how much he was willing to grovel. "A victim of circumstance and poor judgment. Blame whomever you'd like, Agent Larsen. Ruined lives sadden me. Period."

"Doesn't it make you angry?" he asked, forgetting about the apology for the moment. He had to understand how she could feel anything other than disgust for someone who might have killed an innocent girl.

"Yes, it makes me angry," she said, turning to face him. Her eyes, that odd mix of brown and green and gold, studied him closely. "It makes you angry too," she said after a long moment. "Perhaps we're not so different after all, Agent Larsen."

He tried to dismiss her words with a laugh, but they seemed to have taken root in his head. "Time to go," he said, with a glance across the street to where more Diablos had gathered.

She followed his gaze, took in the sight of the group. "Agreed." Then she stuffed her notebook into her satchel. "Why do you hate them so much?" she asked, jerking her chin in the direction of the Diablos.

"I don't hate them," he said. "But when they break the law, steal, sell drugs, kill each other, it's my job to make sure they don't get to do it again. It's very simple, Doc. Don't try to read something into it that isn't there."

"Nothing about you is simple, Agent Larsen," she said with a tight smile. "Nothing at all."

What the hell did she mean by that? She was the complicated one. He unlocked the Bureau car, climbed in, and tapped his fingers on the steering wheel while he waited for her to join him. He didn't need a damned sociologist playing mind games with him. He'd had enough of that to last a lifetime. But like it or not, this woman was proving to be a valuable source of information, so he was going to have to learn how to get along with her. An apology seemed like a good first step.

"I'm sorry," he said as she settled into the passenger seat.

Slowly, she swiveled her head in his direction, her eyes widening in surprise. "For what?"

"For being such a judgmental asshole."

Trevy Barlow stared at him, too polite—or too offended—to utter a word.

Well, fuck me, he thought as he stared back at her. Maybe he should have kept that last bit to himself.

SEVEN

Slouched against the red brick wall of the Academy of Learning charter school, Bandit waited as far from the front doors as possible. He stuck his hands in his pockets and hunched his shoulders against the wind. After spending Thursday night outside with only rats and trash for company, he was half-frozen. He welcomed the numbness.

Another twenty minutes passed before the first students began to arrive. Voices spilled out into the damp air as they piled into the building, some with enthusiasm and others with the quiet determination to get through another endless day. What Bandit remembered most about school was the helplessness that had dogged him from the moment he stepped through those front doors. He sucked at reading in two languages. Teachers talked too fast and used fancy words when plain ones would do. Sometimes they called on him just to make sure everyone in the class knew he was an *idiota*.

But mostly they ignored him.

It had been a relief when the principal suspended him for fighting. He had decided against returning when the suspension was over, and not even the weight of his mother's disappointment had changed his mind. The only thing he'd enjoyed was art class. The smell of the paints, the feel of a brush in his hand, the smudge of charcoal on his fingers…

He scanned the crowded walkway for Lola's sister Cecilia.

Just when he thought he'd missed her, she walked right past

him, her eyes fixed on the open door like a prize was waiting for her inside. A giant present just for her. He couldn't understand it. He reached out and grabbed hold of her backpack. "Ceci, wait."

Cecilia shook free of his grasp and whirled around, battle shining in her dark brown eyes. She was small for fourteen, but strong and quick. Just like Lola had been. He pressed his hand against the dull ache of grief that had settled in his gut. Ceci gave her head a little shake that sent her straight black hair swinging over her narrow shoulders.

"Bandit," she said, the fight going out of her. "What are you doing here?"

"I need to talk to you."

"Now?" She glanced at the oversized watch on her wrist. "I'm going to be late."

"It's important. Please, Ceci." Her mouth, the exact same shape as Lola's, turned down. He thought she was going to refuse, so he added, "It's a matter of life and death. I swear."

Sensing her surrender, he pulled her farther from the school building.

"What's so important?" she hissed, her breath clouding the air between them.

"I need that key. The one Lola wore around her neck. Did the cops give it back?"

"They're keeping everything until they find the person who killed her," she said with a wobble in her voice. "An FBI agent even asked Mama for permission to examine the car."

"Car?" FBI Agent Larsen had asked him the same question on Sunday, but the trip to the police station had given him enough time to figure out that he'd stay alive for longer if he kept his lips zipped. So he had told the agent he wouldn't talk to anyone except Lola's teacher...and then he'd gone into hiding. "What did your mother tell him?"

"What do you think she told him? There's no car. Lola just found the key somewhere." Cecilia studied him with shrewd, dark eyes. "But that's not true, is it?"

"I gotta get that key, Ceci. It's a matter of life—" Bandit's breath stalled in his throat.

"And death?" Ceci finished for him, her eyes narrowed. "So you said. Why is it so important?"

"Razor wants it."

"What's Razor going to do with some worthless old key?"

Her questions made his stomach churn. Didn't she know that too many questions could get you killed?

"Don't ask," he said, his voice sharp. She stiffened and half turned away, her eyes fixed on the school. Bandit could feel her need to escape. He tightened his grip on her arm. "The less you know, the better. Do you want to end up like Lola?"

Tears filled Ceci's eyes and spilled over onto her cheeks. She dashed them away. "I'm going to college. I'm not going to be like Lola. Stay away from me, Bandit. You're the reason she's dead. You and the Chingazos Locos."

It was true. Ceci had only given voice to what he already knew. Still, the words sliced through him. He swallowed down the bitterness that rose in his throat. The late bell rang. Cecilia tried to push past him, but he didn't release his grip. He wasn't through with her yet.

"Let go, Bandit. I need to get to class."

"Not today," he told her, tightening his fingers around her arm. "Your sister's dead and her funeral's tomorrow. Your mother needs you at home."

"Mama?" She stopped protesting and let Bandit pull her toward the bus shelter at the end of the block where a Metrobus was slowing to a stop. "Did she send you?"

Bandit bit back a snort of disbelief even as he increased his pace and signaled for the bus driver to wait. Had Ceci forgotten how much her mother hated him? He had ruined Lola's life. Even Ceci knew it.

And now it was Lola's turn to ruin his. "I haven't talked to your mother." Shit. What was he going to do if Mrs. Sanchez was at home? "She's at work, right?"

"Yes. Where are we going?" Ceci stopped in front of the bus's open doors.

"To your apartment." He was sure he'd find the spare key for the BMW somewhere in Lola's room. If only he felt the same certainty about the stolen money. Well, the Sanchez apartment was as good a place as any to start his search.

Bandit pushed Ceci ahead of him. She climbed the first step into the bus and looked back at him. "Why? The key's not there, Bandit."

"Life and death, Ceci," he reminded her. The less she knew, the safer she'd be.

She locked eyes with him before looking away, her lips flattening into a grim line. Ceci was a fast learner. Wordlessly, she climbed into the bus and paid the fare for both of them.

The Sanchez apartment was spooky quiet, and it felt like a place that would suck all the happiness out of anyone who was stupid enough to enter. Without checking to see if he was following her, Cecilia walked down a short hall to the room she had shared with her sister. "Mama told me to pack up Lola's things." She pointed to two black garbage bags. "Not so much." Her voice trembled with unshed tears. "Look through them if you want."

Bandit lifted one of the bags and untied it. The clothes inside were neatly folded. He pulled out a pink shirt and held it against his face. Lola had been wearing it the last time he kissed her. He breathed deeply, but when he couldn't find even a trace of her scent, he let it fall from his fingers. Beside him, Ceci lunged for the shirt and caught it before it touched the floor. Ignoring her heated glare, he dumped the contents of the bag onto the floor and searched each piece of clothing. Nothing. No money. No key.

What had he expected to find? A treasure map sewn into one of the seams? He grabbed the other bag. This one was filled with costume jewelry, shoes, and stuffed animals. An oversized cross studded with fake diamonds spilled onto the floor, its heavy chain of cheap metal uncoiling like a snake across the top of his boot. It had been one of Lola's favorites. Before she started wearing the key on its pink velvet ribbon. He kicked the cross onto the growing pile.

Nothing.

Desperation mounting, he turned to Cecilia, who was still

clutching the pink shirt to her chest. "Where's the rest of her stuff?" This couldn't be it. How could Lola's whole life fit into two garbage bags? He wanted to howl with rage at the unfairness of it all. But he didn't have time to waste. No key. No money. No life. He booted a stuffed bear out of his way. It was satisfying to sink his foot into something so soft. He drew back his leg again. He wanted to grind his heel into it until there was nothing left but stuffing.

Ceci threw herself on the stuffed animal and cradled it in her arms, acting like he'd kicked a puppy.

"This was for her baby."

Her words cut through him. He paused, sweat dripping down the side of his neck. The soft brown bear was about the size of a baby. His baby. The baby he hadn't wanted. The baby Lola had tried to protect by stealing the money. Now Lola and the baby were both dead. And soon he would join them.

Unable to look at the bear any longer, he turned away. *Think*, he told himself. There were other places Lola could have stashed the bills.

"What are you doing?" Ceci asked when he pulled the mattress off the double bed that she and Lola had shared. Nothing was hidden between the mattress and box springs. He ripped the sheets off the mattress and ran his hands over the top and along the sides, searching for openings where she might have stashed the money. Or even a slip of paper with a bank account number. Anything that would give him guidance.

Nothing.

Breathing hard, Bandit heaved the mattress away from him. He couldn't leave the Sanchez apartment empty-handed. Even if the money wasn't here, the spare key had to be. Where would Lola have put it for safekeeping? Trying to think like her, he zeroed in on the scarred dresser made of pasteboard. He pulled out the top drawer, dumped Ceci's neatly folded clothes onto the floor, and flipped it over to look at the bottom. Nothing. He repeated the process with the next drawer. And the next.

"Stop it." Ceci tugged on his arm, but he shrugged her off with a hard shove. He heard her cry out as she landed in the pile of

Lola's stuff. He ran his hand along the back of the last drawer.

Nothing. He pulled the dresser away from the wall. Nothing. Lying flat on his stomach, he slid his head and shoulders underneath and felt around with his hands. Nothing.

Ceci jumped on him. Her little fists delivered hard, fast jabs of pain to his kidneys. He bucked her off and started to push himself out from under the dresser when she launched herself at him again. When he grabbed the two back legs of the dresser to steady himself, something sharp bit into his fingers. There was blood beading at the tip of his middle finger when he pulled his hand away. *Dios*, had Lola taped razor blades to the furniture?

"¡*Páralo*! Stop," he roared at Ceci, who continued to pound her fists against his lower back. The loud wails that poured from her mouth made him want to cover his ears.

"Shut up, shut up," he muttered as he gathered his strength to dislodge her once and for all. Then he froze, his entire body poised on the edge of discovery. "Lola," he breathed her name out like a prayer.

With shaking fingers, Bandit reached for the back leg of the dresser and carefully traced the object that was secured there with a piece of tape. Not a razor blade, as he had first thought—a car key. Bandit ripped it off the leg and clutched it tightly in his hand. "*Basta*," he shouted at Ceci. "Enough."

Ceci rolled off him, utterly quiet now, drained of emotion. She rubbed her tear-stained face against her sleeve. "Did you find what you were looking for?"

"No," he said, slipping the key into his pocket. Ceci was better off not knowing.

Exhausted, he looked at the mess he had made. Where the hell was the money? He'd have to let Razor know it wasn't here. That should keep Lola's family safe from the Chingazos, anyway. It was the least he could do for them.

"You better help me clean up," Ceci said, thrusting the stuffed bear at his face. Amazingly, it smelled like Lola. Memories of her rushed through him, knocking him to his knees. His fingers curled into the soft brown plush. He wanted to keep his face buried in its belly. Instead, he tucked it inside his jacket.

"I don't want to have to explain this mess to Mama," Ceci said, her hands on her hips. "I'd guess you wouldn't want that either."

EIGHT

The ambassador's residence on Foxhall Road hummed with energy on Saturday evening. Trevy swallowed a bite-size crab cake and forced a smile for the newly credentialed Spanish ambassador, who was standing across from her. The harmonious sound of the string quartet, strategically placed on a dais in the far corner near the floor-to-ceiling windows, blended with the drone of conversation as diplomats, businessmen, and politicians worked the room.

Although attending this reception wasn't exactly hardship duty, Trevy would rather be almost anywhere else. And she wasn't doing a good job of hiding it. She could tell by the pointed look her brother shot her when she snagged another hors d'oeuvre from the tray of a passing waiter. It was his silent plea to do more than stand next to him like a potted plant. Still, she couldn't help it. The festive atmosphere of the party was such a jarring counterpoint to her fresh memories of Lola's funeral service, which she'd attended just hours before. And the warning Ceci Sanchez had whispered into her ear before Trevy left the church wouldn't leave her thoughts.

Trevy sent JC a narrow-eyed glare, but her brother didn't seem to notice. He'd already turned to address a comment to Ambassador Hermosa's twenty-something daughter Sophia. Small, curvy, and beautiful—with a hint of brainy—the Georgetown law student had been the focus of JC's attention from the moment the ambassador introduced them. Trevy shrugged and washed the caviar down with a sip of sparkling wine.

Mrs. Sanchez had dressed her daughter in a frothy pink gown that Trevy suspected had been Lola's Quinceañera dress. In death, with her eyes shuttered and all signs of the letters that had been carved in her forehead artfully covered with makeup, Lola looked more like an innocent seventeen-year-old girl than the mature-before-her-years young woman Trevy had come to know. Damn it, she wanted to remember Lola as she'd been in life—bubbly, plainspoken, determined—rather than as the still shell of a girl in an open casket. Lola drained of life.

The ambassador was busy giving a lengthy recap of a recent meeting with the secretary of state, so there was no chance of escape for Trevy. Restless, she shifted her gaze to her brother. She hadn't told JC anything about the funeral. He and her upstairs neighbor, Rafael Montoyez, had left at dawn this morning to go rowing on the Potomac River, following that with a late breakfast at The Four Seasons.

Casting about for a distraction until she could make a polite exit, her gaze landed on Rafael. Even from across the room, she could tell that his charm meter was set on full blast. For a moment, she watched as the Spanish diplomat paused to exchange greetings with a businessman while his assistant Miguel Navarro, a younger, slightly shorter, less expensively attired clone of his boss, jotted notes in a small leather-bound agenda. Then they moved on to their next target. And the next.

At last the ambassador finished his story. Her brother surfaced from his newest infatuation long enough to send another prodding glance her way. *Mingle.* Trevy gave him a mock salute with her wine glass and turned, hoping to retreat to the ladies' room. If she took her time, she could burn up at least a quarter of an hour.

But Rafael appeared by her side before she could make good on her escape plans. With just a light threading of gray in his dark hair and closely cropped goatee, the Spanish diplomat had eased into middle age with the same fluid grace with which he propelled himself through the tightly-knit, powerful Foreign Service community. He took her by the elbow and pulled her a step away from the circle of supplicants surrounding the ambassador.

"Aren't you enjoying the party, *querida*?" Rafael said. "I'll admit that the ambassador's stories can be a bit tiresome. Be glad you didn't come to the embassy with JC on Thursday. We were subjected to a recollection that rivaled the soliloquy from *Henry the Sixth*. Wouldn't you agree, Miguel?"

"Since I'd been sick with the flu for most of the week," Rafael's assistant said, his mouth turning slightly petulant, "I couldn't say."

"That's right. A lucky escape for you. Five days of bed rest just to avoid a couple of hours with the ambassador."

"Rafael, don't tease Miguel," Trevy said, noticing dark circles under the poor man's eyes. "The ambassador is delightful. I enjoy hearing about trade negotiations."

"Really," Rafael said skeptically, "then why the sad face? Is it JC? Your brother can be high maintenance, but he goes back to Moscow soon, no?"

"Wednesday," Trevy confirmed. "It's not the company or JC, Raphael. Forgive me, I'm just a little distracted tonight." She had planned to leave it at that, but somehow the words bubbled up in her throat anyway and she heard herself adding, "I was at a funeral this morning for one of the girls in my literacy class. She was killed last Sunday."

"One of your *chicas perdidas*?" Rafael touched her shoulder, his concern stamped on his face.

Her lost girls. That was what he called the teenagers she taught at the community center. Trevy frowned and glanced back at JC, worried he might overhear, but he was too busy charming Sophia Hermosa to listen to her conversation with Rafael and his assistant.

"My condolences," Miguel Navarro murmured sympathetically, but Trevy could tell he was annoyed that she'd brought it up. Talk of death was about as welcome at an embassy reception as illness or religion.

"Killed?" Rafael asked, seizing on her careless choice of words. "Have the police arrested the murderer?"

"No." End of story. End of the conversation. Or so she thought when Rafael's expensive Swiss watch chimed the hour, momentarily distracting him. Trevy looked to Miguel, expecting him to step into the conversational void and suggest it was time for Rafael to schmooze with one of the many suits milling about.

But Miguel was also checking the time on his lookalike watch, so he missed the opportunity to steer his boss back on track.

"Until the police make an arrest," Rafael said after the last notes from his watch faded away, "you must be careful, *querida*."

"I am careful," Trevy said, ignoring the urge to remind him that she was thirty-two, not two. "The FBI and the D.C. police are working together on the case. I'm not in any danger." Agent Larsen was convinced the Diablos would retaliate for the Vega murder, but Trevy still hoped the threat of drawing MS-13 into the fray would be enough to prevent further violence.

"What if the gangs think you're assisting the police with the investigation?" Rafael's dark brows arrowed downward. "You know what can happen to witnesses. Terrible things. Remember a few years ago, that young girl who was found along the bank of the Potomac River. Beheaded. Am I correct, Miguel?"

"Beheaded," Miguel agreed with a brusque nod.

The teenager had testified against an MS-13 gang member accused of murder and a long list of other crimes including extortion, money laundering, drug dealing, and human trafficking.

But Trevy wasn't a witness. And she needed to end to this conversation before JC figured out that they were talking about gruesome gang slayings instead of embassy gossip. "I don't know who killed Lola Sanchez. I'm not in any danger."

Agent Larsen hadn't verbally acknowledged her at the funeral, so no one knew she was helping him. Even now Trevy could feel the heat lingering from his frustrated gaze when their eyes had met as she filed past him at the end of the service. He had stood in the back of the church for the entire ceremony, studying the faces of everyone who stopped to say a few words to the Sanchez family.

"If you say so." Rafael sounded only half-convinced.

"I do," Trevy insisted, despite the continued unease she felt about the frightened words Ceci had whispered into her ear when it was Trevy's turn to offer condolences to the Sanchez family. Words that had sent Trevy's gaze straight to Razor's tattoo-stained face.

Before Rafael could challenge her further, Miguel cleared his throat. "Here comes Señor del Fuego," he murmured discreetly and stepped aside to make introductions.

"Señor del Fuego," Rafael said, seamlessly slipping into his official role, "the U.S. Trade Representative agreed to meet us in California to tour the facility you're interested in purchasing."

Miguel consulted his agenda. "We arrive in Santa Rosa at noon on Monday. I'll finalize the itinerary and deliver the briefing books to your apartment while you're attending the ambassador's dinner tonight." He turned to a clean page in his notebook, and Trevy took note of his relieved smile. His boss was back on message.

While Rafael and Sr. del Fuego discussed the wine industry and the Spaniard's strategy for gaining a foothold in the U.S. market, Trevy surreptitiously glanced around the room in search of her brother. He'd disappeared…and so had the ambassador's daughter Sophia. How like JC to indulge in a flirtation when he was booked on a flight back to Moscow on Wednesday.

Relaxing now that Rafael's attention was no longer on her, she took a sip of wine and let her gaze fall onto a medieval tapestry that dominated the wall to her right, directly behind the diplomat. Woven in silken threads, the bloodthirsty design was eerily reminiscent of a crime scene. Danger seemed to lurk everywhere these days…

What if the gangs think you're assisting the police with the investigation? Rafael's question had struck a nerve. And if Agent Larsen was right, it was only a matter of time before the Diablos would retaliate. Even if she wasn't in any danger, her girls certainly were.

Maybe even Lola's sister.

Trevy was not going to be able to wait for the gang task force to find Bandit, she realized. Agent Larsen needed to hear what Ceci had told her.

NINE

BANDIT STOOD IN the dark across the street from the New Hope Community Center, waiting for Razor's girlfriend Angel. The brightly lit building mocked him with its promise of warmth. Of safety. All false promises. He hadn't been inside the center since the night of Lola's death. Only a week ago.

It felt like years had passed. And, thanks to Lola, every minute had been hell on earth. He zipped his Raiders jacket to keep out the cold. Shouldn't be long now. The key he'd found in Lola's room had been passed from him to Razor to Angel, who would be doing Lola's job. He slid more deeply into the shadows of the building. A streetlight was broken. Black pooled on the sidewalk like a stain. Then the wide double doors of the community center banged open and the *chicas* spilled out. They were laughing and talking.

All except for Angel. She paused in the open doorway, eyes searching for someone. Him? Ashamed to be caught hiding in the shadows, Bandit stepped into the light and Angel called *adios* to the others. He watched her cross the street. Tight jeans, hips swaying with every step of her fuck-me heels, her black jacket unzipped as if the cold didn't bother her. Her shirt was made of some kind of sparkly stuff that drew his eyes to her tits. And the long gold chain that disappeared into the low-cut vee.

"*Hola*, Bandit," she said, her red lips turning up at the corners. "Were you waiting for me out here in the cold?" She tossed her long wavy black hair over her shoulder and looked at him through heavily made-up dark eyes. Beautiful and scary at the same time. Bandit swallowed hard.

"Did everything go okay?"

"Worried about me?" she teased, her smile broadening. "That's so sweet." She ran a cherry-red fingernail up the front of his jacket and lightly scratched the beard stubble on his chin before pulling the long chain out of her cleavage and swinging the car key on the end of it in small circles close to his face.

Sweat pooled between his shoulder blades. He stiffened, resisting the urge to step away. *Dios*, he hoped Razor wasn't hiding somewhere nearby, watching them. Angel's little show had nothing to do with flirtation. She was flexing her muscles, toying with him. If he dissed her by jerking away, he was as screwed as he'd be if he made a play for her. Life kept throwing shit at him. Thanks to Lola, he owed Razor ten thousand dollars. And he had killed a girl. Not even a Diablo. Just a thirteen-year-old girl with even shittier luck than him. Razor had shrugged it off, but it was eating away at Bandit. Some days, he almost wished Razor would get it over with and kill him. Almost.

Angel threw her head back and laughed. *Bitch*. Even her laugh was sexy. The large hoops in her ears swung violently, catching the light of the street lamp. She pressed against him and whispered, "Poor Bandit, you don't know what to do with me, do you?"

Another question he was better off not answering. He breathed in her perfume and smiled weakly. "Give me the phone. Razor's waiting for me."

Maybe Razor's name would remind her that she should be careful too.

"I'll take it to him."

Holy *Cristo*, she was cutting him out of his job. Her idea? Or Razor's? Bandit caught her by the arm. "Show me the phone," he said, his voice tight with panic. "Now."

"Chill," she said with a cold look that froze his balls. Then, with a huff of annoyance, she dug the phone out of her coat pocket. "Satisfied?"

Bandit studied the small flip phone cradled in her palm. A black plastic throwaway. Same as always. A new burner for each shipment. Only Razor knew the password to access the voice mail that would give them the lowdown on when and where to pick up the next shipment of contraband cigarettes.

How long would it take before Angel convinced Razor she could drive the shipment to New York too? A hard knot of fear formed in his stomach. He didn't have a fucking clue where Lola had stashed the money she'd stolen. The next shipment was going to cost Razor ten thousand dollars of his cut. With each unfolding hour, it became more and more obvious to Bandit that he'd outlived his usefulness. A smart *vato* would disappear while the going was good—the farther away, the better.

But the few dollars left in his wallet wouldn't even cover a bus ticket to Maryland, so instead of escaping while he could, he made a grab for the phone.

With a fast backward swing of her arm, Angel whipped the burner out of reach and shoved him back a step.

"I take my orders from Razor. Not you," Bandit said, desperately searching for the words that would convince her to give him the phone.

"It's too cold to stand outside arguing." Angel slid the phone back into her pocket and zipped up her jacket. She gave him a strange look, like maybe she felt sorry for him. "You can come with me, Bandit." As she walked away from the community center, he hurried to catch up.

Three blocks later, a black Navigator slowed to a crawl alongside them. Razor was supposed to be waiting at some dive motel on Rhode Island Avenue. What was he doing here? It wasn't like him to be anywhere near the community center on Sunday evenings. He never put himself on the line when someone else was willing to do his dirty work. Someone expendable. Someone like him. Or Lola. Even Angel.

Bandit aimed a questioning glance at Angel, but she just shrugged her shoulders and stepped up to the car as it rolled to a stop.

"*Hola*," Razor said through the open window. He looked past Angel, his eyes zeroing in on Bandit. "You got the phone?"

"No, I—" Bandit bit down on the words when he saw Razor's expression darken. So it *had* been Angel's idea to cut him out. "I mean, yes, Angel—"

She held it out to Razor. "I told Bandit I could bring the phone to you without an escort, but he insisted on coming."

Razor shifted his gaze from Bandit to his girlfriend. After a long beat of silence, he grabbed the phone. "I don't like you messing with the plan, Angel. Next time, Bandit brings it to me."

"But he's got a big target painted on his back," Angel said, shooting him a smirk before she climbed into the back of the truck. As she closed the door, he heard her add, "What are you gonna do if Bandit gets picked up by the cops again? He's no use to you if he can't drive the shipment.

Still rooted to the sidewalk, Bandit watched Razor consider her point. At least Angel thought he was good for something.

"From now on, Angel delivers the phone," Razor decided, "and Bandit drives the shipments." He powered on the phone and keyed in the voice mail code. "Get in, Bandit."

Resigned, Bandit climbed into the back, next to Angel. He should have run when he had the chance. There would be a shipment to drive to New York later tonight. Not long after that, Bandit would find out if he was more useful to Razor than the ten thousand dollars that would be coming out of the Chingazos's cut.

As if reading his mind, GQ, Razor's right-hand man, looked back at Bandit from the passenger seat and mouthed, "Stupid fuck."

"What's this shit?" Razor lobbed the question toward the backseat like a grenade ready to detonate on impact. He held out the phone, the volume cranked high enough for them all to hear the message. Three words: "Wait. *Soy Trece.*"

"Wait for what?" Bandit's insides tightened. Beside him, Angel kept her mouth shut. Smart *chica*.

In the rearview mirror, Razor's eyes narrowed into slits of fury. "If we lose this deal…" Razor didn't need to finish. Bandit knew the rest. He was a dead man. Hell, he was a dead man anyway. He turned his head to stare at the blur of light and shadow outside his window.

"*El Trece* wants to wait for things to cool off," GQ said as they idled at a red light. He took the burner from Razor and pulled out the battery. Bandit felt the knot in his chest loosen. Razor usually listened to GQ. "Two murders in a week gets the cops heated up. *El Trece* will have something for us next week."

GQ lowered his window and pitched the cell phone into the road, where it would be crushed under the wheels of an oncoming car.

"I'm sick of this waiting shit." Razor complained. He turned in his seat to glare at Bandit. "Clock's still ticking, homie." He flipped open his knife and tapped the four-inch blade against his broken front teeth. "Ten thousand dollars. Tomorrow."

"Then kill me now," Bandit said. His bravado surprised both of them. But Bandit was tired of living on the edge of fear. He was a fugitive, broke, desperate, and lonely. He missed Lola even though he blamed her for the shithole his life had become. At least she hadn't lived to see him turn into a killer…

Thoughts clicked behind Razor's shark eyes. Bandit knew he was weighing the pros and cons of killing him. He held his breath and waited, not sure which outcome he would prefer.

The blare of a horn interrupted the stare down. Green light. Razor hit the gas. "No, I still need you," he said, and Bandit breathed a sigh of relief. So that was the answer then: He still wanted to live more than he wanted to die. Maybe he was as *loco* as Razor. "By next week, you better have the money that bitch stole from *El Trece*. And don't get caught by the cops."

An hour later, Bandit let himself into the two-bedroom apartment that he, his mother, and his two younger brothers shared with the Ortiz family: ten people in all when Señor Ortiz wasn't down in Florida or Texas picking oranges and strawberries. Cold enough, hungry enough, to risk spending the night at home despite Razor's pointed warning, he breathed in the delicious smell of onions and browned meat. He could hardly wait to load a plate full of whatever his mother had made for dinner.

Ma, arms elbow-deep in soapy water, was in the kitchen with two of the Ortiz girls. Seven-year-old Brenda dried the dishes and Elizabeth, her elder by two years, put them away in the cabinet. She had to stand on an old metal folding chair to reach the shelves. Catching sight of Bandit in the doorway, Ma dried her hands on her apron and stepped away from the sink.

"Hector, where have you been?" Her dark brows drew together, deepening the lines on her face. She looked past him and called, "Javier, come finish up for me."

"Ma, I got homework," Bandit's eleven-year-old brother shouted from the bedroom he shared with their mother and six-year-old brother Jorge.

"Homework?" She raised her voice to be heard over the cartoons blasting full volume in the bedroom. "Do you think I can't hear the TV? Get in here. Help Brenda and Elizabeth with the dishes. Then you can *start* your homework."

"*Sí, Madre*," he said, coming into the kitchen, his face like a thundercloud. The Ortiz girls giggled, making Javier's scowl deepen, but he didn't say a word. Sometimes it was better to act like the other family sharing your living space didn't exist. That's what Bandit always did. That and stay away from home as much as possible.

Tonight, though, the deaf and blind act wasn't working for him. Not when the two youngest Ortiz boys were chasing each other around the living room like wind-up toys gone *loco*. Ma pulled him away from the little monsters.

"The police were here," she said, swatting him on the side of his head with the flat of her hand. Not enough to hurt, just enough to show she was upset. "They want you to go down to the police station to answer some questions. Why didn't you tell me about Lola? I had to hear the news from Señora Ortiz." She pulled him into a tight hug that made him feel safe. Then she spoiled the illusion by whispering, "Are you in trouble?"

He shrugged and knocked her arms away. *Mierda*. He had to get out of here. He had been wrong; even one night at home was too risky. Benny Ortiz, a five-year-old bowling ball of flailing arms and thick black hair, plowed into him as Bandit took a step back toward the front door. Three-year-old Nicky threw himself on top of his brother and screamed, "Mine! Mine!"

Bandit shook them off and they tumbled to the floor in a mass of kicking arms and legs. Nicky tugged at something fuzzy and brown that Benny was hugging to his middle. A stuffed animal, Bandit noted with disgust. They were fighting over a stupid stuffed animal.

"If you want it, take it, crybaby," Benny challenged, tightening his grip. Nicky tugged the toy and cried harder.

"Hector, I have leftovers. Come get something to eat," Ma said, over the chaos of clanking dishes, fighting brothers, and loud cartoon music. "Turn that down," she called out to Jorge.

"I already ate, Ma," Bandit lied. No way could he choke down even one bite. He had to get away now, before the cops came back.

In a last-ditch effort, Nicky lunged forward to latch onto the stuffed animal with his teeth, then fell backward, a furry brown leg hanging suspended from his mouth.

"You wrecked it, you big fat baby." Benny held up the torn toy and let out a wail.

That's when Bandit realized it was Lola's bear. His baby's bear. He snatched it from Benny. How had the little monsters found it? He'd stuffed it so far underneath the couch no one should have been able to find it.

But the little fuckers had.

"That's mine." Rage boiled through Bandit. The bear was ruined. *Jesús Cristo*, he couldn't even take care of a stuffed animal. How pathetic was that? Bandit wanted to hit someone, starting with Benny.

But Ma stopped him. With a firm push, she sent Benny to the Ortiz family's bedroom. Then she picked up Nicky and held him while he wailed, the bear's torn leg still clenched in his teeth. The girls huddled in the kitchen doorway and stared at Bandit. Brenda giggled. "Hector has a teddy bear." Elizabeth nodded her head and giggled too, one hand over her mouth. She was old enough to be afraid of him.

Bandit threw the ruined bear out the open door. It hit the wall with a solid thwack and slid to the floor. He kicked it ahead of him like a soccer ball as he walked down the hall. He had to get out of there before he hurt somebody. Before the cops came back for him. Before Ma figured out he was neck deep in shit and sinking fast. Before he started bawling like the little Ortiz monsters.

"Where are you going, Hector?" His mother followed him to the open door.

"Leave me alone." Bandit kicked the bear down the stairs and out onto the sidewalk. When he leaned down to pick it up so he could shove it into the trash can on the corner, a tiny notebook fell out of the torn seam where the bear's leg had been attached and bounced off his boot.

The stuffed bear forgotten, he grabbed the notebook and thumbed through it. Lola's scrunched handwriting covered the pages. Bandit moved closer to the streetlight. His back pressed against the metal pole, he squatted down on his haunches and turned to the first page. The letters looked like meaningless black squiggles. More like a secret code than simple words and sentences. Shit. He forced himself to take a deep breath and slowly sound out each letter as if his life depended on it.

Because it might.

TEN

MONDAY AFTERNOON, CRUZ sat in the back of the mostly full auditorium. A man in a dark suit was bound to look out of place, but only a couple of students cast curious glances his way before returning their attention to the front of the lecture hall and Trevy Barlow. This morning's topic was transnational street gangs and terrorist organizations. Two hundred kids were transfixed. He found himself being drawn in against his will, and he almost wished he'd arrived before the last ten minutes of class. Who would have guessed Dr. Do-Good was such a rock star?

As soon as Trevy Barlow finished her lecture and shut down her microphone, students converged on her instead of heading for the exits. Cruz sat unmoving in the back and waited. After five minutes, he saw her glance at her watch. *That's right, Dr. Barlow, you're late.* She'd called him at 8:30 that morning to ask if he would meet her after her afternoon class. He watched her disengage from the throng of students. All but one took the hint. A shaggy-haired, earnest do-gooder in the making tagged along after Trevy as she left the auditorium through a side door. Cruz followed at a distance as they moved down a narrow hallway to her office in the basement of the sociology department.

"I only have a few minutes before my next meeting, so we might have to finish during my office hours," Cruz heard her say as he approached. *Wrong, Dr. Barlow, fifteen minutes late and counting.* He stepped into the open doorway. Trevy Barlow was standing behind the student, peering over his shoulder at the screen of the kid's laptop.

"Jake, this is good," she said with unfeigned enthusiasm that was puffing up the student's ego. Christ, the kid looked like he was ready to move mountains for her. "I like the topic you've chosen to explore. I think the problem is that your approach is too broad. You might consider—"

He tuned out her words, letting her precise upper-crust voice wash over him as he checked out her small office. It could easily have doubled as a broom closet. There was barely enough room for her desk and a tall metal filing cabinet. His phone alarm vibrated in his pocket, a reminder that he'd pissed away nearly half the time he'd allotted for this meeting with Dr. Do-Good. Next on his to-do list was some face time with the assistant U.S. attorney handling the Sanchez case. Tick-tock, he didn't have time to waste. He rapped his knuckles on the doorframe. Dr. Do-Good glanced up and saw him. She ran a hand through her hair and gave him a wary smile. A tingle of uncertainty ran through him. Why had she sent for him? The kid followed her gaze and his expression hardened. *Yeah, sharing sucks, kid. Too bad. Time for you to scram.*

"Am I interrupting?" Cruz asked.

The student snapped his laptop shut and stood. "Thanks, Dr. Barlow. Can I send you a draft to read Friday?"

"Absolutely, Jake. My office hours are from four to five-thirty today if you have more questions."

Cruz waited in the doorway until the kid cleared out. Then he shut the door and sat in the extra chair in front of her desk. "What've you got for me, Doc?"

Trevy moved behind her desk as if she needed to put a barrier between them. She took a deep breath and cut to the chase. "Razor has a new tattoo on his face. Two teardrops."

"Already noted, Dr. Barlow." His expectations for learning something important clicked down two notches. He'd been at the funeral too. He hoped this wasn't the reason why Dr. Do-Good had wanted to see him. Did she think he was too dense to notice the gangbanger's new facial art? "You think he's claiming responsibility for shooting Samantha and Charlie Vega?"

She shook her head. "Not Charlie Vega. He survived. I meant Lola."

Whoa. Now that *was unexpected.* He kept his expression neutral. "Yeah?"

"After the funeral, Ceci Sanchez—Lola's sister—told me she thinks the Chingazos were involved in Lola's murder."

"Why?"

"Before school on Thursday, Bandit waylaid Ceci to find out if the police had returned the key on the pink ribbon that Lola always wore around her neck. Razor wanted it."

"Did Bandit tell Ceci why?" he asked, leaning forward, his hands gripping the edge of the desk. The key in question had been cut from a locksmith's blank and had no distinguishing marks or key codes that could be used to search car manufacturer databases. He watched her eyes, looking for any hint that she wasn't being straight with him. She shifted her chair back a couple of inches, but maintained eye contact.

"A matter of life and death. That's what he told her." Her eyes flicked up and to the right. Recalling the memory, not lying. "When Ceci told him that the police hadn't returned the key, Bandit made her take him home so that he could search Lola's room. He tore the place apart."

"Did he hurt her?"

"Scared the hell out of her. Does that count?"

"It counts. Ceci should have called me." Damn it. He was sick and tired of people holding out on him. How was he supposed to help them if he didn't have any information? He wasn't fucking clairvoyant. "Did Bandit take anything?" Cruz knew the gang members weren't going to find the key—it had been tagged and stored in the evidence warehouse—but he was interested in why Razor wanted it. And if there was a copy, as Bandit's search indicated, it had to have some significance.

"Just a stuffed bear that was Lola's." Trevy bit down on her bottom lip and held his gaze. "Ceci's afraid, Cruz. Afraid what happened to Lola might happen to her—especially if word leaks out that she's talking to the FBI and pointing a finger at the Chingazos."

He sat back and crossed his arms, the sound of his name on her lips—Cruz, not Agent Larsen—momentarily distracting him. He gave himself a mental shake. *Stay on track, pal.* "What do you know about this key?"

"Nothing." She tapped her fingers on the desk and exhaled loudly. She was frustrated. *Welcome to my world, babe.* "A few weeks after Lola started coming to my literacy class, I noticed her wearing a car key on a long velvet ribbon. So I asked her about it. She looked at me as if I'd lost my mind. 'A car? Don't be *loco*,' she told me. Apparently the key was a flea market find. The cool, retro shape reminded her of a Tiffany key. I suspect she was being ironic."

"Tiffany key?"

"Charms shaped like keys. Haven't you seen them? Tiffany makes them in gold and silver. The really expensive ones are diamond-studded." He suppressed a snort. Yeah, like he popped into the high-end jewelry store on a regular basis. "They're popular with teenage girls in the more affluent neighborhoods of the city. They wear them on long chains draped around their necks. Why on earth would Razor want Lola's necklace?"

"You think Razor killed Lola," Cruz said, ignoring her question, "and was smart enough, organized enough, to pin it on the Diablos?" He tried the idea on for size. It wasn't impossible. Especially if Lola had something that belonged to the gangbanger. But it had to be something more valuable than an old flea market key.

"I would never underestimate Razor. He's capable of extreme violence when threatened and he has a finely honed instinct for survival."

"Ever seen him wearing a dark parka with a hood?"

"Yes, but that doesn't mean—"

"Yeah, yeah, I get it. So does half the male population of D.C.," he said with an impatient wave of his hand. "You know I'm going to have to talk to Ceci about this."

Before she could protest, he added, "Don't look so worried, Doc. I'll be discreet. The Chingazos won't find out." Then he leaned forward and touched her hand. She looked so desperately in need of reassurance that he couldn't help himself. Their gazes met. And in that moment, he read trust in her gold-green eyes.

"Thank you, Trevy," he said, tightening his grip. For an instant, she held onto him as if she didn't want to let go. He forced himself to release her fingers. "You did the right thing when you called me this morning," he told her. He stood up. The meeting was over, but something important had changed between them. When had she begun to believe they were on the same team? For the first time since Lola Sanchez's death, he felt a faint glimmer of hope. She was beginning to trust him.

His first stop after leaving Trevy Barlow's cramped office was Ceci Sanchez's school. He enlisted the help of the principal to facilitate a private meeting with Ceci and her mother in the principal's office. And although the meeting went smoothly, Ceci didn't tell him anything he didn't already know.

After leaving the school, he spent an hour with the assistant U.S. attorney assigned to the cases before walking over to MPD headquarters on Indiana Avenue for an up-close-and-in-person meeting with the chief of police, who was more than happy to pin the gang task force's lack of progress on the FBI. Not only had Cruz failed to solve the Sanchez homicide before the mayor's deadline, he had also failed to prevent the Vega murder a few days later. The chief was making sure that everyone knew where to point the finger of blame: squarely at Special Agent Cruz Larsen.

A hell of a way to start the week.

Several hours later, when twilight was starting to creep in, Cruz was sitting in the FBI Washington field office, a phone receiver pressed to his ear. He leaned back in his government-issue chair as he listened to Lou Alvarado's update on the new developments in the Vega case. The gun he'd found in the storm sewer had been reported stolen two years ago.

"No readable prints," Alvarado said. No surprises there. Readable prints on a gun were the exception, not the rule. "No DNA either. I'm still waiting for the ballistics report."

Damn. "At least I found the gun. What about those paint prints on the spray can?"

"Inconclusive. Two might belong to Hector Bonilla, might not. The paint was too thick for the techs to verify a positive match."

"Nothing about this case is going to be easy, is it?" Cruz pushed back from the computer and rubbed his neck to ease some of the stiffness. Even if ballistics checked out, they didn't have strong physical evidence linking Hector Bonilla—or any Chingazos Locos—to Samantha Vega's murder.

"You don't like it easy, man." Alvarado laughed. "Never have. Not even in our Ranger days."

"Screw you," Cruz said without heat. But just to rib him back, he added, "Are you sure no one spotted you at the Sanchez funeral?"

"You insult me. I'm a detective, not a uniform. I was part of the scenery. Nobody pays attention to a homeless drunk, sitting in a bus stop shelter."

"Let's go over the action outside the church again. Who, what, where."

"Razor arrived in style in a black Lincoln Navigator with spinning rims. He's one mean-looking dude."

Cruz grunted in agreement. Samantha Vega had been gunned down by someone in a black SUV. Coincidence? The evidence Alvarado was rolling out supported a retaliatory strike by the Chingazos, but the new information from Ceci Sanchez suggested otherwise. "And you checked the vehicle for bullet holes?"

"That's right. I couldn't get too close. Razor's lieutenant GQ stayed with the car the whole time, but I was close enough to snap a picture of a ding on the passenger-side mirror. A strip of paint the size of my pinky's missing. A forensic photographer is taking a look at the photo for me to determine whether a bullet could have done the damage."

Physical evidence that could help them build a case against the Chingazos. Now that he had secured Trevy Barlow's cooperation, they needed to flush the gangbanger out of hiding so he could spill all his secrets to her. "I thought for sure Bandit would attend the funeral."

"Well, he wasn't hiding in Razor's SUV. I counted fifteen people in the Navigator—including four in the cargo space in the back. There was no room. Accept it, Cruz, the dirtbag skipped his pregnant girlfriend's funeral."

"He didn't vanish into thin air," Cruz said, his voice level despite his growing frustration. "Maybe he got out of Dodge."

"Or maybe he's dead."

"Real helpful, Lou." Bandit had links to two homicides in a seventy-two-hour period. If he was dead, so were his secrets. It was time to fill Alvarado in on the new lead.

"Cecilia Sanchez came forward with some information. Razor sent Bandit to the Sanchez apartment looking for Lola's key."

"That's not good."

"Yeah, we need to take another look at that key. Lola was up to something in that parking garage that got her killed. That key might be more important than we had realized."

Alvarado's silence on the other end of the line raised his hackles. "What are you thinking, Lou?"

"The murder weapon's been temporarily misplaced."

"The ribbon and the key? Tell me you're joking. How the hell does evidence get temporarily misplaced?"

"The question is why the hell doesn't it happen more often?" Alvarado's voice was still calm, unperturbed, slightly amused. Typical Alvarado. "We'll find it. You know what the evidence warehouse is like. Someone put it in the wrong place. It'll turn up eventually."

"Hardly a comfort. You want to let the U.S. Attorney's office know? They'll kick our asses into next week for wrecking the prosecution's case before we've even made an arrest. Hell, I'd like to kick some asses myself."

"I know, man, but what can I do?"

"Find that goddamn key," Cruz suggested. "It might be the one piece of evidence that pulls everything together."

"Do you want to bring Razor in for questioning?"

"Not yet. If word leaks that I met with Ceci Sanchez right before Razor was brought in for questioning, he might go after her." Trevy Barlow was right to be concerned about the girl's safety. Razor had a finely honed instinct for survival, and he wouldn't hesitate to use violent means to silence Lola's sister if he considered her a threat.

And Cruz had promised Trevy Barlow he wouldn't endanger Ceci. But Alvarado didn't need to know that.

"Just keep a surveillance team on Razor. Maybe he'll do something to give us an excuse to bring him in. In the meantime, find Bandit. He's the weak link."

Alvarado sighed. "If he's still in the area, he'll turn up eventually."

"Sooner would be better," Cruz said and hung up the phone. He swiveled in his chair to face his desk, only then realizing that someone had entered his office while he was talking to Alvarado. The man was leaning against the wall near the open doorway. With his movie-star handsome face and expensive suit, he looked like he'd just stepped off the cover of one of those men's magazines. He returned Cruz's stare, his expression undisturbed, as if he had every right in the world to be there. He looked vaguely familiar. Cruz searched his memory until an image from his background search on Dr. Do-Good surfaced, and a name clicked into place. Jean-Claude Barlow had come to pay him a visit. How interesting.

Cruz raised a dark eyebrow and waited for Trevy Barlow's brother to break the silence.

A smile touched the corner of the man's mouth. "I hope you don't mind"—he said smoothly, a diplomat to the core—"I didn't intend to disturb you." He looked around the office at the stacks of files that covered every available surface: chairs, tables, the floor. "And there was no other place to wait."

"The hallway would have sufficed," Cruz said, refusing to play this polite game.

"I'll remember that next time."

"There's going to be a next time?"

The amusement vanished from Barlow's eyes in an instant. Cruz caught a glimpse of the hard core Barlow hid behind his handsome face and perfect manners. "That depends on you."

"How so?" Cruz reminded himself that he needed to tread carefully. Why the hell was Trevy Barlow's brother paying him a visit? Unless he'd caught wind of her involvement in the Sanchez case. Had she told him? He didn't imagine her family would be too pleased to find her in the middle of a homicide investigation, especially given the recent escalation in gang violence.

"JC Barlow." The diplomat pushed away from the wall and stepped closer. He tossed a business card on the desk and held out his hand.

"Cruz Larsen," he said, ignoring the card. He fought the urge to stand up and shake the man's hand. Damn sneaky bastard's ambush tactics didn't merit common courtesy. "But I guess you already know that."

"Yes. I'm Trevy's brother."

"I figured as much. What brings you all the way from Moscow to my humble abode?" Cruz asked, making use of the facts he'd uncovered about JC Barlow while researching Trevy's background. If Barlow's advantage was surprise, his was information.

"Hmm, so she's told you about me. I wish I could say the same about you." He leaned a hip against Cruz's desk. "I'm in town to find a place to live. I'm being reassigned to Washington for a few months before my next posting."

"To?" Mr. Slick was trying his best to intimidate him.

"Tegucigalpa," he said like a native Honduran. "The Public Affairs section."

"Might be dangerous," Cruz ventured. With over four hundred miles of unpatrolled Atlantic coastline and an unstable government, Honduras was ideally situated for black market trafficking to the U.S., and Europe via Africa. Not to mention Russia's renewed interest in making friends in Central America.

"The Cultural Affairs Office? Hardly."

Cruz's gut was telling him that Barlow's low-level, super-safe cultural affairs post was a CIA cover, but he decided to play along. "Are you here in an official capacity, JC? Do you need the assistance of the FBI?"

"No," he said. Without asking permission, he moved a stack of files off the visitor's chair and sat down. "You strike me as a man who appreciates straight talk. So I won't dance around the issue. I was there in Montrose Park when you met Trevy last week." His bluntness surprised Cruz. The diplomat had taken off his white gloves.

"You were following her?" Cruz feigned outrage just to throw JC further off balance.

"She seemed upset and it wasn't like her to leave me for another appointment. Not when I had just arrived in town. And I could tell she was lying about something."

"So you followed her. She's a grown woman, you know."

"Yes, a grown woman who's made it her life's purpose to try to help dangerous people who probably don't give a damn whether she lives or dies."

Seemed to be a family trait, Cruz was tempted to observe, but he swallowed the words and let JC continue his rant.

"Until I saw her climb into the car with you, I thought maybe she was meeting a gang member or going into a dangerous part of town to study the latest wall of graffiti."

Was it possible JC's visit to his office had nothing to do with the Sanchez case, and everything to do with his guilt for not being there for his sister? The whole damned family seemed to have made a habit of living at least ten time zones away from Trevy.

"How do you know we weren't?" he challenged, skirting dangerously close to the truth. He *had* taken Trevy to a dangerous part of town to do exactly that.

"I recognize a government car when I see one," JC said referring to the piece-of-shit Bureau car. "It wasn't too hard to verify." After standing abruptly, JC started to pace in front of the desk, careful not to knock over any of the piles. "I can't believe Trevy is dating a federal agent... That's beside the point, though. Why all the sneaking around? Are you ashamed to be seen with my sister?"

"Whoa." Cruz held up a hand to halt the conversation. It had swung from annoying to bizarre. He wasn't sure which issue to address first. He started with the most obvious misunderstanding.

"Dating? Trevy told you we were dating?"

JC stopped and fixed his narrowed eyes on him. "Are you telling me that you're not?"

Cruz had less than half a second to make up his mind. Had Trevy invented this story to keep her brother from finding out what she really was up to? He was fairly certain that good old Jean-Claude would try to interfere if he thought Trevy was putting herself at risk by helping the gang task force solve a couple of murders. And he still needed her help to make Bandit squeal.

"Easy there, Jean-Claude, I'm not taking advantage of your sister, if that's what you're thinking."

"Better not be," he muttered, settling himself onto the edge of the desk once again, his composure restored. "I prefer JC."

"What I'd like to know, *JC*, is what's wrong with your eyesight?"

"My eyesight?"

"Why would you think I'd be ashamed to be seen with Trevy? She's a beautiful woman." Too beautiful.

"I never said she wasn't," JC said, shifting uncomfortably. "I guess a brother doesn't always see his sister the way others might. Here I thought that she was hiding herself away in academia. Perhaps I was wrong."

"Why would you think that?" he asked, unable to keep the hostile edge from his voice. Christ, had the dude never bothered to attend one of her lectures? She was freaking magnetic. There was no better way to describe her.

"I'm treading on dangerous ground," JC said with an elegant shrug of his shoulders and a smile meant to disarm him.

But Cruz wasn't going to let the guy off the hook. For some reason that he didn't care to examine too closely, it made him angry to see Trevy's brother dismiss her so easily.

"Let me guess…you thought that your 'not unattractive' sister"—he used his fingers to make air quotes—"knew she couldn't cut it in diplomatic circles so she chose a field where brains mattered more than looks and a high tolerance for bullshit. Am I close, Jean-Claude?"

"Ouch," JC said, raising both hands in surrender. "Closer than

I'd care to admit. Does that satisfy you, Agent Larsen?"

"Call me Cruz," he said with a wave of his hands. He was going to let Jean-Claude off easy this time. This little sidetrack had served its purpose. Dating? Jesus, what had Trevy been thinking? Cruz smiled and settled back in his chair. JC was on the defensive now, and Cruz was firmly in the driver's seat.

"Don't sell Trevy short," Cruz said, warming to the boyfriend act.

"I know she's a remarkable woman. I'm glad to see you do too." Then JC placed both hands on the surface of the desk and leaned forward to add, "I'm meeting Trevy for dinner in half an hour. Come with me. We'll surprise her."

Cruz opened his mouth to refuse, but one look in JC's eyes made him snap his jaws shut. Good old Jean-Claude had neatly turned the tables on him without getting one hair out of place. If Cruz refused, it would seem like he didn't want to be seen with Trevy...his girlfriend. "Let me clear my desk."

"Is that possible?" JC asked with a smirk. He knew he was back in charge, the sneaky bastard.

"No." Cruz stood up, grabbed his suit jacket off the back of his chair, and put it on. "Let's go."

As he followed JC out of the room he wondered what kind of reception he was going to get from Trevy. This was her fault. She was the one who had told her brother he was her boyfriend.

Paybacks were hell.

ELEVEN

BANDIT WAS TIRED, hungry, cold. And he stunk worse than week-old trash. Still, the past twenty-four hours hadn't been all bad news. He'd manage to read Lola's journal from cover to cover—even the boring parts. Page after page of plans. Plans for a better life for herself and the baby.

Bandit couldn't help but wonder if her plans had included him.

But that didn't matter now. He'd found what he was looking for on the last page. *The money is safe with Trevy Barlow*, Lola had written.

Maybe God hasn't abandoned me yet, he thought as he closed the notebook and stuffed it in his pocket. Or maybe God didn't have anything to do this. Bandit pulled up the hood of his sweatshirt and hunched his shoulders, settling deeper into the limited warmth of his Raiders jacket, which had once been his pride and joy. Now it was stained and torn. Ruined from too many nights spent sleeping outside. He'd toss it in the nearest trash can if it wasn't so fucking cold out.

Early evening. The dark streets were crowded with cars. People brushed past him, their strides long, purposeful in the cold wind, eager to find the shelter of home or one of the stores that lined the block. It was a good time of night to blend in.

He moved down the block, keeping to the shadows as much as possible. Would Lola's teacher give him the money if he asked her for it? No, too risky. She might turn him over to the cops so she could keep it for herself. Ten thousand dollars was a lot, even to someone like her. Should he tell Razor about her involvement? He'd know how to convince her to give it back.

Food first, Bandit decided as he drew even with an overflowing trash can. He couldn't think while hunger gnawed at his empty belly. Trying to look casual, he sifted through the top layer and struck gold: a white bag with red stripes and golden arches. He fished it out and shuffled on down the street.

Saliva pooled in his mouth. He looked inside the bag and found the remains of a chicken sandwich and French fries. An apple pie— unopened. For an instant, Bandit felt like he'd won the lottery. He grabbed the apple pie and ate half of it in one bite. Cinnamon and apples burst on his tongue. The sweet pie filling oozed between his lips. He wiped the sticky goop off his face while he turned to look over his shoulder to make sure there weren't any cops around. The coast was clear. He popped the other half of the pie in his mouth as he trudged past the brightly lit McDonalds in the middle of the block.

Not too far away, a shadow spilled from the alley, forming a black rectangle on the brightly lit sidewalk. That was where he planned to fade into the dark. He pulled the chicken sandwich out of the bag. Only a few bites left, but he didn't dwell on what wasn't there. He shoved it into his mouth and chewed, his cheeks pouched out like a squirrel he'd once watched gathering nuts at the playground when he was younger. So long ago it almost seemed like someone else's life.

Several yards from the alley entrance, he tossed the crumpled bag into a wire trash can. Two points, he silently awarded himself. He stepped around a lady carrying two plastic bags of groceries in each hand and looked up into the face of a cop. For half a second, maybe less, their eyes locked, and then Bandit ducked his head. Chewing furiously, he kept walking. He wanted to run, but knew he would draw attention to himself if he moved too fast. He fought the urge to look back over his shoulder. It would be a dead giveaway that he was a wanted man.

The food turned to glue in his mouth. Swallowing was impossible. He used his tongue to shove the half-chewed sandwich deeper into the pockets of his cheeks. Hopefully his puffy cheeks would help distort his features. Holding his breath tight in his lungs, he took two more steps. *Easy does it*, he told himself. Almost there.

He took another step. Just a couple of feet from safety now. His heart beat a loud tattoo in his ears. Don't look back. Easy. Easy. Sweat dripped into his eyes and trickled down his neck.

One more step and his foot would be inside that dark rectangle of shadow that was the alley. Slowly he released the air from his lungs. He worked the food into a ball in his mouth, preparing to spit it out the moment he was out of sight.

"You there!" he heard a voice call out, so close behind him that it took every drop of willpower to keep from swiveling his head to look back.

One more step. Keep moving.

"Hey, Raiders Jacket, I'm talking to you. Hold up!"

Oh, shit.

A hand grabbed him from behind, spun him around, and slammed him against the wall. "I told you to hold up. Let's see some identification."

Bandit's breath sawed in and out of his lungs.

"Jesus, you stink." When the cop turned his head in disgust, Bandit saw his chance. He rammed his head up under the chin of the taller man. The cop's teeth snapped shut with a sickening click of bone against bone. Momentarily stunned, he let go of Bandit, who shoved him aside and ran.

People scattered out of his way, hiding in store doorways or behind parked cars. No one wanted to be caught in the middle of whatever was going down. A quick glance over his shoulder confirmed what Bandit knew in his gut: He didn't have long to disappear. The cop was already keying his radio—calling in backup. If he didn't scram now, he was going to be taking a ride to the station. Assaulting a cop would be added to his growing list of offenses.

In his hurry to get away, he had run in the wrong direction. Now the cop stood between him and the alley. Bandit quickly looked left, then right. The other end of the block seemed miles away. *Hide*! *Hide*! the voice in his head screamed, drowning out all other thoughts. He ran past the McDonalds, past the check cashing place. He needed to disappear and he was running out of options fast. Last on the block was Smitty's BBQ, then a dirt parking lot. He pulled open the glass doors of Smitty's and immediately skirted the line at the register.

Bandit had been in Smitty's a million times before. Small tables filled the rectangular space to the right of the register, and a short hallway at the back led to the restrooms. If he could make it to the men's room before the cop caught up with him, he could escape out the back window into a maze of alleys he knew like the worry lines on his mother's face.

The seating area was mostly deserted. Three guys were eating ribs at a table near the back, but they pretended not to notice him. In this neighborhood, it was safer not to see too much.

He had almost reached the back corridor when he heard the cop push the door open and shout, "I'm looking for a man in a black Raiders jacket. Short. Possibly armed…"

Mierda. Bandit glanced back. At the same time, he ran headlong into an obstacle that hadn't been there a half second before. His feet went sliding out from under him, and he hit the floor, the air whooshing out of his lungs. What the fuck? He stared down at the girl lying under him, the brim of her Smitty's BBQ hat covering one eye. An empty trash bag was gripped in her hand.

"Bandit?" It took him a moment to realize that he was staring into the round face of Rosa Reyes. One of Lola's friends. He had tripped her while she was pulling an overflowing plastic bin from the fake wood paneling that hid the trash from view. The only good part about being on the floor was that he was beneath the cop's line of sight.

"No one saw anything?" the cop's voice prodded. "This guy's dangerous."

Bandit pushed away from Rosa. He didn't have time for explanations. The men's room wasn't too far away. He could still make it if he crawled along the floor, using the empty tables and chairs as cover.

Rosa grabbed his jacket. He tried to shake free, but she was stronger than she looked. Another second and the cop would see him when he walked past the take-out line to question the dudes in the seating area. "Let me go," he panted. "The men's room, is the window barred?"

"In here," Rosa hissed. She shoved him toward the empty trash bin.

"No," Bandit protested. Christ, he'd be trapped. "The back window," he said, hoping she'd understand that he wanted to escape through it.

But then the loud crackle of a police radio cut through the agitated thrum of voices at the front of the fast food restaurant —"Backup on its way. ETA one minute"—and there wasn't any choice. Time was up.

Rosa knew it too. "Quick." She shoved him inside the square bin and closed the flimsy wooden door. She even leaned against it.

"Where'd he go?" The cop's voice was so close now, Bandit was afraid to breathe. He squeezed his eyes shut and counted his heartbeats. He was a dead man.

No one answered until Rosa spoke up. "Who?"

"A guy with a fist tattooed on the back of his neck."

"I saw him," she said, and for half a second, Bandit thought she was going to betray him. "He went that way." Bandit couldn't see her, but he imagined her pointing toward the rear hallway.

"What's back there?"

"Restrooms. Kitchen."

"Is there a back way out?"

"Through the kitchen. There's an alley in the back."

"Which way did he go? Restrooms or kitchen?"

"I didn't see. I was busy with the trash."

The cop swore under his breath and keyed his radio. "Check out the alley in back." His voice faded as he ran toward the rear exit.

After what felt like a year, but could only have been five or ten minutes, Rosa whispered, "He's gone." She pushed open the swing lid that had "Thank you" stamped on the front, letting in a sliver of light. "But you'd better wait here a little longer to be sure."

Bandit could almost breathe again as he looked into Rosa's kind brown eyes. She was not pretty like Lola, but those eyes almost made up for it.

TWELVE

WHEN THE CAB pulled to a stop in front of the most expensive French restaurant in the city, the back of Cruz's neck began to itch. He hated places like this, where the maître d's and waiters acted like they were doing you some kind of favor when they let you through the doors. Suddenly, his perfectly adequate suit felt cheap; his pants, wrinkled. Hell, he'd rather hang out with the parking valet.

And from the smug look JC Barlow sent his way as they walked past the parking valet, Barlow knew it. Shit. Was that Barlow's game? To show his sister that Cruz was beneath her?

And then there she was, Dr. Debutante, looking like she belonged in this exercise in snobbery. She was seated in a fancy French version of a booth. The table was set for two. JC sat across from her, leaving Cruz to squeeze in next to Trevy while the waiter added another place setting and handed them menus.

"I ran into a friend of yours," JC said blandly, "so I invited him to dinner."

Trevy tried to smooth her features into an expressionless blank. Too bad she didn't quite succeed. She glanced up at Cruz and her lips parted to utter the question that was stamped on her face: *What are you doing here?*

Cruz could feel the weight of JC's assessing gaze, so he did the first thing he could think of to shut her up. He pressed his lips against her open mouth.

The unexpected kiss surprised her into immobility. She stared at him, her fairy eyes confused, watchful. He closed his eyes to keep her out of his head, brushing his mouth against hers until he felt her melt into the kiss. She felt good, too good. Forcing himself to release her, he slid his lips across her cheek. Her skin was so soft, he couldn't help but notice, and she smelled insanely good. His mouth settled close to her ear.

"Quit acting so surprised," he whispered. "You should have clued me in this afternoon."

Instead of straightening once he'd delivered his message, he nuzzled her neck, enjoying the havoc she was wreaking on his nerve endings. His body approved and was taking advantage of the fact that his brain had obviously short-circuited.

"Your hair smells like flowers," he murmured and then straightened. *Jesus, get some control, Larsen.*

With her fingers pressed to her lips, Dr. Do-Good looked as uptight as a virgin on her way to a chastity convention. What the hell? This had been her idea. Hadn't it?

"Your brother couldn't wait for you to introduce us, Trevy." He left his arm along the back of her seat, a deliberate invasion of her space. She tried to surreptitiously scoot away, but he let his fingers dangle near her shoulder, anchoring her in place with the threat of even greater contact.

"He decided to pay me a visit at my office. Wanted to know if my intentions were honorable." Cruz smiled at Trevy, who was finally catching on. She glanced at her brother when he added, "Isn't that right, JC?"

"Something like that." Disapproval momentarily flickered in JC's eyes before his diplomat's mask slid back into place. Yeah, JC definitely thought his sister was too good for him. Cruz didn't disagree, but coming clean to JC at this point would create more problems than it would solve.

Trevy smiled at Cruz, a fake smile that he couldn't interpret. He wrapped a silky lock of her caramel-colored hair around his finger and tugged lightly. A warning to choose her words carefully.

We'll talk later, her eyes warned back. Shifting her attention to JC, she said, "How did you find out about Cruz? I don't recall mentioning him."

Cruz's fingers stilled in her hair. So Trevy hadn't come up with the lie? His day had just become a thousand times more complicated. And now he owed her another damned apology.

"Why all the secrecy, Trevania?" JC went on the offensive. A good ploy, but Trevy refused to take the bait. She shrugged her shoulders and tossed her head to dislodge her hair from Cruz's fingers.

"I'm not the one who's sneaking around, Jean-Claude," she said pointedly. Cruz gave major points to Trevy. She wasn't intimidated by her brother. Good for her.

JC sighed. "I'm sorry, Trev, but you're a terrible liar. I knew something was up when you pretended to forget about that meeting last week, so I followed you. I was there when you met Larsen in the park."

"JC! Do I invade your privacy?"

"Sorry, Trev," he said again, not sounding the least bit sorry. "I worry about you. I was afraid you were meeting with some gang member or—"

"That's my job. It's what I do."

"Do you have any sisters, Larsen?" JC said, pulling Cruz into their argument.

"No."

"Brothers?"

"No."

"You're an only child?"

"That's right," Cruz said, his eyes fixed on JC. What the hell was the slippery bastard up to now? No way was he joining Team JC, not when he could be on Team Trevy.

"Really, JC," Trevy protested in an attempt to shut her brother up.

But JC ignored her and continued the interrogation. "Still, you can understand why a brother might worry about his sister, want to watch over her. You're in law enforcement because you want to protect people from harm. Am I right?"

"Yeah," Cruz agreed cautiously.

"Good," JC sat back, a satisfied gleam in his eye that raised his hackles. Was JC worried he might actually harm Dr. Do-Good? Could the guy be any more insulting?

A glance at Trevy confirmed that JC's subtle barb had not gone unnoticed. The look of disgust she shot her brother went a long way toward soothing the sting.

"JC, you invited Cruz to dinner, not an interrogation." Her thigh brushed against his when she tapped her foot against her brother's shin in warning.

It was almost impossible to ignore the sparks of heat that shot up his leg, straight to his groin, so Cruz nearly missed it when JC said, "I don't want to see you repeat the mistakes you made with your ex-husband."

Whoa, JC doesn't fuck around, Cruz thought as he fought to keep his expression neutral. The asshole went straight for the jugular. No holds barred, even for his sister.

"For God's sake, JC," Trevy said, her voice low and angry.

"You didn't tell him?" JC challenged. "How long did you say you've been seeing each other?" His eyes zeroed in on Cruz like a heat-seeking missile.

"That's none of your damn business." Trevy threw her napkin on the table and started to rise.

Without breaking eye contact with JC, Cruz grabbed Trevy by the wrist. Couldn't she see what her brother was doing? He had gone into overprotective mode because he was worried about his sister getting hurt again. And he probably felt a little guilty about living so far away from her. But that didn't excuse his behavior. It was one thing for JC to ambush Cruz, but, for reasons he didn't care to analyze, he minded a lot when JC turned his aim on Dr. Do-Good.

He tugged on Trevy's arm, forcing her to sit. Without releasing her, he reached up with his other hand to capture her chin between his thumb and fingers and gently turned her face until she was looking at him. She was flushed, her eyes half wild with anger. And shame. Feelings he understood all too well. Tenderness uncurled inside his chest. He released Trevy's wrist to lace his fingers with hers. Palm against palm, he could feel the rapid beat of her pulse.

"I know about Trevy's ex-husband," he told JC. Trevy's fingers tightened on his, but she didn't say a word, so he continued.

"Montgomery Fordham," Cruz said, reciting what he'd learned from the background check he'd run on her. Taking a gamble, he said, "Foreign Service stud who cared too much for his career and not enough for his wife. Trevy is well rid of him."

Based on JC's grunt of agreement, Cruz knew he'd gotten it right. The guy had married Trevy for her connections. Between Ambassador Barlow and JC, there'd been plenty for Fordham to like. It had only taken six months of marriage for Trevy to figure out that the bastard was using her.

"What backwater is old Monty Fordham calling home these days?" Cruz said to keep JC from noticing that his sister seemed to have been struck mute. A temporary condition, he was sure.

"He left the foreign service," JC said tightly. "MoFo is running for the open U.S. Senate seat in Texas."

A puff of air escaped Trevy's pursed lips. "For God's sake, JC, are you satisfied? My life is an open book." She cast a sidelong glance at Cruz. Uncertainty had replaced the shame that darkened her eyes. He could almost hear the words that were dying to leap out of her mouth: *You know about my ex?* When she tugged her fingers free of his grip to open her menu, he let go of her hand.

"What looks good?" Trevy asked in an effort to change the subject. "I'm starving."

Interesting. Judging from JC's overprotectiveness, her family was not happy with her career choices or her very short-lived marriage. Cruz opened his menu to give himself time to consider the significance of that. No wonder she hadn't corrected JC's misinterpretation of their relationship. She didn't want JC interfering in her life any more than Cruz did.

His eyes shifted to the words on the menu. Shit. The whole thing was in French, and apparently this place was too fancy for translations. Discomfort flared again. He didn't belong here. Yeah, he knew enough to keep from looking like a total barbarian. Napkin in your lap. Chew with your mouth shut. Never lick your fingers. But this...well, this was asking too much.

The smug bastard and his sister ordered in fluent French, and then it was Cruz's turn. The waiter looked down his long nose at him and said in an accent as phony as a fifteen-dollar bill, "*Monsieur?*"

Cruz pointed to the open menu. "I'll have that."

"*Très bien, monsieur. Qu'est-ce que vous voudriez—*"

"Just the entrée," Cruz said, using the one French word he knew, his Texas drawl growing more pronounced despite his best efforts. He could feel Trevy's gaze on his face. He clenched his jaw, his bottom teeth grinding against the top with enough pressure to create sparks, and forced himself to meet her eyes.

Instead of scorn—or worse, pity—she smiled at him. A warm smile that turned her fairy eyes gold. He barely noticed when the waiter took his menu because she was leaning toward him. Then she murmured into his ear, "It's my turn to apologize."

"For what?"

"I'll forgive you for being a judgmental asshole if you'll forgive me for descending from a long line of insufferable ones," she said. And she brushed her mouth across his.

Cruz smiled against her lips. For a moment, he forgot that he hated snooty French restaurants and interfering brothers. Or even that he had two murders to solve. All he could think about was pulling Trevy closer and kissing her perfect mouth again.

And he would have if they had been alone.

THIRTEEN

ROSA'S SHIFT AT Smitty's ended at eleven, but she volunteered to stay late and lock up. Al, the night manager, was more than happy to let her. After she finished mopping the floor and cleaning the prep area, she opened the trash bin to let Bandit out.

He wasn't there.

Guessing he'd snuck into the restroom after hearing Al leave for the night, she knocked on the door to the men's room—two slow raps followed by two rapid. Then she pushed it open.

The bathroom was empty.

"Bandit?" she said in a loud whisper. A cool breeze brushed over her, drawing her eyes to the open window. With chapped fingers, she yanked up the zipper of her jacket until it closed just below her chin. She hated winter, and the cold, damp rain was almost worst than snow. A wave of homesickness surged up inside her. She missed the heat of San Salvador. Washington D.C. wasn't the Promised Land. She was only sixteen, and yet it seemed like she would never outrun the violence and poverty that followed her like a dark cloud.

"Bandit, it's Rosa," she hissed into the silence, not really expecting an answer. Bandit had taken off without a word. She shouldn't be angry with him. It was almost laughable that she'd thought she could protect him when it was a daily struggle just to take care of herself.

"Damn you, Bandit." She crossed to the window, slammed it shut and locked it. Now she would have to walk all the way back to her family's apartment in the cold, dark night. Alone. If she had left at eleven, she could have gone part of the way with one of her coworkers.

The stiff rubber soles of her Payless sneakers squeaked as she walked across the tile floor and yanked open the door. Why did she even care? She should be glad that Bandit was gone. He was nothing but trouble. Hadn't Lola's death been enough of a warning? And there were rumors that he was the one who had shot that girl, the Diablo's sister. But Rosa didn't believe that. Bandit had a gentle soul. An artist's soul. And Razor was the one who wore more teardrops on his face while Bandit had only added a small L surrounded by a black heart to the back of his hand. She shoved against the door to the women's bathroom. She'd better check on that window too.

From her vantage point in the doorway of the women's restroom, she could tell that the window was closed and locked. She had already turned to leave when a hand grabbed her by the elbow and pulled her inside. The door swung shut behind her.

"Is everyone gone?" Bandit asked, trapping her between the door and his body.

Rosa put a hand on her chest. "Don't scare me like that. I thought you'd left. The window in the men's room was open." Her heart was beating so rapidly that she had trouble catching her breath. She leaned back against the door for support.

"That was what you were supposed to think. I didn't want anyone to get second thoughts about calling the cops back. Is everyone gone?"

"Yes." Rosa turned her head and took a breath through her mouth. *Dios*, he smelled terrible. Bandit took the hint and moved back a few steps.

"*Gracias*, Rosa," he said, brushing past her and out the back door.

He was halfway down the alley behind Smitty's before Rosa caught up with him.

"Bandit, wait."

He turned, pressing his body deeper into the shadows. "What?"

"Where are you going?"

"Hell if I know. You'd better get home, Rosa."

He sounded annoyed, but Rosa gathered her courage and said, "You could sleep on the couch at my place."

"No thanks." He turned to go.

She grabbed his arm. "Everyone will be asleep by now. You could leave first thing in the morning. No one would know."

"Why?"

She frowned. "My mother works the late shift. She won't be home until seven. I'll get you up before six—"

"No. Why are you helping me?"

Rosa hesitated, surprised by the question. Why was she helping him? Her mother would be furious. And so would her father if he had been home. But he was down in Florida for the month, picking tomatoes. The number one rule in her family was to be invisible. That meant staying out of trouble and away from the police. By helping Bandit, she was putting her whole family at risk. Her mother didn't know about her recent brush with the law at the New Hope Community Center. If she did, she wouldn't let her continue to meet with Trevy and the other girls on Sunday evenings.

"Lola was my friend," she said at last. When she felt his arm stiffen beneath her fingers, she wished she had kept quiet. He turned his face away from her and sniffed. Rosa tightened her grip on his arm. He jerked free and pressed his face against the rough brick wall, his shoulders shaking in silent sobs. She raised a hand to touch his back. "Bandit."

Thoughts she barely understood raced through her head. Why did she care? He was nothing to her. He belonged to Lola, now as much as ever. She was a fool to think anything different.

And if he had done what they said—killed that girl—he was permanently beyond her reach. Nothing she could do would save him. Still, she couldn't turn away from him. All the longing that vibrated inside her spilled out, and she wrapped her arms around him, pressing her cheek between his shoulder blades. He was dirty and smelly, but she barely noticed. When he turned and buried his face in her hair, she felt him sink into the warmth of her body.

Whispering tender words into his ear, she stroked her hand along his nape, where his hair was soft as a baby's.

Finally, his crying subsided and he rested limply against her. "Let me help you, Hector."

He pulled away, wiped his nose on the sleeve of his jacket. "Go home, Rosa. Forget you ever saw me."

"I can hide you from the police."

He laughed, a harsh sound like a rusty gate swinging shut. "Who cares about the cops?"

"They almost caught you tonight," Rosa reminded him.

"Maybe I should have let them. I'll be dead soon anyway. Why the hell should I put it off any longer?"

"No, don't say that," Rosa drew back in shock. "Don't ever say that it. It's a sin."

"What's one more?" He shrugged. "I'm a dead man, Rosa. Whether the cops catch me or not, I'm dead."

"Because of that girl?" Even now Rosa didn't want to know the truth, but she couldn't stop herself from asking.

"No, because of this." He slapped a small notebook into her hand.

She opened it. "What is it?"

"Lola's diary."

"I don't understand. You're a dead man because of something Lola wrote in here?"

"Lola stole ten thousand dollars. She wrote about it."

"Burn the notebook. Burn it right here. No one will ever know. I swear I won't tell."

"Too late. *El Trece* knows. Razor too."

"Lola stole from *El Trece*? Give the money back. You can't spend it if you're dead, Bandit."

"Christ, Rosa, I know that, but I don't have it."

Rosa pressed her hand against the cover and then opened it. Foolish Lola. Always the risk-taker.

"What are you going to do?"

It was too dark in the alley to read the scrunched handwriting in the journal, and before she had the chance to decipher it, Bandit grabbed it and snapped it shut. He flicked his finger against the tattered cover. "Don't worry about me. I've got a plan."

"You do?"

"Trevy Barlow's got the money. Lola said so in the book."

"You're going to ask her to give it to you?"

He shook his head. "Too risky." Bandit slid the notebook into his pocket. "She could turn me over to the cops and keep it for herself."

"She wouldn't keep the money. Not if she knew it was stolen. She probably doesn't know what to do with it now that Lola's gone."

"Get real, Rosa. Nobody gives back ten thousand dollars. Not without a gun to the head."

"You're not going to hurt her, are you?"

"Not unless I have to. I'm gonna steal it when she's not home. Razor can help."

Rosa grabbed his arm. "Don't tell Razor. He'll hurt her."

Bandit didn't answer.

"Don't tell him. I'll help you."

"You? No."

"I will. I bet you don't even know where Trevy lives." She could tell it wasn't something he'd thought about.

"Where does she live? Tell me."

"I don't know, but I can find out."

"Forget it, Rosa."

"Then I'll think of something else. Give me a week."

Bandit didn't answer. He just shook his head.

"Please, Bandit. Please. You owe me."

She watched his heavy brows knit together. He didn't like being reminded that she'd rescued him, she could tell. Then he shrugged. "You have until next Monday. Otherwise I give the notebook to Razor."

FOURTEEN

OUTSIDE THE MOVIE theater on Wednesday evening, half a dozen members of the Chingazos Locos gang had taken over the sidewalk in front of the art deco façade, forcing passersby to cut a wide path around them. Behind the wheel of her BMW, Trevy eased off the accelerator as she neared the group. There was Rosa. She stood at the edge of the Chingazos, not quite part of the mix, while the bolder girls like Angel and GQ's girlfriend Maria held center court, shouting out comments to GQ as he tried to impress them with tricks on his skateboard. The vibe of the teens was mostly harmless, especially without Razor around to ratchet up the stakes. So why had Rosa called her twenty minutes ago with an urgent request for a meeting?

Then Trevy spotted Bandit.

She almost didn't recognize him. His face was drawn and dirty and his clothes hung on him like they were two sizes too big. Trevy forced herself to look away from him so she could find a place to park along the busy commercial block on Connecticut Avenue. Was Bandit the reason Rosa had called her? Not for the first time, Trevy wondered what Lola Sanchez's boyfriend had wanted to tell her that he couldn't, or wouldn't, tell Cruz Larsen.

A hundred yards past the Chingazos, Trevy maneuvered her car into a no-parking zone and cut the engine. She should let Cruz know Bandit had resurfaced. But just as she was reaching into her bag for her phone, she saw Rosa separate from the group and head toward her. Trevy decided to hold off. Maybe she could talk Bandit into going down to the police station with her after she spoke with Rosa.

Trevy climbed out of her car to join Rosa on the sidewalk.

"I'm so sorry, Trevy," Rosa said, skipping past pleasantries. Her eyes darted nervously toward the milling teenagers. "I didn't mean for you to come all this way tonight. I thought maybe we could meet somewhere tomorrow. Some place convenient for you."

"No worries, Rosa. I was on my way home when you called." She had just dropped JC off at BWI for his evening flight. "What's up?"

Rosa pressed her lips together and glanced toward the group. Bandit was watching them. He and Rosa locked eyes for an instant before Bandit turned abruptly and stepped closer to the rest of the teens. Was there something going on between the two of them? Nothing good could come from that for Rosa. She could jeopardize her chances of becoming a permanent resident if she wasn't careful. But now was neither the time nor place for that conversation. "Rosa?" she prodded. "Is this about Bandit?"

"No," the girl said, startled, "I need your advice—" Rosa's words were cut short by a shout from the street.

"*¡Chingazos putos!*"

Trevy swiveled to look.

Holding his arms outstretched in front of him, a guy in a dark parka strode toward the group and shouted another slur. Trevy had less than a second to register the gun in his hand before white muzzle flashes and a string of loud pops filled the air, mixing into a discordant symphony with the kids' screams and shouts of confusion.

A few kids dropped to the sidewalk. Others scattered in every direction. Trevy grabbed Rosa and pulled her into the street and behind the small BMW. A high-pitched scream cut through all of the other sounds and went on and on, even after the gunfire had stopped.

"Don't move," Trevy ordered before crawling to the front end of the coupe. Keeping her head low, she peered around the fender to see what was happening. Three of the Chingazos Locos had rushed the gunman and were taking turns punching and kicking him. He lost his grip on the gun, which went sliding across the sidewalk. Angel used her foot to shove it off the curb and it landed with a thunk under the BMW.

"Call 911," Angel shouted over the din. Trevy looked past her. There was a body on the ground by the movie theater ticket window. Long black hair spilled across the cement. The wounded girl writhed in pain, her screams momentarily drowned out by the sirens of the approaching first responders. Trevy narrowed her eyes to cut the glare of the streetlights. Oh, God, it was one of her students. Maria.

At the first sound of sirens, more Chingazos took off, Bandit in the lead. Forgetting about the danger, Trevy ran to Maria. She stripped off her coat and draped it over the teenager's torso, then knelt beside her and spoke softly into her ear. "Help is on the way, Maria. It's going to be okay."

"She's going to bleed out if we don't do something." Angel knelt beside her. She was right. Blood was pooling under Maria's leg at an alarming rate.

"Give me your scarf," Trevy said, but Angel was already unwrapping the cheap nylon from around her neck. Together, they used it to fashion a tourniquet above the wound on Maria's thigh. Angel added her jacket to Trevy's, then pressed her hands against the wound.

As they worked, Maria's screams faded into low moans that were even more frightening. Trevy pulled off the cotton T-shirt from under her sweater and wadded it up, pushing the younger girl's hands away so that she could use the material to put more pressure on the wound. She released a sigh of relief as a fire truck barreled to a stop in front of the movie theater, immediately followed by four patrol cars, blue lights flashing.

The rescue vehicles cut their sirens, but more approaching alarms blared in the distance. The shouting escalated, and she glanced back in time to see GQ leap to his feet and dash toward the side alley, shouting for the other Chingazos to follow. No longer under attack, the gunman pushed himself to his knees. The hood of his gray parka had fallen back and Trevy could see that he was just a kid. Early teens. Blood streamed from his nose and mouth, soaking the red bandana hanging askew on his chin. Los Diablos Rojos.

"Keep the pressure on," Angel told Trevy. Then she launched herself at the LDR gang member before he could escape. "I got the shooter," she shouted to the policemen, who were already piling out of their vehicles, guns drawn. "His gun's under the orange BMW."

Another fire truck arrived with an earsplitting blast of sound, followed seconds later by an ambulance. *Hurry up*, Trevy wanted to shout as a pair of EMTs headed toward Angel and the gunman first. The shooter was lying face down on the sidewalk and one of the cops was slapping his wrists into cuffs. After getting a thumbs up from the paramedics, the officer yanked the kid to his feet and stuffed him into the back of a cruiser. At the same time, two paramedics finally unloaded a stretcher from the back of the ambulance and ran toward Trevy and Maria.

"Leave me the fuck alone," Angel shouted as a policeman barred her from joining them. Ignoring her loud protests, the officer dragged her to an empty cruiser while the medics set up next to Maria.

"I'm Bill. I'm a paramedic," he said, reaching for Maria's wrist. His partner removed the coats to better assess the teen's condition. "What's your—?"

A siren drowned out the medic's voice as the police car with the gunman left the scene.

"What's your name?" the paramedic asked Maria again, drawing Trevy's attention back to the injured girl. Maria moaned and tried to push them away.

"Maria. Her name is Maria Tejada," Trevy said when the EMT glanced over at her. He lifted the balled-up shirt Trevy had been using to keep pressure on the bleeding wound.

"Okay, Maria, can you tell me where you're hurt?" he asked.

"My leg," Maria managed to croak out in a voice thick with pain.

"Anywhere else, Maria? Your head?" The paramedic shined a light in her eyes, checking her pupils.

The teen shook her head. "Leg. Hurts. Bad."

"We're here to help you. My partner Holly is going to take a look at your wound." The female paramedic was already cutting off Maria's jeans. She quickly applied a pressure bandage to the gunshot wound.

"Maria, we're going to take you to the hospital," Holly said as she fastened a collar around Maria's neck and then slid a body board under her. On the count of three, the paramedics hoisted her onto the stretcher.

"Is she going to be all right?" Trevy asked, following them to the ambulance.

"We'll take good care of her," the woman told her with a quick backward glance.

An MPD officer intercepted Trevy. "Come with me, ma'am." He gestured toward one of the patrol cars. "Let's get you out of the cold."

Trevy saw that Angel was still sitting in the back of another patrol car. Rosa was nowhere to be found, but Trevy was not surprised. If anything, she was relieved that Rosa had extracted herself from the mess. She was trying so hard to make an honest life for herself. The last thing she needed was borrowed trouble. The officer opened the back door of the empty cruiser and Trevy climbed inside.

The heater was cranked to full blast. Warmth seeped into her and for the first time that evening she realized how cold she was. The officer sat in the front seat and entered her name and address into his laptop. She told him about Rosa's call and what she had seen when she arrived.

"My car's right over there." Trevy pointed. "If you're finished —"

"The orange BMW?" He clicked through a few more screens.

"Yes."

"That's a no-parking zone," he observed. "I'm going to have to give you a citation."

Seriously? After all that had happened, he was worried about parking enforcement? She watched him tap on the keyboard, inputting more information. A couple of minutes later he handed her the ticket.

"Two hundred and fifty dollars?" she said, unable to believe her eyes. "For parking in a no-parking zone?"

"Your car's blocking emergency vehicle access."

Trevy clamped her jaw shut to keep from making the situation worse. "Can I go now?" she asked between clenched teeth.

"I'm going to have to ask you to wait here."

"But I need to get my phone so I can call Special Agent Larsen. He's investigating the Chingazos—"

"He's already been notified," the officer said, interrupting her, "and he wants to talk to you. You can wait here where it's warm." Then he left the car, clicking the locks shut before he walked away.

She sat in the car stewing. There was nothing else she could do. Her phone and keys were in her car. Her coat was still lying on the ground where the medic had dropped it. All she had was this damn parking ticket. Angel looked equally frustrated, detained in the back of another car. Cruz had probably asked to question her too.

More police vehicles arrived on the scene, including an unmarked car driven by Detective Alvarado. He acknowledged Trevy with a brief nod before heading toward the crime scene investigators who were piling out of the large white van double-parked alongside her BMW. Great. Now she *couldn't* leave.

The crime scene unit and the uniformed officers worked the scene, putting up yellow tape to rope off the perimeter, collecting evidence, and recording every last detail. Under Alvarado's supervision, the MPD officers fanned out across the long block, talking to people in the crowd that had formed around the crime scene tape. TV news vans from the local stations set up outside the perimeter.

Nearly an hour later, long after the media and the crowd had slowly dispersed, a familiar beige sedan rolled to a stop next to her prison on wheels. Special Agent Larsen got out of the vehicle, a grim expression on his face. He ducked down to look at her through the side window. "Are you okay?" he asked, his voice muffled by the glass.

"Yes, but what took you so long to get here?"

"I was at the District station," he said with a touch of defensiveness, "questioning the shooter."

"Well, you missed your chance to talk to Bandit."

"Bandit's here?" He swept the scene with his eyes.

"Not anymore—"

"Shit," Cruz muttered. "I'll be right back." Trevy watched him make a beeline for Detective Alvarado and the MPD officers who were helping the crime scene investigators collect evidence. Then he headed over to the patrol car to question Angel.

It wasn't much longer before the evidence technicians packed up the white van and drove off. Angel was released and disappeared into the night. Soon most of the other uniformed officers followed suit. All that remained were the two MPD cruisers, the detective's car, and the beige sedan. The quiet was unnerving after all the noise and activity. Would this night never end? Swamped by a wave of fatigue, Trevy closed her eyes and leaned her head back against the seat. Warm air kept pumping out of the heater, making it hard to breathe. Her heart hammered against her ribs in alarm. Light-headed, she cupped her hands over her nose and mouth to slow her breathing, and lowered her head to her knees. The parking ticket, which she'd been holding clenched in her fist, fell to the floorboard.

Just as her panic began to subside, she heard the click of power locks and then the sound of the car door swinging open. Her head still resting on her knees, she turned her face toward the cold air. It rushed over her, cool and sweet. Sucking in a deep breath, she opened her eyes. Her gaze collided with Cruz Larsen's. Crouched in the doorway, he lifted his hand to brush a strand of hair out of her eyes.

"You told me you weren't hurt, damn it," he said. Despite his rough tone, his touch was gentle as he slid his fingers along her throat to rest against her pulse point.

"I'm fine." She straightened. "Really." Now that she wasn't trapped in the overheated patrol car, she could feel her heart rate returning to normal.

Cruz stared at her face and then his gaze darted lower. "Jesus,

Trevy, you're covered in blood."

She followed his gaze to her sweater. Rusty smears stained the pale yellow cashmere. Her hands too.

"Maria's. Not mine," she said as a cold, clammy shudder rippled through her.

"Easy now," he murmured, rubbing warmth into her hands.

"Is Maria going to be okay?"

"Her injuries are serious. A broken femur and muscle damage."

"I should go to the hospital." Trevy pulled her hands from his and retrieved the parking ticket from the floorboard. "Do you know where they took her?"

"Washington Hospital Center," he said. Trevy set one foot on the ground, but instead of moving out of her way, Cruz stood up and braced his hands on the door frame. "Not so fast, Doc. I still have to take your statement."

"Can't that wait until tomorrow?" She set her other foot on the ground.

"No, first your statement, then I'm going to take you home so you can get some rest."

"My car's right over there." She pointed with the parking ticket and after he glanced at the BMW, his eyes fell on the crumpled paper in her hand. "I'll drive myself home *after* I go to the hospital —"

"What's that?" He tugged the ticket from her fingers and slanted it toward the light. "MPD gave you a parking ticket?" His voice was heavy with disbelief. "What the fuck?" he added under his breath.

"Yeah," she said with a flat laugh and held out her hand. "I parked illegally. I didn't think I would be here long and—"

"Wait here," he said, pinning her with a hard look that stifled further explanations. She let her hand drop.

All *Sturm und Drang*, Cruz marched over to the MPD officer who had issued the citation and slapped the ticket against the man's chest. Words were exchanged. Heated words, judging from their body language. Detective Alvarado joined the fray and the discussion continued until the patrol officer threw up his hands in surrender.

When Cruz returned, the ghost of anger still on his face, he pulled her from the cruiser and, after a brief detour to retrieve her coat from the sidewalk, led her to the BMW. "Where are your keys?"

"In the ignition."

He opened the passenger door and gently guided her into the car. "Buckle up," he said and draped her coat across her legs.

"I can drive my own damn car," she protested as he shut the door.

Ignoring her, he crossed to the driver's side and settled himself behind the wheel.

"You better be taking me to the hospital."

He cranked the starter and took a deep breath before turning to her. "I know you want to see Maria, but she's in surgery. And then she'll be in recovery. For hours. You're not family, so you'll have to wait for visiting hours. Tomorrow. The best thing you can do for her is to tell me what happened while I take you home." He fished his smartphone out of his jacket pocket. "Tap AudioNote and start with your name, address, the date, and the time."

She took the phone. "The hospital first. Just to check on her status."

"If you show up at the hospital looking like that, they'll try to admit you. You need to clean up before you go anywhere."

His words penetrated and, for the first time, Trevy thought about how other people might react to her appearance. Maria's blood was on her hands and her clothes. She turned the rearview mirror until she could see her reflection. There were even more rusty brown smudges on her face.

"I can't go home," she said.

"You're going home." His voice was as unyielding as steel as he repositioned the mirror.

"No, not looking like this. I couldn't bear all the questions. Please, Cruz, please take me somewhere else first. Just so I can wash my face and hands."

He tapped his fingers against the steering wheel, four quick beats, the last more forceful than the others. "I know I'm going to regret this," he grumbled, running a hand through his hair. Without looking at her, he said, "You can get cleaned up at my place. It's not far."

As they pulled away from the curb, she opened the app on his phone and tapped *record*. "Trevania Barlow, 1005 Thomas Jefferson Street, Washington, D.C., February 26th, 11:30 p.m. I dropped my brother off at the Baltimore-Washington International Airport at nine…"

Cruz sipped coffee and stared at his laptop screen. His concentration was shot to hell. All his brain had room for were thoughts of Trevy Barlow upstairs in his loft. Naked. He scrubbed a hand down his face as if it might erase the image of her wrapped in a towel, her skin flushed from the heat of the shower, her curves unmistakably outlined because she'd wrapped the towel so tightly around her torso. It had only taken her a few moments to walk from the bathroom to the stairs leading to the loft, but he wasn't sure the image would ever leave him.

He could hear her moving around up there. He pictured her letting the towel fall from her body, the sway of her breasts as she reached for the clean button-down shirt and sweatpants he'd left on the bed. *Get it together, Larsen,* he told himself and pushed away from the table. Every molecule in his body was pulling him toward the foot of the stairs. Instead, he went into the bathroom to collect her discarded clothes. The sweater was ruined, so he stuffed it into a garbage bag. Her jeans might be salvageable, so he'd throw those into his washing machine along with—Holy Mother of Jesus, she had forgotten her underwear. He scooped up the scraps of pale blue lace. Should he take them up to her? She'd want them, right? Then again, he liked the idea of Dr. Do-Good without any underwear. It made her seem less…good.

He shook his head. What the hell was his problem? Nothing, he reminded himself. And for good measure, he reminded himself again. Nothing. He shoved her jeans and underwear into the washing machine, added soap, and started the wash cycle. Feeling ridiculously virtuous, he returned to the kitchen.

There was a knock on his door. Three sharp raps. At the same time his cell phone buzzed and a text message from Alvarado appeared on the screen. *Let me in.*

"Cruz?" Trevy poked her head over the loft railing. She was dressed in his shirt. Nothing more. Although it covered her from shoulders to knees, his whole body tightened, instantly aroused by the sight. Especially since he knew she wasn't wearing anything beneath it. *You're killing me, Doc. You know that, right?* But he kept his eyes on her face and his thoughts to himself.

"It's Detective Alvarado," he told her, the words acting like a cold shower. "Your clothes are in the washing machine. Why don't you lie down on the bed and rest?"

"I'm too keyed up to sleep," she said and disappeared from sight. She came down the stairs a moment later, dressed in sweatpants that were at least three sizes too big. "I hope you don't mind, but I borrowed one of your ties for a belt." She lifted the shirt to show him the striped tie and he caught a glimpse of her smooth, flat stomach.

Killing me, he thought again, forcing himself to look away. "There's coffee in the kitchen," he told her and went to let Alvarado in.

"What took so long?" Alvarado complained, marching into the apartment. He pulled up short at the sight of Trevy. "Dr. Barlow, I didn't realize you were here," he said, sending Cruz a what-the-fuck look.

"Call me Trevy," she said, setting her mug of coffee on the kitchen table before she sat down. "Cruz let me use his bathroom to clean up so I wouldn't have to walk through my apartment building covered in blood."

"Thoughtful of him." Alvarado shot Cruz a knowing look before tossing him the keys to his Bureau car. "A patrolman parked it right out front."

"Have you been able to confirm whether Charlie Vega is a member of Los Diablos Rojos?" Cruz asked to move the conversation along.

"Samantha Vega's brother was the shooter?" Trevy said, alarm sparking in her pretty hazel eyes.

"Yeah, the brother," Alvarado confirmed. He helped himself to coffee and joined Trevy at the table. "He was wearing LDR colors, but he's not talking. He's listening to his public defender's advice."

"He was wearing a dark parka," Trevy said, stifling a yawn, "just like the guy who was seen marking the wall next to the community center."

Cruz leaned a hip against the counter and studied Trevy. She looked about ready to fall asleep sitting up. Fighting the pull of exhaustion, she'd propped both elbows on the table and was resting her chin in the cup of her hands.

"That's why I stopped by." Alvarado aimed a tightly controlled grin at Cruz. "The crime scene techs found traces of blood and lipstick on Charlie Vega's parka. Even some paint residue on one sleeve. They sent it to the lab to test it for Lola Sanchez's DNA. The U.S. Attorney's office is pushing for a quick turnaround, so we should have the results by the end of next week."

"The Vega kid didn't look strong enough to me," Cruz said. The scrawny teen didn't have the strength to subdue and strangle a woman who outweighed him by twenty or thirty pounds.

"Well, the AUSA likes him for it," Alvarado said. "If the DNA's a match, she wants to convene a grand jury to charge Vega with Lola Sanchez's murder."

Well, that news wasn't all good. "Does the AUSA know about that misplaced piece of evidence we discussed?" Cruz asked.

Alvarado expression turned sour. "I got a detective going through every box and bag in the evidence warehouse. But if the DNA matches, our case is solid with or without the ribbon and key."

"I'm not so sure, Lou. Vega's motive for shooting at the Chingazos tonight is crystal clear, but why would he have killed Lola Sanchez? Bandit's testimony is what we need for a breakthrough." More likely than not, the gangbanger knew what had been going down in the parking garage on Sunday and how Lola was mixed up in it.

"Why wouldn't Charlie Vega be strong enough to shoot Lola?" Trevy asked before Alvarado could respond. "And does it really matter that Lola's key has been misplaced? She wasn't murdered for a flea market trinket."

Oh shit. They were all tired and it had made them careless. Cruz looked at Alvarado and then shifted his gaze to Trevy. He could almost see the wheels turning in her head as she rewound the conversation.

"The killer used the key to carve CL *Puta* on Lola's face. That explains the traces of blood on the jacket," she said, putting together the clues. "But you can't stab someone to death with a key. Can you?"

Keeping his expression carefully neutral, Cruz neither confirmed nor denied.

"Even if you could, there would have been blood on the parking garage floor if that's how she was killed." Her face tightened. "I don't remember seeing any when I went into the garage to get my car that night. So, if Lola wasn't stabbed or shot —"

Her eyes welled suddenly and Cruz knew she'd put it all together.

"Oh my God, Lola was strangled. The murder weapon is the pink ribbon."

"We haven't gone public with that information," Alvarado said. "Only the family knows, and we've asked them to keep it to themselves until the investigation is over."

"I won't tell anyone." Trevy put her head on the table. But not before Cruz caught sight of the tears spilling down her cheeks. Shit.

"Let's widen the BOLO on Bandit. After tonight, I wouldn't be surprised if he's left the area," Cruz said while he tried to think of some way to comfort Trevy. He looked at Alvarado and lifted both his hands in a what-do-I-do-now gesture.

Alvarado shrugged and said, "In the meantime, the chief's ramping up patrols in Southeast to discourage any retaliatory strikes from the Chingazos Locos."

If that gave any comfort to Trevy, it didn't show. Her shoulders shook and he could hear the quiet, breathy sobs she was fighting back. Desperate to comfort her, Cruz pushed away from the counter and spanned the distance that separated them. Carefully, as if even the slightest pressure might set off an explosion, he laid his palm against the curve of her back.

"Doc, it's not all bad news. If Detective Alvarado's theory pans out, then we have Lola's killer behind bars. Justice and the chance for closure are important. It will help the Sanchez family move on. And as an added bonus, I won't be bugging you anymore."

He gave her back a gentle pat, ready to withdraw. But instead of comforting her, his words made her cry even harder.

He didn't get it. Lola's killer in jail. That should make her happy. That should make them both happy, right? So why didn't he feel any better than she did?

FIFTEEN

Sunday, March 2

AFTER CLASS ON Sunday evening, Rosa lagged behind when the others left the classroom, and dropped her book on the floor to capture Trevy's attention.

Trevy came over and kneeled down next to her. "Rosa, please tell me who hurt you," she said, her voice gentle, her eyes furious.

Rosa just shook her head. Gingerly, she touched the side of her mouth. It had taken quite a lot of convincing to get Bandit to backhand her. It had hurt like hell. Still did. But in order to convince Trevy, she knew she'd need real injuries. The rest was easy to fake. The shuffle. The slight hunch as if her ribs were sore. Trevy's concern had covered her like a warm blanket from the moment she walked through the door that evening.

"I tripped, that's all."

Trevy's indignation was soothing. It felt good to know that she cared enough to be angry for her. Rosa almost felt guilty about her determination to trick Trevy. Almost.

"I don't believe you, Rosa. First Maria, now you. Did a Diablo do this?"

"No," Rosa said quickly. If Trevy thought her injuries were from another retaliatory strike by the Diablos, she might insist on involving the law. For Rosa's safety. And that of the other girls.

"It's like I said." Rosa let a little fear creep into her voice. It wasn't too hard. She *was* afraid. Afraid that her plan wouldn't work.

Then Bandit would go to Razor for help, and Trevy would get hurt. "I tripped."

"Someone hit you. I want to know who." Trevy held out the book.

Rosa lifted her eyes to meet Trevy's for the first time that evening. "Not here," she whispered. She tugged her book from Trevy's fingers and stood up.

"We'll go get a cup of coffee somewhere."

"No, I'm afraid—" Rosa bit off the sentence as if she had said too much. "I gotta go."

"Where then?"

"Nowhere," she said, hoping she wasn't overplaying her part. This had to work.

Except Trevy didn't take the bait. She didn't look too happy about letting her walk away, but she didn't try to stop her as she slowly shuffled out of the room. What was she going to tell Bandit? She had been so sure that their plan would work this time.

Rosa was halfway out the door of the community center when Trevy caught up to her.

"Tell me who did this to you, Rosa. We'll figure out how to make sure it never happens again."

"I can't," Rosa said. This time, the uncertainty in her voice was real. Maybe this wasn't such a good idea. Although Trevy didn't come right out and say it, Rosa suspected that the part about making sure it never happened again would involve the police.

"Whoever hurt you could do it again," Trevy told her. "Let me help you. Is it safe for you to go home?"

"Ceci Sanchez will help me," she lied, naming the last person Trevy would want her to involve in this mess.

"Ceci?" Trevy asked, looking horrified. She and Trevy both knew that Lola's sister was the only one of them that had any real chance of escaping this place where just surviving was a victory of sorts. "Please leave Ceci out of this."

Rosa shook her head. *Be brave.* Bandit needed her help. And so did Trevy, even if she didn't know it. And she'd already come up with a plausible lie to tell her teacher. One that wouldn't get anyone in trouble. Herself included.

"We could go to your place," Rosa suggested. She watched Trevy's face as her teacher wrestled with the dilemma she had created. Endanger Ceci. Or herself.

Bandit waited in the alley behind the community center just like Angel had told him to. She wanted him out of sight while she delivered the disposable phone with *El Trece's* message to Razor. Soon, Razor would show up to take him to the warehouse. He would need to drive the shipment north later tonight, if all went according to plan.

Headlights spotlit the alley. Bandit ducked next to the dumpster, trying to make himself as small as possible until he was sure it was Razor's rig. The dark SUV rolled past him and pulled to a stop.

"Get in," Angel said through the open back door.

Bandit didn't have time to do more than climb into the backseat. He pulled the door shut as the Lincoln Navigator roared out of the alley and merged into traffic.

"What's the deal with Rosa?" Razor said. "Angel saw her leave with that teacher."

Half worried, half hopeful, he tried not to react to the news. He was counting on Rosa to find a way for him to get into Trevy Barlow's home; otherwise he'd have no choice but to tell Razor everything.

Bandit glanced at Razor's girlfriend, looking for some sort of clue about whether the shipment was ready for delivery. But she was staring out the window, ignoring him. Not good. As usual, GQ was riding shotgun.

"Rosa?" Bandit asked, answering Razor's question with one of his own, pretending the girl was nothing to him.

"You deaf or just terminally stupid?" GQ tossed over his shoulder.

Like a model citizen, Razor flicked on his right turn signal and shifted over into the next lane. Traffic was fairly light as they headed west on New York Avenue. The light turned yellow, but Razor sped through the intersection before slowing down.

"No, I—" Bandit stared at the back of Razor's head, trying to read his mood. "Don't we have a shipment to load and deliver?"

Razor turned around and scowled at him. "No."

Bandit's heart sank. Razor didn't need to keep him alive if there wasn't going to be a shipment. Maybe now was the time to tell Razor about Trevy. He took a deep breath and sent a silent plea to *Santa Maria* to keep Rosa safe.

"Next week." GQ tossed the words over his shoulder and then glanced at Razor, who gave him a slight nod. "So be ready."

Bandit tried to still the racing of his heart. He'd been a breath away from betraying Rosa. Even though Angel was watching him, he made the sign of the cross and whispered an *Ave Maria*.

"You got one more week to get me the money. Don't fuck up."

One more week. There was one more week for Rosa's plan to work…

That was when he realized that Razor was following an orange BMW.

Fool. Shit for brains. Not even *Santa Maria* could help a sinner like him.

Traffic picked up as they crossed the bridge over the Rock Creek Parkway and entered Georgetown. They followed the orange car down M Street, the main thoroughfare lined with trendy shops, restaurants, and bars. Even at this hour on Sunday, the sidewalks were busy, although not as busy as they would be in the warm days of spring and summer. Razor brought the car to a stop when the traffic light turned red.

The BMW was two cars ahead. Bandit stared at the people who stood on the corner waiting to cross the street, huddled together against the damp wind that blew off the Potomac River. He fought the urge to yank open the door and lose himself in the crowd even as his fingers crept to the door handle. If he timed his escape to the moment the light changed, Razor would have to choose between losing sight of the orange car or letting him go. He increased the pressure of his fingers on the metal handle, his eyes fixed on the glaring red light.

What about Rosa? The thought had him hesitating. Was he

going to abandon her?

Her problem. He tightened his grip on the door handle. Every man for himself. Wasn't that the motto of the street? But Rosa… sweet, shy Rosa with those kind brown eyes. She had saved him—more than once—and she didn't deserve whatever Razor had in mind.

But he couldn't help her if he didn't get away from Razor first. That settled it. He would make his escape now and find Rosa later. They could go into hiding together. He didn't have time to sort out the details though, because the light was changing. It was time. He yanked the door lever and pushed with his shoulder.

Nothing happened.

"Going somewhere?" Razor asked, his shark eyes still fixed on the BMW.

GQ snickered and Angel yawned.

"Those child safety locks on the back doors sure come in handy." Razor's flat tone sent a shiver of dread racing down Bandit's spine. He was trapped. And now they knew he wanted to escape them.

Helpless, he watched as the BMW shifted into the left lane and moved slowly down the block to the next light. Razor held his position in the right lane and dropped back even further when the orange car signaled a left turn and slowly nosed its way into the intersection. Oncoming traffic made the turn difficult. As the light turned yellow, the BMW slipped through the intersection and down a small side street that led toward the canal. Razor muscled the Navigator into the left lane and waited for the light to turn green.

GQ swore under his breath, but Razor silenced him with a slice of his hand through the air. "Watch," he hissed.

Even Angel seemed interested as the orange coupe halted halfway down the block and turned into an underground parking garage. "Nice place," she said, her voice a mixture of admiration and envy.

When the light turned green, Razor didn't turn down the small side street as Bandit had expected. He drove another couple of blocks, then made a left on Wisconsin Avenue. A quick right and they were in the brightly lit parking garage for the Georgetown Park shopping mall. The garage was mostly empty at this time of night. Only the restaurants in the mall were still open. Razor parked the SUV in a secluded space far from the elevator and stairs that led to street level. He turned in his seat and fixed his gaze on Bandit, his eyes like two black holes in his narrow face.

"What's Rosa doing with Trevy Barlow?"

Bandit shrugged. "How the hell should I know?"

GQ reached across the seat and grabbed him by the front of his jacket. He made a game show buzzer sound. "Wrong answer. Try again."

Still trying to tough it out, he swallowed his fear and said, "Ask Angel, maybe she knows."

Angel glared at him and punched his arm. "Chickenshit."

"You and Rosa are up to something sneaky and Razor don't like being kept out of the loop," GQ said, shifting his grip to Bandit's neck.

Razor bared his teeth and got up in Bandit's face. His beery breath made Bandit want to puke. "Do you think I got fucking shit for brains? What's Rosa doing with that teacher?"

It was time to let Razor in on the plan to get the money back from Trevy Barlow. Bandit felt a brief stab of guilt—Rosa had trusted him to do the right thing.

But what she hadn't understood was that sometimes the price for doing the right thing was too high. And Bandit had no intention of paying with his life.

SIXTEEN

THE SPORTS BAR on Seventh Street was crowded for a Sunday night. College basketball was the draw. The Maryland Terps were leading. But not by much. Cruz didn't give a damn. He carried two beers to a booth and slid in, his back to the large TV screens that were a major part of the décor.

"Hell of an idea to meet here," Cruz groused as he set the beers on the table. Alvarado grabbed one, his gaze fixed on the action unfolding on the wide screen.

"You're just in a bad mood because the AUSA decided not to add murder to the other charges Charlie Vega's facing," Alvarado said and took a long swig. "Foul! That was a damned foul. Did you see that, man?"

Alvarado slapped the table with the flat of his hand, and Cruz grabbed his beer before it could be knocked over. Alvarado was a rabid Terps fan. His wife didn't like it when he yelled profanities at the TV, particularly when their daughter was around, so he snuck out to bars like this one whenever he could. Apparently, decorous behavior sucked all the fun out of watching sports.

"I never liked him for the Sanchez murder anyway, but now we're back to square one with the mayor breathing fire up our asses."

"You gotta admit that kid's lawyer is doing a great job."

"Yeah, tracking down the evidence to prove that Charlie Vega didn't have possession of that parka until a week after Lola Sanchez was killed at the community center was top-notch investigative work."

"Or divine intervention. You should have seen the look on the chief's face when I told him about the affidavit from Vega's priest. WTF!" Alvarado half-stood and pointed. "He walked, man. The ref is blind."

Cruz took a long sip of his beer and glanced over his shoulder at the screen. Fifty-three seconds until half-time. "That parka could be a game changer."

"Hell yeah, for Charlie Vega," Alvarado said, not looking away from the game. "Now instead of life, he's looking at eight to ten years. With time off for good behavior, he could be back on the streets in half that time."

"I was talking about the Sanchez case."

"You're grasping at straws," Alvarado said, glancing away from the game for a moment to look at Cruz.

"What about all the materials we collected from it? It's hard evidence that could lead us to Lola's killer."

"If the lab report comes back with a DNA match to Lola Sanchez, we might have something. Still, we can't directly tie the damn coat to her killer."

"So what do you suggest we do? Wait around twiddling our thumbs until the lab results are in? We've got no witnesses. MPD has misplaced the murder weapon. You got a better lead?"

Alvarado shook his head. "MPD's been tracking the Chingazos' movements for the past two weeks. Razor and his lieutenants have been camping out in a different motel in Northeast every couple of nights. Nothing illegal about that."

"Maybe not, but it means something big is afoot. Otherwise they'd stay in the same no-tell motel until they wore out their welcome and got booted out. Maybe Lola Sanchez was mixed up in that something and it got her killed."

"Bandit knows about it," Alvarado said. "You're right about him. He's the witness we need."

"Well, we don't have Bandit, but we do have the parka," Cruz said, not ready to concede defeat. "It could give us intel on Lola Sanchez's killer that will help us track him down."

"Yeah? Sounds like FBI profiling mumbo jumbo."

"Think about it, Lou. This guy's a planner. He steals a car, kills Lola Sanchez in the parking garage, and then dumps the car at the Metro station…but not before scratching LDR graffiti on the hood. He makes a clean getaway, so he can ditch that coat anywhere in the city. But what does he do? He waits for a new opportunity. When he hears about the drive-by shooting in LDR territory, he packs the parka into a box the very next day and mails it to the church collecting donations for the Vega family. Someone's going to a lot of trouble to stir up the rivalry between the Chingazos and the Diablos, and I want to know why."

Alvarado tapped his mustache as he considered the point. "If that's true, then the Sanchez girl wasn't targeted because of her gang affiliation. The killer had some other motivation."

Cruz shrugged. "I'm just saying we need to follow up on *all* leads, even the long shots. Our guy didn't count on the priest keeping a log of every package donated. That was lucky for us. Since the mailing box hadn't been recycled yet, we know our guy used stamps, which have to be hand cancelled. I already did a little legwork and tracked the postmark to the post office next to Union Station. We can subpoena the transaction records and security tapes to help us track the package back to its source."

Alvarado groaned. "Do you have any idea how much mail passes through that post office every day? It'll take weeks, months even, to go through all those records. My eyes hurt just thinking about it." He swept his hand toward the screen. "I'll have to get glasses to watch basketball."

"You got a better idea?"

"No."

"We'll focus on all transactions that include postage for a medium flat-rate box."

"That's narrowing it down?"

Ignoring Alvarado's question, he continued, "Once we've identified some possible transactions, we'll be able to zero in on specific parts of the post office surveillance tapes. Do you think your eyesight's up for that?"

"If our guy's as smart as you think, he'll be wearing something to hide his face from the cameras. Maybe even a disguise."

"Then let's hope one of the clerks on duty remembers something about him. Buying stamps for a priority mail package can't be an everyday event. That could be mistake number two."

"Okay, I'm in." Alvarado shifted his gaze back to the TV to check the score. "Since we're going to the judge for subpoenas, why don't we ask for a warrant for GPS surveillance on Razor? He's moving around so much, my guys are doing overtime keeping track of him."

"Can't hurt to try. We've got a ballistics report that matches the bullet casings from the Vega drive-by to the 9mm I found near that Chingazos tribute in LDR territory, plus the forensics report on that bullet graze on the side view mirror of Razor's SUV. The judge should have no problem with signing a warrant."

Cruz took another swallow of beer and glanced up at the game. The clock had stopped at seven seconds for a free throw. Between foul shots and time-outs, fifty-plus seconds had been stretched into almost five minutes. Unbelievable. This was why he didn't watch basketball.

Alvarado was leaning forward, his hands gripping the table. "In, in," he chanted as if he could control the ball by the sheer power of will.

Finally, the buzzer signaling halftime sounded. Alvarado had a satisfied grin on his face. The Terps were ahead by six. He finished his beer. "I'm getting another. Want one?"

"Naw, I'm going to take off pretty soon. Tomorrow's a work day."

Alvarado frowned. "You need to get laid, buddy. You're way too uptight. How long has it been?" He paused by the table. "At least a couple of months, I'd guess. Whatever happened to that redhead you were dating? What was her name? Jackie, Janice—"

"Nicole," he interrupted to put an end to the torture. "Her name was Nicole. She dumped me six months ago for an NSA wonk. The FBI wasn't glamorous enough for her. Said it was like dating a cop."

"Ouch," Alvarado said with a laugh. "That's cold."

"Go get your beer before half-time's over," Cruz prompted before Alvarado could further analyze his love life. Or lack thereof. He knew his friend didn't mean anything by it, but his wisecracks were a bit too on-target. Meaningless sex had gotten old for Cruz, so he hadn't bothered to replace Nicole. Instead, he'd focused all his energy on his job.

And then he'd met Trevy Barlow. In his mind, he replayed that kiss in the French restaurant. He could still remember how good she tasted. How sexy she'd looked days later, standing in his home, wearing nothing but his shirt. A sense of possession had washed over him then…and it haunted him still. If he had asked her to stay, would she have said yes? Now, he would never know. Regret rose in his throat, choking him.

Fortunately, Alvarado returned to the table with his beer, saving him from becoming a total sop. Thirty seconds into the second half, Alvarado's phone blared out the Maryland Fight Song. As he fished it out of his pocket, he said, "Crap, it's probably my bride calling to tell me to come home."

But when Alvarado looked at the number on the screen, he swapped his henpecked-husband face for his cop face. "Alvarado here."

The call was short. "Fucking craptastic," Alvarado said when he hung up, the Maryland game forgotten. "That was Detective Lewis. He's called in to report he followed Razor to Georgetown Park."

"The shopping mall?" That was the last thing Cruz had expected to hear. He tried to picture Razor with his tattooed face and major attitude blending in with the well-heeled crowd at the upscale Georgetown mall. "Is he alone?"

"No, his girlfriend's with him. Angel Mendez. And his second-in-command, GQ."

Cruz didn't like the idea of Razor and pals hanging out in Trevy Barlow's neighborhood. A wave of protectiveness swept over him. *Don't overreact*, he warned himself. "Where are they now?"

"Lewis followed them to the pizza place in the mall."

Swearing under his breath, Cruz stood up and tossed a few

dollars on the table for a tip.

"Hey, where are you going, Larsen?"

"I have a sudden craving for pizza."

"My team's on top of the situation," Alvarado called after him as he headed for the exit. "Razor doesn't have to be your problem tonight."

But Alvarado didn't get it. The kid's impromptu trip to Georgetown wasn't the only problem riding his ass tonight. The burn in his gut wasn't going to ease up until he knew Dr. Do-Good was safe.

Oh man, he was so fucked.

SEVENTEEN

As THEY SAT side by side on the couch in Trevy's living room, Rosa tried to explain how she'd gotten a fat lip. "Amigo shopping," she said and launched into a story about a drugged-out white guy grabbing her purse and hitting her across the face with it.

"Amigo shopping?" Trevy's brows drew together in a slight frown.

Rosa twisted her hands in her lap and lowered her eyes to peek at Trevy from the cover of her lashes. "Yeah, that's what they call it when guys walk around looking for Latinos to mug."

"I know what it means." Trevy's frown deepened. "It's a serious crime, Rosa. People like that need to be stopped. The police—"

"No," Rosa said sharply, dropping all pretenses. She met Trevy's gaze straight on. "No police. You know what will happen."

"What do you think will happen, Rosa?"

"The police will go through the motions of looking for this guy. They won't find him, but they'll sic Immigration on me. I'm the one who'll be punished. I'm the one who'll go to jail or be deported. Not this guy who did this to me."

In her fury, Rosa almost forgot that she'd made up the story about the mugging. She felt a twinge of guilt when she noticed her teacher's worried frown. Rosa wiped the palms of her hands on her jeans. She didn't like lying, not to Trevy.

"The immigration laws have changed, Rosa. But you need to stay out of trouble. Hanging out with gang members is not—"

"I have to pee," Rosa said to stop the lecture. All this

deportation talk was giving her the jitters. What in the name of God had she gotten herself into? This was too risky.

Inside the large bathroom, Rosa counted to one hundred, flushed the toilet, and ran the water over her hands. Unable to resist the fancy soap in the shape of a flower, she rubbed it between her palms until the scent of lavender filled the bathroom. Rosa usually had to share a bathroom with eight people. On a good day there was more than a sliver of plain white soap on the edge of the sink next to the mineral-stained faucet. She dried her hands on the soft towel—the softest she'd ever felt—then held it to her face to breathe in the clean flowery scent. For a moment, she let herself wonder what it would be to live like this every day.

Reluctantly, she reached for the door. It was too late to turn back. She knew what she had to do. Lie to Trevy, steal the key to her apartment, get the hell out. She started to hang the towel on the rack by the sink, then changed her mind. She pulled up her shirt and flattened the towel against her stomach, smoothed her stretchy yellow shirt over it and checked her reflection in the mirror. Frowning at a bulky wrinkle, she yanked up her shirt again. This time she shifted the towel to her back, covered it with her shirt, and studied the effect. Better. Barely noticeable. Later tonight, she would spread the flower-scented towel on her lumpy foam pillow.

Rosa opened the bathroom door and poked her head out into the hallway. Instead of returning to the living room, she tiptoed down the short hall in the opposite direction. She paused in an open doorway to stare into the dark room. It was some kind of office with books lining the walls and a large desk covered in stacks of papers and folders. She glanced over her shoulder to make sure she was alone, then crept down the hall.

A phone rang somewhere in the apartment and she started guiltily. When Trevy answered it on the third ring, Rosa released the breath she'd been holding. She'd have another minute or two to check out the rest of the apartment. But Bandit had told her not to try to find the money. That was his job. All she needed to do was steal Trevy's key.

So she retraced her steps to the living room and settled back onto the couch. Trevy was still on the phone, and Rosa could hear her voice streaming in from the kitchen. Trevy laughed and said, "No, Kate, I don't want to hear all the gory details. My department meetings aren't any better."

Trevy's friend sounded like she wasn't going anywhere fast. She had to be talking nonstop, because Trevy was silent except for an occasional mumbled answer.

This was Rosa's chance to swipe the apartment key. She rose up from the soft down cushions and slunk toward the table by the front door. *Grab it quick*, she told herself. *Don't think about it.* She slid her fingers along the smooth surface of the table while turning her body toward the kitchen just in case—

Rosa froze. Trevy was standing in the doorway, the phone still pressed to her ear. She smiled ruefully at Rosa and pointed toward the phone. "Sorry," she mouthed. She motioned Rosa into the kitchen. Lightheaded from the sudden rush of blood to her limbs, Rosa slid her fingers away from the keys on the hall table and reluctantly followed Trevy.

The kitchen was all steel and granite and gleaming wood. There had to be at least two dozen yellow roses in the vase on the kitchen table. Trevy pointed to a kettle steaming on the stove. "I'm making tea," she said, covering the receiver. "Would you like some?"

Rosa nodded. That had been too close. Way too close. The shrill whistle of the kettle startled her and her heartbeat kicked up another notch.

"Lunch tomorrow sounds great," Trevy said. With the phone wedged between her ear and her shoulder, she turned to take the kettle off the heat. "The Capitol Hill Grill works for me. What time?" She poured the water into a ceramic teapot shaped like a lily of the valley.

Trying to regain her composure, Rosa looked around the kitchen. She'd have to explain to Bandit why she hadn't been able to get the key for him.

And then she thought of Bandit going to Razor for help.

A shiver chased down her spine. She couldn't let that happen. Razor would think nothing of hurting Trevy, maybe even killing her.

But what could she do? Steal the key on her way out the door? No, that would never work. Trevy would see her.

Think, she told herself. She looked around the kitchen, taking note of the pretty flower plates decorating one wall, the oven mitts that were shaped like a bouquet of daisies, and the ceramic tulip magnet with a hook on the side of the stainless steel refrigerator. Trevy sure liked flowers—

Rosa's eyes returned to the magnet. There, dangling within reach, was a key. That had to be the spare for the apartment. Rosa couldn't allow doubt to creep in. She glanced at Trevy, whose back was still turned.

"I really have to go, Kate." Trevy reached into a cabinet filled with china. Rosa could see delicate tea cups decorated with pink and green flowers.

Not letting herself worry about getting caught, Rosa snatched the key off the hook. The tulip magnet slid askew, but there wasn't time to straighten it. She said an *Ave Maria* and shoved the key into her pocket as she moved to the other side of the room.

"See you tomorrow." Trevy clicked off the phone. "Sorry for the interruption, Rosa," she said as she set two pretty teacups on the counter and poured tea into them.

"It's okay," Rosa said. The apology only made her feel guiltier. Rosa took a quick sip from the teacup before she could ruin everything by confessing the truth to Trevy. She wasn't just doing this for Bandit, she reminded herself. Trevy needed to be protected. She just didn't know it yet.

It was nearly eleven by the time she left the apartment. When she refused a ride home, Trevy pressed a twenty-dollar bill in her hand and insisted on calling a cab for her. In no time at all, Rosa was back in Northeast, standing in front of the apartment building where her family lived. But before she could reach the front door, someone dragged her off the cement walkway and tugged her into the shadows near the side of the building. In her struggle to get free, her head banged against the rough brick wall and she bit her tongue so hard she tasted blood.

"It's me, Rosa," Bandit whispered into her ear. She slumped in relief, sliding down the wall until he caught her and held her against his wiry body. "I'm sorry I scared you."

She shook her head. Fear turned into exhilaration. "I did it, Bandit. Trevy lives in Georgetown." As she reached into her pocket to pull out Trevy's spare key, she recited the address and apartment number that she'd memorized.

"Did she suspect anything?"

"No. She's meeting a friend for lunch tomorrow on Capitol Hill, but I didn't hear the time. I'm sorry."

"That helps a lot, Rosa. Really." He pocketed the key.

"It's not going to be easy, Bandit," she said, the initial glow of success fading. "There's a security guard in the lobby you'll have to get past to reach the elevators. And don't you have to drive to New York tonight?"

"No, next week."

"Bandit," she clutched his arm, ready to tell him to forget this crazy plan. But then she remembered all the reasons why she'd agreed to help him. "What are you going to do now?"

He scrubbed a hand over his face. He looked so tired. "Don't worry about me." He reached out and touched her lip where it had begun to bleed again. "I'm so sorry, Rosa."

And she could tell that he meant it.

"Come inside with me."

Bandit shook his head. "I'm poison, Rosa. You should get away from me. I wish I'd never let you help me in the first place."

"Where else are you going to sleep? Under a bridge? In a dark alley? It's too cold."

He shrugged. "Razor has a motel room. He wants me to stay close until I deliver the shipment next week."

Rosa planted her hands on her hips. "You didn't tell Razor, did you?"

For a long minute, all he did was stare at her. "No," he said at last. And then, as if he couldn't resist, he added, "Razor can go to hell. I'm coming with you. But just for tonight."

One night at a time, she would keep him safe. Trevy too. After Bandit used the key to retrieve the money Trevy had been holding for Lola, Rosa would help him disappear. Maybe she'd even go with him. They could go somewhere warm. California. Arizona. Texas. They could make a new life. She'd get a job. He could sell his artwork…

"Rosa," he said, and that was when reality set in, making her dreams of the future vanish like smoke. "It's cold. Let's go inside."

EIGHTEEN

ON HER DAILY run the next morning, Trevy was deep in thought as she picked up the pace, leaving the uneven brick sidewalks for the dirt and gravel path that meandered through Montrose Park. A few flurries chased through the air, and the wind felt like it was trying to push her back home. The temperature was near the freezing point, but Trevy was warm—all but the tip of her nose. Overhead, bare branches swayed in the wind, clacking in discordant rhythms that matched the questions churning in her brain. How could she help Rosa?

She expelled a heavy breath, her frustration taking the form of a white puff of smoke. Who had mugged the girl? To say that her neighborhood wasn't the safest was an understatement. Crime happened there every day. Very likely every hour. Still, she couldn't shake the feeling that Rosa had been trying to manipulate her for some reason. The sound of heavy footfalls approaching behind her interrupted her thoughts. Suddenly more aware of her surroundings, Trevy quickened her pace and glanced back.

It was Cruz Larsen.

"Hey, Doc, wait up," Cruz called as he spanned the distance that separated them.

Today he was dressed in running gear, his dark hair covered by a gray cap. Trevy slowed and smiled at him. She hadn't forgotten his kindness the night Maria was shot.

And the kisses they'd shared in that restaurant…even if the show had been for JC's benefit.

They started to run side by side, their breaths mingling in the cold air. The wind blew her scarf into his face. Before she could grab it back he tucked it into the collar of her jacket, his light touch shooting heat throughout her body.

"I didn't expect to see you again." Trevy had assumed Cruz had already moved on to a new investigation. Wasn't that what he'd promised her the night of Charlie Vega's arrest? She glanced over.

Interest radiated from Cruz's green eyes. "Did you miss me?"

Realizing how revealing her statement had been, she had the ridiculous urge to hide her face in her hands. The fact that she hadn't stopped thinking about him for even a day since he stormed into her life a couple of weeks ago was pathetic. She sped up and he matched her pace.

"Is this another race? We already know how that will end." His lips curved upward, revealing a slightly crooked incisor that marred the perfection of his white smile. Oddly enough, it only made him more attractive.

"Pretty sure of yourself, Agent Larsen." She increased her pace again. Maybe she could outrun her embarrassment.

He effortlessly lengthened his stride to keep up with her. "I think you should join a gym."

The non sequitur confused her. "A gym?"

"Yeah, you know, one of those fitness places with treadmills. You could run to your heart's content without worrying me."

His eyes narrowed slightly, as if he regretted adding that last bit.

"You worry about me?" Trevy grinned at him. She couldn't help it. Her lips just turned up at the corners in defiance of gravity. Maybe she wasn't the only one who was having a hard time with the idea that they no longer had an official reason to see each other. "That's so sweet."

Instead of looking embarrassed, his face grew hard. "Don't read too much into it."

"I would never make that mistake," Trevy lied, her smile faltering. "Why would you be worried? Isn't Lola's killer behind bars?"

"It's not safe to run alone in isolated areas—"

The path divided ahead. The right fork curved up a steep incline, a shortcut that looped back to the park entrance and would cut her run in half. She veered in that direction, increasing her pace so that she didn't have to listen. He followed her sudden change in direction easily. She glanced over at him when he caught up. "The real reason, Cruz. Don't give me some official bull."

Her stride lengthened as they ran down the other side of the steep incline. The path wound through the woods for a bit and then leveled out near the perimeter of the park. The sounds of the city penetrated the thin screen of trees that surrounded the running path.

"Charlie Vega didn't kill Lola Sanchez. The AUSA isn't adding murder to his charges."

Her annoyance vanished instantly. They kept running side by side, slower now, as Cruz told her about the priest who had come forward with evidence proving that Charlie Vega hadn't possessed the suspicious parka at the time of Lola's death.

"But he's still in jail, right?"

At Cruz's tight nod, some of her tension eased. One less danger for her students. "He pled guilty to assault with intent to kill. He'll be locked up for a long time."

"Then what's the problem?" she asked.

"Razor's developed a taste for M Street Pizza."

"Razor was here in Georgetown?" Her chest tightened, and she slowed to a walk. What if Rosa had lied and Razor was the one responsible for hurting her? Could her visit have been a ruse? Had Trevy led the leader of the Chingazos Locos to her doorstep? "When? How do you know?"

"Around nine-thirty last night. He's under surveillance."

By nine-thirty, she and Rosa had been sitting in her living room, safe from prying eyes. "Was he alone?"

"His girlfriend and another gang member were with him," Cruz said, adjusting his stride to match hers.

"Is that all he did? Buy a pizza and leave?"

"Yeah, he was gone by the time I got there."

"What does that have to do with me?"

In answer, Cruz lifted an eyebrow. *Figure it out*, his expression said.

"Razor wanted a pizza. It's not like he killed someone to get it." She halted, her lungs suddenly burning like they were on fire. She bent over to catch her breath.

Cruz put a steadying hand on her back. She inhaled noisily before straightening to face him.

"He didn't kill anyone, did he?" She could hear the rising panic in her voice, but there was nothing she could do to control her fear. Oh, God, no. Not Rosa. She should never have let her take a cab back to Northeast alone.

"No."

The fear drained away so rapidly that she felt lightheaded. She sagged and Cruz gripped her shoulders, easing her into a sitting position at the base of a large poplar tree by the side of the trail. She leaned her head back, stared into the canopy of bare branches overhead, and tried to slow her breathing. It took a long time before she felt herself regain control. "Then what's the big deal?" she asked, still a little breathless. "It's a free country. Why shouldn't Razor be able to buy a pizza wherever he likes?"

"You don't think it's a little strange that he came all the way to Georgetown, mere blocks from your home, to buy a pizza?" Cruz crouched down in front of her, his face level with hers.

"I doubt they deliver to his neighborhood," she said, forcing herself to meet his hard green gaze.

Irritation flared in his eyes. "Don't be a smart-ass, Trevy. Is it possible that he knows where you live?"

"No."

Cruz didn't look convinced. "Do any of the Chingazos know where you live? Or maybe one of the girls you teach?"

"No," she said and looked away. He didn't need to know about Rosa. It could only lead to trouble for the girl and her family. Besides, Trevy reasoned, Rosa had been at her apartment while Razor was picking up his pizza, so she couldn't have told him anything. It was just a coincidence. An unsettling one, but a coincidence nonetheless.

He reached out and set two fingers under her chin. Slowly he applied pressure until she turned her head to face him. "Not one of those girls knows you live in Georgetown, even if they don't know the exact address?"

"They know that I teach at GW," she said, sidestepping the question.

The skeptical twist of his lips told her he noticed. "Would I find your address if I searched for it on the Internet?"

"No. My brother JC owns the apartment and I pay extra to keep the phone number private. Given the nature of my work, I do take some precautions."

He mumbled something that sounded a lot like, "Wonders never cease." Did that mean he believed her?

"I'm not giving up my morning routine just because Razor decided to buy a pizza in Georgetown last night," she said, going on the offensive. "I like to run outside before my classes. It clears my head. It wouldn't be the same on a treadmill in a gym."

"Then you can count on my company, Doc."

"Every morning?"

"Every morning."

"Rain or shine?"

"Think of me as a running version of the mailman," he said with a tight smile.

But Cruz Larsen didn't look happy. Not one bit. He could at least pretend to like the idea of spending more time with her.

"See you tomorrow. Six a.m. I won't wait for you."

"I'll be there," he said. And she knew that was a promise she could take to the bank. There was something surprisingly attractive about that straightforward dependability, that unvarnished honesty.

But that didn't mean she wasn't going to make him pay for his show of reluctance.

"Oh, and I plan to run an extra half hour tomorrow to make up for cutting today's run short," she tossed over her shoulder as she ran down Thirty-First Street toward her apartment.

"Try not to sound so happy about it," he grumbled as he matched his stride to hers all the way back to M Street.

After leaving Cruz Larsen standing on the sidewalk in front of her apartment building, Trevy walked through the front door of the lobby. There was no one there. She looked around for the security guard who usually manned the desk.

"Good morning, Joe," she called out when she spotted him. He was hurrying across the lobby toward her. Although she didn't want to admit it, even to herself, she was a little spooked by the knowledge that Razor had been so close to her home last night, so she was glad to see him.

"Did you have a good run, Dr. Barlow?" Joe walked with her to the elevator and pushed the call button. "Winter's hanging on hard this year."

"Do you think we'll get snow today?"

"Forty percent chance. I wouldn't mind. Anything to get a break from all the construction going on in 2C," he grumbled. "Workmen in and out through the service entrance. They've got me running back and forth all day."

Trevy made a sympathetic sound and smiled at him. The elevator doors opened and Rafael Montoyez stepped out, wheeling a heavy suitcase behind him.

"Trevania," he said, greeting her with a kiss on each cheek, "what a delightful surprise."

"Mr. Montoyez, do you need a cab to the airport?" Joe asked, reaching for his suitcase. "Let me help you with that."

"Not necessary, Joe. My flight doesn't leave until the afternoon. I'm driving from the embassy." He turned his gaze on Trevy. "Miami. Two days of blue skies, turquoise water, white sandy beaches."

"It sounds…" The embassy paid him for this? Trevy thought of JC's future post in Honduras and her mouth tightened. "…warm."

"Why the frown?" Rafael touched her shoulder, his dark eyes searching her face. "Isn't it your spring break? Why don't you join me? JC thinks you're working much too hard."

"I promised my editor I'd finish the first round of revisions on my book before my classes start up again, and I'm going to need every minute of break to work on it."

"What better place to revise your book than on the beach? Miguel can reserve a room for you in our hotel. Diplomats from all over Latin America will be there for the mini trade summit. Perhaps you'll see a few old friends from your embassy days."

She forced a smile. "I also have a hundred midterm papers to grade. I'm afraid I don't have time for a vacation."

And she didn't want to be a part of that world—the world of her ex-husband Montgomery Fordham. At first, enthralled by his movie-star good looks and sophistication, she'd mistaken his charisma for a genuine desire to make the world a better place. It had only taken her six months into their first diplomatic post as a married couple to figure out that underneath all that star power wattage was a shameless self-promoter.

It was not a mistake she intended to repeat.

Cruz Larsen was the opposite of her ex-husband in so many ways. Was that why she couldn't stop thinking about him? Well, it didn't matter. Once Lola's murderer was behind bars, Cruz would move on to another case. And that would be the end of their association. She shook off the thought and returned her attention to Rafael. "Safe travels, Rafael," she said with a small smile.

"*Adiós, querida.*" Rafael left her with a farewell wave as he wheeled his bag toward the garage elevator.

Minutes later, Trevy unlocked the door to her apartment, shucked off her outdoor gear, and headed into the kitchen. Her mind still stuck on Cruz and the news he'd shared with her, she snagged a water bottle from the fridge and drank until nothing was left. Setting the empty bottle on the counter, she glanced at the refrigerator door. The tulip magnet with the hook for her extra apartment key was askew.

And the key was missing.

NINETEEN

FOR NEARLY AN hour Monday morning, Bandit crouched in the shadows behind the hardware store on Twenty-Fourth Street until it opened at 8:30. After making a copy of Trevy Barlow's spare key, he hoofed it several blocks west to Georgetown. The light from the rising sun was all but smothered by a low cover of clouds that threatened a late winter snowstorm. Cold air burned his skin.

Groggy, his head throbbing from another long, sleepless night on the Reyes' lumpy couch, he ducked into a narrow alley across the street from the upscale apartment building where Trevy Barlow lived. He wasn't warm, but at least he was out of the wind. When his phone vibrated against his hip, Bandit pulled it from the pocket of his baggy jeans. "Yeah."

"Where the fuck are you?" Razor shouted, and the ache in his head exploded like a mule kick. Last night, Razor and his posse had left him chilling in the Navigator deep in the lower level of the mall parking garage while they got something to eat. The plan had been to crash at a motel on Florida Avenue. Razor had wanted Bandit close at hand. But Bandit had only waited ten minutes before leaving to meet Rosa back in Chingazos territory. Now Razor was pissed. Apparently he hadn't thought Bandit had the *cojones* to do more than follow orders like a scared little rabbit.

"Waiting for Rosa to bring me the key," he lied to buy himself time. Razor expected him to hand over the key to the apartment so that he had the final say-so on who to send to search for the money. And when. Bandit couldn't let that happen. Even though he'd betrayed Rosa, he still owed it to her to keep the other Chingazos out of Trevy Barlow's home. Especially Razor and GQ.

"You better not be frontin' me," Razor said before he broke the connection. There was no need for him to add, "Or I'll kill you." Bandit knew exactly how little his life was worth if he didn't find the money. He fingered the two keys in his pocket and stared at the entrance to the brick building. Rosa had told him there was a security guard in the lobby. How the hell was he supposed to get to the elevator without anyone noticing? The beat of what felt like a thousand tiny hammers inside his head kicked up a notch. Oh, yeah, and he had to avoid getting caught by the cops.

Or killed by Razor.

Think, he told himself. It was a little before 9:00, and he knew Trevy Barlow had a lunch meeting. Plenty of time for him to figure out a way in. No need to panic. Yet.

His gaze swung away as a strong gust of wind pushed down the street, whipping up trash. A plastic shopping bag became airborne, and the wind flattened it against his head. He squelched a grunt of disgust and yanked it off.

A large white van turned onto the street and pulled over to the curb not far from where Bandit was hiding. Damn. He could no longer see the front door of the apartment building. More rotten luck. He stared sourly at the sign on the side of the van. C&G Interiors. If he had a can of spray paint, he wouldn't mind messing with the exterior of the van. All that white space was just begging for his tag.

Settling back against the wall, he watched the workmen pile out of the van and cross the street in a slow-moving pack. Six *vatos*. They headed down the narrow alley that separated Trevy Barlow's building from the low brick box of an office building next door. Shit, the truck would be parked there for hours and he wouldn't be able to see when Trevy left the building. He'd have to find another hiding place.

Fate was a cold bitch. He slunk over to the recessed doorway of a small shop with a For Lease sign in the window. At least no one would be showing up any time soon to open the place for business.

He hunkered down, trying to take up as little space as possible, and pulled the hood of his sweatshirt up to cover his hair and hide his face.

Half-assed plans circled his brain and died almost as quickly as they formed. If it wasn't so damned cold…if his head didn't feel like the inside of a fucking kettledrum, then maybe he could come up with a solid strategy for getting past the front door of the apartment building. If he didn't think of something soon, Razor was going to feed his guts to the fish in the Potomac River. And then Rosa and Trevy would be next.

Around noon, the metallic grind of a heavy garage door opening penetrated Bandit's half-frozen state. He straightened in time to see an orange BMW halt briefly at the top of the ramp before making a right turn onto a narrow side street. Trevy Barlow was on the move. Bandit's muscles protested as he shot to his feet and shuffled to the edge of his hideaway. His feet felt like wooden blocks inside his sneakers.

The right rear turn light blinked on and off as the orange car merged onto M Street. Just like Rosa had said: Trevy Barlow was heading to Capitol Hill to meet a friend for lunch. Ignoring the hunger that was eating a hole in his own stomach, he slumped against the wall and took stock of his situation. The good news was that Dr. Barlow's apartment was empty. Bandit figured it would take at least twenty-five minutes, maybe more in midday traffic, to cross the city to Capitol Hill. Another hour for lunch. Then twenty-five minutes for the return trip. Ten minutes short of two hours to get in and out of her apartment. The bad news was that none of his lame plans to get into the building were likely to pan out. He needed a new plan fast.

Or a miracle.

Neither seemed likely.

Five minutes passed. The guys from C&G came back outside and climbed into the back of their van, leaving the double doors wide open to the frosty air. From his vantage point in the doorway, Bandit could see inside. He watched them pull sandwiches out of crumpled bags and pour a steaming liquid into Styrofoam cups. His stomach grumbled. Saliva pooled in his mouth and he swallowed hard.

The hot smell of cigarettes seeped into the air. He filled his lungs, hoping to steal some of the warmth. But the smoke-scented air was thin and cold. What would Razor do if he didn't find a way to get into Trevy Barlow's apartment today? Push him harder to hand over the key? Or slit his throat, and then send someone else to find the money?

If he was a superhero…Spider-Man…he'd climb straight up the wall to Dr. Barlow's window and slip inside before anyone noticed.

But superheroes didn't gun down innocent girls in drive-bys. They didn't lie to their friends. They didn't skulk in dark alleys.

A shameful tightness behind his eyes felt suspiciously like unshed tears. *Mierda*. He wanted Mama. When she wrapped him in her arms, he felt…safe. He shook away the thought. She couldn't help him now. Maybe no one could.

Twenty minutes later, the construction dudes left the van and walked across the street, laughing and talking as they went. Bandit stepped away from the awning to peer around the front of the vehicle. It had been two weeks since he'd worked a job. Hiding out from the cops was a cold, lonely affair. He would have given anything to trade places with one of those lucky bastards.

Holy shit.

Suddenly he knew how he was going to get inside.

Ignoring the usual hum of activity in the hallway outside his office, Cruz shifted in his chair and reached for his half-eaten sandwich. His eyes glued to the computer screen, he finished his lunch in a couple of bites while he scrolled down endless columns of postal transactions coinciding with the date the dark parka was mailed to the Vegas' church. Every now and then, he paused to jot down the timing of a promising cash purchase so he could review the Massachusetts Avenue post office's security tape later. Then more scrolling.

As the numbers rolled down the screen, Cruz's thoughts

drifted. MPD's sighting of Razor in Georgetown still disturbed him. Something in his gut told him there was a problem no matter what anyone had to say about coincidences.

And then there was Bandit. The gangbanger had vanished again. No one had seen him since the night Charlie Vega had gunned down one of Trevy's students. Was he dead? It was a distinct possibility. Cruz's gut was warning him that the investigation was on the verge of moving in new and unexpected directions. That Razor was playing a deeper game than a turf battle with a rival gang.

And somehow, Trevy was caught up in all of it.

Cruz leaned forward, his chair squeaking in protest, and snagged a pen to write down another time sequence to check on the security tape. The phone rang. He minimized the file on his screen and reached for the receiver. "Larsen."

"It's JC Barlow," came the cool patrician greeting. "We might have a little problem, Larsen."

Shit. The muscles in Cruz's neck stiffened, making his tie too tight. "Is that so?" He loosened the knot and waited for JC to elaborate.

"Trevy called me. The spare key to her apartment is missing."

"And I should be worried why?" he said, his voice still relaxed despite the slight spike of anxiety that shot through him.

"I thought you might know where it is."

Cruz laughed. He leaned back in his chair and rested his feet on his desk. "Sounds to me like you're on a fishing expedition, Jean-Claude." His exaggerated good-ole-boy drawl was guaranteed to grate on JC's nerves. "Are you asking me if I'm shacking up with your sister? I had you pegged as a guy with a little more subtlety."

"Fuck subtlety, Larsen." Bingo. JC was not so cool when his own sister was involved. "Do you have the spare key?"

"No."

"Shit."

"Not the reaction I was expecting. I thought you'd be pleased to know that our relationship hasn't reached the point of key sharing."

"Shut it, Larsen. This might be serious."

Serious? Cruz dropped his feet to the floor and straightened, his amusement vanishing.

"What's going on?" he asked, the drawl dropping from his voice.

"I wish I knew," JC said. "Trevy thought I'd forgotten to return the extra apartment key before I left for Moscow."

"Maybe she misplaced it." Cruz's hand tightened around the receiver. On the surface this news was hardly cause for alarm, but in light of all the trouble swirling around Trevy, he couldn't very well ignore it either. "Where does she usually keep it?"

"On the hook of that ridiculous flower magnet she keeps on the refrigerator. You know, the one that looks like a tulip."

"Yeah," Cruz agreed, hoping this wasn't another one of JC's little tricks. Since he'd never been inside Dr. Do-Good's apartment, he had no idea what her kitchen looked like, let alone some flower magnet on the fridge. "What do you want me to do, JC? Open an official investigation?"

"I don't know," JC admitted. "The missing key was a big enough deal for Trevy to call me to ask about it. And when I told her I didn't have it, that I remembered hanging the key back on the magnet, she got very quiet. Too quiet. When I asked her who else had been in her apartment, she just changed the subject. Something's off. I'm worried."

And now, so was Cruz. "When did she notice the key wasn't in its usual spot?"

"This morning, after her run."

In his mind, Cruz replayed the conversation he'd had with Trevy in Rock Creek Park. He hadn't missed her evasion when he'd asked her if any of the Chingazos knew where she lived. He could only think of one reason why she would have lied: to protect one of her girls. It was all he could do to keep his feet planted firmly on the ground when all he wanted to do was find Trevy Barlow and... what?

"One of these days that heart of hers is going to get her in a lot of trouble," JC said, and Cruz couldn't help but agree. Two dead girls, an escalating gang war, and Trevy Barlow smack in the middle of it.

"Your sister's too trusting."

"I agree."

He did? Cruz had a terrible feeling that he'd walked into a trap without realizing it.

"What are you going to do about it?" JC asked.

Me? he wanted to protest. *Why me?* But he knew why. He'd gotten himself into this mess when he'd gone along with the farce that he was Trevy's boyfriend. And like it or not, he wouldn't be able to focus on anything else until he knew Trevy was secure and the missing key was a false alarm.

"I'll go over to her apartment to make sure she's okay," Cruz said. "I'll even help her find the damned key."

TWENTY

TREVY WAS IN a bad mood by the time she drove into the garage underneath her apartment building. Kate had cancelled their lunch plans for a last-minute meeting with her faculty advisor to discuss her dissertation. But not before Trevy had already driven across town to the Capitol Hill restaurant where they'd agreed to meet. Tamping down on her irritation, Trevy steered into her parking space while mentally rearranging her schedule for the afternoon. Now she no longer had an excuse to put off tackling the revision notes from her editor. Oh, joy.

Her phone started ringing as she got into the elevator, but when she plunged her hand into her satchel, her fingers could only find her wallet and a tube of lipstick. By the time she located the phone, it had stopped ringing. And then it instantly powered off. She'd forgotten to charge it after Rosa left last night.

Damn.

Frustrated, Trevy stalked out of the garage elevator and crossed the lobby to the one that would take her to her apartment.

"Hey, Doc, hold up," a familiar voice called out and she looked over to see Cruz Larsen rising from one of the overstuffed chairs in the waiting area. And just like that her bad mood vanished. *Along with half your brain cells*, she told herself as she altered course to meet him by the reception desk.

"Two visits in one day, Agent Larsen? I don't know whether to be flattered or alarmed."

"Neither. Why aren't you answering your phone?"

"You're such a smooth talker. Be still, my beating heart," she said and fluttered her lashes dramatically, partly to provoke him and partly to cover the fact that she actually liked his no-bullshit way of speaking. And maybe he was starting to develop the tiniest bit of appreciation for her as well, if the flash of amusement in his green eyes was any indication. His lips quirked up just the tiniest bit before his cop mask fell back into place.

"Got a minute?"

"Sure."

They took the elevator to the sixth floor. Once they were inside her apartment, Cruz paused in the doorway to the kitchen, looked down the hall toward the bedrooms, and then crossed over to the living room windows to take in the view. His thorough perusal of her apartment's layout sent a quiver of alarm through her. Something was wrong. She perched on the edge of the sofa, her fingers twisting into knots.

At last, he dropped into one of the wing chairs that flanked the gas fireplace and pinned her with his steady gaze. "I had a very interesting chat with your brother about a half hour ago."

"JC called you? Why?" she asked an instant before comprehension flooded her cheeks with heat. "He asked you about my missing key?"

"He's worried."

"He doesn't need to be."

Cruz sighed. "Trevy, I need you to be straight with me. Bad shit is happening. Two girls are dead. Another is in the hospital. And Razor's cruising through Georgetown."

"What does that have to do with my missing apartment key?"

"Hell if I know." He leaned forward, his arms resting on his knees. "But what I do know is that every single one of these events has one thing in common. You."

"Me?"

"Yeah, so can you save us both a lot of aggravation by being on the level with me? Is it possible that there's a link between that missing key and the Chingazos?"

Their gazes tangled in a silent stare-off. She lost when she looked away. Confession time.

"I brought a girl from my literacy class here last night. Just for an hour or so." She huffed out a breath when his dark brows arrowed downward in disapproval. "Someone beat her up and I wanted to help."

"You could have helped her by taking her to the police station to file a complaint instead of bringing her to your apartment. Now she knows where you live."

"I'm sorry, it was reckless."

"Reckless? Try insane."

Instead of bristling at his insult, she touched his hand. He was worried about her, and it felt good to have this man's concern. "I wouldn't do it again."

He covered her hand with his. "I'd like to believe you."

And then she realized just how foolish she'd been. Not only had she endangered herself, she'd also damaged her credibility. And that felt even worse.

He stood up and walked away from her.

"Where are you going?"

"To the kitchen. I want to check out this flower magnet that JC said he hung the spare key on before leaving for Moscow. And then we're going to do a very thorough search of your apartment. I want us to know beyond a doubt that the key is actually missing."

"The magnet's on the fridge," Trevy told him, following him into the kitchen.

"I see it," Cruz said, stopping so suddenly that Trevy walked into him. "Is this your idea of joke?" he asked, slowly turning to face her.

"Joke?" Trevy didn't like the way he was looking at her—like he couldn't decide whether to be furious or relieved.

"What do you mean?" She leaned around him. The spare key was dangling on one of the leaves of the tulip magnet, just like it always was. "It's back."

"What the hell, Trevy?"

"It's right where it's supposed to be." She reached out, but Cruz grabbed her hand.

"Leave it."

"I swear it wasn't there this morning. I spent an hour looking for it after I called JC. Then I left to meet a friend for lunch." She rubbed her temple with her free hand.

He looked at her for a long moment before giving a tight nod. Relief flooded her body. He believed her.

"Who was here last night? A name."

She knew it was her turn to trust him.

"Rosa," she told him. "Rosa Reyes."

He pulled out his cell phone. "I'm calling Detective Alvarado. You're going to report this."

"Report what? Why would Rosa break into my apartment without taking anything?"

Cruz held her gaze for a moment. Instead of answering, he said, "After I talk to Alvarado, I'm going to call in a security expert to change all the locks and install an alarm system."

Trevy could see that protest was futile. *Oh, Rosa, what have you done?*

And why?

A quarter of an hour later, Lou Alvarado and the MPD crime scene unit arrived. After Detective Alvarado greeted Trevy, Cruz pulled him aside and brought him up to speed. The members of the CSU moved through Trevy's apartment, layering a fine silt of black dust over every light-colored surface and white dust over every dark surface. It was messy, tedious work. Trevy stood off to the side, her arms folded across her chest.

Nodding his head in her direction, Alvarado said, "CSU counted eight hang-up calls from you on Dr. Barlow's landline voice mail. Real professional, Larsen."

"Zip it," Cruz said, not in the mood for ribbing from his task force partner.

Alvarado laughed and stuffed his notebook into his pocket. "Time to check out the security cameras," he said as he started for the door. "You coming?"

"I'll join you in a few minutes," Cruz told him and walked over to Trevy. He put a hand on her arm and let the reassuring warmth of her seep into him. "Detective Alvarado is going to make a copy of the security camera footage from the last few days. I'll need you to view it—"

"That's everything," the head of the CSU interrupted. "We'll run the fingerprints and let you know what we find."

While the crime scene unit filed out, Trevy moved through her apartment. A fine coating of dust covered everything. Cruz could only imagine what she was feeling as she surveyed the mess. Violated. Scared. Angry. Those were all common emotions victims experienced after a break-in.

He watched her as she went into her kitchen pantry and pulled out cleaning supplies. After spraying the countertops with a cleaning solution, she began to wipe them off. Cruz entered the kitchen and lifted her chin. Tears were welling in her eyes. She blinked furiously, trying to hold them at bay, but one escaped in a trail down her cheek. He brushed it away with his thumb and tried to think of what he could say to comfort her. He wished he could tell her that he didn't think Rosa Reyes was involved. But that would be a lie.

Trevy jerked her chin free and went back to scrubbing the countertop. He stood behind her for a moment longer. He was certain the teenager Trevy was trying so hard to help had set her up. A betrayal like that could gut a person. For someone like Trevy, who cared so deeply, it must be unbearable. And yet she was hanging on to her self-control. Words of sympathy weren't what she needed right now. There would be time for that later.

Grabbing a few paper towels from the roll on the counter, he said, "I'll clean up the bathrooms."

"I don't feel safe in my own home." Her words halted him in his tracks, and he turned to look at her. She was wiping the fingerprint residue from the refrigerator doors with long punishing strokes. Now he was the one who felt gutted. *Damn it!*

"You'll be safe, Trevy. I'll make sure of that."

The phone rang and she threw the dirty paper towel on the counter. She hesitated a moment before reaching for it and that seemed to make her more upset. "Hello," she said. "Yes, I'm expecting him. Please send him up. Thank you, Joe."

Despite everything, her manners remained intact, Cruz was amazed to note.

"Your security guy is here," she told him.

"That'll be Sam Jacobs. He's top-notch. He'll make this place so safe even the White House gatecrashers couldn't get in."

Trevy's lips curved into a slight smile and he felt like he'd won the lottery.

After Cruz let Sam into the apartment and explained the security setup he wanted him to install, he headed for the door. "I need to check in with Detective Alvarado," he told Trevy. No way could their B&E suspect have entered the apartment building without being captured on film. His money was on Rosa Reyes. "I'll be back in half an hour."

"Cruz," Trevy surprised him by taking his arm as he opened the door. "Is Detective Alvarado going to question Rosa?"

He had been hoping to address this issue later, when Trevy wasn't quite so raw. But now that she'd mentioned Rosa, there was no point in delaying the inevitable. "Yes, we need to figure out what's going on here. That's part of keeping you safe, Trevy. I won't pretend it isn't. You're going to have to tell me where to find her."

"I'm so afraid for her. Cruz, you don't understand."

Even though she couldn't bring herself to say it out loud, he knew Trevy was worried the police would arrest the teen. And that would mean her fingerprints would be entered into the system. If she was here illegally, it would mean game over for a path to citizenship. She'd be heading to a detention center before the week was out. Maybe her family too.

"I understand all too well. I'll try to keep her out of the system, but I can't make any promises. Especially if she stole your key." Or trespassed to return it.

He watched conflicting emotions flit across her face and wondered if she would refuse to give him the information. Then she said, "I don't know where she lives, but she works at Smitty's BBQ. You'll be able to find her there."

Something eased inside of him. So she *did* trust him. Until that moment, he hadn't realized how much that mattered. *Well, hell.*

"I won't be long," he said and left her with Sam before he could say something stupid that would ruin their new rapport. Women were so damn complicated.

Seconds after Cruz stepped into the lobby, the door in the wall behind the security desk swung open. "What took you so long?" Alvarado said and waggled his eyebrows. "Get in here and see if you recognize anyone."

Cruz followed him into the small room. One wall was lined with monitors that were showcasing activity in the lobby, the service entrance, the parking garage, and the elevator doors. After a quick glance at the monitors, he said, "No cameras in the elevators or the hallways. What about the stairs?"

"Nope, just the entrances and exits."

Cruz gestured to the computer monitor where Alvarado had been watching the footage from the last few days. "Spot anything unusual?" Like Rosa Reyes?

"Not a thing." Alvarado rubbed his eyes. "There's a week's worth of video. It all looks so normal it practically put me in a coma, but maybe you'll see something I'm missing."

"There's no way our B&E suspect could have avoided the cameras entirely." Cruz tapped the keyboard and started viewing the footage from the beginning of the day. And shit, Alvarado was right. A typical Monday morning. Nothing more than a boring stream of residents and occasional visitors coming and going, the start of another work week.

No Rosa Reyes.

After ten minutes more of staring at the screen, Cruz could feel his brainwaves shutting down. "We could make a fortune selling this footage to insomniacs," he grumbled.

Alvarado laughed in commiseration.

Then Trevy Barlow's image filled the screen. She was leaving the building for her morning run. He pressed a button on the keyboard to slow the footage to real time when she reappeared on the screen, this time walking back into the building. He watched her talk to the security guard, who walked her to the elevator. The elevator doors opened and a man in a dark overcoat stepped out, wheeling a large suitcase behind him. When the man stopped to greet Trevy with a kiss on each cheek, Cruz hit the button to freeze the frame.

"Cozy." He said it a little too casually, and Alvarado gave him funny look. He tried to shrug away the twin jolts of anger and envy that stabbed through him. Trevy Barlow was nothing more to him than a member of his team, he reminded himself. A very temporary member.

Yet, he couldn't stop himself from envying the lucky bastard. Cruz wanted to be the guy she greeted with such easy familiarity.

Alvarado returned his gaze to the screen for a minute and then flipped through a few pages of his notebook until he found what he was looking for. "The lobby guard told me this guy lives on the seventh floor," he said. "Penthouse apartment. Rafael Montoyez. Works at the Spanish Embassy. Trade attaché. Travels a lot." Alvarado traced a circle around the on-screen couple with his finger. "What do you think? Could they be lovers?"

Trevy and the trade attaché. How perfect. His gut tightened at the thought. But if Trevy and the diplomat were an item, JC wouldn't have been so quick to accuse Cruz of stealth-dating his sister. "I don't think so," he said, tamping down on emotions he'd just as soon ignore. He unfroze the frame. "How about this group?"

Cruz tapped the screen and Alvarado leaned closer to watch over his shoulder.

"C&G Interiors," Alvarado told him. "I'll check them out, but according to building security they've been in and out of the place for months. A remodel job on the second floor that's taking forever."

They watched more footage. Trevy left and returned from her luncheon. Then Cruz backtracked to Sunday's footage. More of the same old, same old. Until Rosa Reyes stepped out of the elevator and into the lobby with Trevy at her side. Cruz pointed her out to Alvarado. "There's the girl from Trevy Barlow's literacy class. The one who lied about her name and address. If she stole the key from Trevy's apartment, who did she give it to?" He pushed back from the monitor and looked over at Alvarado. "I hate complicated."

Alvarado laughed and slapped him on the back. "Not buying it. You don't like it any other way."

"Well, maybe I'm a changed man. Make me a copy of the Sunday and Monday footage. I'll go over it with Dr. Barlow. Maybe that'll shake something loose."

And they would have plenty of time to look at it. Until he knew what was going on, Trevy Barlow was going to get FBI protection 24/7, and he was assigning himself to the first shift. He stood up and squared his shoulders. He'd better go back to his apartment to pick up a few essentials. Then it was time to break the news to Trevy.

Sam Jacobs jotted a few notes on a clipboard before sliding it into his briefcase. "That about does it," he said to Trevy, who followed him to the door. She was about to open it when a loud knock came from the other side, startling her.

"It's Larsen." His voice was muffled by the closed door. After stepping in front of Trevy, the security guy opened the door.

"Good timing, Larsen. I was just leaving."

Relief weakened Trevy's legs. She leaned against the wall for support. The sight of Cruz filling her doorway made her feel safer than any new locks ever could. Ridiculous but true.

"Thanks, Sam. I owe you," Cruz said.

"I'm keeping track." Sam laughed. "Trevy, I'll be back first thing tomorrow to install the alarm system. Is eight too early?"

"We'll be here," Cruz answered for her. Jacobs just nodded and left, disappearing down the hallway.

Trevy leaned against the door jamb and folded her arms across her chest. "*We* will?" she asked Cruz, not bothering to hide her irritation at his presumption. "It's spring break. What if I had plans?"

"Do you, Doc?"

"No."

"Then what's the problem?" he asked and, for reasons she couldn't explain, she felt her annoyance slip away. Besides, she couldn't deny that she would feel safer if he dropped by first thing tomorrow morning. After a long night alone, she'd be more than happy to see him darken her doorway. So why fight?

Conceding defeat, she said, "No problem at all. Thank you, Cruz, I'm sorry to add to your workload"—*two murders, a drive-by shooting, and now a break-in*—"I'll see you at six tomorrow for our morning run." She glanced over at the windows in the living room. Snow was beginning to collect on the sills outside. "Looks like the winter weather is picking up…You'd better get going."

Instead of leaving, Cruz snagged a canvas duffle bag from the hallway and then walked into the apartment, shutting the front door behind him.

"Where do you want me?" He eyed the couch. "I can sleep pretty much anywhere, but I'd be lying if I said I wouldn't prefer a bed." He smiled disarmingly.

Trevy stared at the overnight bag he'd slung over one shoulder. "You're sleeping here?" she said stupidly.

"Until I know what's going on, I don't want you here alone."

Being alone in this apartment tonight was not on her top ten list. But it was too much to ask of Cruz. Maybe Rafael would let her spend the night in one of his spare bedrooms. The penthouse apartment was so large he wouldn't even know she was there.

Then she remembered that Rafael wasn't home, that he was in Miami.

"You don't mind?" Trevy asked. Maybe he was right. She'd let him stay the night. But once the locks were changed and the new security system was in place, she'd have to be prepared to let him go.

No matter how safe he made her feel.

"I don't mind." He moved past her. "I want to stay, Trevy."

"You do?"

He shrugged. "I don't want you to be alone."

"Oh," Trevy said in a small voice, not sure how to reply. *Don't read too much into it*, she warned herself. *He's just doing his job. Nothing personal. The last thing you need to do is lose your heart to this man.* "There's a daybed in my office. You can sleep there."

TWENTY-ONE

HOURS LATER, A nightmare woke Trevy and she wasn't able to get back to sleep. Part of the problem was Cruz. Asleep on the daybed in her office, his presence seemed to alter the very air in the apartment. She felt like she was breathing him in with every inhalation, which made relaxation impossible.

When the liquid crystal digits of her bedside clock reshaped themselves into a four and two zeros, she gave up on trying to fall asleep and decided to try working on her disaster of a book. After pulling on a long-sleeved T-shirt and a pair of yoga pants, she headed for the kitchen, where she'd left her laptop and chapter notes the night before. She had been planning on getting an early to start on her revisions. Just not this early.

Yawning, she powered up her laptop and opened the working draft of her book on gang linguistics. The end product of two years of in-depth research, it was flat and uninteresting, completely lacking the soul of her previous projects. If only she knew why…

She pulled up her revision notes and glanced through them for the umpteenth time. *Include more real-life examples*, her editor had written.

She minimized the draft document and brought up the file chronicling her anecdotal data. She had worked with fifteen different area gangs and crews, and her data showed that the cultural roots of the gang members were more important in shaping each gang's hierarchy and position in the community than the social influences they had in common. The high-level takeaway was that one-size-fits-all gang intervention programs were ineffective. The programs needed to be tailored to the unique characteristics of each gang.

For two hours, she worked back and forth between her draft document, her research files, and her revision notes. On the last page of her chapter notes, she came across a handwritten note: *Insert Lola Sanchez—6 mo. period reading level improved to grade 8— functional literacy—GED possible.* Out of nowhere, a hard tight ball formed in her throat and her eyes burned with unshed tears. She let her head fall to the table and, unable to hold back the wave of sorrow, she wept for Lola and Samantha Vega, for the grinding dysfunction that would destroy many more girls just like them, for the futility of her own efforts. For herself.

She didn't know how much time had passed when she felt his hand stroking her hair. Cruz knelt by her side and whispered, "Hey now, *cariña*, you don't need to be afraid. We'll find your intruder."

All Trevy could do was shake her head as a fresh flood of tears streamed from her eyes.

"I promise we'll find him. You're safe now." He stood and left the room for a moment, returning with a box of tissues that he set on the table next to her laptop.

"That's not it. I'm not crying because I'm afraid." Trevy yanked a tissue from the box and blew her nose. "I'm crying for the utter waste—the goddamn tragedy of these kids' squandered lives. And what do I do to try and stop it? I teach sociology classes to bored undergrads who are taking my one-hundred-level courses to get their humanities requirement out of the way. I spend years researching gang dynamics and interviewing members so that—how did you put it? Oh, yes, I study them and then write books. Nothing of real importance. Nothing that will change lives or stop the violence."

"I was just being an ass, Trevy. Why would I be familiar with your work if I thought it had no value? Two of your books and several of your white papers are required reading for gang task force members."

"No, no, you were right," she said, dabbing at her eyes with a fresh tissue. "More pearls of wisdom to pad my academic résumé. And deep down inside, I knew it too. That's why I started that literacy group. I tried to get word out to all the local gangs and crews, but only eleven girls were interested. All affiliated with Chingazos Locos. Eleven—that's all. I thought, okay, it's a small start, but it's a start. If I could help improve their literacy—both in Spanish and English—I could help them get their GEDs, which would give them opportunities."

She sniffed. "What a complete fucking pie-in-the-sky failure. Lola is dead. Her baby, Samantha Vega—more collateral damage. Bandit is God only knows where; Maria is in the hospital. And then there's Rosa...

"It's like I'm out there sticking my finger in a leaking hole while a tsunami breaches the levee. And what am I doing about it?" She slashed a hand through the air and brought it down hard on the table. "Sitting here in the comfort of my home and feeling sorry for myself because the first draft of my book sucks. Quitting would be such a relief."

"Trevy—" he said, pushing back the wet strands of hair that clung to her cheek, then cupping her face gently within the warmth of his hands; "—it may not feel like it right now, but what you do matters. It's just that you can't save the world all by yourself, not in a month, not even in a hundred years. Dry your eyes, Doc. Let's get some coffee and work on saving the world one little piece at a time."

Making the coffee helped settle her. When it was ready, she poured a cup and turned to face Cruz. Loose gray sweats hung low on his hips, and a faded black T-shirt was pulled tightly across his broad chest. He was leaning against the doorjamb, looking disreputable. And wildly attractive with his sleep-tousled dark hair and sharp green gaze. He was watching her, waiting for some infinitesimal sign that she was back in control of herself.

She held out a coffee mug. An invitation. He rubbed a hand across his beard-stubbled face, as if to wipe away his drowsiness, and closed the distance between them until their bare feet nearly touched. He grasped the handle of the mug, his fingers wrapping around hers. For a moment, the world stopped and Trevy forgot to breathe. Her body felt strangely buoyant, as if shedding all those tears had made her light enough to float to the ceiling. Then he stepped away, his gaze locked with hers, anchoring her, and she reached into the cabinet for another mug. As she poured coffee into it, she could feel the expectation build in the air between them. He wanted something from her. But what?

"Cream? Sugar?" she asked. The intimacy of the scene was unsettling. It was a little like waking up in the middle of someone else's life. It was a foreign land, mysterious and unexplored. And she was no diplomat. Nobody knew that better than she did.

"Black is fine," he said, taking a sip. His gaze over the rim of the mug was inscrutable. He was studying her as one might a particularly aggravating puzzle.

Uncomfortable, she glanced away, her eyes catching on the small digital clock on the coffeemaker. Almost six-thirty. "I'm sorry I subjected you to that little pity party." With a rueful smile, she lifted her eyes to meet his and added, "I hadn't planned on guests." Before he could reply, she said, "I'm going to get changed. A run will help clear my head."

"You plan on bringing a shovel?" he asked, stopping her.

"Shovel?"

"Yeah, look outside. It's snowing."

Trevy pulled open the shade on the window by the sink. He was right. A foot of snow had transformed the landscape into softly curving white domes and bumps. The air was still thick with it.

"Snow day," she confirmed before dropping back into the chair and staring at her laptop. "I guess I should get back to work."

A leaden weight settled in her gut. Her book.

"Seriously?" Cruz set his coffee mug on the counter and crossed his arms. "And waste all that untracked snow. Get on your boots, *chica*. We're going outside."

"But you don't have boots. Your feet will freeze."

"Doesn't matter. It's after six. Who knows how many kids are already heading out there while we burn time. Get a move on, Doc."

And for the first time, she didn't mind him calling her Doc.

Everything between them felt different. She could feel a smile spreading across her face.

"It can't be more than twenty frigging degrees out here," he said under his breath when they stepped out the front door. Trevy ignored him. But why shouldn't she? It had been his brilliant idea. Hell, who was he kidding? He wouldn't trade the discomfort of this outdoor trek at the crack of dawn for anything, not when it brought the smile that had lit her face from the inside out, wiping away the lingering traces of defeat from her hazel eyes. A smile that made him want to follow her through pelting snow and knee-high drifts just to see it again. A smile that made him want things he couldn't have. Ever.

Overnight, the city had turned into a ghost town. The streets were deserted, and not even a single footstep marred the small white mountains of snow. He followed Trevy, her red hat and jacket a colorful beacon in a white world. Twirling, she tilted her face up to the falling snow and opened her mouth. His gaze fixed on the pink of her tongue, the stinging cold snowflakes melting there, powerless to survive against the warmth of her mouth.

With a muffled curse, he forced himself to look away. The cold seeped into his running shoes. Alvarado would laugh his ass off if he could see him slipping and sliding in a frigging March blizzard when spring was only a couple of weeks away. The wind picked up as they rounded the corner. M Street was as empty as the side streets. Letting Trevy get a few feet ahead of him, he made a snowball and tossed it at her back. She yelped in surprise and whirled to face him, eyes bright with pleasure. For a moment, he forgot that he hated cold weather. He stared back, frozen and warm all at once.

Laughter bubbled out of her like fizzy champagne. She stooped to make a snowball and then threw it at him. Thwack. Cold exploded on his lips and cheeks, stinging his eyes and nose. Direct hit. He would never have guessed she had a ruthless streak. He would have expected it of her brother, but not Dr. Do-Good. Today she was full of surprises.

He wiped the snow out of his eyes as she stood there, her mouth a frozen O, her eyes dancing with a mixture of hilarity and horror. She didn't know whether to laugh or run. When it was almost too late, she turned and did both.

He raced after her. Having the advantage of boots, she widened the distance between them. But not for long. She made the rookie mistake of looking over her shoulder, so she didn't stand a chance when he launched himself at her, catching her around the waist, rolling when they hit the snow to cushion her fall.

On the ground, he kept rolling until she was underneath him, his body pinning hers. She looked up at him with wide eyes, snowflakes caught in her lashes. Her lips were the color of double cherry pie. He was warm where their bodies touched and cold everywhere else.

"I think we're in the middle of the street," she said with a soft hitch in her voice that stirred the leashed hunger inside him.

Snow dripped from his face and melted onto her lips. When she swept the droplets away with the tip of her tongue, every cell in his body quickened. She tightened her arms around him, pulling him closer until their mouths almost touched. He wanted her. To hell with the consequences.

And that's all it took. That feeling of being poised on the edge of control scared him back to his senses. *He* ruled his emotions, he reminded himself. Not the other way around. Another kiss would complicate their relationship and he couldn't risk it. Not when this case was so unsettled…not when her security was so at risk. His fingers closed around the snow, shaping it into a ball. Lightly, he brushed it against her lips.

Her eyes widened in surprise. The desire was still there, but now it was counterbalanced with confusion. She turned her face away from the cold snow and he let it slide across her cheek to the soft skin behind her ear. Shrieking, she writhed against him. He rolled off her—if she kept doing that, there was no way his newfound control would last—and she flung another handful of snow at him.

"Playtime's over," he said and pulled her to her feet. Her whole body was shaking with laughter as he hauled her down the street.

"You fight dirty," she said, her eyes lit with amusement, disarming him again.

"So do you." His lips curved upward despite his best intentions not to be charmed.

She nodded. "That's why you always want me to be on your team."

"I'll keep that in mind," he said dryly, then forced his mind onto safer terrain. "I'd like you to come inside to watch the security footage with me. It might help us figure out who broke into your apartment."

The shadows returned to her eyes, and the knowledge that he was the one who'd put them there was like a punch to the gut. Still, he reminded himself, it was safer this way.

For both of them.

TWENTY-TWO

"PAY ATTENTION TO even the smallest details," Cruz was saying. They sat side by side on her couch, careful not to touch, staring at the laptop on the low table in front of them. "We're going to start with Sunday, the day Rosa came over."

Why didn't he kiss me?

The words kept repeating in Trevy's mind as she stared at the screen. Her lips still tingled with the memory of his warm breath, followed by the slide of the cold snow across her mouth. Outside in the snowstorm, she had been on the verge of giving in to the attraction that arced between them—invisible but powerful—when Cruz suddenly put on the brakes.

Leaning forward, he inserted a DVD into the drive, then pressed play. Trevy forced herself to concentrate on the images from the apartment's security cameras. There she was heading down to the lobby in her running clothes. The time stamp on the bottom corner of the screen indicated that it was 5:56 a.m. Not much happened in the building while she was out, which wasn't too surprising considering that it had been a Sunday morning. For most people it was a time to sleep late, read the paper in bed. Make love. She shoved the treacherous thought away. The image on the screen switched to the parking garage elevator. A middle-aged man walked from his car to the elevator. Trevy thought he lived on the second or third floor. Late night, from the looks of him. Sleeping at the office again.

Then the image shifted to the camera by the front door. There was Mrs. Wilton, the widow from 5B, taking her bichon frise out for her morning walk. Trevy yawned and lifted her coffee mug to her lips. She cast a sideways glance at Cruz, but he was staring intently at the screen as if it were a complicated code that he could crack by sheer force of will.

With an inward sigh, Trevy returned her attention to the screen. Several minutes ticked by and then Trevy was on the screen again. It was 7:15 p.m. on Sunday evening. She tracked her progress. She left her floor in one elevator, then crossed over to the other one. Her image disappeared as the doors closed, only to reappear when she stepped into the parking garage through the open doors.

"That's when I drove to the New Hope Community Center," she told Cruz, whose only acknowledgment was a grunt, his gaze fixed on the screen.

A steady stream of people came and went as the footage continued on fast forward through the evening hours. And then Trevy entered the elevator in the garage with Rosa by her side. The comings and goings thinned to a trickle. Rosa was alone when she left the lobby later that evening.

"I'm sorry," Trevy said, turning toward Cruz, "I don't see how this is helping. You already know Rosa was here on Sunday night. This doesn't prove she took the key." *Although really, who else could it have been?* an insistent voice whispered in her head.

"You believe that, Doc?" Cruz's sidelong glance matched the skepticism in his voice.

Slowly, Trevy shook her head. He was right. Rosa *had* taken the key. She was sure of it; she just didn't know why.

"Let's look at Monday. Maybe you'll see something I'm missing." He sped up the timing and hours shrank to seconds. "Tell me about that morning. All the details you can remember."

"I woke up at 5:45 and left the apartment around 6:00 for my morning run. You caught up with me in the park."

While she talked, she watched the images flicker across the screen. Cruz slowed the video down when he reached the part where she returned from her run. The date stamp matched her recollection. Rafael, dressed for travel, stepped out of the elevator and leaned forward to kiss her cheeks. The move looked possessive, the conversation intimate.

"Rafael Montoyez," Cruz said and hit pause. "Is there something going on between you and the diplomat? Something JC doesn't know about?"

"What? He's a colleague of JC's," she protested. "We live in the same building. We're just friends."

"Maybe he'd like to be more than a friend," he muttered under his breath as he sped up the video footage. Then he surprised her by adding, "Can't say I'd blame him."

Their gazes met and held, his eyes daring her to pretend she hadn't heard him. What could she say in response to such an oblique declaration? And why had he gone from avoiding her kiss earlier in the morning to saying things like that?

After a long beat of silence, Cruz glanced away and the moment was lost. When he clicked play, the images on the screen began to move again.

"I was back upstairs by seven-ten. I grabbed a bottle of water from the refrigerator." She didn't tell him about how edgy and spooked she'd been after their talk—after learning that Razor had been cruising Georgetown while Rosa sat in her apartment, evading all questions about who had hurt her. "As the door swung shut, I noticed the magnet was crooked. I realized the key was missing when I reached over to straighten it."

"Then what did you do?"

"I looked for it. I searched the floor, my junk drawer, all the usual places. And then I called JC."

And JC had called Cruz, her pretend boyfriend. Only the feelings that rushed through her whenever she saw Cruz, thought about him, touched him weren't pretend. They were very real, and they were getting harder to ignore. *Get over it, Trevy.* "I spent the rest of the morning grading papers."

"Where were you going?" Cruz had frozen the footage at 11:58 a.m. yesterday. On the screen, Trevy was entering the lobby from the upstairs elevator.

"Meeting someone for lunch."

"Who?"

"Kate Davis. She's also just a friend, in case you were wondering."

"I guess I deserved that," he said with a rueful smile, and the tension between them ratcheted down a notch. "She works at the university?"

"She's teaching classes this semester while finishing her PhD."

He pressed play again and they watched as the workmen renovating 2C entered the lobby through the service door, presumably returning from their lunch break. Several more people came and left the building through the front doors.

"That's been going on forever," Trevy commented.

"What?" Cruz slowed the frames.

"2C is remodeling. The job was supposed to be finished by Christmas, but now it's anyone's guess. It gets pretty noisy at times. Sometimes I have to escape to my office at the university to get any work done."

"*That* broom closet," he said as the footage switched to the camera focused on the parking garage elevator. Trevy's image reappeared on the screen. The time stamp in the corner read 1:10 p.m. "That was a quick lunch."

"Kate had to cancel. Faculty meeting." The camera showed Trevy entering the lobby.

Then Cruz, as they headed into the elevator together to go upstairs to her apartment.

"Well, you know what happened after that," Trevy said and Cruz stopped the DVD.

"We went upstairs to talk," he said, more to himself than to her. "I wanted to confirm that the key hadn't been misplaced."

"And we found it hanging from the magnet on the refrigerator as if it had never been missing."

"That means our suspect had roughly seventy minutes to get in and out of your apartment." He ran through Monday's footage again, starting at the moment when Trevy left the building to meet her friend for lunch.

"Where are you?" he muttered as he watched, his eyes

narrowing in concentration. Images from the different cameras flickered across the screen. When he reached the part where he and Trevy met in the lobby, he stood up and walked to the window.

She glanced back at the screen. The footage was still on fast forward, and she watched as it continued to scroll through to late afternoon. The workmen from 2C were leaving through the service entrance.

"Damn, this is driving me crazy," Cruz said, shoving a hand through his hair. "What am I missing?"

Trevy studied him as he paced. He looked tired, discouraged. A quick glance at her watch confirmed they had been at this for a couple of hours, only stopping once, when Cruz's friend Sam Jacobs had called to tell them he wouldn't be installing the alarm system this morning because of the snowstorm. Her eyes hurt from the strain of staring so intently at the screen.

"Six workmen," Trevy said, trying to lighten the mood. "I can't imagine what they're doing in there all day, but at least I can reassure 2C that they're putting in a full day."

Cruz pivoted, his gaze locked on hers. "Are you sure?"

Trevy laughed. "Yeah, I'm sure. I saw the time stamp. They left after five yesterday, even though it was already starting to snow."

"Not that," Cruz said. "Six workmen?" He pushed some keys on the laptop, then watched the footage of the workmen leaving for the day. He froze the image. "You're right. There are six."

"So?"

He didn't answer her right away. Instead he pushed rewind until he was back to the image of Trevy leaving for lunch. Soon after, the workmen filed in through the service door, their lunch break over.

"One, two, three, four, five, six," Cruz counted. A man wearing a black jacket over a gray hooded sweatshirt brought up the rear. "Seven." Cruz froze the footage. He turned to Trevy, his green eyes brilliant with discovery. "There's our guy," he said.

Trevy studied the figure on the screen. The camera had captured him in partial profile, but the hood covered his head and hid most of his face. "One of the workmen broke into my apartment?" Trevy leaned toward the screen as if that might help her identify the man. A tiny spurt of hope bloomed. *Not Rosa*, she thought. Thank God.

"I doubt he's one of the workmen." Cruz fast forwarded and caught the same man leaving through the service door at 1:05 p.m., five minutes before Trevy returned from her cancelled lunch. He paused the image and pointed to the time stamp on the corner of the screen. "I was here." Frustration vibrated in his voice. He grabbed Trevy by the shoulders. "Sitting in the fucking lobby. Christ, I probably scared him off when I called your landline."

Repeatedly. Eight hang-ups in a two-minute period, Trevy remembered from when she'd reviewed her voice mail messages later that day. She felt a shiver of dread scrape down her spine as Cruz released her and turned his gaze back to the image on the screen. If she had arrived a few minutes earlier and Cruz hadn't been waiting for her, she might very well have been hurt or even—

She cut off the thought. No point in getting hysterical after the fact.

"It's a Raiders jacket," Cruz said, drawing her attention back to the screen.

"Bandit," they both said at the same time, their eyes locking.

"Well, at least we know he's not dead," Cruz added. "I was beginning to wonder."

"Why would Bandit break into my apartment?" And why had Rosa helped him?

"That's what I intend to find out," he said, his mouth flattening into a grim line.

The late season snowstorm stalled over the Washington area for another day before pushing into the northeast by mid-morning Wednesday. Sam arrived at Trevy's apartment at noon to install her security system, and Cruz greeted him at the door.

"About time," he commented, shrugging into his suit jacket. He was anxious to track down Rosa. Sam could keep an eye on Trevy while he installed the security system, giving him the chance to go to Smitty's and then swing by his office.

"I've got to go out for a while—"

His cell phone rang, so he waved the security expert into the living room, where Trevy was grading papers, and answered. It was Alvarado calling with an update on the Chingazos. Since the judge had inexplicably turned down their GPS warrant, two alternating teams of MPD detectives had spent the last thirty-six hours freezing their asses off in a snowy motel parking lot while Razor and pals hung out in a warm room on the first floor.

"I'm on the nine-to-five shift," Alvarado said. "So far Razor and his pals have been keeping a low profile."

"Any sign of Bandit?" Cruz glanced over his shoulder as he put on his overcoat. Jacobs was showing Trevy the specs for the security system.

"Nope. Just Razor, his lieutenant, and two females. They checked into the motel at ten p.m. on Monday, just ahead of the storm."

"No visitors?"

"Nope."

"Anything unusual?"

Alvarado consulted with the other detective. "Nothing except for the rug they carried into the room when they checked in on Monday."

"Rug?"

"Yeah, the gangbangers carried a rolled-up rug into the room."

A rolled-up rug? Cruz had a bad feeling he knew where to find Bandit. "I'm coming over. Call me if you have to leave before I get there."

He disconnected the call and went to tell Trevy he was leaving for a few hours.

"Don't worry about me. I have papers to grade," she said. The look she gave him when she said it was a strange mix of hope and fear, though, and he couldn't shake the feeling that she didn't quite trust him not to stir up trouble for Rosa. It was still bothering him ten minutes later as he headed to the Northeastern quadrant of the city.

Only the main thoroughfares had been plowed. What should have been a fifteen-minute drive took Cruz almost three times that long. Alvarado had said their stakeout car was parked in the far corner of the motel parking lot near a snow-covered van.

Cruz scanned the lot as he approached it. The van would shield his unmarked Bureau car from the direct line of sight of the motel's office. He forced the front-wheel drive sedan through the snow, skidding to a stop next to the MPD stakeout car before pulling up Alvarado's number on his phone and hitting call.

"Yeah?" Alvarado answered on the first ring.

"What room?" Cruz asked, glancing over at the detective, who was sitting in the passenger seat of the stakeout car. He had his binoculars trained on the row of doors.

"109."

Cruz could see the door just past the van. Paint was peeling off it in long strips. "Who's in there now?"

"Razor and his lieutenant GQ."

"That it?"

"Yeah, the girlfriend and her pal left a few minutes ago."

"Angel Mendez?" Cruz had interviewed her twice now. First at the New Hope Community Center the night of the Sanchez homicide, and again at the theater when Charlie Vega shot one of Trevy's students.

"That's right. No record. Possibly illegal."

"And her friend?"

"She's a new addition. We don't have a name yet. Short, round face, doesn't look old enough to drive."

"Could be Rosa Reyes." If it was, there'd be no point in visiting Smitty's today.

"I couldn't get a good enough look at her to confirm it." Alvarado paused and then added, "No sign of Bandit yet."

That didn't surprise Cruz. It was hard to move around if you were dead.

As they watched from their separate cars, the door to room 109 opened and Razor and GQ emerged, kicking at the snowdrifts as they made their way to the Navigator parked in the row closest to the motel. GQ used his hands to push the snow off the driver side door so that Razor could open it, then did the same for the passenger side door. The two climbed inside.

The front and back windshield wipers swished back and forth, snow flying from the car in an explosion of white. The tires spun, making a high-pitched whine as Razor tried to muscle the SUV over the foot of snow carpeting the unplowed parking lot.

After a few minutes of futile effort, GQ climbed out and stomped over to the office. He was carrying a shovel when he returned. Not a wide flat snow shovel, but one meant for digging holes. Snow shovels in March were hard to come by in D.C.

Once the path behind the rear tires had been cleared, GQ opened the door on the passenger side, tossed the shovel in, and hitched himself onto the seat. The rest of the windows were still covered with snow when Razor backed out of the parking space.

"Idiots," muttered Alvarado into the phone. "They can't possibly see well enough to drive."

"See you later," he added a few moments later as the stakeout car pulled out of the parking lot in pursuit of the Navigator.

"Right," Cruz said before disconnecting the call. "I'm going to scope out the room. They left without their rug."

And if his hunch was right, without Bandit.

No one tried to stop Cruz when he approached the first-floor room and knocked on the door.

No answer.

He knocked again. "FBI," he added this time, just in case Bandit was there, conscious, and ready to cooperate. Cruz pressed his ear to the door and listened. Seconds ticked by. Still no answer. He pulled out his phone and dialed Alvarado. "No one's home, Lou. My hunch about Bandit didn't pan out." Even Razor wasn't brazen enough to leave a dead body in a motel room for the cleaning staff to find. "I'm heading back to Trevy Barlow's apartment to check on her security system. I'll be there if you need me."

"Is that what they're calling it these days?" Alvarado said. "Dude, you got it bad."

You have no idea. Cruz shook his head as he ended the call. Who was he fooling? Certainly not Alvarado. Just to keep his thoughts from veering down that dangerous path, he rapped his knuckles against the door and, one last time, pressed his ear against the cold surface. He was about to retreat to the car when a faint moan from inside the hotel room captured his attention.

Was someone hurt? Maybe Bandit was alive but injured?

That was all the invitation he needed to enter without a warrant. He used a credit card to jimmy the flimsy lock. His gun drawn, he pushed the door open with his free hand and went into the room low, his gun ready.

Except for empty pizza boxes and beer cans, it was deserted. Had he imagined the moan? Keeping his back to the wall, he slid past the unmade beds to the closet. A metal bar. No hangers. He kicked at the bedspreads that were heaped on the floor. What a mess. The yeasty smell of spilled beer was the top note above lingering aromas of weed, cold pizza, and firmly entrenched mildew.

The bathroom door was closed. Was Bandit hiding in there? "FBI," Cruz announced again. "Come out with your hands up."

The only sound in the room was an anemic wheeze from the heating unit before it shut off. Cruz kicked the door open, slamming it into the wall. He counted to ten and then peered inside.

Empty.

The toilet seat was up, and a dark gray blanket was balled up on the floor near the bathtub. The rug? Cruz moved closer.

Three plastic rings held a mold-speckled beige shower curtain in place, blocking his view of the tub. What had been rolled up in that blanket? Cruz grabbed the curtain and ripped it down with one swift yank.

There was a body in the tub. Face down, hands tied behind the back, duct tape wrapped around the wrists and ankles. Cruz aimed his gun at the dark head and said, "FBI, don't move," even as he reassessed the situation. He recognized the Raiders jacket. Shit.

Bandit looked dead. And dead men don't moan. Alvarado was going to roast his balls for not taking the time to get a search warrant.

Careful not to disturb the body, he reached down and pressed his fingers against Bandit's neck. Shocked, he drew back his hand. Bandit's pulse was slow but strong. When Cruz rolled him over, he didn't stir. *Drugged*, Cruz decided as he holstered his gun and hoisted the gangbanger out of the tub.

No longer worried about preserving the scene, Cruz dragged him out of the bathroom. He was going to hand deliver Bandit to the MPD for questioning. And this time he was going to get some answers.

After glancing outside the room to make sure no one was nearby, Cruz left Bandit in the room and moved his car closer to the motel.

It was later than he'd thought. Nearly two. Sam Jacobs had probably left Trevy's apartment by now. A sense of urgency grabbed him by the throat. He didn't like the idea of her being alone—security system or not. Razor was up to something and Rosa was helping him. As soon as Bandit started talking, they could arrest Razor. Then maybe he could stop worrying about Trevy, and he could end his short stay in her apartment before he got too used to having her in his life. He had been doing just fine solo before he met Dr. Do-Good. The sooner he got back to the old normal, the better it would be for both of them.

Bandit was heavy. Cruz half-carried, half-slid him out of the room and then propped him against the trunk of his car while he opened the back door. Bandit's limp body refused to cooperate when he tried to get him into the backseat. Cruz had to go around to the other side of the car, place one knee on the backseat for leverage, and pull Bandit by the shoulders until his body was stretched across the seat. Cruz pulled himself out of the car and shut the door. He had to call Alvarado to let him know he was bringing Bandit to the station. But first he needed to get out of the cold.

A gust of wind blew snow off the car roof and into his face, momentarily blinding him. He swiped a hand across his eyes. *Jesus, could life get any more difficult?* He reached for the door handle to the driver side door.

And then pain exploded in the back of his head in a burst of white light.

TWENTY-THREE

"HELP ME WITH him," Angel hissed to Rosa. *Madre de Dios, the girl was about as useful as an ice sculpture.* "Grab his arm."

"Did you kill him?"

Angel shrugged, wishing the cold would freeze Rosa's mouth shut. The whole way back from the 7-Eleven where they'd waited while Razor and GQ led the cops away from the motel, Rosa had bitched nonstop about leaving Bandit drugged and tied up in the bathtub. But lately he'd become too unpredictable for them to allow him to roam free. What did Rosa think would happen to him if he ended up in police custody? The entire smuggling operation would be in jeopardy and Rosa could start picking out her outfit for Bandit's funeral. He was far better off unconscious and immobile.

Angel eyed the dark-haired man sprawled at her feet. What should she do with him? One thing was for sure. She couldn't leave him lying out here for anyone to see. She bent over and grabbed him underneath the arms, but when she stepped back, she slipped in the snow, landing heavily on her backside. She was strong, but he was too big for her to move on her own.

From her position on the ground, she looked up at Rosa. "Help me, damn it. Quick, before someone sees us." Rosa's whole body jerked and her eyes widened. Angel used the girl's terror to prod her into action. "Do you think the cops will believe that you were an innocent bystander?"

Beneath her knit cap, Rosa's face turned white as the snow. Gingerly, she reached down to grab an arm. "He looks familiar."

Angel scrambled to her feet and grabbed the other arm. Ignoring Rosa's comment, she started to drag him toward the motel room.

"Remember, Angel? He was there the night Lola died. Look at his face."

Angel didn't have to look at his face. She remembered him all too well. Special Agent Cruz Larsen.

"What are we going to do with him?"

"Let's get him inside. Hurry."

His feet dragged in the snow, making a trail to the room. The girls were out of breath by the time they lugged him across the worn carpet, shutting the door behind them. Angel dropped to her knees beside the agent and reached into the front pocket of her jeans. She forced three small white pills between his lips, past his teeth, and under his tongue.

Panting, Rosa said, "Shouldn't we put him on the bed?"

Angel searched the agent's overcoat and suit pockets until she found what she was looking for—the car keys and his phone. For a moment, her fingers hesitated on the holstered gun, then moved on. Taking it would stir up more trouble than she could handle. She glanced up at Rosa while she turned the smartphone over and pulled out the battery. "No." Angel stuffed the phone back where she'd found it. Standing up, she said, "Let's get out of here. Wait for me in the car."

"Car?" Rosa's round face screwed up in a frown. "That's not part of the plan. I thought we were going to move Bandit to another room in this motel."

"Our plans have changed." Wasn't that obvious? How could Rosa have gotten by for so long with so little natural talent for survival? Angel opened the door and pointed at the beige sedan. No way could she leave Bandit and the Fed in the same motel.

"Oh," Rosa said. Her eyes grew round with comprehension.

"Yes," Angel said wearily as she pushed Rosa out the door, "we're stealing his car."

Rosa didn't say another word. She just climbed into the front passenger seat of the car.

Angel rounded the hood and slid behind the wheel. She stuck Larsen's key into the ignition and cranked the engine before glancing back at Bandit. The sleeping pills she had given him that morning hadn't worn off yet. It was fortunate that there had been three left for the agent. He should be out of commission for hours.

After pulling out of the parking lot, she paid careful attention to the rearview mirror. There was almost no traffic on the streets. It would be hard for someone to follow her without her catching on. But she had to ditch the car as soon as possible. She watched as a silver SUV gained on her. Her breath caught in her throat even as she told herself that there was nothing to worry about. But she didn't exhale until the truck passed her, the driver speeding recklessly on the slippery road.

The tension eased out of her shoulders as she put more distance between them and the motel, heading to another part of the city. Another cheap motel almost identical to the one they'd left behind. This one closer to Eastern Avenue and the Maryland border. She sent Rosa to the office with enough cash to rent a room for a couple of days. Rosa returned with a key.

Another flea-bitten night with too much beer, cheap pot, and bad pizza, Angel thought as she and Rosa struggled to get Bandit into the room. It had been pure luck that they'd returned to the motel in time to see Bandit being dragged from the room by the FBI agent. If she hadn't acted so quickly, their plans would have been ruined. Bandit wouldn't have been available to drive the shipment of cigarettes to New York on Sunday, and he probably would have spilled his guts to the police before the ink on his fingers dried. Not for the first time, Angel wished Razor had listened to her when she'd warned him that it was risky not to replace Bandit with her. But Razor wouldn't agree to let her drive the shipment alone, and there was no way he or GQ were going to take the risk when Bandit was willing and able. Now it was too late.

They dumped Bandit on the floor of the motel room, both of them breathing hard from the effort. Angel shook her head in amazement when Rosa pulled a flat pillow from the bed, gently tucking it under Bandit's head. How could kindness survive anywhere in this tough world? Her cell phone in her hand, she sank down on the lumpy bed. *Forget about Rosa*, she told herself. She needed to call Razor.

But what to tell him? She tapped a long red fingernail against her front teeth. She couldn't imagine what he'd do if he stumbled upon the unconscious man in the other motel room.

Scratch that, she knew exactly what would happen if Razor found the agent. He would kill him. He wouldn't stop to think about the consequences or whether the cops would have enough evidence to link him to the murder. Or even worse, uncover the smuggling operation. All Razor would think about was eliminating the threat. He'd slit the Fed's throat and never look back.

Razor could ruin everything if she didn't manage him carefully. She knew what she'd have to do and it made her feel more than a little sick inside. But this was no time to lose her nerve. She pushed away the weakness, pulled out her cell phone, and dialed.

TWENTY-FOUR

CRUZ DIDN'T KNOW where he was. His brain felt sluggish, disjointed, his thoughts incoherent. Then instinct and training kicked in. Until he knew whether he was alone, he didn't move. He was cold, but not overly so. The mild discomfort of a poorly heated room. The worn carpet was rough against his fingers, doing little to cushion the hardness of the cement underneath.

Without altering his breathing, he identified the scents in the air. Beer, pizza, and…filth. Fragments of memory came rushing back, the disjointed pieces snapping into place. Room 109. Bandit trussed like a turkey. He opened his eyes a fraction and scanned the dark room. He was alone.

He sat up. Too quickly. Sharp pain stabbed the back of his head. Ignoring the ache, he pushed to his feet and staggered to the door. He felt drugged, out of it. What time was it? He flicked on the lights. Cockroaches scattered, scurrying into the closet and bathroom. Cruz tried not to think about them crawling over him while he lay unconscious on the floor. He glanced at the alarm clock on the rickety bedside table.

Midnight. Out for ten hours. He explored the lump at the base of his skull. Jesus, had an anvil landed on him Wile E. Coyote style? He glanced at his fingers. No blood. His vision was fine too. His hand automatically went to his holster. The gun was still there.

All good. Strange, but good. Except that he felt like a bear resurfacing after a long winter's hibernation.

Trevy. The name clanged in his head like an alarm. The

throbbing ratcheted up a notch. He forced himself to stay calm, to detach from the worry. She had been alone for most of the day, but her apartment was safe. The locks had been changed. She had a new security system. The guards in the lobby were on code red.

But what if Trevy had left the building? One of the Chingazos could have grabbed her. His brain flashed to an image of Bandit lying in a bathtub. What if —

Fuck detachment. It wasn't working. He reached into his overcoat pocket and pulled out his cell phone. First a quick call to Trevy. Once he knew she was fine, he could concentrate on the rest.

Someone was going to a lot of trouble to keep Bandit away from the police. The only surprising thing, really, was that the gangbanger was still alive.

Nothing happened when Cruz powered on his phone. It took him a moment to realize it was lighter than it should have been. He turned it over. The battery was missing. Whoever had knocked him out had been thorough. Disturbingly professional.

The room phone was on the bedside table. He reached for it and punched in two numbers before he realized the line was dead. On closer inspection, he noticed the severed phone cord dangling over the edge of the table.

Stumbling out of the room, he slid on the snow-covered sidewalk and went down on one knee. He pushed himself back to his feet and looked around. After a moment, he located the motel office. The cold air cleared away some of the fog in his brain as he made his way through the snow to find the manager. Except the door was locked.

He banged his fist on the cold metal surface. Nothing. He added a few kicks for good measure. More nothing.

Unless you counted the pounding pain in his head.

Cruz leaned in to read the metal sign fastened to the door at chin level: *Office closed after midnight. For assistance call 202-410-7031.*

This night kept moving higher on his list of top ten shitty life experiences, he thought as he searched the half-empty lot for his car and reached into his pockets for his car keys. Then he remembered he'd parked it in front of the motel room so he could stuff Bandit into the backseat. Fuck.

No Bandit. No phone. No keys. No car. He shoved a hand into the back pocket of his suit pants. Amazing. His wallet was still there. Whoever had hit him over the head hadn't bothered to rob him. Or steal his gun.

Unfortunately, that worried him more than it comforted him.

It took him five blocks to find a pay phone to call Alvarado to report the carjacking and what came after. When Alvarado picked him up twenty minutes later, he had more bad news. His MPD surveillance team had lost track of Razor and his inner circle. And God only knew who had taken Bandit. Alvarado wanted to drive Cruz to the emergency room, but he persuaded his friend to take him to Georgetown instead. He didn't know Trevy's phone number by heart, so he figured it would be easiest just to drop by.

It was well past one in the morning by the time Alvarado dropped him off in front of Trevy's apartment building. "You sure you want to be doing this? It's not too late. I can drive you home."

"Hell if I know, Lou." He climbed out of the car anyway and waved to Alvarado.

"Call me in a few hours," Lou called out before he drove away.

Cruz stood at the curb for a moment to survey the brick building and its perimeter. Everything appeared normal. No crime scene tape, no flashing lights. The sixth-floor windows were all dark. The tightness in his chest eased ever so slightly.

A punishing wind bit into him as he slipped and slid on the walkway to the front door. Any part of him that wasn't frozen hurt. The night guard's shift had ended at midnight, and the security lights were on in the lobby. He should have listened to Alvarado. It was obvious that nothing was amiss. Trevy was snug in her bed, protected by a new security system and locks to keep out the bad guys. Fatigue and the aftereffects of whatever drug he had been given had dulled his wits. But he had no way of calling his friend, so he continued to the front door of the building and pressed the buzzer labeled 6A.

Trevy answered on the fourth ring.

"Hello." Her low voice sounded sleepy and slightly distorted by the intercom system. He imagined her standing at the front door of her apartment, her hair sleep-tousled, her body warm. He couldn't think of anything nicer than Trevy in her bed. How he'd like to wrap her in his arms, letting her warm body melt away the numbness that had sunk into his bones hours ago. Her fresh scent of flowers and soap would chase away any remnants of that dirty motel room where he'd awoken. The sharp stab of longing surprised him. He shook it off, reawakening the dull throbbing in his head.

"Hello," she said again. This time he heard an edge of anxiety in her voice.

"It's Cruz."

He heard her exhale. Relief? Surprise? Irritation? He'd told her he would be back in a few hours. And now he was waking her up in the middle of the night. He was supposed to be protecting her, not robbing her of sleep. *Damn fine job you're doing, Larsen.*

"Are you okay? I expected you hours ago."

"Buzz me in. Please, Trevy. I'll explain everything when I get upstairs."

Barefoot, a pale blue robe wrapped snugly around her body, Trevy waited for him with her door cracked open. He moved past and stumbled toward the dark living room. If he didn't sit down immediately, he was going to fall flat on his face. He unbuttoned his overcoat and sat heavily on the couch, falling sideways anyway, his head landing on the soft seat cushions. That was better.

Her bare feet moved into view. He studied her toes. Her nails were unpolished, a healthy pink. He let one of his hands fall forward until he was touching her foot. Warmth flowed through his fingers and up his arm.

Whoa. He was getting turned on by a woman's feet. That was a new one.

"Are you drunk?"

He let his gaze travel up the length of her robe, lingering on the swell of her breasts before settling on her face. He couldn't help but wonder if she was naked underneath the silky material that clung to her curves in all the right places. The look of concern he'd noticed in her eyes when she was standing in the doorway had faded a bit. She took a step back, her arms folded across her chest. His hand slid off her foot.

"Don't be mad, Trevy," he said and closed his eyes to shut out her face. He was too tired to deal with her ire. "I'm not drunk."

"I'm not mad. I'm worried," she said. He could smell the flowery perfume of her hair. He opened one eye, surprised to find her kneeling before him. She was worried? About him? Her eyes were puzzled, as if she couldn't quite understand it herself. She pushed a lock of hair out of his eyes, and her fingers felt so good against his head that he leaned into them.

"Your skin is so cold. What happened to you, Cruz?"

"Someone hit me. On the head. And drugged me. I think."

Her eyes widened as if she didn't believe him, so he added, "Stole my car and my damned suspect too."

"Rosa?"

"Not Rosa. Bandit."

"Bandit hit you?"

"Naw," he said, his voice slurring a bit. He lifted a hand and placed it against her lips to stop the interrogation. Her warm breath against his fingers gave him a jolt. For a moment their gazes caught and electric tension zipped between them. He let his fingers skim across her cheek and follow the graceful line of her neck. As he rested his hand at the base of her throat, the heat of her making him feel half-drunk, he felt her pulse quicken.

He shook his head to clear it and tried again. "I found Bandit passed out in the bathtub of an empty motel room in Chingazos territory." He narrowed his eyes, his fingers lightly stroking the pulse at the base of her throat before he pulled away. Touching her was too distracting. For both of them. "I was moving him to my car when someone hit me from behind. I woke up in the motel room just after midnight."

"And Bandit?"

"Gone."

"Do you need a doctor?" Her eyes softened. She was all concern now. She sat back on her heels and waited for his answer.

"You volunteering, Doc?"

She gave him a get-serious look and started to rise to her feet. "I'm volunteering to drive you to the emergency room."

"I'm fine, Trevy," he said, even though it was far from true. He sat up and shrugged out of his overcoat. Putting his hands on his knees to keep his balance, he closed his eyes for a moment as the throb at the back of his head ratcheted up a few notches before settling into a low-grade ache.

"You don't look fine to me." Still kneeling in front of him, his legs bracketing her on either side, she reached for his head. God, her touch felt so good; it nearly made him forget all the aches and pains in his body. He wanted nothing more than to wrap his arms around her.

"Look at me," she said, momentarily distracting him. Oblivious to the battle that raged inside of him, she calmly studied his eyes. "Your pupils seem fine. How many fingers am I holding up?"

He looked at her hand. "Three."

"How many now?" She waved four fingers in front of his face.

He grabbed her hand. "My vision's fine, *Doctor* Barlow." Trevy frowned at the slight emphasis. "Want to check my heart rate too?" He pressed her hand against his chest.

Her slender fingers were warm, even through his layers of clothing. She leaned closer to him, a half smile curving her lips, her eyes still simmering with worry.

"You're incorrigible." She tried to slide her fingers from underneath his, but he tightened his grip. He liked the feel of her hand on his body, her breath on his face.

"Is that your expert diagnosis, Doc?"

"Yes," she said and laughed.

He kissed her while she was laughing. He had intended for it to be a small kiss—one taste of sweetness in a rotten day. But then her hands were in his hair, stroking his face, pulling him closer…

Trevy kissed him back with the same fierce passion he'd felt building inside him for days, weeks. Cruz pulled her into his arms and fell back onto the couch. He couldn't fight this any longer, not when her soft breasts were pressed against his chest and her tongue was in his mouth, brushing against his, warming him from the inside out. Melting him like spun sugar.

She tugged his suit jacket off his shoulders, trapping his arms while she dragged her petal-smooth lips down his throat, pressing soft, urgent kisses against his thundering pulse. A low moan that might have been her name escaped his throat. He pushed up against her, loving the feel of her body sliding along his, her mouth slanted across his. Kissing him as if stopping would kill her, she straddled his lap.

The thought of how far removed he was from that dirty motel room where he'd spent half the day unconscious flashed through his head. Christ, death had come way too close for comfort this time. But he didn't want to think about how easy it would have been for Razor or one of his compadres to kill him while he was out cold on the floor, so he shoved the thought away, surrendering to a pleasure so intense he thought he might lose control before he managed to get the rest of his clothes off.

She jerked his jacket lower, freeing his arms so he could loosen his tie and pull it off. His button-down shirt followed, and then he yanked his T-shirt over his head and wrapped her in his arms. She was soft and warm against his chest. Still half frozen, he fumbled to untie the knotted strip of silk at her waist. Once he did, he pushed the loosened robe off her shoulders. So there *was* a nightgown underneath, but it was just as diaphanous as the robe. Sliding the thin straps down her arms, baring her to the waist, he pulled back to drink her in with his eyes.

"Beautiful," he said, holding her narrow wrists. She was so delicate. And yet surprisingly aggressive in taking what she wanted from him.

She freed her wrists and slid her hands up to his shoulders. "You're the beautiful one."

"Trevy," he said, enflamed by the touch of her mouth and her hands on his skin. He grabbed the hem of her nightgown and yanked it to her waist.

"Now, Cruz," she said against his mouth, pressing her hips into his. He felt himself getting harder, hotter than he'd ever thought possible, and he knew that he wasn't going anywhere. Not without Trevy. He unclipped the holster from his belt and set it on the side table before reaching into his back pocket for his wallet.

Insane laughter boiled up in his throat. No matter what a major fuck-up the evening had been, at least one thing had gone right: Whoever had attacked him hadn't stolen his wallet. Because right now the only thing that mattered was the condom neatly stored behind his credit cards. He was going to die, incinerate, if he wasn't buried deep inside Trevy within the next ten seconds.

Her touch burned his skin as she undid his belt and unzipped his pants. He lifted his hips to help push down his boxers. Then she wrapped her fingers around him and he hissed with pleasure as she stroked him, her fingers applying soft pressure. It was almost more than he could bear. He brushed her hands away so he could roll on the condom and thrust himself into her heat.

So good. So good. A thousand times better than he had imagined.

TWENTY-FIVE

PLEASURE STILL THRUMMED through Trevy hours later when she slipped out of bed, careful not to wake Cruz. Even though it was well past noon, she was still on spring break, so she was in no hurry when she left the room to find her robe. After making a pot of coffee, she returned with Cruz's discarded clothes and set them on the slipper chair near the window before allowing herself to turn and gaze upon his sleeping body. She liked the way he looked sprawled across her bed, the sheet twisted around his narrow waist.

She felt at ease for the moment, yet she wondered how it would be between them when he awoke. Sex was sex, she reminded herself, tightening the belt on her robe. Not a declaration of undying love. Her marriage had taught her that.

So why did this feel different? She sank down on a corner of the bed, forgetting that she didn't want to wake him. He shifted his legs, kicking the sheet loose from his waist, and she touched the warm skin of his back, watching her fingers trace the elegant line of his spine from his powerfully muscled shoulders to his lean hips. He was a beautiful man. But it wasn't just his beauty that drew her to him. It was the intelligence that gleamed in his eyes, the steadiness of his gaze, his willingness to listen to her even when he didn't agree, even when she was falling apart. Although they had started out at odds with each other, somewhere along the way, they had become a team. They were working toward the same end—freeing kids from the stranglehold of destructive lives. They only disagreed on the means of getting there.

He had been in danger yesterday, and the thought of what might have happened to him chilled her to the bone. She wanted to loosen her robe and press herself against the heat of him, wrap her arms around him and hold him close. Reassure herself that he was safe. That there would be time for them to discover where this attraction between them would lead. She tugged the sheet lower, her fingers halting as she brushed against the dark stain on the small of his back.

A crudely inked tattoo. Her breath caught in her throat as she traced the entwined LV. Los Vatos.

Los Vatos was a well-established Latino gang that was predominant in the western part of the U.S., particularly in Texas. Compared to Los Vatos, the Chingazos were preschoolers. Were there other markings? After that first frenzied joining on the couch, they had moved to the bedroom. In the dark, she had learned the shape and feel of his leanly muscled body through touch, not sight.

She examined the clean lines of his back and neck. No, no other tattoos. Whatever he'd done to earn those letters must have been a long time ago, but it still stung to discover that he had been keeping secrets. She wasn't entirely sure how she felt about that. Did he think she wouldn't care? Or that it would scare her away? The sight of his naked body stretched out on the rumpled sheets was suddenly too much for her. She stood up, needing to put some distant between them so she could think.

Before she could step away from the bed, his hand caught her wrist. "I thought I'd dreamed you." His voice was sleep-roughened. Desire warmed his eyes, turning them dark with a thin ring of pale green rimming his pupils. Even now, with a jumble of conflicting emotions leaping through her, she felt her body respond to him. She still wanted him. She tugged against his hold. He let go.

With a sigh, he rolled over on his back, one arm shielding his eyes. "I know what you're going to say. Last night was a terrible mistake, right?" He let his arm flop to the mattress. His gaze was direct when he looked at her again. "I'm not going to apologize." His lips tightened into a flat line.

For a moment, Trevy was speechless. He thought she blamed

him for taking advantage of her? She was the one who should be apologizing. He had stumbled into her apartment still dazed from the combination of a head injury and some kind of drug. She should have done the responsible thing and pulled away when he kissed her.

"No, that's not it. I don't want an apology," she told him.

"You wanted it as much as I did," he said. She hated the blush she felt creep from the back of her neck to the edge of her hairline. She had been the one to supply the condoms after that first time on the couch. No one could have been more surprised than Cruz. Not that he'd complained. He'd laughed instead, pulling her tightly against him as if he never wanted to let her go.

"Yes." She agreed. What was the point of pretending she hadn't desired him every bit as much as he'd desired her? She turned her back on him and stood.

"Then what is it, Trevy?" Her easy agreement seemed to defuse his mood; his voice was less tense now. She could hear him pushing back the covers, walking toward her on bare feet. He settled his hands on her shoulders and started to nibble tiny kisses up her neck. His touch sent a massive wave of desire through her, weakening her resolve to keep him at arm's length. "Talk to me," he said, pressing a kiss against her ear.

"Los Vatos," Trevy said. "Why didn't you tell me?"

His fingers tightened on her shoulders for an instant before he stepped away.

Her back was to him, but he could see her face reflected in the mirror above her bureau as he sank down onto the bed. Cruz squeezed his eyes shut and pressed his fingers against the dull ache in his temples. He had just gone from a state of deep contentment, in which his only concern was how long it would take to get Trevy out of her robe, to the utter certainty that she would never let him touch her again.

Why didn't you tell me? It was a good question. Had he thought the truth would push her away? Or maybe he'd been afraid that it wouldn't...

"I was a teenager rebelling against my gringo father." The words shot out of his mouth before he could stop them. Tired excuses that he thought he'd left behind long ago. When he opened his eyes again, Trevy had turned to face him. But for once she was the one with emotions tightly shuttered behind a blank mask while his own raged out of control. "I thought Los Vatos understood me. Kind of like a family where I fit in."

"What about your mother?"

"Her name was Gabriella Cruz. She was a journalist. She died when I was six. Gunned down in Mexico City while investigating links between local government officials and the leader of a powerful drug cartel." His headache shifted from dull to skull-splitting. He welcomed the distraction from a pain that went so much deeper.

Perhaps it was the blow to his head that had made him so careless about the tattoo. No, that wasn't it. Trevy was the only woman he'd ever been with who would immediately recognize the tattoo and understand what it meant. He couldn't deny that a part of him had wanted to her to see it, to know him in a way no other woman had.

"You were born in Mexico?" she asked, not through with the interrogation. Oh, no, not Trevy. She was thorough. Well, he'd give her what she wanted. The least he owed her was the truth.

"Yeah, my mother hooked up with an American journalist who was sent across the border to cover a Pemex oil spill in the Gulf. Ten months later, around the time when the well was capped, I arrived on the scene. Diego Larsen Cruz. My father only stuck around long enough to put his name on my birth certificate. When he returned to Texas, he never looked back."

"When did you come to the United States?" Trevy wrapped her arms around her waist and watched him with an unreadable expression on her pale face. She was withdrawing from him, and that knowledge felt like a stab in the gut. He took a deep breath, steeling himself to finish the job.

"After my mother was killed, it wasn't safe for me to stay in Mexico City. Bad things tended to happen to the children of rebels and reformers. My uncle smuggled me across the border to Texas and found my father, who had long since been fired from his big-city paper and was eking out a living as a part-time reporter in West Texas. The only thing he did full time was drink.

"He was about as happy to reclaim his cholo son as I was to discover that my father was a bigoted alcoholic with an amazing capacity to carry grudges. He told everyone my name was James Larsen, but I insisted on Cruz. Hell if I know why. It was the only battle with him I remember winning. He beat me black and blue for it, but he couldn't beat it out of me."

Trevy nodded. "You had lost everything, your mother, your home, your friends. All you had left was your identity. Your sense of self. Of course you clung to your mother's name."

To his amazement, the guarded look in her eyes was fading. That wouldn't do. No, no, no. He didn't want her understanding. He wanted...

Hell, he didn't know what he wanted. He felt exposed. Vulnerable.

"Whatever you say, Doc," he said, attempting to pull his armor back into place.

Trevy stiffened just as he'd known she would. It was probably for the best. Trevy Barlow was too good for him. He'd known that all along.

"How old were you when you joined Los Vatos?"

"What's with the twenty questions?" He considered adding, *Writing another book?* But he couldn't bring himself to take it that far. Not when he knew how much those words would hurt her.

And he couldn't do that, not intentionally.

"How old?" she asked again, pushing him. *What the fuck, might as well spill your guts.* There was nothing unique about his sordid past. And Trevy deserved to know what type of man she had allowed into her bed, her life.

"I was the son of an alcoholic journalist and a dead Mexican. The entire middle school administration must have heaved a collective sigh of relief when they passed me on to the high school the next town over. It didn't take Los Vatos long to find me. I was fourteen."

"Did you finish high school?"

"I got booted out at sixteen. A locker search turned up a knife."

"Was it yours?"

He raised an eyebrow. Was she kidding? "It was mine." He could practically see her brain churn as she tried to make up excuses for him. Well, he wasn't going to let her. It was time for Professor Barlow to take off the rose-colored glasses. Life wasn't neat and tidy. And his past was a messy shithole of anger, resentment, and mistakes.

"I was a bad kid. I intimidated people. I got into fights. I stole." He stood up from the bed, and she raised her eyes to hold his gaze. He could tell she didn't want to believe him.

"What about your uncle?"

He shrugged. "Disappeared. Happened to a lot of Mexican journalists' family members. Still does."

"You were grieving for your mother, you were alone in a foreign country, and your father sounds completely dysfunctional."

"Fuck the excuses. I made bad choices, but I was old enough to know what I was doing. I liked the wild life, the thrill, the power."

"Then what made you change?"

"The school of hard knocks. Two weeks before my eighteenth birthday, I got caught shoplifting. I'd gone into JC Penney to get a new pair of boots. Notice that I didn't say buy, Doc.

"Usually it was so easy. Pick a busy Saturday and a department store advertising a big sale. Ask for the boots you want in your size. Try them on. Tell the salesperson you need a different size. Then ask to try on a different style. When the salesperson goes into the back to get another pair, you put your old boots in the empty box and slide it under the seat. It's so busy that no one notices you walking out of the store in your brand new boots. The box with your old shoes stays under the chair until the end of the day. Someone puts it back on the shelf. Days pass, maybe even weeks, before the switch is noticed. If anyone remembers you, well, it doesn't matter, you're long gone."

"If it was so easy, why'd you get caught?" She unfolded her

arms and held her hands up for emphasis.

"Bad timing," he said, the corners of his mouth edging into a grim smile. "An off-duty police officer was buying shoes that day. He noticed me walk away without paying. He had the advantage of surprise when he took me out with a well-aimed kick to the middle of my back. I was busted."

"Jail time?" Her delicious lips shaped the words as if she had tasted something rotten. She finally looked rattled. Just a few more details and she was sure to turn away in disgust. He ignored the sharp twist in his gut. She deserved someone without all the scars he carried inside. Broken pieces that had healed, but would always, always be there.

"Since I was nearly eighteen and my father had kicked me out the year before, the juvenile court judge offered me a deal. I could serve my time in a detention center or get my GED and enlist in the army. It was a real wake-up call. I was lucky I hadn't killed anyone. Yet. If I'd continued living that way, *la vida loca*, it would have been only a matter of time. I could spend my life fighting and stealing. Or I could spend my life fighting and serving my country. The army seemed like the smarter choice."

"An ex-gang member becoming an FBI agent...do you know how remarkable that is? How remarkable that makes you?"

Her reaction shouldn't have surprised him, but it did. Jesus, when didn't she surprise him? He dismissed her words with a snort of self-disgust. "Don't kid yourself, Doc. The army worked out for me because I was tough. I liked to fight. All I lacked was discipline. And they sure as hell drilled that into me. I had a talent for fighting, so I went to Ranger School and fought in Afghanistan and Iraq. After three tours of duty, I'd had enough. Used the GI bill to get a college degree in computer science and finance. Then the FBI recruited me. End of story. Nothing heroic, Doc."

"Tattoos can be removed."

"I keep it to remind me."

"Remind you of what?"

He thought for a moment. No one had ever asked him that.

"What I'm capable of," he said and then immediately regretted his honesty.

The apartment phone rang, giving him a break. Trevy answered. She listened for a moment before handing him the receiver. "It's for you."

Their eyes met. Hers were dark and solemn, seeing entirely too much for his comfort. Even though his tattoo now felt like a glowing brand, he turned his back on her. "Yeah?"

"What the hell's up with you?" Alvarado's question exploded into his ear. "You were supposed to check in with me this morning."

"I got delayed." Cruz glanced at the clock on the bedside table and winced. Jesus, it was nearly three in the afternoon. He wasn't even sure what day it was. Wednesday? No, Thursday. He spotted his shirt and suit pants draped over the back of a chair. Last he remembered, his clothes had been left in a heap in the living room. Trevy must have brought them into the bedroom for him. "I'll meet you at the station in a half hour."

He grabbed his pants and stepped into them as he spoke. A realization hit him hard: He'd revealed more of himself to this woman than he had to any other living soul. What the hell was wrong with him? Why not just stab himself in the heart and be done with it?

Better you than her, a little voice in his head whispered before Alvarado drowned it out. "Forget the station, Larsen. Cecilia Sanchez is missing. I'm heading to the high school to talk to the principal."

Shit. "I'll meet you there."

"No, someone needs to talk to the mother. Think you can get your sorry ass over to the Sanchez apartment without my help?" Alvarado sounded more like his platoon sergeant today than his task force partner. Cruz figured he deserved the jab, so he kept his lips sealed and listened as Alvarado brought him up to speed on the timeline.

"Oh yeah," Alvarado added when he was done briefing Cruz, "we found your car in PG County. It's been towed to the impound lot. You can have it back as soon as the CSU is done with it."

"Bandit?"

"No sign of him. And we put out a BOLO for Razor."

"I want to know the minute either of them turns up."

"You and me both," Alvarado said before ending the call.

Cruz handed the phone back to Trevy. "I've got to go."

"This discussion is not over." She followed him out of the bedroom.

"Cecilia Sanchez is missing." He retrieved his gun from the side table in the living room, his tie from the floor, and his overcoat from the couch. "I've got to talk to her mother. Stay here until I get back."

"I'm coming with you."

TWENTY-SIX

NOW THAT HE'D been saved from their little heart-to-heart, Cruz could breathe again without feeling like someone had wrapped a tourniquet around his chest. "Mrs. Sanchez got one of those automated calls from the school," he said, filling Trevy in as she drove them to the Sanchez apartment, "you know, the ones that go out when kids skip class."

"Has anyone talked to Ceci's teachers?"

"Detective Alvarado is on his way to the high school."

"I can't believe she would skip school," Trevy said, her eyes on the road. "Ceci's an honor student. She wants to be the first person in her family to go to college."

"Violence has a way of changing people."

Trevy wanted to argue the point. He could see it in the swift glance she shot him. "Make a left at the light," he said before she could get the words out. He was in no mood for psychoanalyzing Cecilia Sanchez.

Trevy took the hint and they traveled in silence the rest of the way.

"This is it," he said when they drew up alongside the fifteen-story brick building where the Sanchez family lived. Trevy maneuvered the car into a parking space and they both climbed out. Mid-afternoon, the sidewalk was deserted. Stepping over a low snow bank of rapidly melting gray slush, Cruz led Trevy past a liquor store and a Laundromat. They entered the Section 8 housing through a metal door next to a storefront with a check-cashing sign in the window. The Sanchez apartment was on the second floor, up a narrow staircase reeking of mildew and neglect.

Midway down the hall, Cruz stopped and knocked on a door. He held his federal ID up to the small peephole. "Special Agent Larsen and Dr. Barlow to see Mrs. Sanchez," he said in voice just loud enough to carry through the flimsy door. It opened almost immediately.

"Please come inside." Mrs. Sanchez's worried gaze touched on him for an instant before zeroing in on Trevy, who was hard to overlook in her bright red coat, jeans, and stylish black boots.

Mrs. Sanchez reached past him to pull Trevy into the apartment.

"Dr. Barlow," she said, lapsing into rapid Spanish, "have you seen Cecilia?"

"Not for a couple of weeks." Trevy said, holding Mrs. Sanchez's hand in both of hers for a moment before sticking them back into her coat pockets.

"At Lola's funeral," Mrs. Sanchez supplied the words Trevy had left unspoken. Deep grooves bracketed her mouth, and the stark pain her dark eyes made Cruz want to look away.

"I'm sorry." Trevy glanced back at him. The look on her face told him she knew how worthless the sentiment was. Sorry wasn't going to get the job done.

It was cold in the apartment, and Mrs. Sanchez did not offer to take their coats before she waved them into the small, tidy living room, which was bracketed by a galley kitchen to the left and a short hallway to the right that probably led to the bedrooms. Trevy sat at one end of the couch that faced the TV. Mrs. Sanchez sat next to her. That left the folding chair for him. He eyed it with caution. It looked too flimsy to hold anyone over one hundred pounds, let alone a full-grown man. He ignored the creak of protest when he settled onto the seat and focused his mind on the business at hand.

"Señora Sanchez, when did you last see Cecilia?" Cruz asked, continuing the conversation in Spanish. He pulled a pen and a small notepad from his suit jacket pocket.

"Monday morning when she left for school." Mrs. Sanchez was

perched on the edge of the couch like she couldn't decide whether to sit or stand. The coiled tension in her body radiated outward, silently communicating her desperation. "I went to work soon after and didn't get home until midnight. I thought she was asleep in her room."

"You didn't check?" Cruz asked, just to confirm the timeline.

"No, Ceci's door was shut."

"When did you realize she wasn't home?" Trevy angled her body toward Mrs. Sanchez and touched her hand. A gesture of comfort that made Cruz grateful she was with him.

"Not until noon on Tuesday. We were snowed in, so I let her sleep late." Mrs. Sanchez pulled a crumpled piece of notebook paper from her sweater pocket and handed it to Cruz. "I found this note in her room when I went to wake her up."

Cruz read the note and then passed it to Trevy. He watched some of the worry ease from her face as she read it.

"Ceci said she was spending the night at a friend's house. Maybe she's still there, Señora Sanchez," Trevy suggested, handing the note back to him.

But Mrs. Sanchez was already shaking her head. "At first I thought the snowstorm was keeping Ceci away from home. But when the school called on Thursday to report an unexcused absence, I knew something was wrong. That's when I called the police."

"Señora Sanchez, has Cecilia ever gone missing for any length of time before today?" Cruz asked.

"No, Cecilia never gave me a moment's worry. It was always Lola who came and went as she pleased. Sometimes for days at a time. I couldn't always be here to make her obey me."

"No one is judging you, Señora Sanchez," Trevy said, picking up on the defensive tone in the woman's voice.

"That's right." Cruz shifted on the chair, trying to find a more comfortable position. When it creaked, he held his breath. As if in silent agreement, they all waited for a moment to see if it would collapse beneath him. When it didn't, he asked, "Did you check with her friends?"

"No," Mrs. Sanchez twisted her hands in her lap. Her face colored and for the first time since they'd arrived, her eyes filled with tears. "No," she whispered again and looked away from both of them.

"It's okay," Trevy leaned to one side to pull a tissue from her bottomless pit of a purse she'd set on the floor near her boot clad feet. The black satchel had more in common with Mary Poppins's carpetbag than it did an ordinary handbag. Trevy handed the neatly folded tissue to Mrs. Sanchez. Of course it was covered with tiny pink flowers. Did Trevy own anything that wasn't decorated with or scented like flowers? His mind tracked to the silk nightgown he'd stripped from her body just hours before. It had been covered with small blue flowers. He tried to banish the image from his brain. He had no business thinking about that now. Maybe never again.

"You shouldn't blame yourself," Trevy said, almost as if she could hear Cruz's thoughts. His eyes whipped to her face, his heart beating out a fast rhythm of alarm. But she was looking at Mrs. Sanchez. He took a deep breath and released it slowly. Of course, she was. *Pull it together, Larsen.*

"*Gracias.*" Mrs. Sanchez dabbed her eyes with the tissue. "Please excuse me for a moment," she said and left the room to gather her composure.

"Blame herself for what?" Cruz asked as soon as Mrs. Sanchez was out of earshot. He stuffed his notepad back into his pocket and waited for Trevy to answer.

"Mrs. Sanchez has a full-time job cleaning houses during the day and then works part-time in the evenings cleaning offices at one of the downtown law firms."

"Doesn't leave much time for her to get to know Cecilia's friends. Is that what you're getting at, Doc?"

"Exactly." Trevy bobbed her head and a lock of shiny caramel hair slid forward across her cheek. He couldn't help remembering how good that thick mane of silk felt brushing against his skin. "I wouldn't be surprised if Ceci keeps that information to herself anyway. Don't judge Mrs. Sanchez too harshly. She's doing the best she can."

Unable to help himself, he admired the graceful sweep of her hand as she tucked the tawny strands behind her ear. Exasperated, he blew out a breath of air and rested his elbows on his knees, leaning toward her. "I'm not judging her, Doc. I'm trying to do my job. Sometimes that means asking questions that make people uncomfortable. Or even upset."

"I understand perfectly," Trevy said, her hazel gaze locked on his.

After a moment, Mrs. Sanchez returned to the room. Instead of resuming her seat on the couch, she handed Trevy two pieces of paper that looked like they'd been torn into a hundred pieces and taped back together again. Cruz watched a faint crease appear between Trevy's eyes as she scanned the pages. "Oh, poor Ceci," she said, looking up at Mrs. Sanchez. "You think this is why she ran away?"

"I know it is," Mrs. Sanchez said with a nod.

Trevy handed the pages to Cruz. It was a World History paper. He read the title: "The Role of the Fourth Estate in Revolutionary France." The first page was filled with red marks and comments. The pages crackled when he flipped to the second page, his eyes traveling straight to the large red D at the bottom of the page, followed by the words *See me after school.*

"She has World History before lunch on Mondays," Mrs. Sanchez said. "The school said she didn't go to her afternoon classes, and none of her teachers remember seeing her after lunch."

"At least we know she came home at some point on Monday," Cruz said, handing the history paper back to Mrs. Sanchez. She took the crumpled essay and rolled it into a tube. "We'll find her, Señora Sanchez. I wouldn't be surprised if she comes back on her own. In the meantime, the police are looking for her."

Instead of reassuring her, his words seemed to make Mrs. Sanchez even more upset. "Cecilia is ruining everything. I don't want her cleaning offices like me. I want her to work in an office. She can't afford to make mistakes."

Cruz didn't know what to say. Mrs. Sanchez was right, but he couldn't fix Cecilia Sanchez's missteps. All he could do was find her before she lost even more ground. Trevy rose and wrapped an arm around Mrs. Sanchez's shoulders. Though she was no Amazon, she towered over the older woman. She bent her head to catch Mrs. Sanchez's gaze. "Mistakes can be overcome."

Then she looked straight at Cruz. *Message delivered loud and clear, Doc.*

"No, no, it's too late." Mrs. Sanchez slapped the rolled-up essay against her palm, a counter beat to every word she spoke. "First the bad grades, then the missed classes. Pretty soon she'll drop out. Just like Lola." She crumpled the paper and threw it across the room.

Trevy took Mrs. Sanchez by the shoulders and gave her a gentle shake. "If one door closes, we'll find another. Just don't give up on her."

The anger drained from Mrs. Sanchez's face, leaving her expression flat with defeat. "But I don't know what to do."

"Then we'll help you," Trevy told her. "But first we have to find Ceci." She looked past Mrs. Sanchez to him. The fight in her eyes heated him from head to toe. This woman was a warrior.

He nodded, accepting her silent challenge. "Count on it," he said so that Mrs. Sanchez could hear him too.

TWENTY-SEVEN

THE ASSISTANT DIRECTOR of counterterrorism ordered Cruz to the FBI headquarters for a meeting the next day. No agenda for this Friday morning get-together, not even a hint. Cruz had a bad feeling he wasn't going to be happy when he found out why he was on the receiving end of a high-priority summons, but he arrived on time and was shown to an empty conference room. He sat cooling his heels for the next twenty minutes, and then she entered the room. Not the AD. A young Latina teenager with a killer body. Her shiny red shirt and dark blue jeans looked like they'd been spray-painted onto her body, and black hair waved past her shoulders.

Where the hell was the AD? He lifted his eyes to her face for an answer, and recognition jolted him like a high-voltage wire. This was no teenager. Mid-twenties, he reassessed. Definitely undercover.

Angel Mendez. She was posing as one of the teenage dropouts Trevy Barlow was trying to save…and Razor's girlfriend. Holy shit.

Anger sizzled just below the surface of his skin as he realized a deeper game was in play. Why hadn't he been informed that the Bureau had someone else working his case? He eased back in his chair, feigning indifference. Angel sat across from him.

"Will the AD be joining us?"

She arched one elegant eyebrow in reply. Her dark, intelligent eyes and cold smile told him all he needed to know. He had been called in to meet with her.

"Okay, Angel," he said, ready to stop playing games. "What are you doing fucking with my investigation?"

Angel laughed. She studied him as she tapped her red fingernails against the mahogany table top. The little clicking noises irritated him, but one glance at her dark eyes told him it was intentional. He held himself still as he waited for her answer. He sure as hell wasn't planning to dance to her tune. The sooner she figured that out, the sooner they could cut through the bullshit.

"You're the one fucking with *my* investigation." She threw his words right back at him, confidence radiating from her. She thought she held all the cards.

"Last time I checked, I was the one heading up the gang task force. Who sent you in undercover?" *And why the fuck did no one tell me?*

Her smile was thin, cold. "Agent Larsen, don't get into a pissing contest with me. You'll lose."

"Pretty sure of yourself." Of course she was. Weren't they sitting in the AD's conference room? Still, he wanted to rattle her chain, so he added, "You won't mind if I verify it with the AD?" He pulled out his cell phone before he remembered that it didn't have a battery. Shit. He tossed it on the table.

Angel smiled and shifted in her seat to pull something out of her back pocket. Her jeans were so tight that he was amazed there was room for anything else. Curious in spite of his growing fury at having been played by his own team, he watched as she placed a sealed evidence bag on the table.

Through the clear plastic, he could see a car key on a pink velvet ribbon.

"Tampering with evidence is a felony," he said flatly, suppressing a fierce surge of anger.

"Relax, the chain of custody's intact."

"Good to hear." He leaned forward to slide the bag closer to him, just out of her reach. He and Alvarado were still sifting through postal transactions, hoping to find a solid lead on Lola's killer. He wanted the murder weapon back where it belonged, in the evidence warehouse. And he wanted another crack at figuring out the key's significance. "I have a lead on a possible suspect. As soon as I find Bandit—"

"The MPD surveillance on Razor has been called off"—she interrupted before he could finish his thought—"the BOLO too."

"Don't worry, your boyfriend's safe." *For now.* Cruz couldn't filter the sneer out of his voice. "Bandit's the guy we want."

"Back off, Larsen. He's off limits too."

"It was you!" he said as all the pieces clicked into place. He stood so quickly his chair fell over. "You knocked me out."

"You were endangering the operation." She tossed his cell phone battery on the table. "I can't let you question Bandit until we wrap up this phase. Another week, tops."

"He might be dead by then." Cruz snapped the battery back into his phone with more force than necessary, then sat back down.

Angel shrugged.

Cruz held up the plastic evidence bag by one corner. For some reason the key dangling from the end of the ribbon, the murder weapon in the Sanchez case, was important to Angel's operation too. "Then tell me why you don't want us to have access to this piece of evidence."

"No can do." Angel shook her head, the expression on her sex-goddess face as unyielding as steel. "And I need it back." She pointed to the evidence bag.

"Why all the cloak and dagger shit?" Cruz needed a better reason to dance to her tune. "You're deliberately making it impossible for me to get a killer off the streets."

"Don't make me pull rank on you, Agent Larsen."

"And you can do that?"

"If I need to." She held out her hand, her lethal nails pointing at him. "I have the assistant director's full support," she reminded him.

His grip tightened on the evidence bag. "You're not FBI," he said.

"Very perceptive, Agent Larsen." She wiggled her fingers. "The key."

"Not until you tell me what's more important than getting a killer off the streets."

Angel blew out an exasperated breath. "You're not going to

make this easy, are you?"

"No, I don't like working with people who knock me out and drug me. What did you use, by the way?"

She laughed; it wasn't a happy sound. "Chill, Agent Larsen. I slipped a couple of sleeping pills under your tongue. Completely harmless."

He raised an eyebrow but didn't say anything. Harmless? She'd left him unconscious in an unlocked motel room in Chingazos territory for several hours.

Dropping her outstretched hand on the table, she sighed. "Okay, I guess I owe you one."

"Damned straight." If Razor had found him before the sleeping pills had worn off, he'd be dead.

"I'm not FBI," Angel confirmed.

Too soon to tell if that was going to be good news or bad. "DEA?"

"All you need to know is I've been detailed to ATF for the duration of this op."

That would have been his next guess. The Bureau of Alcohol, Tobacco, and Firearms was one of hundreds of investigative agencies across ten federal departments, and none of them were team players. Unless they had to be.

"Not good enough." Cruz shook the bag.

"Okay, this investigation is too important for you to fuck it up with your misplaced concern for law and order."

"I'm all ears."

Annoyance radiated from Angel, but her voice was cool as she said, "I've been working on this operation for almost a year now, six months undercover."

She was a fast worker. Not only had she infiltrated the Chingazos Locos gang, she'd managed to become Razor's girlfriend. She had to be tough to play house with that punk.

"The Chingazos are the middlemen in a cigarette smuggling and money laundering scheme. They deliver shipments of contraband cigarettes with counterfeit tax stamps to a buyer in New York City and courier cash back to D.C."

"No shit?" Cruz leaned forward, resting his arms on the table. That explained how Razor could afford his luxury SUV. A carton of cigarettes in New York City sold for about a hundred bucks after city and state taxes were added in. Smuggled cigarettes with counterfeit tax stamps could be bought on the black market for considerably less, and still sold at a high enough price to generate a healthy profit for everyone involved. A whole truckload had to be worth a couple of million dollars.

"Who's the target?"

"A high-level player in the Bidarte Network," she said, referring to an emerging transnational crime syndicate whose black market profits rivaled those of the most successful international corporations. "The network's supplying the contraband cigarettes, and our target's off-shoring millions of dollars from the profits to fund a group of militant Basque separatists in northern Spain."

"Tell me something that makes sense," Cruz said. "The paramilitary wing of the separatists signed a cease-fire a few years ago. Now it's just a lot of hot air and political maneuvering."

"Yeah, well, nothing lasts forever. Years of recession and the Spanish government's austerity plan have re-energized a radical splinter group of separatists. They believe Spain broke the terms of the cease-fire when it sold its sovereign rights to the European Union for a bailout from the European Central Bank. Once we have our target in custody, we'll be able to use him to learn more about the Bidarte Network. The syndicate is highly decentralized, but the target has a direct line of communication to the very top. He can help us identify the next level of leadership. And if we get really lucky, we'll get enough good intel to shut down the entire network. Rumor has it that the Bidarte Network has infiltrated the governments of every G20 nation, as well as Spain and key emerging nations in South America and Africa. That's what's more important than getting a murderer off the streets."

"Then arrest the bastard and let me get on with my investigation. What's the holdup?"

"It's complicated."

"Bullshit. Make the arrest. Deal with the complications later."

She ignored his comment. "The Sanchez murder delayed the takedown. Our target got nervous, backed off the timetable. Now that things have cooled down, he's ready to make his move. Another shipment of cigarettes will be ready for delivery on Sunday. Once money changes hands, we'll make our arrest."

"And what do you want from me?" The words were hard to force out. Angel was right; counterterrorism trumped murder one every time. He tossed the evidence bag on the table.

"Nothing." She slid it toward her body, covering it with her hand as if she expected him to snatch it back.

"Nothing?"

"Exactly. You can have your evidence back—Bandit and Razor too—after we have our target in custody."

"Deal. As long as you leave Trevy Barlow out of this mess. It's too dangerous."

"Can't. She's part of it, like it or not. If Trevy Barlow doesn't go to the New Hope Community Center on Sunday like she always does, the target might get spooked and pull the shipment. Permanently. We can't risk losing our link to the Bidarte Network. All you have to do is wait until Monday to pick up your investigation where you left off."

"I'm watching out for Trevy," he warned, not liking the passive role Angel had assigned to him.

"Then you're going to look like a fool, Larsen."

"Am I?"

"Yes." She paused, clearly engaged in a mental debate with herself. More fingernail tapping ensued, and then she looked up at him as if she'd finally made up her mind. "There's a reason why Bandit broke into Trevy Barlow's apartment."

"And that reason is?"

"Ask Bandit on Monday."

"And if something goes wrong?"

"Nothing will go wrong." She patted the evidence bag.

TWENTY-EIGHT

FOR THE PAST forty-eight hours, Cruz had been aloof, his cop face locked in place. Trevy glanced over at him as she cut off the ignition. He gave her a tight, impersonal smile that she returned in kind before unfastening her seatbelt and climbing out of the BMW.

What was the deal with this new, super-polite version of him? She was getting damned tired of it. She walked to the rear of her car and opened the trunk. Unlike him, she didn't have an on/off switch for her emotions.

The Saturday afternoon shopping trip had been necessary. Otherwise they would have had to split the last yogurt in the fridge, eating wilted baby lettuce as their salad course. But the Safeway on Wisconsin Avenue was hardly a hotbed of crime, so Cruz hadn't needed to come. He had insisted on it anyway.

"I'll get those," he said, moving to stand beside her as she opened the trunk. He swept his eyes right and left like they were returning from a mission deep in enemy territory, then reached for the paper grocery bags. Apparently he felt some obligation to watch over her until Bandit was apprehended.

Don't do me any favors, the words were poised on her tongue, ready to spring out at him like poisoned darts until she remembered the six-pack of beer he was carrying in one of those bags. Maybe his diligence had nothing to do with her safety and everything to do with Dos Equis. Trevy closed the trunk with a little more force than necessary.

"Thanks," she said, adopting his tone of supreme indifference despite the tight clutch of hurt in her chest.

A wave of vertigo swept over her as she contemplated all the mistakes she'd made with him. She should never have let him kiss her... No, it was kissing him back that had pulled her in so fast and deep. She didn't get his cool detachment. Had their night together meant so much less to him than it had to her? She grabbed hold of the rear fender to steady herself.

Cruz shot her a curious glance over his shoulder as he walked toward the elevator. "Keep up," he said.

"Aye-aye." She shot a mock salute at his back that he wasn't supposed to see, but he turned unexpectedly to make sure she was following orders like a good little soldier.

"Is there a problem?" he asked, his dark brows arrowing downward over his glittering eyes.

"I'm not one of your subordinates."

He blew out a breath, exasperated. "Christ, Trevy, don't you think I know that?"

The slight crack in his composure, the first since they'd left her bed on Thursday to go in search of Ceci Sanchez, sent a thrill thrumming through her veins. She wanted to make more fissures until the wall that had been erected between them crumbled into dust. Reaching past him, she pushed the elevator call button.

Waiting for the elevator, she cast a sideways glance at him. There were shadows under his eyes. Cruz stared straight ahead, a miles-away expression firmly back in place on his face. She knew he was thinking about his cases. Rosa had quit her job at Smitty's and dropped out of sight before Cruz could question her about the break-in. And the police still hadn't found Ceci. The thought was enough to settle Trevy down. Cruz had been working nonstop searching for leads, but nothing had presented itself.

"Headache?" she asked, concern for him trumping her hurt feelings. Heat rose in her face when he turned his head to look at her.

"Nope." His answer was accompanied with a shrug of his shoulders that rattled the contents of the paper bags he was holding.

"You might have a concussion."

"Nothing's wrong with my head, Doc," he said with such forced flatness that she knew he was lying. She looked away, fighting the urge to touch the faint lines that bracketed his mouth.

Back off, Trevy, she warned herself, then ignored her own advice by adding, "I still think you should let a doctor make that call."

"What do you want from me, Trevy?" he said, meeting her eyes.

"I want you to stop pretending that nothing happened between us." The words were out of her mouth before she could stop them.

"That's why you're poking at me? You think I'm too cowardly to own up to my actions?" The solid wave of frustration emanating from him knocked her back. "Christ, Trevy, did it ever occur to you that—"

The soft ping of the elevator cut him off, and the moment was lost when the doors slid open with a quiet hum and Rafael Montoyez's assistant barreled out, head down, and ran straight into Trevy. Miguel Navarro grabbed Trevy by both shoulders to steady her. At the same time, she was startled by the loud clank of glass on glass as the four bags Cruz was carrying hit the cement floor in an explosion of sound.

Her gaze shot to Cruz. The fierce possessiveness she read on his face took her breath away, but the look vanished as soon as Cruz determined there wasn't a threat.

Miguel Navarro released her immediately. Dressed for the office, he was wearing a dark wool coat over a blue pinstripe suit, a cashmere scarf, black leather gloves, black lace-ups buffed to a mirror-like shine, and an aggrieved expression that didn't disappear even as he apologized. "Forgive me," he said, stepping aside so that Trevy and Cruz could enter the elevator. "Rafael is in a temper about some documents I left at his office. We're working through the weekend to get ready for the Latin American economic summit in Mexico City next week. Did I hurt you?"

"No harm done," Trevy assured him. Cruz held the elevator door open with his foot and reached for the bags he'd dropped while Miguel's gaze traced a path from her to Cruz to the grocery bags. He didn't comment, but Trevy could only imagine what he was thinking. Dressed in weekend wear, jeans and winter jackets, they looked pretty domestic, like a real couple.

Except it was all a brittle façade.

"Good luck with your meetings, Miguel," Trevy called out over the loud buzzer signaling that the elevator doors had been held open too long. Then she glanced back at Cruz. He jerked his chin toward the wood-paneled interior, a silent order to get inside so he could release the door and stop the annoying sound. She tamped down on the urge to salute him again. He was right, after all, so what could she possible hope to gain from riling him? "I hope Miguel pays more attention while he's driving."

The buzzer shut off after Cruz released the doors and followed her into the elevator. "The guy's an accident waiting to happen," he said and reached past her to push the Lobby button.

As soon as they were inside the apartment, Trevy paused to reset the alarm before following Cruz into the kitchen. He took the lead in restocking the refrigerator, including the six-pack of beer that had somehow survived the crash landing on the garage floor, while Trevy put away the rest of the supplies. Except for the bottle of burgundy. She set the wine on the counter and turned to thank Cruz for his help. He was already eyeing the tall stack of accordion folders stuffed with documents he'd left on the kitchen table. The vase of pale yellow roses had been pushed to one side, she noticed, to make room for his laptop and case files.

"We're not done yet," Trevy said when Cruz pulled out a chair, ready to shut her out. Again. She'd be damned if she'd let him. "We're making *boeuf bourguignon* tonight."

"That sounds way above my pay grade," he said. "Got any cans that need opening? I'm your man." The expression of alarm on his face was oddly satisfying. Maybe her words in the garage had made it a little harder for him to pretend she was nothing to him. She wondered what he had been about to say before they were interrupted by Miguel.

"It's just a fancy way of saying beef stew. It'll have to simmer for a couple of hours, so we need to get started now if we want to eat before midnight. Since you're so good at opening things, why don't you start with the wine?" She twisted her hair into a messy bun and anchored it with a pen, then slid the bottle of burgundy in his direction. "The corkscrew's in the drawer next to the refrigerator."

His only answer was to drop his hand from the chair and head for the drawer. Not anticipating his sudden movement, Trevy pushed away from the counter and walked straight into the hard wall of his chest. His hand stroked down her back, steadying her.

For a moment, neither of them moved. A delicious warmth flooded through her. He wasn't ignoring her now. Slowly she let her hands, which had pressed up against him, fall to her sides.

The motion seemed to shake him free of the invisible force that had held them pinned together. Wordlessly, he stepped back and she moved past him to the refrigerator. She heard him open the drawer to retrieve the corkscrew, and glanced over her shoulder in time to catch him staring at her, the heat of his gaze burning into her skin.

Suddenly breathless, she tightened her grip on the door handle of the refrigerator and looked away. *Boeuf bourguignon*, she reminded herself. Mentally checking off a list of ingredients, she set an onion, carrots, celery, mushrooms, and a few sprigs of fresh thyme on the granite countertop. Then she leaned down to open the bottom drawer where she kept her cutting boards. As she straightened to set the wooden board on the counter, she cut another sideways glance at Cruz. He looked perfectly composed, as if he hadn't almost set her on fire with his gaze just moments before. The bottle of wine was open, the cork set neatly beside it.

"That looks like a lot of vegetables, Doc. Are we inviting the entire apartment building for dinner?"

"It won't seem like as much once we chop and sauté them." She handed him a knife. "Start with the onion. It should be coarsely diced. You do know how to dice an onion, right?"

"Cut it into little squares." Cruz eyed the onion as if it were the enemy and he need to stage a takedown.

"Peel it first," Trevy advised before crossing to a cabinet by the stove to pull out a heavy metal pot she could use to sauté the meat and vegetables before transferring the stew to the oven.

"I knew that," he said and Trevy turned to hide her smile. She didn't want him to know how easily he could charm her.

While Trevy browned the cubes of beef, Cruz chopped the rest of the vegetables. When it was time to deglaze the pan with red wine, Trevy poured a cook's glass for herself. She felt herself relaxing as they worked in companionable silence. It had been a long time since she'd made stew, but she knew the recipe by heart. She increased the heat to bring the wine in the pan to a boil, inhaling the fragrant mix of herbs and tender vegetables as she stirred the mixture. She never cooked like this for herself anymore. It was too much trouble for one person. She was struck by an unexpected pang. She had been alone for too long.

"What do I do with this?" Cruz asked, breaking into her thoughts. Trevy glanced at him. He was holding up the sprig of thyme, a dubious expression on his face. "Do we really need this twig?"

Trevy laughed and Cruz shot her a half-smile. "Strip off the leaves and add them to the stew."

Cruz pinched the sprig between his thumb and index finger and ran his fingers along the stem, scattering leaves across the countertop. He tossed aside the denuded stem, then brushed the leaves into his palm and dumped them into the pot. "Like that, Doc?"

"Interesting technique." She stirred in the herb before covering the simmering stew with the lid, then opened the oven and hoisted the heavy pot inside. "This needs to cook for two hours. We can roast the potatoes about twenty minutes before we eat."

"It smells good enough to eat now." Cruz crossed over to the refrigerator and pulled out a beer.

"Trust me, it'll taste much better in a couple of hours."

"Promises, promises," Cruz said. He lifted the beer to take a long, deep swallow, and she couldn't take her eyes off the strong column of his throat. She remembered how it felt to press her lips against that tender place where his neck curved into the solid muscle of his shoulders. Then she noticed he wasn't drinking and she raised her eyes to his.

"Are you sure you should be drinking after your head injury?" she asked. Her voice sounded breathless even to her own ears.

Cruz didn't answer at first. It was almost as if he couldn't hear her. The heat of his gaze streamed into her like an invisible current. He shook himself as if to break free and raised the bottle for another pull. "It'll take more than a couple of beers to kill me, Doc."

A chill ran down her spine as she thought again of how he had been attacked and left unconscious. Defenseless. Anything could have happened to him.

Clean-up duties were all that remained. Trevy carried the cutting board and knives to the sink that was already filled with dirty utensils. She added hot water and soap.

"I'll dry," Cruz offered. He grabbed a towel.

"That's okay," Trevy told him. The routine of washing the dishes would help settle the anxiety churning in her gut. "I've got it covered."

"If you're sure." He cast her a quizzical glance.

"I'm sure," she said, willing him to let it drop.

"Okay," he said and took a seat at the kitchen table in front of his laptop and files.

Not exactly what Trevy had in mind, but it would have to do. She took her time washing the dishes, drying them, and putting each item in its proper place. Then she started to clean all the counters, slowly but surely restoring order to the kitchen. By the time she was done, the room was filled with the aromatic smell of the stew. It reminded her of home and family. Of people who cared for each other.

Without meaning to, her eyes found Cruz. He was hunched over his laptop like he wanted to find a way to climb inside the screen. He ran a hand through his hair, making the thick strands stand out in every direction. Feeling the weight of her gaze, he looked up and the heat of his frustration flashed through her.

"Any luck finding Bandit?" she asked, leaning against the counter.

"Nope." He immediately returned his attention to the computer.

All the earlier camaraderie between them had fallen away. They were back to single-word answers and uncomfortable silences. Trevy crossed her arms. "What are you looking at?"

Cruz met her determined gaze and sighed. "The DNA results are in. We found Lola Sanchez's blood and traces of her lipstick on the parka Charlie Vega was wearing when he was arrested."

"That's good news, isn't it?"

"Only if I can figure out who had the parka before it was mailed to Charlie Vega's priest," he said. "He saved the box, so we know it was mailed in D.C. the day after Samantha was shot."

"Does that mean you know which post office it came from?" Trevy pushed away from the counter.

Cruz answered with a terse nod, then added, "The stamps on the box were hand-cancelled at the branch post office next to Union Station before it was sent to the Brentwood distribution center."

More good news. So why was he frustrated?

"That's one of the largest post offices in D.C.," she said after a moment, moving to stand behind him. "Is that making it hard to track down the suspect?"

"Using postal transactions records, I was able to narrow down a few likely time periods. I've been studying the post office's security footage for my UNSUB—"

"UNSUB?"

"Oh, sorry, unknown subject," he said and turned his laptop so she would have a better view of the screen and the surprisingly sharp image of a man handing a package to the clerk behind the service counter in the large post office. "I think I found him mailing the package at 3:23 p.m."

"This is Lola's killer?" Trevy pulled out the chair next to his and sat down.

"Maybe, but there's no way to identify him." He hit the play button and pointed at the screen. "For one thing, I can't see his face. He's angled the brim of his baseball cap like he knew what would show up on camera. Based on the height of the counter, I know he's about five foot ten, but even that might not be real. He could have lifts in his shoes for all I know."

Trevy watched the video. The suspect turned away from the camera and walked out of the frame. Cruz was right. There wasn't much to go on. "Did you talk to the clerk?"

He raised one eyebrow. "What do you think?"

"And?"

"And none of the clerks working the counter that day remember him."

"Rewind it. Let me watch it again. Maybe I'll see something."

"Sure, why not? I've watched it so many times, I see it when I close my eyes." With a few clicks of the touchpad, Cruz restarted the footage, then leaned back in his chair. "I'm just not picking up on anything that's going to help me find this guy."

Trevy studied the full five minutes of footage. The man Cruz had singled out as a possible suspect stood in line with his package, walked to the counter, handed the package to the clerk, and bought stamps with cash. Cruz wasn't exaggerating; the guy seemed pretty anonymous. Trevy leaned in and replayed the video.

"Is he left-handed?" she asked when the man reached into the left front pocket of his jeans to pull out a wad of cash. She paused the feed to glance back at Cruz.

"I don't think so." Cruz sat up and pointed at the screen. "In a few seconds, you'll see him peel off a twenty with his right hand and give it to the clerk."

As she reached out to restart the video, she noticed something she'd missed before. The suspect's sleeve had caught on his jacket, revealing part of his wrist. "I can see the edge of his watch when he gets the cash out of his pocket. Can you zoom in?"

Without a word, Cruz resized the image and did something to make it clearer. Amazing. Trevy leaned closer. She could only see part of the watch, but the logo was quite distinctive.

"That looks like a Girard-Perregaux."

"I love it when you talk dirty, Doc."

Her breath caught in her throat. She turned her head. Only a whisper of space separated them now. When they were this close she could see the darker green striations in his eyes. The ferocity of his gaze drew her to him, and she had to fight the urge to span the distance between them with a kiss.

"It's a watch. Swiss," she said, trying to ignore the way he was making her feel. "That strap looks like alligator to me. And you can just make out some of the letters on the face. See the *aux* and part of the logo on top?" She pointed at the tiny ruby chip on the watch face. "Most Girard-Perregaux watches have that double-sided arrow with a ruby in the center."

When she felt Cruz's attention shift to the enlarged image, she tried to ease away from him without being obvious. At the same time, he reached for the keyboard and his fingers slid across hers, sending warmth dancing along the nerve endings of her too-sensitive skin. Cruz jerked as if he'd felt it too. Then he tapped on the keys with a little more force than necessary to open a search engine, pulling up the Girard-Perregaux website beside the image of the watch on the video feed.

"Well, I'll be damned," he said. He rubbed his eyes for a moment and exhaled before clicking on the buy button on one of the watches. He whistled and looked over at her. "Pricey."

"Uh-huh," Trevy agreed, leaning in to get a closer look. She studied the image of the suspect on the split screen. "Could that be Razor? Judging from the fifty-thousand-dollar SUV he's driving, he has a lot of disposable income for a guy with no visible means of employment."

"How tall is he?"

"About my height."

"That'd be what, five-five, five-six?"

"I'm five-six," Trevy said.

"Too short." Then Cruz added, "Razor, not you, Doc."

"I know what you meant." Their heads so close they were nearly touching, she kept her eyes on the partial image of the Girard-Perregaux watch. Something about it tugged at her memory, but her sense of déjà vu vanished when Cruz shifted in his chair and his thigh brushed against hers.

"This guy's smart," he said, and there was a rough edge to his voice that further scattered Trevy's thoughts. He paused to clear his throat. "He's resourceful, highly organized. He manipulates the environment to suit his purposes, rather than reacting to it. Does that sound like a gang member to you?"

Trevy shook her head, and the pen anchoring her messy topknot slid free. It hit the floor with a clatter, sending her hair in a disheveled curtain over her shoulders. Loose strands brushed against Cruz's face, catching in his beard stubble. He grew very still, then took a deep breath. A muscle in his cheek tightened before he sat back in his chair, increasing the distance between them.

"What's wrong?" Trevy asked, alarmed by the pained expression on his face. "Is it your head?"

"In a way," Cruz said and gave a stifled laugh that sounded more like a groan.

"Don't underestimate gang leaders," Trevy said, trying to recapture the thread of their discussion.

But Cruz wasn't listening to her anymore. He was taking slow, deep breaths as if he needed to calm himself. So was his head hurting again or not? For a moment, she'd almost thought…

Chair legs scraped against the floor as he swiveled to face her, heat sizzling in his eyes. Mesmerized, she felt herself tumbling into their dark centers. Then he was reaching for her, his hands tangling in her hair, bringing his mouth down on hers in a hot, claiming kiss. Warmth suffused her as his hands slowly slid to her shoulders and traced a path along the sides of her breasts to her waist. She angled her face to get closer and he lifted her onto his lap, her legs straddling him.

In one last, futile effort to control the irresistible urge to let desire sweep her away, she set her palms against the hard wall of his chest and pulled her mouth free. "I didn't think you wanted me anymore."

"I'd have to be dead not to want you," he said, a dangerous glitter in his eyes.

"You make it sound like a bad thing."

"It is," he whispered. His hand stroked down the length of her hair as he skimmed his lips along the side of her neck. Her head fell back, every bone in her body melting. "For you."

"Why?" She rubbed her lips against the silky strands of his thick hair. "I want to know you. Let me in." She trailed kisses along the curve of his ear, then pushed aside his collar to reach that sensitive spot where his neck and shoulders met. He shivered in response and pulled her tighter against him, fitting his hips against hers.

"No," he said, burying his face in her hair, breathing her into his lungs in long, deep inhalations while his fingers nimbly unfastened the front of her shirt, yanking it free from her jeans. "You already know too much."

The angles in his face sharpened as he traced a finger along the swell of her breasts above the edge of her lacy bra. His breath ratcheted up a notch before he looked up at her through the black fringe of his impossibly long eyelashes. Oh, how she longed to give in to the sensations stirring deep inside her. She let him slide her shirt from her body.

When he leaned forward to shove the computer out of the way, she closed her eyes to keep from thinking. One by one the stacked files fell to the floor in a solid thud-thud-thud. She had only a minute to imagine the papers, spreadsheets, and photos spilling across her kitchen floor before he lifted her onto the now empty table. She kept her eyes shut, not even opening them when she heard his chair crash to the floor.

She let him push her back until she was lying on the polished wood. Then his warm breath brushed against a tender spot behind her ear. "You smell so good, like a bouquet of flowers," he whispered as if they had all the time in the world. *Hurry, hurry*, she thought. She didn't want time to come to her senses, didn't want to remember what it felt like when he shut her out. His fingers feathered over her closed eyelids and outward to her temples. She held herself motionless as he made a trail of soft kisses across her shoulders and along the delicate skin of her inner arm to her wrist.

"I can't be near you without wanting to touch you," he whispered, picking up the thread of their conversation. "Isn't that enough for now?"

Was it? He rested his open mouth against her rapidly beating pulse, his breath heating her skin. She wanted to tell him yes.

"*Plus encore*," she told him, unable to resist the greedy need for him. The words bubbled out of a deep, primitive place inside her. "*Je veux tout.*"

"I have no idea what you just said, Doc," he said with a husky laugh that vibrated through her. "But it sounded sexy as hell."

She opened her eyes and smiled up at him. An invitation. Cruz stood between her legs, his shirt hanging open, his large hands clenching her hips. He was so strong, so beautiful. She could smell the sweet perfume of the nearby roses mingling with the clean scent of him. And all around them was the thick aroma of simmering stew. *Don't overthink this,* she told herself. She pressed her hands against his ridged stomach and then slid them higher, over the thick muscles in his chest. *He's yours for now, isn't that what's important?* His weight sank into her as he covered her with his body. She pushed his shirt off his shoulders and he freed his arms from the sleeves.

"You destroy me, *cariña*," he said, his voice thick with desire. He brushed his thumb across her lower lip. "All it takes is one smile and I'm a goner. I'll give you what you need. I promise."

And that was enough to bring her back to herself. She knew he'd keep his promise, but what exactly was he promising? A moment of pleasure followed by more days of awkwardness as she tried to guess what was going on his mind and he did his best to keep her from finding out?

"You have no idea what I need," she said, her sense of self-preservation reawakening. "Let me go."

He braced his arms on the surface of the table, bracketing her between them. "Tell me, Trevy, what do you want?" Anger and frustration vibrated in his voice. "Do you need poetry? Love notes? Moonlight serenades?"

She shook her head, but he didn't seem to notice.

"If hearts and flowers are your thing, I'm not your guy." He started to push away from her, but she clutched his shoulders.

"Did I ever ask for hearts and flowers?"

"Then what? Let me in on the secret, Doc."

"I just need to know that you care about *me*." She stroked the side of his face as he looked down at her with hot, angry eyes. "That you won't disappear when the investigation is over."

He jerked his head back as if he'd been struck.

"How can you not know that I care about you?" he asked, utterly baffled. "What do you think this past week has been about?"

"I thought you were just doing your job."

He raised an eyebrow in disbelief. "I'd catch bullets with my teeth if you asked me to."

"Oh." It took a moment for the meaning of his words to sink in. "I didn't know."

His gaze softened when she wrapped her hands around his biceps to pull herself upright. She touched her forehead to his and stared into his eyes. Then she kissed him.

"Lie back," he said against her mouth. She let him push her down on the table. The wood was warm and smooth against her skin. Her legs dangled off the edge. He smiled down at her—a wicked, beautiful smile full of unspoken promises—and her heart thumped hard in her chest. He pulled a yellow rose from the vase on the table and brushed the loosely furled petals across her lips to the hollow of her throat, across her collarbone and down the sensitive skin of her inner arm to her wrist.

"Does that feel good?" he asked. He touched the rose to the pulse beating rapidly in her throat.

"Yes," she said, trying to take in enough air to answer him.

His smile spread to his eyes. He stripped the petals from the rose, one after another, and dropped them in a scattered trail across her torso. "This is how soft your skin feels."

The scent of roses filled her nose. With sure fingers, he finished undressing her. Then he unzipped his jeans and let them pool around his knees. She circled his hips with her legs and pulled him closer, desperate to show him how much he meant to her.

He resisted long enough to retrieve a condom from the wallet in his back pocket and then he was so deep inside her that there was no beginning or ending, just wave after wave of pleasure. And something more. Something so right, it defied naming. Her heart pounded against his. She felt him smile against the curve of her shoulder as his fingers lightly traced her hipbone. "I don't think I'm ever going to be able to smell beef stew and roses without getting a hard-on, Doc."

No hearts and flowers for her. And she was glad. Those things were fragile and easily bruised. This was better.

This was real.

TWENTY-NINE

Sunday, March 9

CRUZ GAVE TREVY a ten-minute head start and then followed her all the way to the New Hope Community Center in his piece-of-shit Bureau car. He was still half a block away when she turned her orange BMW down the ramp and into the parking garage below the community center. Technically, he wasn't supposed to be anywhere near the community center tonight, so he parked the Bucar on a cross street two blocks away. Letting her leave without him was one of the hardest things he'd ever done.

Lying to her about the reason was the second hardest. He'd wanted to kiss the confused look off her face as he stumbled through some lame excuse about needing to pick up a few reports from his office. He waited in his car a few more minutes, until it was quarter till eight. Trevy should be inside the building by now. He jammed a dark baseball cap on his head and switched off the interior lights before easing himself out of the car and sliding into the shadows. Staying low, he ducked into the dark alley a few feet away and waited. He had a two-part plan. First, make sure Trevy got from point A to point B and back again without any trouble. Second, stake out the community center to see what the Chingazos Locos were up to—more specifically, Angel.

A battered sedan that could have been the long-lost twin of his car rattled past and then the street was empty again. The taillights winked in the distance when he stepped out of the alley, hunching his shoulders forward to disguise his size as he crossed the street. Under the brim of his cap, his eyes were watchful. The security door at the foot of the ramp was open and the entrance to the community center's garage was a quiet, dimly lit hole. That bothered him. A lot. Security was supposed to have been heightened after Lola Sanchez's death. And that meant that the garage door should be kept shut after hours. He decided to take a quick look-see and then return to his hiding spot in the alley.

Cruz glanced around and ducked into the parking garage when he didn't see anyone. A spooky feeling of déjà vu swept over him. It had been a Sunday the last time he entered this garage. Three weeks ago. Only this time, it was personal.

A sliver of unease snaked along his spine at the sight of Trevy's car, which was parked under the lights near the elevator. His professional detachment was shot to hell. What would he do if something bad happened to her? What if…

He took a calming breath. She was safe inside the community center, he reminded himself. As long as she didn't alter her routine, she wouldn't be in any danger.

Time to head back to the alley. But as he neared the exit, the loud clack-clack-clack of stiletto heels approaching froze him in place. Angel? With only seconds to hide, Cruz fell back against the wall and crouched down behind the dented front fender of the only other car in the garage: a dark green Subaru near the exit. It belonged to the community center's security guard, Cruz remembered. No one would be coming to move the vehicle while Trevy was still in the building, so it was the perfect place to hide. It didn't hurt that it gave him a clear view of the first floor of the parking garage and all the entrances and exits.

Ignoring the cold air that was seeping in through the seams of his clothes, he tried to relax. It wasn't long before Angel Mendez came into view, her stilettos forcing her to take small steps down the steep incline of the ramp. Although she was making no effort at stealth, Cruz could tell by the way she was swiveling her head from left to right that she was on high alert. Everything inside him turned to ice when Angel sashayed over to Trevy's BMW and unlocked the driver side door. While his brain struggled to catch up with his eyes, he watched her push the seat forward and lean into the car.

How the hell did Angel have the key to Trevy's car? The answer to the question momentarily blew out all the circuits in his brain. Then one by one, the tangled knot of this case began to unravel in his mind. Lola's key was not a flea market find. It belonged to the orange BMW. That's why Razor had sent Bandit to search the Sanchez apartment. That's why Angel had removed it from the evidence warehouse.

Keeping his head low, Cruz shifted to get a better view. When Angel straightened, she was holding something in her hand. A cell phone. The Bidarte Network operative and the Chingazos were using Trevy's car as a transfer point for the cigarette smuggling operation. That explained what Lola Sanchez had been doing in the parking garage that night. He felt a flare of fear for Trevy. She was neck deep in shit and didn't even know it.

As Angel walked toward the garage exit, she slid the cell phone in her jacket pocket. Cruz counted to sixty, then followed. Keeping close to the exterior wall, he peered around the corner, expecting to see Angel enter the building. She was nowhere to be seen. Had he waited too long? He didn't think so. Angel wasn't going to be breaking any land-speed records in those six-inch heels she was wearing. He remembered the fire door on the other side of the community center. Three weeks ago, the night of Lola Sanchez's death, it had been propped open. Keeping low, he used the bushes in front of the building as cover as he crossed to the other side.

No one was there and the fire door appeared to be locked. Now what? Angel hadn't just disappeared in a puff of smoke. He hugged the wall and continued to walk around the perimeter of the building. As he neared the back alley where Lola's killer had been seen tagging the wall, he heard voices. Slowing his pace, he crept closer.

On the other side of the dumpster, he heard Angel say, "Scoot over. I'll drive." A door slammed and then an engine caught. He boosted himself onto the lid of the dumpster and used his elbows to slither to the edge in time to see Angel slip behind the wheel of a rental truck. Bandit was in the seat next to hers. Wasn't Angel supposed to be in the community center classroom pretending to learn enough reading and math to pass the GED?

The agent must have moved up the delivery schedule for the contraband cigarettes. But why? He didn't know what Trevy would do when her student didn't show up, but he didn't like the fact that it made her actions unpredictable. He stayed on top of the dumpster for another five minutes until he was sure that the action had moved off-site. Then he returned to the parking garage and hunkered down in his hiding space behind the guard's car near the exit, waiting for Trevy to emerge from the building.

While he waited, he used his time to sort through what he'd learned. Now he knew why he kept hitting dead ends. He had been following false leads. LDR keyed across the hood of the black Camry. The slur etched into Lola's forehead. The drive-by shooting that had killed Samantha Vega. None of it was about retaliation. It was about protecting Lola's killer.

But what had Lola done to get herself killed? Had she double-crossed Razor?

At an impasse, Cruz returned to the question that worried him the most. Who was the hidden actor who had access to Trevy's car? He thought back to the signature line that had been spray-painted beneath the tribute to Lola. *Somos B, R, G, 13. We are Bandit, Razor, GQ, Thirteen.* Had that been a clue to his identity? Cruz reviewed a mental list of what he knew about the Bidarte operator. He was someone with a high degree of mobility and the resources to move the cash from the smuggling operation into offshore accounts. Smart, sophisticated. A strategic planner. Someone with access to Trevy's car. Did he live in her apartment building? Did she know him?

Holy shit. *Somos B, R, G, 13.* M was the thirteenth letter of the alphabet. *We are Bandit, Razor, GQ, Montoyez.* The Spanish diplomat.

Like a punch to the gut, he realized Angel and her whole fucking ATF team had left Trevy Barlow unprotected for nearly a year while a transnational criminal masquerading as a foreign diplomat used her to set up his smuggling and money laundering operation. In other words, Trevy Barlow was expendable.

But not to him.

Trevy stuck to her lesson plan on compounding interest even though only seven girls occupied the desks facing the whiteboard. Financial literacy was an important topic, but Trevy's mind kept straying. Although Maria was at home recuperating, Angel and Rosa's absences were less easily explained. None of the girls had admitted to knowing the whereabouts of the two teens. And Ceci Sanchez was still missing.

At exactly nine, Trevy dismissed the class and rode the elevator down to the parking garage in the basement of the New Hope Community Center. Despite the girls' lack of concern, Trevy was on edge as the elevator descended into the underground garage. She missed Cruz's steady presence by her side. And she was much too smart to believe the lame excuse he'd given her about picking up reports at his office. Especially after he'd spent days shadowing her every move.

And then there was last night...

Was he running away from the unexpected turn their relationship had taken? Was it too much to expect him to trust her with his battered heart? The elevator doors parted and she stared into the cave-like parking garage. Her thoughts jumped back to the missing girls. The garage door was broken again and darkness pooled at the end of the open exit ramp. Her keys in one hand, she dug around in her bag until she found her cell phone. With the comforting knowledge that 911 was just a button push away, she forced herself to leave the elevator. Too bad her dark thoughts weren't so easy to banish. Where were Rosa and Angel?

And Ceci?

She unlocked the old orange coupe, eager to be inside. Turning slightly, she tossed her bag into the back and sank onto the cracked leather seat. The phone still gripped tightly in her hand, she shifted to swing her legs into the car when something from the darkness beneath the car closed around her ankles like a trap being sprung.

Hands—they were hands.

A startled cry escaped her lips. Her keys fell under the pedals with a clink and her cell phone skidded across the cement floor of the garage. The frantic beat of her heart pounded in her ears as she clutched the steering wheel and tried to kick her legs free.

The hands tightened painfully and began to pull, jerking her out of the car. Panting with fear, she landed hard, tearing her jeans, skinning her knees. Pain shot up her legs.

"Leave me alone," she screamed.

The harsh scent of gasoline mingled with the smell of her blood and the metallic taste of fear. Oh God, what was happening? *Cruz*, his name echoed inside her head, a silent SOS. Pointless. He wasn't here and 911 was now out of reach.

Just as suddenly as they'd grabbed her, the hands released her. She scrambled to her feet and lunged toward the open door of her car. If she could just get inside—

Arms clamped around her waist, lifting her off the ground. She kicked out with both her legs, but instead of freeing her from her attacker's hold, they banged against the car door, slamming it shut. Her attacker set her down, trapping her between his body and the car.

"*Quiero mi plata*," a guttural voice demanded. Then the man's hands were in her hair, jerking her head back with such force that she cried out in pain.

"I don't—"

"Shut up."

She pressed her lips together and looked into a face without a trace of human emotion. Even in the dark, she could see the tattooed tears on his cheeks. He pulled back his lips in a mockery of a grin, exposing the sharp pointy teeth of a predator. *Razor*.

"Don't hold out on me, *puta*." He shook her with such force that her legs slid out from under her and her head slammed against the door.

He wants money. Trevy tried to make sense of it through the pain. Hot sparks of light danced before her eyes.

"I have fifty dollars." Would that be enough for Razor? "It's on the backseat of my car. In my bag. Take it."

He bared his teeth again, and a harsh grating sound issued from his chest. He was laughing, Trevy realized in horror. She had never seen Razor laugh. The stink of his breath brushed her face as he yanked her to her feet. "Wrong answer, *chica*."

"I can get more. There's an ATM machine on the next block."

He tightened his grip on her hair. "I want the ten thousand dollars Lola stole from me."

Lola had stolen money from Razor? Why would he think she knew where it was?

"I don't have it."

"You're lying." He slapped her with the back of his hand, the hard edge of his knuckles landing like a punch.

"Touch her again and you're a dead man."

It was Cruz.

The quiet menace in his voice was the most beautiful sound she'd ever heard. It cut through the pain, the fear. She didn't understand how he could have gotten here so quickly, but at the moment, she didn't care. She locked her eyes on him. He stood in firing stance, his gun aimed squarely at them. He'd know what to do.

Anchoring her to him with one arm, Razor turned to face Cruz. Trevy raised her leg and was preparing to deliver a backward kick to his knee when the snick of his knife snapping open stopped her. Four inches of cold steel pressed against her throat. She could feel the sharp edge bite into her skin. Not hard enough to cut her, just enough to grab her attention. She lowered her foot back to the cement floor.

"Ten thousand dollars," Razor said.

"Let her go." Cruz's voice was utterly calm. "Then we'll talk about the money."

"Do you think I'm stupid?" Razor pulled her closer. "If the bitch tells me where she hid the money, then maybe we'll talk. Now put down your gun real slow. Kick it to me."

"And if I don't?"

"Then she gets cut. Nothing too bad for starters. Maybe just a few scratches across her cheek. She'll still be pretty enough." He lifted the knife from Trevy's throat to nick her cheek, flicking the blade so quickly that for a second all Trevy felt was a tiny sting. Then the pain deepened. She bit down on the inside of her cheek, determined not give Razor the satisfaction of knowing how much the cut burned as a warm trickle of blood traced a path down the side of her face.

Cruz aimed his gun at Razor's head, but from Trevy's perspective, it felt an awful lot like he was aiming at her. She held her breath and forced herself to stay still. Razor pressed his face against hers and laughed. "Go ahead, take the shot if you think you're good enough."

Oh, God. Trevy closed her eyes. "Do it, Cruz. Do. It."

Trevy heard Cruz swear under his breath. Then Razor said, "Slowly now. Your phone too. No tricks or the bitch pays."

She peeked between slitted lids to see Cruz slowly lower his gun to the ground. Then his phone. With both hands held out in front of him where Razor could see them, he straightened and kicked the gun toward them.

"Don't try anything," Razor warned, his eyes on Cruz.

The knife was still pressed to her throat, so Trevy was forced to crouch down when Razor bent to retrieve the gun.

He immediately turned the weapon on Cruz. "Get behind the wheel," he ordered. Then he shoved Trevy into the cramped backseat of the BMW and pushed in after her, the muzzle of the gun pressed against her spine. "Where are the keys?"

For a moment Trevy couldn't remember. A trembling began deep inside her body as she considered the order of events. Frozen in the moment, she couldn't remember anything that had happened before or after Razor's attack.

"Where, bitch?" Razor snapped his knife open again with his free hand and swung the blade across the front of her coat in a clumsy left-handed swipe. A cry of surprise escaped her throat as the heavy fabric tore from shoulder to hem.

"They're here," Cruz said, his voice frantic, "on the floor."

"Get them and start the car." Razor pocketed his knife. He held up the gun so Cruz could see it in the rearview mirror. "You know the score. No tricks or the bitch pays."

Cruz cranked the ignition and put the car in reverse. "Where are we going?"

"Someplace where we can talk without being disturbed. Take a left out of the garage."

Ten minutes later Razor directed them to a windowless brick warehouse off New York Avenue, not far from the Maryland border. The place had seen better days. Cruz followed the rutted driveway to the loading docks at the back.

"Stop at the last bay," Razor told him.

Cruz did as instructed. Then, keeping his hands on the steering wheel where Razor could see them, he turned back to look at them.

"Eyes straight ahead," Razor ordered in a sharp bark.

Cruz sent one last glance her way before complying. "What now?" he asked, the anger in his voice tightly controlled.

"This." Razor lashed out and brought the butt of the gun down hard against the side of Cruz's head.

With a low groan, he slumped in the seat.

Razor reached forward to nudge Cruz with the muzzle of the gun. He didn't move.

"You killed him," Trevy screamed, reaching for Cruz. Razor shoved her onto the floor.

"He's not dead. Yet. Where's the money?"

"I don't have it."

"Tell me." He slapped her.

"I don't know—" His fist caught her low in the stomach. The air whooshed out of her lungs. Hot pain speared through her, turning her thoughts to ash. She could barely understand Razor's words.

"Tell me." He shoved her, slamming her head against the side door panel this time. Black spots clouded her vision, and her breath came in sharp, shallow pants. She couldn't speak. She couldn't even catch her breath. But that didn't matter. She didn't know where the money was. And as soon as Razor figured out that she was telling him the truth, he would kill them both.

THIRTY

THE MOTEL DOOR banged against the wall and Razor exploded into the room. "The bitch won't tell where she hid my money."

GQ, sprawled on one of the beds, looked up from the TV show he was watching. It was just after midnight. On the other bed, Rosa squeezed her eyes shut and pretended to sleep. But not before checking to make sure that Ceci Sanchez, who was lying next to her, followed suit. The door slammed shut.

The next sound was a beer can opening, followed by noisy swallowing sounds. Crumpling metal. The dull thud as the empty can hit the wall near the two double beds.

"Watch it, *carnal*," GQ said without heat. Another beer can was opened. "Hurt the bitch. She'll tell you so fast it'll make you dizzy. Where is she?"

"In the warehouse."

"You left her there?"

"Yeah, you got a problem with that?"

"No, I guess it'll be okay. Cigarettes are gone. Better hope *El Trece* don't find out. Something tells me he wouldn't like it."

"Yeah, well, who's gonna tell him?"

"Someone like Trevy Barlow don't go missing—"

Rosa gave Ceci a small warning pinch when she gasped, even though the news made her own insides churn. *Dios, they had Trevy.* How had they found out that she had the money Lola stole?

The answer wasn't hard to come by. Bandit must have lied to her. Anger and fear formed a toxic brew inside her stomach.

"—without someone raising a stink. The cops gonna be sniffing. If they find her—"

Rosa swallowed back the bile burning a path up her throat. It was all her fault. Her fault that Trevy was trapped in the same dirty warehouse where hours ago she and Ceci had helped Bandit, Angel, and GQ load the U-Haul truck with cartons of cigarettes. Her fault that Ceci was lying next to her, just as vulnerable to Razor's psycho whims as the rest of them.

"We've got time," Razor assured GQ before gulping down his beer. He crumpled the can and threw it against the wall. It landed, with a metallic clang, on the other empties. "We'll get rid of her after she gives me the money."

Rosa should never have trusted Bandit.

She was stupid. Unforgivably so.

She peeked at the other girl through her lashes. Ceci was holding herself so still that Rosa couldn't even tell if she was breathing. The wet track of tears leaking from her eyes was the only sign that her self-control was fraying. Poor Ceci. If Rosa hadn't been so determined to send the girl home to her mother on Sunday instead of letting her hide out in the Reyes apartment for another night, Lola's sister wouldn't be stuck in this hotel room. Rosa had planned to walk with Ceci all the way to the Sanchez apartment before heading to the New Hope Community Center for the evening literacy class. Instead, GQ had been waiting outside her building, leaning against the illegally parked Navigator. When he insisted on giving them a lift, Rosa knew they were in trouble.

Razor sank into the chair next to GQ's bed, and the two of them steadily drank their way through the rest of the beer. Rosa forced herself to push away her regrets. There'd be plenty of time to play the blame game later. Right now she had to think. Hard. Her options were bad; the only way to save them might also get her deported. Still, she had to take the chance. She was going to have to go to the police and tell them what she knew.

She'd start with that FBI agent. She still had the card with his phone number on it. The one he'd given to her the night of Lola's death. Maybe he could save Trevy. Maybe he could save them all. When the volume swelled during the commercial break and Razor got up to go to the bathroom, Rosa put her mouth next Ceci's ear. "As soon as they pass out, we're leaving."

Ceci didn't make a sound. She just gave a barely perceptible bob of her head and tightened her hold on Rosa's hand.

The cold woke him. That and a rhythmic clicking sound that kept time with his super-sized headache. He cracked open an eye to search the darkness for familiar outlines that might help him figure out where the hell he was. But the blackness pressed down on him, trapped him inside the pain that originated at his temple and radiated outward. The second blow to his skull in less than a week. His head felt like it had been used as a piñata at a party for major league baseball players.

And what the hell was that god-awful chattering? The sound reminded him of rattling bones, conjuring an unwelcome image in his head of a loose-jointed skeleton dancing a gruesome jig. Forcing himself to stay focused on the priorities—*assess, plan, act*—Cruz tried to touch the wound at his temple, only to discover that his hands were bound behind his back, which went a long way toward explaining why he was lying on his side on a hard cement floor that felt like a sheet of ice. The good news—he wasn't dead—was hard to appreciate when every part of him that wasn't frozen hurt like a motherfucker.

And then, as if his mind was playing a game of word associations, an image of Razor flashed through it. And that was very bad news. Pieces of memory slowly reordered themselves. The details were still a little fuzzy. The harder he tried to concentrate, the more his head ached. Had he been carjacked? The last thing he remembered was driving to the warehouse while Razor pointed a gun at him from the backseat. On Razor's orders, he had driven around to the back of the building and parked near a loading dock. That must have been when the gangbanger had knocked him out. It wouldn't have taken much force to render him unconscious while he was still recovering from a previous blow to the head.

Cruz forced himself to take deep, steady breaths though his nose to try to clear the fog from his brain so that he could think past the pain. With each passing moment, more memories came creeping back to him. He had been knocked out with his own weapon. The gun he'd surrendered to Razor. In doing so, he'd broken the ironclad rule of his profession—an agent never surrenders his weapon. But he had risked it all—his reputation, his job, even his safety—to ensure that Trevy would not be alone with Razor. And that sudden thought sent a surge of panic through him.

Where was Trevy? Had Razor left her in the warehouse or taken her somewhere else? Was she hurt? He was supposed to protect her, goddammit. He formed her name in his mouth, but all that escaped was a muffled groan. His mouth was covered with duct tape. He wiggled his jaw and felt the adhesive stretch and then hold. Frustration replaced panic, and he thrust his legs forward in an attempt to swing into a less supine position. They touched something. No. *Someone.* The chattering stopped, replaced by a groan. Trevy. Relief flooded him. More good news. He had just been given a second chance to save her.

Frigid drafts swept along the floor of the room. Trevy made another sound and rolled into him. Then the dancing skeleton sounds started up again, closer to his ear this time. Trevy was shivering so violently that her teeth were chattering and every muscle in her body was trembling. Compared to him, she was small and thin, with the lean muscled physique of a runner. No excess body fat to keep her warm. And Razor had sliced open the front of her coat. Hypothermia was a real danger. He wondered how long they'd been lying here in the dark.

Trying to see her, he moved his face closer. It was useless. The windowless warehouse was much too dark. For an instant he rested his forehead against hers and her trembling lessened, but the coolness of her skin alarmed him. He murmured a soothing sound, but he knew that she was going to freeze to death unless he acted fast. He brushed his nose across her cheek and then into her hair, breathing in her flowery scent. Something sticky touched his cheek.

It took him a moment to realize that the strip of duct tape across her mouth had come loose.

When he rolled away from her, she let out a muffled protest and tried to get closer. He issued a short, sharp sound in his throat. She must have understood because she stopped moving, giving him a chance to scoot back toward her, close enough to touch her face with his hands. His fingers were clumsy, tight and numb. Pain shot through his shoulder as he worked the corner of the tape.

Trevy, smart beautiful Trevy, got with the program and pressed the side of her face against his fingers to give him more leverage. He stroked her cheek with the backs of his fingers, a silent apology, then yanked the tape with a quick downward pull of his hand. That had to hurt the cut on her lip from Razor's smack, but she only made a small sound.

"I'm okay," she said, pressing her face against his hand to reassure him. He felt the warm trickle of blood from her reopened cut and anger sizzled deep inside of him. "Roll over so I can get the tape off your mouth too."

She turned on her side and waited until he touched his mouth to her fingers. It took her several tries to get the tape off his mouth, taking a good amount of his facial hair with it.

"Thanks," he said and immediately began testing the strength of the tape wrapped around his wrists. "Try to pull your hands apart."

"It's no use. They're wrapped too tightly."

"Same here," he conceded with a loud exhalation.

"Your head?" she asked, her voice sharp with concern.

"It's fine," he lied.

"Then it must be harder than I realized," she said with a touch of tartness. She could obviously tell he was lying. "Are you cold?"

"A little."

"Me too."

He snorted at her answer. "Yeah, between the two of us, we could keep the emergency room busy for an hour." Stifling a groan, he flipped onto his side and lifted his arms away from his back. "Scoot in next to me."

He felt her snake-crawl into the circle of his arms, her front pressed to his back. He pulled her closer and covered her hands with his. He wanted to give her a chance to warm up before he turned his attention to getting the tape off his wrists.

"Better?"

"Mmm." She settled her cheek against his back, right between his shoulder blades. "What time is it, do you think?" she asked.

"No idea. Did you get a chance to look around when Razor dumped us in here?"

"The walls are lined with empty shelves. There aren't any windows or doors, just the metal roll-up door at the loading dock."

"Any trash, bits of metal, broken glass?"

"Not that I noticed. I only had a couple of minutes while Razor brought you in from the car. And even then it was pretty dark. Just a little light from my car's headlights."

"Did Razor say when he'd be back?" Because there was no doubt in his mind that Razor would be. After all, he thought there was ten thousand dollars on the line.

"No."

That didn't surprise him. He figured they had no more than a few hours before the gangbanger returned for another go at Trevy. Although why Razor thought she had Lola's stash was another missing piece of the puzzle. He opened his mouth to ask her about it, but she beat him to it.

"Cruz, do you know what Razor was talking about?"

"The ten thousand dollars?"

She nodded against his back and snuggled closer, probably trying to absorb as much of his heat as possible.

"Razor's gotten the Chingazos involved in cigarette smuggling," he said, choosing his words carefully. If the ATF team was closing down the operation today, it would all be public knowledge by the time he and Trevy got out of their warehouse prison. And if they didn't get out... Well, then it wouldn't matter if he told her. Dead people were the best at keeping secrets. But his mind shied away from that train of thought. If he gave up on them now, their chances of coming out of this alive would decrease to nil. "Lola must have been stealing from the profits."

"Oh," she said. And then after a moment, "I still don't understand."

"Understand what, Doc?"

"Why does Razor think I have the money?"

"I'm still working that one out."

"How does Parka Guy fit in if Lola was stealing from Razor?"

"I doubt Lola was stealing from Razor." His bet was on someone much higher up the food chain. Someone like the Bidarte operator running the smuggling ring. "Have you ever noticed Rafael Montoyez wearing a watch?"

"Well, yes," she said, clearly confused by the question.

"Just humor me, Doc. What does it look like?"

"It's really quite beautiful. It's Swiss—" She sucked in a breath. "The watch Parka Guy was wearing. That's why it looked so familiar. But that's crazy… Rafael is my friend. He isn't a killer. He's a diplomat."

"Take off your rose-colored glasses, Doc." His grip on her fingers tightened for an instant before he forced his hands to relax. "Killers come in all varieties. Some are even diplomats."

"But Razor's the one who's after the money."

"If Lola was stealing from the supplier's take, who do you think the big boss would expect to make good on the loss? Think, Trevy." When she didn't respond, he answered for her. "The leader of the Chingazos. Lola was killed as a warning to Razor to get his house in order and claw back the stolen profits."

"But that would mean that Rafael is running the cigarette smuggling operation. There must be other people around town who own that watch."

"You won't like this," Cruz said, preparing her for more bad news. He told her how the cigarette supplier was communicating with the gang. How he'd watched with his own eyes as Angel unlocked Trevy's car to retrieve a cell phone from under the seat. He was careful to leave out any mention of Angel's true role. He might not like her tactics, but agents didn't burn other agents.

"They were using my car?" He could hear the shock in her

voice, the disbelief. "Rafael has a great life. A great career. Why would he jeopardize that to smuggle cigarettes?"

"Recently it was brought to my attention that someone has been under investigation for over a year now for ties to a radical splinter group of Basque separatists. So there's your motive. He's using the Chingazos Locos to smuggle cigarettes, and his diplomatic cover to move the money offshore to fund terrorist cells in Spain. Lola Sanchez steals from him, so he kills her. We know the killer was wearing that parka because we found her DNA on it.

"We've got film of a guy mailing a package on the same day the parka was sent to the church for the Vega family." He continued to present the evidence as if she were the AUSA and he needed to convince her to bring charges. "The cash transaction made on that day and time matches the dollar amount of the stamps on the package. The guy on film is wearing an expensive Swiss watch that Rafael Montoyez also wears. You and Montoyez live in the same building. He has access to the Chingazos through you. There's the connection to Lola."

"The number thirteen," Trevy said. He felt her stiffen and he knew she was remembering the signatures on the tribute Bandit had painted for Lola. "The letter M is the thirteenth letter of the alphabet."

"M for Montoyez," he said.

"JC has an extra key to the car. I suppose he could have given it to Rafael to hold in case I ever locked myself out," she said, slowly filling in the missing pieces. He added that little snippet of new information to the growing list of evidence in his head. It was obvious that she didn't want to believe it—and who could blame her?—but there were too many coincidences to ignore. She was the common denominator.

"I'm a mule." The desolation in her voice cut into him. "I'm a part of it."

"Easy, Trevy," Cruz soothed. He would have given everything he had to take away her pain. Her shaking increased, but this time it wasn't from the cold. He tightened his hold on her. "No one blames you."

"I blame myself. Stupid, predictable Trevy Barlow. There's no way of hiding this from my family. JC is right to worry about me. I'm just an idealistic Pollyanna, not fit for anything but life in an ivory tower."

"I don't know about the rest of your family, but JC's an idiot."

She stifled a teary laugh against his back and he felt an unexpected surge of relief. "I love my brother."

"Well, then he's a lovable idiot," he said, just to see if he could make her laugh again. And when her laughter vibrated against him, this time stronger, he was ready for the warmth that flowed through his body. He held onto it like he'd been given a gift.

He didn't have long to savor the feeling. After a few minutes of silence, Trevy started as if someone had poked her with a needle. "Rafael's not the killer," she said. This time her voice sounded different. The doubt was gone. Trevy was a smart woman. She wouldn't sound so sure of herself without good reason. And that worried him. A lot. What had he overlooked?

"Explain."

"The parka was mailed on Thursday, right? That was the same day JC arrived in town. I remember because it was also the day you took me to see Lola's tribute in the Diablos' territory. Before I left to meet you, JC told me he was going to the embassy with Rafael to meet the new ambassador."

"So?"

"The meeting was at three that day."

"Did JC tell you how long the meeting went?"

"No, but Rafael did. We talked about it a few days later at an embassy party. He was complaining about the ambassador boring them both to tears. Rafael wouldn't have had time to drive from the Spanish Embassy to the post office near Union Station."

Had he been wrong about Montoyez? "I'll have to talk to JC," Cruz said, adding it to his mental to-do list. If Montoyez could use JC as his alibi, nothing would be able to resuscitate the case he'd been prepared to build against the diplomat.

But at this particular point in time, building a case against the guy hardly topped his list of priorities. He'd worry about Montoyez after he and Trevy were out of this warehouse.

"Are you giving me the silent treatment, Doc?" he asked after several minutes passed without any reaction from Trevy.

"What? No," she pressed her body closer to his, "I was just thinking."

"About?"

"Parka Guy's watch." He noticed that Lola's killer was back to being Parka Guy—some nameless, faceless killer who was not Rafael Montoyez. She seemed convinced of the diplomat's innocence. But the guilty party knew her routines and had access to her car. It *had* to be Montoyez, right?

"I need to look at the video again to be sure," she said with a sigh. "Maybe it's nothing."

"Tell me anyway," he said. "We can check later." Cruz trusted his instincts and hunches. Sometimes they were all that stood between an open case and a closed one. And he realized with some surprise that he trusted hers too.

"Rafael's assistant Miguel Navarro has a knockoff Girard-Perregaux watch that looks almost identical to his boss's. I saw him wearing it at an embassy party a couple of weeks ago. He copies the way Rafael dresses and talks. And he wasn't at the ambassador's meeting with Rafael and JC. Supposedly he was home with the flu, but he could have gone to Union Station that afternoon without anyone noticing."

If Trevy was right, he had a new suspect to check out. "Why does it matter that Miguel's watch is a fake?" Cruz said, wanting to know more.

"A lot of Girard-Perregaux watch faces have this double-sided arrow with a tiny ruby in the center. But not Rafael's. It's an Opera Three. There aren't arrows on the face, just a thin bar with the ruby. And then there's the *au passage*."

"The o-what?" he asked. God, he loved it when she used that sexy French accent. Her voice was very close to his ear and her warm breath sent a shiver through him. It made him remember what it felt like to have her warm delicious skin pressed against his, her smooth contralto voice whispering over him, exciting every nerve ending on his body. He craved her touch, even now. Especially now.

"*Au passage*," she said again, and he tamped down his unruly libido, forcing himself to listen to what she was telling him. "It's a French phrase referring to the musical chimes that mark the passing of the hour. Rafael's watch has a miniature music box inside that can be set to play Mozart or Tchaikovsky each hour. I heard the chimes play on his watch at the party. Miguel checked his watch at the same time, but it was silent. And it had the double-sided arrow on the face, not the bar. If I'm remembering correctly, Parka Guy's watch looked like the same knockoff Opera Three."

"Montoyez's assistant has access to your apartment building's garage," Cruz said, flashing back to the day when Miguel Navarro came charging out of the garage elevator, nearly flattening Trevy in his haste.

"Rafael must have given him the security code. What if the *trece* in *Somos B, R, G, 13* means Miguel? What if he's Lola's killer?"

"Then I'll arrest him, and he'll be charged with murder. His diplomatic immunity won't protect him." But that wasn't what was burning a hole in his gut. What if Angel Mendez and ATF were going after the wrong guy?

But none of that would matter if he didn't figure out a way for them to escape this empty warehouse before Razor returned.

THIRTY-ONE

Monday, March 10, 2:30 a.m

BANDIT WAS DEAD tired when he pulled the U-Haul truck filled with three hundred cartons of contraband cigarettes packaged as gourmet dog treats to a halt in front of the high chain-link fence enclosing the warehouse. At two-thirty in the morning, the Bronx sky was still dark. He and Angel seemed to be the only living beings in this small city of warehouses not far from the railroad tracks. They'd made good time traveling up I-95 from Washington to New York. Five hours. Angel climbed out of the cab and walked up to the chain-link fence to punch in the six-digit number to open the gates. Bandit waited for her to climb back into the cab before driving the truck through the opening.

"Over there." She pointed to the left side of the warehouse. "Park in the back."

Bandit did as he was told. When the truck pulled to a stop, Angel got out and walked up to the nearest garage door, where she entered another code into the keypad on the wall. The door opened with a metallic rattle that sounded loud in the darkness. Inside was a blue compact car with New York plates. Almost as good as invisible. The keys were already in the ignition. Angel got in and started it, then backed it out of the garage.

Bandit knew the drill. He pulled the truck into the empty bay, turned off the engine, and left the keys in the ignition.

"You drive," Angel said. She marched over to the keypad beside the open garage door and, pausing to yawn, punched in the code. The door rattled shut. "I'm tired."

Who the hell did the bitch think she was, anyway? It was his job to punch in the codes. And Lola always took the first shift driving so he could sleep. Since he'd driven the whole way there, Angel should be sliding behind the wheel now, not giving him orders like someone had made her the boss of the universe. But Razor's girl didn't seem to care about the way he and Lola had handled things.

Lola. The memory of his trips with her brought a sharp jab of grief. He climbed behind the wheel.

"Pop the trunk," Angel told him, walking to the back of the car. Bandit fumbled in the dark, searching for the trunk release with one hand, using his other hand to grip the gear shift. If he threw the car into reverse, he could knock that bossy bitch flat and get the hell out of there. Alone. With all the money. Two fucking million dollars.

Angel rapped impatiently on the trunk.

"Hold on, hold on," Bandit called out through clenched teeth. Shifting the gear into reverse, he looked over his shoulder, his foot sliding off the brake. *Mierda.* Angel was no longer behind the car. He stomped down on the brake. So where the fuck was she?

In answer, the driver side door jerked open, and Angel reached across him to pull the key out of the ignition. The car wasn't in Park, so the key was locked in place. Afraid to meet Angel's eyes, afraid of what she might read in his face, Bandit kept his head down and slid the car back into Park. Angel didn't pull away and the weight of her gaze smothered him, making it impossible for him to breathe.

Then, without a word, she yanked the key out of the ignition and walked to the back of the car. Did she suspect something? Bandit watched her lift two rolling suitcases—one large and one small—out of the trunk and set them on the ground.

This wasn't part of the drill. He and Lola never took the suitcases out of the car. All Angel had to do was unzip the luggage to make sure the cash was there. Lola had always checked the money while he parked the truck in the garage. Fool that he was, he had trusted her. And she had fucked him over. Anger twisted in his gut.

He rolled down the window. "The money stays in the car," he shouted. "Always."

"Chill," Angel snapped back. She waved a thick stack of bills in his direction. "Did you forget about the ten thousand?"

No, he hadn't forgotten. He watched her toss part of the Chingazos' cut into the bigger suitcase for *El Trece*. Another nail hammered into the lid of his coffin.

Satisfied, Angel returned the luggage to the trunk and slammed the lid shut. She climbed into the passenger seat and tossed the keys to him. "Let's get out of here. Wake me up when we get to Delaware."

Sure thing, bitch, Bandit thought, but he kept his mouth shut.

The miles rolled underneath the car. Out of habit, Bandit kept to the speed limit. But would it be so bad if the cops pulled him over for speeding? His odds of surviving behind bars were looking a hell of a lot better than his odds of surviving Razor.

He owed the gang leader ten thousand dollars, and time was almost up. Razor wasn't going to wait much longer. Trevy Barlow's apartment hadn't been the answer to his prayers. Even though the nonstop ringing of her phone had spooked him into running out of there like a scared *pendejo*, he had already searched every inch of it. The money was not there. He was starting to think he'd read Lola's journal wrong. He sucked at reading. Why had he thought this time would be any different?

But maybe there was another way. A way that didn't involve the cops or Razor.

More than halfway down the Jersey Turnpike, he glanced over at Angel. Her eyes were closed, her lips parted, her breathing slow and natural. Asleep. His fingers tapped a nervous beat on the steering wheel, keeping pace with the plans whirling through his brain. It was seven o'clock, but Daylight Savings Time had kicked in yesterday, so it was still dark. The sun wouldn't rise for another fifteen or twenty minutes. Early morning traffic was still light on this stretch of highway. A large blue sign loomed ahead. Ten miles to the next rest area.

Perfect. He might just have enough time to save himself.

Bandit eased the car onto the shoulder. Dead to the world, Angel didn't stir. All he had to do was shove her out of the car while she was still asleep. Then take off.

Careful not to touch her, he reached across her to open the passenger door. It was locked. A setback. He positioned his fingers against the lock and pushed. It disengaged with a loud pop. He held his breath, waited a minute.

When Angel didn't move, he unfastened her seatbelt. *Dios*, she was a safety freak. He would never have guessed that tough-as-nails Angel would worry about locking her car door and wearing her seatbelt. The world was full of mysteries, he thought sourly as he prepared himself to act.

Angel shifted, and her eyes opened a slit. "What's going on?" she mumbled sleepily.

Mierda. Bandit drew back as if he'd been slapped. What now? His mind frantically scurried for an answer. Something that wouldn't make her suspicious. "Go back to sleep. I need to take a leak."

"Make it quick," she muttered, curling her legs underneath her and settling her head against the window. Her eyes fluttered shut. Bandit heaved a sigh of relief and got out of the car. She was too sleepy to have noticed that she was no longer wearing her seatbelt.

Time for a new plan. He'd take a whiz. Then he'd yank her out of the car and throw her into the ditch. That should give him enough time to get back behind the wheel and drive away.

It was probably for the best, anyway—it would be a long time before he felt safe enough to stop again. He walked a few feet closer to the tangle of weeds and low bushes that lined the road. When he was a good distance from the car, he turned his back and eased down his zipper. A steady stream of piss pooled on the frozen ground.

There was a whisper of movement behind him. He glanced over his shoulder. Angel. He hadn't even heard the car door open. He fixed a smile on his face.

"Almost done," he said. He stuffed himself back in his pants. What was he going to do now? Could he get to the car and take off before she realized what was going on? With only seconds to improvise, he whipped around, his fist plowing through the air on a collision course with her face. She wouldn't be prepared. She'd go down like a boxer in the last round.

Her arm shot out to block his punch, and she kicked him in the knee. His leg buckled instantly, the pain nearly unbearable. She followed him to the ground. He had no more than a moment to wonder if Angel had been pretending to sleep before her hand closed on his neck, almost a lover's caress. Then she squeezed, and his world narrowed to black.

"Dumb-ass." Angel wiped her hands on her jeans. Straightening, she looked over her shoulder at the highway. No sign of headlights. Good. Even the truck traffic was light at this hour of the morning.

She nudged Bandit with the toe of her stiletto shoe. What now? Cruz Larsen wanted him. Should she hog-tie him and bring him back to D.C.? She dismissed the idea almost as soon as it surfaced. Too complicated. Larsen was going to have to wait a little longer. She pulled her cell phone out of her pocket. She knew someone in the New Jersey state police who could keep Bandit out of sight for the next few hours. Once they'd bagged the major players, she'd send the gangbanger to Larsen as a little present.

Larsen wouldn't be happy, but he wasn't the one making the rules. He'd have to play along to get what he wanted. Angel figured he probably understood that by now.

THIRTY-TWO

THE DARKNESS INSIDE the warehouse thinned to a murky gray as the morning light crept through the cracks in the metal bay door. At some point during the long night, Trevy had fallen into an exhausted sleep that even fear couldn't penetrate. She awoke to the rattle of the heavy doors. Her first thought was Razor. The quick flood of adrenaline made her dizzy as she turned her head. Cruz was no longer holding her in the safety of his arms.

"Cruz?" she called out over the noise of the rain beating down on the flat roof.

"Over here," he answered. He was a dark silhouette against the door of their prison. She watched his shoulders flex and contract as he strained his arms against the metal, making it rattle. "Almost got it," he said. Trevy realized that he was using the sharp edge of the bay door handle to saw through the duct tape binding his hands.

His face darkened as he strained against the handle again, and then a loud ripping sound filled the cavernous room as he pulled his hands apart. He stripped off the tape. In less than five minutes, he and she were both free of their restraints. Trevy rubbed the circulation back into her hands and rolled her shoulders against the stiffness of a long, uncomfortable night. Cruz went straight to work on the bay door, but it wouldn't budge.

"It must have a bolt lock on the outside," he said in disgust. Trevy followed his gaze as he examined the rolling mechanism that raised and lowered the door. There didn't appear to be a way to move the door off its tracks without lifting it. "Time for plan B," Cruz said, apparently coming to the same conclusion.

"Divine intervention?" Trevy asked.

"Something a little more proactive," he deadpanned.

"A natural disaster?"

He raised an eyebrow. "A surprise attack. Razor thinks he has the upper hand, so he doesn't expect anything from us. You're going to stand by the door. When he opens it, be ready to bolt...but wait until he comes inside before you do. He'll expect to see us lying on the floor where he dumped us."

"What if he's not alone? I might not be able to get away."

"You're fast and strong. Just do it. Don't stop for any reason."

"What about you?" she asked, already guessing that she wouldn't like his answer.

"Playing possum. I'll be on the floor. See how the shelves cast shadows against the back half of the storage unit? I'll position myself back there. With any luck he'll think you're on the other side of me and it will draw him deeper into the space. That should give you a head start. As soon as you're outside, run like the hounds of hell are on your heels. Get away from the warehouse, and then work your way to the first commercial building you can find. Call 911. And Alvarado."

"No, we leave together."

"Do you have a death wish?"

"No. Do *you*?"

"Dying is not a part of the plan." He cupped her face in his hands and drew her toward him. Then he touched his forehead to hers. "Trust me, Trevy."

"I do, but—"

"Then you'll go for help while I distract Razor?"

"I don't like your plan."

He answered her complaint with a brush of his lips that deepened into a lingering kiss. "Promise me, Trevy." He pulled back to look into her eyes.

The bay door rattled as someone lifted the bolt lock. Time was up. Razor had returned. Cruz grabbed her by the shoulders and positioned her against the wall to the right of the door before running to the back of the warehouse and dropping to the ground. The door rolled up with a squeaky protest from the rusted metal and worn parts. A bitter blast of wet air burst into the room, sharp as knives.

"Promise me," Cruz mouthed. His eyes flashed with frustration when she didn't immediately signal her agreement, then he narrowed them to slits as the door rose.

Trevy pressed herself against the wall and reviewed the escape plan in her head. Wait for Razor to move toward Cruz. Slip out the open door. Run like hell. She held her breath and counted off the seconds to calm herself, adrenaline pumping through her body.

"*Hola, mes amigos*," Razor called out as he crossed the threshold. He sounded almost cheerful. The rain-dampened morning light glinted off the lethal-looking knife he gripped in his right hand. She was already moving toward the exit when she realized that Razor wasn't alone. He was carrying someone fireman style over his left shoulder. From behind, Trevy couldn't see a face, just long black hair spilling down his back like a curtain.

At first she thought it was Angel. Then Razor slid the teen from his shoulder and held her in front of him like a shield, his knife poised at her throat. Her hands and feet were wrapped with duct tape. Not Angel.

Ceci Sanchez.

Cruz was on his feet in a flash, hands fisted. He glanced past Razor and locked eyes with her. "Run!"

"The *chica* dies if anyone moves," Razor snarled.

Ceci let out a sharp cry of alarm and glanced back at Trevy. Fat tears spilled from her eyes. Eyes that were eerily familiar. *Lola.* Trevy froze, then slowly walked into the warehouse to stand next to Cruz. She brushed her fingers across the whitened knuckles of his clenched hand. "I'm sorry," she whispered.

He stiffened, his fist tightening for an instant before he relaxed his hand and turned his palm to interlace their fingers.

"Things will go better for you if you let the girl go," Cruz said in a calm voice, acting as if he were the one with the upper hand.

Razor flashed his broken teeth in cold amusement before shifting his attention to Trevy. "Where's my money, bitch?"

"The money—"

Cruz squeezed her hand and interrupted. "What money?"

"So, that's the way you want to play it, *vato*?" Razor asked.

"This is no game, *vato*. We know all about the cigarette smuggling. Turn yourself in. Tell us who your supplier is and I'll talk to the prosecutor about pleading down the charges. But I can't help you if you won't let the women go."

"Here's how it's gonna work." Razor tightened his grip on Ceci and held up his knife. "I ask the questions and the bitch answers." He jerked his chin toward Trevy before returning his gaze to Cruz. "I don't like the answers, the *chica* gets cut. You interrupt, the *chica* gets cut. Anybody runs, the chica *dies*."

Trevy read the menace in Razor's flat, emotionless eyes. He would enjoy hurting them. He would enjoy it a lot. She swallowed against the fear that rose in her throat, making it impossible to breathe.

"What if we don't know anything about the money?" Cruz asked.

"Then you better start praying the bitch knows more than you do, 'cause once I'm done with the *chica* you're up next. I'll start with your trigger finger. Better hope you still have some fingers left by the time she squeals."

Ceci was crying in earnest now, a steady swell of sound. Razor kicked the roll of duct tape toward Trevy. "Bind his hands and feet."

Trevy picked up the tape and slowly walked toward Cruz. He held out his hands in front of him.

"Behind your back," Razor instructed.

Reluctantly Cruz obeyed, and Trevy walked behind him to do the binding. She rested her forehead against the strong muscles of his shoulders for a moment as despair washed over her. They weren't going to survive this. First Ceci was going to die. Then Cruz. Then her. She wound the tape around his wrists, careful not to make it too tight.

"Give yourself up. It's the only way," Cruz said.

Instead of answering, Razor slid the blade down the side of Ceci's neck, drawing blood. Her shrill scream echoed off the walls of the empty warehouse.

"Stop it," Trevy shouted, not sure which of the men she was addressing.

"Then tell me where you hid the money." What could she tell him that would keep him from hurting Ceci again? The truth—that she really didn't know—would only get them all killed.

"If you leave now, we won't stop you," Cruz said. "Just lock us in here with Ceci."

"Wrong answer." He raised his knife and pointed the tip at the corner of Ceci's eye.

"No, no," Ceci pleaded. She struggled to turn her face away. "Tell him, Trevy. Please tell him what he wants to know."

"I can take you to the money." The words were out of Trevy's mouth before she could fully think through the consequences. She knew one thing: She would do anything to stop Razor from hurting Ceci and Cruz. Anything.

"Christ, no." Cruz lunged toward her. With his hands bound behind his back, all he could do was trap her against the empty metal shelves. "Don't do this, Trevy," he whispered into her hair with an urgency that shot through her like an electric shock.

She wrapped her arms around him to steady them both and then stepped away. "We'll need a shovel," she told Razor.

"No problemo," Razor said, his teeth gleaming in the low light. "First tape up his ankles. I don't want him moving around while we're gone. Make it quick."

His knife still pressed to Ceci's throat, Razor waited by the heavy metal door. Ceci's sobs of terror floated on the cold air like low-level static.

"He'll kill you," Cruz whispered when Trevy knelt in front him and slowly wrapped a fat strip of silver tape around his ankles. "You know that, right?"

"I don't care."

"Well, I care." The expression on Cruz's face was explosive. "Give me a chance to get *all* of us out of here alive. That's all I'm asking."

"I'm not going to let him hurt Ceci again. Promise me you'll get her out. I can buy you an hour, maybe two."

"Can't you you're ripping my fucking heart out?"

She straightened and touched her hand to his chest. The fierce pounding of his heart matched her own. She knew exactly how he felt.

"Promise me."

"Anything," he said as if the words were being torn from his throat.

Relief flooded through her. He would save Ceci. And himself. That would have to be enough. For a moment, she rested her forehead against the warmth of his chest and breathed in his scent. "I love you," she whispered, sending the words straight to his strongly beating heart. He stiffened for a moment and she wondered if her words had shocked him. Well, it didn't matter. She wanted him to know. "I'd give anything to have more time with you. But not if it means letting Razor hurt anyone else."

"Clock's ticking, bitch." Razor's words broke the spell.

Trevy met Cruz's gaze as she pulled away. She could see the fury and helplessness there, the painful vulnerability. But Trevy knew he wouldn't stay that way for long. She could trust him to do what needed to be done.

"She's lying to you," Cruz said. A last ditch effort to control the situation. "I'm the only one who can take you to the money."

"That's the only reason you're still alive, *vato*. Insurance. If the bitch is lying to me, I'll be back. Alone. And then you'd better be ready to deliver."

Trevy shut out all distractions—the sounds of Ceci's terror, Cruz's angry retort—and steeled herself for the ordeal ahead of her. She had to think of a way to keep Razor busy long enough for Cruz to save Ceci. And himself.

THIRTY-THREE

Monday, March 10, 8:45 a.m.

WITH THE STEADY downpour making visibility difficult, Angel exited the rush-hour-choked Beltway for the less congested George Washington Memorial Parkway in northern Virginia. Keeping to the speed limit, she arrived at Reagan National Airport fifteen minutes behind schedule. Not too bad considering the complications along the way. She followed the signs to the short-term parking garage.

After exiting the car, she locked the doors and opened the trunk, then slid the car key into a small magnetic box with a combination lock. A simple but effective theft deterrent for the short amount of time the car—and the bag she was leaving in its trunk—would be left unattended. She picked up the smaller suitcase and, using its trajectory to the ground to cover her movements, attached the magnetic box to the underside of the car.

Wheeling the luggage behind her, she headed for the airport terminal. As she walked, she pulled the throwaway phone out of the large leather bag that hung from her shoulder. Only one number was stored in the memory. She highlighted it and pushed send. At the beep, she left a message.

"Two, seven, zero, five, C-83," she said. Without pausing for a breath, she added, "Seven, thirty-one, fifty-nine"—the safety code *El Trece* required—before ending the call. Then she keyed in another phone number. "Lot C, space 83," she recited.

With the phone dangling from her fingers, she timed it so that she crossed in front of a shuttle bus just as it pulled away from the curb. She collided with a businessman, who dropped his leather briefcase and caught her by the shoulders to keep her from falling backward into the path of the bus. At exactly the right moment, she dropped the phone into his coat pocket while he made a show of apologizing and ogling her cleavage. The bus slid by with mere inches to spare. She walked to the cab stand. One more task to go. Razor was waiting for his money.

At 8:50 a.m., a voice mail message icon appeared on his phone screen. As he played back the message, Miguel Navarro climbed into the large black Mercedes sedan parked at the curb, a block away from the State Department. He relaxed slightly when a woman's voice repeated the safety code followed by the drop-off location. The most unpredictable part of the transaction had gone as planned. Nothing would go wrong now. He cranked the ignition, turned on the windshield wipers, and pulled into traffic, heading for K Street and the Whitehurst Freeway.

But a slight uneasiness still played along his nerve endings. He had plenty of time to retrieve the cash from Reagan National, which was relatively close to the State Department. Plenty of time. Then he would join his boss and Sr. del Fuego on del Fuego's private plane for a trip to Mexico City. They were scheduled for takeoff at 11:30 from the more distant Dulles International Airport, where Sr. del Fuego's jet was hangared.

Despite the rain, traffic was moving at a steady speed once he crossed the Potomac River and merged onto the George Washington Memorial Parkway. It wasn't long before he parked his Mercedes near, but not too near, space C-83 in the short-term parking garage.

The rental car was exactly where he'd expected it and yet he couldn't shake the lingering feeling of anxiety. Had del Fuego been a little too eager to provide his private jet for the trip to Mexico City? Without looking around, he walked purposefully over to the small sedan. Reaching under the rear bumper, he retrieved the magnetic box and removed the key to open the trunk.

Just as expected, a large black canvas suitcase was inside. He heaved it from the trunk—thirty-three pounds of one-hundred-dollar bills plus five pounds of canvas, metal frame, and wheels—and set it on the ground before returning the key to its hiding place under the bumper. Then, wheeling the suitcase behind him, he strode away from the rental car.

After stowing the suitcase in the trunk of his Mercedes alongside a carry-on bag filled with a change of clothes and his diplomatic papers, he paid cash to exit the short-term parking garage and headed back into the rain toward Dulles International Airport.

He tapped his fingers on the leather-wrapped steering wheel as he waited for the rush of accomplishment that usually accompanied a successful delivery. But it didn't come. Instead his unease grew stronger with each passing mile. Paranoia? With a sigh of annoyance, he keyed a query into his car GPS. It would be foolish to ignore his instincts when they were telling him something about this entire operation was off.

A quick glance at the screen revealed exactly what he was searching for: a suburban shopping center with a supermarket, coffee shop, local shipping store, restaurants, and other small businesses. Two miles later he exited the highway. This little detour would delay his arrival at Dulles by a quarter of an hour, but he could always blame his tardiness on the weather.

THIRTY-FOUR

BOUND HAND AND foot, freeing himself from the restraints the second time proved more time-consuming. Cruz's lower arms were covered with nicks and scrapes from the sharp edge of the bay door handle he used to cut through the duct tape. The fear and anger riding him had made him clumsy and careless. Cruz stripped the tape from his ankles and kicked at the locked metal door even though he knew it was futile. There was no way he could bust the heavy-duty padlock that clanked against the other side of the door like a taunt with every strike of his booted foot. With one final frustrated kick, he turned away. Ceci lay motionless on the floor where Razor had dumped her. At least she'd stopped crying. Thank God.

"We're never getting out of here, are we?" she said in a flat voice filled with resignation.

"Let's get your hands free."

Dim gray light slunk into the warehouse through a small crack of space above the loading bay door. He crouched down next to Ceci and gently rolled her onto her stomach to examine the duct tape wrapping her wrists. He used his nail to scrape enough of an edge loose so that he could pinch the end of the tape between his thumb and finger. Then he pulled and the tape yielded with a scratchy sound as the adhesive stretched and tore. "I'll get us out of here," he told her.

Cruz repeated his actions to remove the binding from her ankles. When Ceci still didn't move, he repositioned her onto her back so that he could make a better assessment of her physical condition.

"It's okay," she said, her brown eyes flat with resignation. "You don't have to lie to me. I know we're going to die in here."

Her words floored him. Ceci was smart. The only way they were getting out of the warehouse was when Razor returned. Trevy would never forgive him for failing, but she'd asked the impossible of him. God damn it. How had he let this happen?

I love you. He could still feel her words ricocheting around inside him like a hollow-point bullet, damaging everything it touched. He already knew what it was like to lose a piece of his heart, and he did not want to face that pain again. Rage swelled inside him as he remembered the helplessness and fear he'd felt as a child when he learned that his mother, who had given everything to help others, was never coming home. This situation was different, but his feelings were exactly the same.

Angry, helpless, abandoned. The three emotions he'd spent his entire adult life avoiding. And loving Trevy Barlow had landed him right back where he'd started all those years ago. Cruz lowered himself to the floor next to Ceci and held out his hand. After a moment, she sat up and placed her small hand in his. A reminder he wasn't alone. His anger began to fade and a sense of calm settled over him. He knew it was temporary, but he eased into it. Trevy had given him this chance to save Ceci. And himself. He wanted to live up to her expectations. That meant shutting her out of his mind so that he could focus on keeping his promise.

The sound of rain on the roof was almost comforting. After a few minutes, a pool of water formed in one corner of the room, near the back wall. He watched as a wet trail slowly traced a crooked line across the cement floor.

"Any chance you have a cell phone hidden in one of those pockets?" he said, pointing at the colorful zippers lining the front and sides of her heavy winter coat.

She shook her head. A wry smile curved her lips for an instant.

"That's what I thought," Cruz said with a matching smile. He needed to keep Ceci away from dark thoughts. The best way to do that was to keep her talking. "How did you end up with Razor? Did he grab you when you left school the other day?"

"No, I went to Rosa's apartment. I knew she'd let me stay with her, no questions. I had to get away for a few days. My mother, the way she looks at me now. It's…suffocating."

"Rosa handed you over to Razor?"

"No, not on purpose. Yesterday she told me I had to leave before she went to the community center. Rosa said she'd walk with me to make sure I got home safe, but GQ was waiting outside her apartment building. He said he'd give us a ride to wherever we wanted to go."

"But he lied," Cruz guessed.

"Yeah, he drove us here."

"To the warehouse? You and Rosa?"

Ceci nodded. "Angel and Bandit met us with a truck. Pallets of dog food were stacked inside the warehouse." So that was how the contraband cigarettes were brought into the city. Cruz made a mental note as Ceci continued, "They were too heavy to carry, so we had to unpack them and load the boxes into the truck."

"How long did that take?"

"At least an hour. Maybe more. There were a lot of boxes. I thought GQ would let Rosa and me go home after Bandit and Angel left with the truck, but he took us to a motel. Nothing was going to happen to us if we cooperated, right? He promised to let us go in the morning. But then Razor came back and everything changed. He told GQ he was holding Trevy Barlow hostage until she gave him the money my sister stole. He never mentioned you."

"I'll bet."

"Rosa and I were going to sneak away as soon as Razor and GQ passed out for the night. But Razor never went to sleep. Then this morning, he told GQ to take Rosa with him when he left to pick up Angel. Razor made me come with him in Trevy's car."

Trevy. Just the sound of her name threatened to drag him back down into that pit of helpless rage. He forced himself to focus on their surroundings instead of entertaining useless emotions. He noticed the water on the floor had reached them, and shifted his boot to keep it from getting wet.

"Do you know where Lola hid the money?"

"No." Ceci frowned. "I didn't even know Lola stole money from Razor. But I think Bandit must have been looking for it too. The day before Lola's funeral, he made me let him into our apartment so he could search through all of her things. Why does Razor think Trevy has the money?"

"My best guess is that he and Bandit have eliminated every other possibility. That leaves Trevy as their last hope."

"Does she know where the money is?" Ceci asked.

"No." Cruz hated to burst that small bubble of hope in Ceci's voice, but lying to the kid wasn't going to help them escape.

"I wonder where Lola hid it. "

"Me too." All he knew for sure was that Trevy had no idea where it was. She hadn't even known she was being used to ferry information between Miguel Navarro and the gang. Did she have a plan beyond giving Cruz and Ceci a chance to escape? If not, why the hell had she insisted on the shovel?

"I would have put it in the bank so nobody but me could get to it." Ceci said, interrupting his train of thought.

He turned Ceci's words over in his mind and dismissed them. Opening a bank account would raise too many questions. "Lola wouldn't have wanted to draw attention to herself or the money. And she would have avoided creating a public record of the funds."

Cruz tried to imagine what he would do if he were a pregnant seventeen-year-old with ten thousand stolen dollars. He would want a place that was secure, but easily accessible for the right people. What kind of place would fit those requirements? Not the Sanchez apartment. Not a bank. Was that where Trevy was taking Razor? To a bank? Did she plan to pay him off with her own money?

Except the shovel didn't fit into that narrative. Frustrated, he got up and paced the perimeter of the room. Twice. Sometimes physical activity helped when he hit a mental dead-end.

"What about a friend?" he asked, looking over at Ceci. "Does she have a friend she would trust with that kind of money?"

Ceci started to shake her head and then her eyes widened. The same thought was forming in Cruz's head, so he wasn't surprised when she said, "She trusted Trevy."

Why did all paths lead back to Trevy? "If I were your sister, I would have trusted her too."

"If she gives it to Razor, he won't have to come back for us." Ceci sounded hopeful.

Cruz stared at the girl, whose pleading eyes begged for him to agree. He thought about what Trevy had said before she left with Razor. *I can buy you an hour, maybe two.* The ache in his head was making it hard to think, but he closed his eyes and forced himself to concentrate.

"Trevy doesn't know where Lola stashed the money. She warned us that Razor would be coming back." He pictured her leaving. She hadn't looked back as she followed Razor out of the warehouse. A slender slice of gray sky had been visible in front of them, the little orange BMW on the horizon, parked in front of the loading dock.

He followed the trail of water back to its source. The orange BMW. A kernel of an idea began to take shape in his brain. Lola had a key to the vintage coupe. Access. And since part of her job was to retrieve the disposable cell phones from the car, she had a reason to access it that wouldn't be questioned by anyone involved in the smuggling op.

"Lola hid the money in Trevy's car," he said, turning to Ceci. "I'd bet my life on it."

The clock was ticking. He had to get them out of the warehouse before Razor returned. Trevy's life depended upon it. All their lives did. He noticed the puddle of water in the corner was still expanding. He traced the wet path with his eyes, following it under the shelves, then up the wall to the roof. There was a leak near the corner. The damaged area had been patched with a flimsy—and now soaking wet—piece of plywood. He studied the metal shelves anchored to the wall.

"Ceci, come here."

The urgency in his voice startled her. "What is it?" she asked.

"There's a hole in the roof." He pointed to the shoddy patch job.

She jumped up and slowly crossed the room to stand beside him. "Can we get out that way?"

"Only one way to find out. Ladies first." He cupped his hands together. "Do you think you can climb up to the top shelf?"

Ceci put her foot in his hands and he boosted her up. She scrambled to the top shelf with the agility of a gymnast. Since the shelves were built to hold heavy equipment, he didn't have too much trouble climbing up behind her. He tugged at the edges of the plywood patch where it was fastened to the underlay, but the nails held. Using his fist, he punched the rotting wood until it split. All he could think about was Trevy…and how much time had passed. Splinters bloodied his knuckles, but he kept at it until the patch was torn away and he could see gray sky through the hole in the roof.

Ceci let out a little cheer.

"Do you think you can squeeze through?" Cruz eyed the opening. It was smaller than he'd hoped, but he lifted Ceci up so she could grab hold of the crumbling underlay.

"It's too little," she said after several attempts to get her head and both shoulders through the opening. Cold, stinging rain drenched them.

"Try again. Hold both arms over your head." He lowered Ceci so she could reposition herself and then lifted her again. At the same time, he tried to puzzle out where Trevy had taken Razor.

Not her apartment. A place where a person could dig a hole to hide something. An isolated place, but not too far off the beaten track.

Ceci kicked him in the shoulder as she struggled to get enough leverage to push her shoulders through the hole in the roof. He steadied her. *Come on. Come on.*

A place Trevy knew well. An image formed in his mind. Montrose Park.

If he could get Ceci out of the warehouse, she could go for

help.

"I'm stuck," Ceci said, her muffled voice drawing his attention back to her. She was wedged in tight.

"Twist a bit. I won't let you fall."

"I can't," she said after more straining.

Cruz hated that word. But it wasn't the girl's fault. Gently, he pulled her free and set her down beside him.

"It's okay." He shed his coat and wrapped it around the wet, shivering girl. "We'll think of something else." But he didn't believe it.

And neither did she. He watched the hope in her dark eyes sputter and die.

THIRTY-FIVE

Monday, March 10, 9:13 a.m.

"STOP HERE," ANGEL told the taxi driver as they turned onto Eastern Avenue. Razor's black SUV was parked on the next block. She paid the fare and climbed out. Wind and rain buffeted her as she reached into the open doorway to tug out the black suitcase. She pushed wet hair out of her eyes and wheeled the bag up on the sidewalk.

Like the mannerless thug he was, Razor stayed behind the wheel and watched her from the shelter of the truck. Or so she thought until she pulled open the back door. GQ was behind the wheel. Even more disturbing, Rosa was in the back. Keeping her face carefully blank, she heaved the suitcase onto the seat beside the teen girl. *Finish the job*, she reminded herself and slammed the door. She climbed into the front seat.

"Where's Razor?" she asked, trying to keep the question casual.

"You got the money?" GQ asked. He put the Navigator in drive and pulled into traffic.

"It's all there. Minus the ten thousand," she answered, even though she wanted to press him about Razor's whereabouts. This end of the op had gone off the rails in her absence. She just wasn't sure how much it mattered. "Don't you trust me?"

"Maybe," he grunted. GQ wasn't born yesterday. But he also wasn't as smart as he thought he was. "Where's Bandit?"

"At the airport, waiting to ditch the rental car," she lied. She pulled a disposable cell phone out of her jacket pocket. "I need to tell him where to meet us. Where's Razor?"

Angel turned to look at Rosa, whose eyes were like a scared rabbit's. The girl's gaze flicked to GQ and then widened in alarm. When Angel whipped around to see what the moron was doing, she caught him staring at his cell phone while the Navigator drifted across the yellow lines at forty miles per hour in the pouring rain. She yanked on the steering wheel just in time to keep them from crashing into oncoming traffic.

"What the hell, GQ?" Angel said, snatching the phone out of his hand. "Are you trying to kill us?"

She read the text message that had distracted him. It was from Razor. He wanted GQ to meet him at R and Thirty-First Street in twenty minutes. With a shovel?

"Give me my phone."

She slapped it back into his hand. A few moments later, GQ pulled into a no-name motel at the edge of the city limits. He handed her a key card. "Room 253. I'll be back in an hour with Razor. Bandit better be here. You and Rosa too."

Yeah, not likely, she thought as she pulled Rosa away from the SUV and headed for the stairs at the far end of the two-story building. She planned to make her exit as soon as GQ was out of sight. Razor was no longer her problem. Let Cruz Larsen sweep up the crumbs. Then Rosa grabbed Angel by the arm. "We need to call that FBI agent. I still have the card with his phone number on it."

"Forget it, Rosa. Go home and stay away from the Chingazos Locos." She shook the girl off and looked at her watch. If she was lucky, she'd be able to get a cab to Dulles Airport in time to watch the rest of her team bust Rafael Montoyez's ass and shut down the diplomat's cash pipeline to the bad guys.

"Razor's got Trevy and Ceci. He's keeping them in the warehouse until Trevy gives him the money Lola stole. We gotta call Agent Larsen."

Oh shit. She pulled out her throwaway phone and shoved it into Rosa's hand. "Call 911."

Rosa took the phone and punched in the numbers. "Where are

you going?" she called when Angel kept walking away from the motel.

"To find Razor. GQ is meeting him at R and Thirty-First Streets with a shovel. Tell the dispatcher everything you know. *Everything.*"

The last of Miguel's tension drained away as he flashed his diplomatic credentials at the Dulles Airport security guard and drove into the private parking lot reserved for passengers flying on charter jets. Sr. del Fuego's assistant was there waiting with an umbrella as he stepped out of his car. He tossed him the keys. "My luggage is in the trunk," he said, moving toward the lounge area of the private hangar.

Security was less stringent for passengers on private or charter jets. That, combined with his diplomatic credentials, guaranteed that his luggage would not be searched before it was loaded into the cargo bay of Sr. del Fuego's Gulfstream.

"Is this your suitcase, sir?" del Fuego's assistant called out as he pulled the large black bag from the car.

"Yes, of course," Miguel said, trying to step around the assistant, but the dolt wouldn't let him pass. Instead he held out a folded piece of paper and said, "I have a warrant to search your luggage. I'm Agent Gallo, Bureau of Alcohol, Tobacco, and Firearms."

Angrily, Miguel snatched the warrant from his hand. *So the assistant was an undercover agent? Had del Fuego played him?* "Your government will regret this. That is a promise." And perhaps del Fuego would as well.

He stuffed the warrant into his jacket pocket. Another agent joined Gallo and said, "Please come with me, sir."

He followed him inside the hangar to a small, windowless office.

Rafael Montoyez was waiting there in the room. And he was in a full-blown rage. His canvas suitcases lay open on a table.

"Miguel, *Madre de Dios,*" Rafael shouted as soon as he stepped into the room, "where have you been? Get the ambassador on the phone." He waved a crumpled document at the agents. "This is an outrage. An act of hostility against the Spanish government!"

Miguel felt the same searing anger that was turning the trade attaché's face the color of a ripe tomato, but he forced his shoulders to relax as Agent Gallo wheeled his suitcase into the room and set it on the table next to Montoyez's luggage. He was protected by diplomatic immunity, he reminded himself. The U.S. government officials couldn't lay a finger on him. He had made sure of that.

The ATF agents unzipped his suitcase, expecting to find stacks of hundred-dollar bills. But when Agent Gallo reached into the heavy case, he pulled out toiletries, energy bars, candy, even a handful of magazines and children's books. "What the hell?" he said, dumping the contents on the floor.

It took every ounce of Miguel Navarro's self-control to keep a smile from curving his lips. "For an orphanage in Mexico City," he said and stooped to gather the items from the floor.

¡Bietan jarrai! He looked to his boss for some small sign of approval. Gratitude, even. Hadn't he done everything he'd been asked? And more.

THIRTY-SIX

Monday, March 10, 9:42 a.m.

CRUZ AND CECI stood in the warehouse, defeat holding them quiet, when they heard the muffled sound of voices on the other side of the warehouse door. Alarmed, Cruz positioned himself near the door with Ceci behind him. Had the Chingazos returned?

Trevy. His gut gave a sharp twist, but he ignored it. There was still Ceci to protect.

The sound of metal snapping as the bolt was cut was all the warning he had before the door rattled open and a SWAT team stormed in, weapons at ready. Cruz slowly set his hands on his head and identified himself. "Cecilia Sanchez is behind me. We're unarmed." He didn't know how it had come to pass, but the MPD had arrived to rescue them.

Bringing up the rear, Lou Alvarado waved the paramedics inside. They quickly ushered Ceci to the waiting ambulance. They would give her a quick exam and then send her home to her mother. The rain had let up, but gray clouds still covered the sky, and Cruz could only guess at the time. Had he used up the two-hour window Trevy had promised him?

"You should get that hard head checked out," Alvarado said.

"Later." He jogged toward the cluster of emergency vehicles, his task force partner by his side. "How'd you find us?"

"Rosa Reyes saved your ass with a 911 call. Although she neglected to mention you. Where's Trevy Barlow?"

"Razor's got her. Did Rosa tell you anything else?"

"Just something about a Chingazos rendezvous on R and Thirty-First Streets. We sent a couple of patrol cars to check it out."

"Christ, I knew it. Trevy took Razor to Montrose Park," he said, filling Alvarado in on the situation with the missing money. "There's an entrance to the park trails on R Street near Thirty-First. We need to find her before Razor hurts her." Or worse.

Alvarado called the dispatcher while Cruz brought the SWAT team up to speed. Minutes later they were racing across the city, the rapid response unit in the lead, sirens blaring. Two blocks away from the park, the sirens cut off and the SWAT unit veered right to approach from the east.

"Take Thirty-First Street," Cruz said. "It's closer."

Up ahead, two cruisers with flashing blue lights had already established the perimeter, and another tactical team was gearing up. Cruz was out of the car before Alvarado could put it in Park. Holding up his FBI badge, he ran past the uniformed officers to the staging area. The sight of Razor's black Lincoln Navigator, parked curbside near the entrance to the running trails, told him everything he needed to know. Trevy was somewhere in the park.

With a cold-blooded killer.

"Hold up, Agent Larsen," the SWAT team commander ordered. Cruz ignored him and kept going. GQ was sitting in the driver's seat while Angel stood in the street, her arm braced against the car door to keep the kid from closing it. They were arguing so intensely that Cruz was able to get fairly close before Angel noticed him. Was he imagining the relief that flashed across her face for a microsecond before it was replaced with a frown?

"Where are they?" Cruz asked. He swiveled his head to sweep the area. Parked cars lined one side of R Street. Trevy's orange BMW should be in the vicinity.

A patrolman came up behind Cruz. "You people need to leave the area," he said in a no-nonsense tone. GQ nodded his head and tried to pull the door shut. "Agent Larsen, Captain Franklin wants to speak to you."

Angel turned and leaned her weight against the open door of

the SUV to keep the gangbanger from clearing the zone. What agenda was the undercover agent working now? Why was she escalating instead of retreating? Whatever. Cruz didn't have time for her games. Not when Trevy's life was on the line. He narrowed his eyes, ready to burn her cover on the spot, when she said to the MPD officer, "It's a free country. I can stand wherever I want."

Did she want to get herself arrested?

GQ cranked the ignition. "I don't want no trouble."

And then the obvious answer hit him between the eyes like a well-aimed two-by-four. That's exactly what she wanted. To be taken into custody so she could extract herself from the situation, pulling GQ out of the game at the same time.

The officer took the bait. "Shut off the car, sir. Come with me. You too, ma'am."

"I didn't do nothing," GQ protested.

"Out of the car, now," the officer ordered.

Angel grabbed GQ by the arm and pulled him from the seat. He stumbled into the street in a flurry of Spanglish curses and denials. Cruz stepped between the Navigator and the car parked in front of it. From the sidewalk, he had a better view of the parked vehicles. No sign of the orange BMW. Did that mean he was too late? Was Razor heading back to the warehouse this very minute, alone?

It wouldn't be the first time someone had disappeared in the narrow strip of wilderness that cut through the middle of the city, only to be found months later by a jogger or a dog walker. Only this wasn't someone. This was Trevy. A chill chased down his spine and he turned, fists clenched, ready to beat the truth out of GQ if necessary. He took two steps toward the trio. The MPD officer had ordered both gang members to lie on the ground. GQ had already been cuffed and Angel was kicking up such a fuss the officer was having trouble tightening the restraints around her wrists. Christ.

"Where's Razor?" Cruz asked again, kneeling beside her.

"I don't know what you're talking about," she said, finally giving up the fight. She rested her cheek against the wet pavement and looked up at him. Then she flicked her gaze toward the end of the street. When Cruz looked in that direction, he instantly saw what he'd been looking for. Near the end of the block, the orange roof of the small BMW was barely visible over the front hood of the white Ford F150 parked behind it.

They were still here.

The MPD officer yanked GQ to his feet. Cruz rose and grabbed the front of the gangbanger's jacket, pulling the kid onto his toes. "Where did Razor take Trevy Barlow?"

"I don't got to tell you nothing," GQ said and then clamped his mouth shut, a *fuck-you* expression written across his face.

The SWAT team captain joined them in time to hear GQ exercising his Fifth Amendment rights. "Get these two out of here. Take them to the station for questioning." He turned to Cruz. "You. Back to the staging area. Unless you'd prefer a trip to the station in the back of a cruiser. Fucking FBI," he added under his breath.

"I think I know where Trevy Barlow took Razor," Cruz said, following the captain back to the staging area. The SWAT team was forming into tactical teams. Alvarado stood nearby, talking to a group of uniformed officers.

Captain Franklin exhaled noisily. "Come with me." He walked over to the snipers, who were studying a map of the park and the running trails. "Tell them," he told Cruz. "And then get a vest. We've got teams in place ready to swarm the park from six entry points. You can join my team as long as you remember who's in charge."

Cruz would have agreed to just about anything to get the team on the move. He told the snipers about the footbridge where he thought Trevy might have led Razor. There was a stretch of lightly wooded land just beyond the bridge. It was just isolated enough that Razor might have believed she'd hidden the money there. And the land backed up to the Dumbarton Oaks' forty acres of gardens, which meant it was Trevy's best hope for a possible escape. If Razor was busy digging for buried treasure, Trevy might have had the chance to get over the fence and onto the private estate.

When the snipers radioed that they were in place, the tactical team entered Montrose Park. The rain had melted the snow from the previous week, but the sloping path was still wet and slippery, slowing the team's progress. It took all Cruz's self-control to follow orders and let the others do their job. Trevy's life depended upon it.

At Franklin's signal, the five-man team paused at a bend in the path. The landscape was familiar to Cruz, and he knew the footbridge was about a thousand yards ahead. He reached for his gun, but his fingers closed on air.

"Why have we stopped?" Cruz asked Franklin while mentally kicking himself for not insisting on a comm unit when the SWAT team member had shoved a flak jacket at him.

"The snipers have visual contact," Captain Franklin told him.

"Is Trevy okay?"

"Healthy enough to dig a hole. She's in a copse of trees on the far side of the footbridge. The target's pointing *your* gun at her while she does the work." Shit, that scumbag had made damn sure that she couldn't escape. Trevy had been right about Razor. The kid was cunning and dangerous as hell. "Our guys are waiting for an opening to take him out."

How long before Razor realized that she could dig all the way to China and he'd still have nothing more than a pile of dirt? Cruz didn't plan on waiting to find out. Every muscle in his body tightened in anticipation of action.

Captain Franklin must have been reading his mind. Or his body language. He narrowed his eyes in warning. "Like I said, let us do our job, Larsen. No interference." Then he signaled the team forward to take cover in a stand of trees across from the footbridge. Cruz could finally see Trevy.

But what he saw didn't make him feel better.

Trevy just kept digging as if her life depended upon it. She was making so much noise with the shovel that there was no way she or Razor would hear the other teams moving in the woods. Then she bent down as if to put more of her weight into the shovel as it bit into the muddy, thawing earth.

Cruz waited, his breath stalled in his throat, for the snipers to take their shot. *C'mon. C'mon.* What were they waiting for?

A crack from a sniper rifle split the air at the same moment

Trevy shoved her body upward in an explosion of motion. She swung the shovel in an arc toward Razor's head. Oh Christ. To hell with orders. Cruz raced toward the footbridge.

The gangbanger dropped to the ground, felled not by the sniper's shot, but the shovel Trevy had swung like a home run champion. She let the shovel fall to the ground, then turned and ran toward the footbridge like the land beneath her feet was turning into air. She was okay. Sweet relief flooded through him.

Blinded by fear and adrenaline, Trevy rocketed into Cruz. He stumbled back a few steps before catching his balance, but not before wrapping her in his arms and pulling her against his body. She lashed out, all sharp elbows and knees. Nothing had ever felt so good.

"Easy, Doc, you're safe. I've got you. You're safe now."

She went slack in his arms. She was breathing hard, her heart pounding against him. And then the trembling set in. "Cruz?"

"Oh God, Trevy," Cruz repeated. He pressed his palms against her shoulder blades and held her to him, buried his face in her hair and breathed in her scent. He felt her sinking into him as if she wanted to crawl underneath his skin. "Oh God, Trevy."

"Ceci?" she asked, her voice muffled in his chest.

"Ceci should be home by now."

"You saved her. I knew you would. Thank you."

Christ, he didn't deserve her gratitude. It had half killed him when she left the warehouse with Razor. And he wasn't the one who saved Ceci. "Rosa is the person you should be thanking. Not me."

As he explained how Trevy's student had come to their rescue by calling 911, he stroked her cheek, more to comfort himself than her. She turned her face into his palm and whispered, "Teamwork."

"She okay?"

Cruz lifted his head to see Alvarado standing next to them.

"Hell yes," Cruz said. Trevy Barlow was more than okay. She'd been kidnapped, terrorized, and held at gunpoint by a sadistic gangbanger, and she'd saved herself. Him and Ceci too. He tightened his arms around her. "My God, Trevy, I can't believe you took Razor out with a fucking shovel."

She put her hand on his chest and pushed away from him to look up into his eyes.

"I did it for you," Trevy said with a smile that arrowed straight into Cruz's heart.

THIRTY-SEVEN

Sunday, a week later

NINE PAIRS OF eyes were fixed on Trevy Barlow as she stood by the whiteboard at the front of the classroom at the New Hope Community Center. Nine dear, familiar faces.

"Let's get started," she said, dry erase marker in hand. Her eyes caught on the empty desk at the front of the room, and out of habit, she lifted her gaze toward the open doorway, half-expecting Lola Sanchez to come barreling into the classroom five minutes late to take her seat, her high spirits and determination charging the air like a fast-moving storm. The girl's absence was a raw, open wound that would take time to heal. No one wanted to forget her...least of all Trevy, but they could only move forward. She turned to the whiteboard and wrote: Three Branches of U.S. Government. "Who can name them?"

"The do-nothing Congress," Maria called out, making the other girls laugh. She had been out of the hospital for a few days and was still getting used to the cast on her leg.

Trevy smiled and wrote Congress on the board. "Two more. Anyone?"

Rosa raised her hand. That was new. "The president," she said.

"Yes, the president and his administration make up the Executive Branch. Very good. And the last branch?" Facing the white board, she waited for one of the girls to call out an answer. Instead she felt their attention shift to the back of the classroom.

When she glanced over her shoulder, she saw that the girls had all turned in their seats to stare at the open doorway. And the man standing there, arms crossed, his cop eyes sweeping the room for trouble.

Cruz Larsen.

Trevy's heartbeat kicked up at the sight of him. She watched his face tighten as his eyes took in her split lip and the small cut on her cheekbone. She ached from the inside out, but her physical injuries would heal. Until then, she would wear them proudly. A badge of courage.

"Sorry I'm late," he said, his deep voice cutting through the nervous chatter as the girls remembered the last time he had visited their classroom. She could almost feel the swell of fear as they exchanged glances and braced themselves for more bad news.

"Is it Angel?" Rosa asked, glancing from Trevy to Cruz, then back to Trevy. "I haven't seen her since Monday."

"No, it's not Angel," Trevy said. "Agent Larsen isn't here to investigate a crime. I invited him." She knew how unsettled the girls were by what had happened, and she hoped talking to Cruz would ease their fears.

"That's right, I'm here to answer questions, not ask them." He uncrossed his arms and gestured toward the hallway. "And I brought someone with me." A few moments later, Ceci Sanchez walked into the classroom.

The girls left their desks to flock around Lola's sister. Cruz looked over their heads at Trevy, and a slow smile spread across his face when their eyes locked. *Oh, my.* Trevy touched a hand to her chest to still the fluttering of her heart.

When the girls had settled down enough to continue, Cruz and Ceci joined Trevy at the front of the classroom. "Don't hold back, ladies. I'm at your mercy," Cruz said.

"Do you know what happened to Angel?" Maria called out.

"Here's what I can tell you," he said. "Angel turned herself in to Immigration and Customs Enforcement on Monday. In exchange for her testimony against the Chingazos Locos gang leaders, all criminal charges have been dropped. For her protection, she entered the Witness Protection Program, though, so she won't be able to contact any of you."

"Not even after Razor and GQ go to trial?" Rosa asked.

"I'm afraid not. She'll be given a new identity to ensure her safety. After their trials, she's agreed to return to Mexico."

"What about our safety?" Maria wanted to know. "Getting shot once was one time too many. What happens when Razor and GQ get out of jail?"

"No chance of that," Cruz said. "At least not any time soon. They're both being held without bail. It'll probably take a year for their trials to get on the court docket. And there are enough criminal charges between the two of them to keep them in prison for several lifetimes."

"And Bandit too," Ceci said, even though no one had asked. Tears welled up in Rosa's eyes before she dashed them away with her fingers. Bandit had confessed to killing Samantha Vega and would be sentenced next month. He would be in prison for decades.

"Without Razor, the Chingazos Locos gang has disbanded and the police have increased patrols in LDR territory," Trevy added. "That should help keep you safe."

Ceci nodded her head. "And the New Hope Community Center received an anonymous donation of ten thousand dollars in Lola's name to install security cameras and fix the broken garage door."

It was news to Trevy. She had been there when the police found and retrieved the money Lola had stashed in the spare tire of the orange BMW. But she hadn't known about the donation. She shifted her gaze to Cruz for confirmation.

His eyes were already locked on her face. Hidden in that hard, green gaze, she detected a hint of uncertainty. He was waiting for a sign of approval, she realized.

Trevy touched her hand to her heart.

For the longest moment, Cruz didn't move a muscle. Then he tapped two fingers against his chest in reply and Trevy felt the heat of the gesture as if he'd reached across the space that separated them.

"Will there be a trial for Lola's murder?" another one of the girls asked, drawing Trevy's attention back to them.

"Miguel Navarro was arrested in Mexico City. He's fighting extradition, but the evidence is on our side," Cruz assured them, glossing over the fact that Spain was still fuming about the covert investigation of their diplomats and ATF was in hot water for another bungled sting operation to the tune of two million dollars. The money had vanished. No one knew where it was, and Miguel wasn't talking. "It may take awhile, but Navarro will be extradited to the United States to stand trial for Lola's murder. Justice isn't always swift."

And, perhaps, not always fair, Trevy reflected. Rafael had been recalled to Madrid. His association with Miguel had blemished his reputation, damaged his career.

Ceci cleared her throat. "Justice won't bring Lola back. I know she didn't always make the best choices, but she was my sister and I loved her. She didn't deserve what happened to her, and it kills me that there's nothing I can do to make it right."

"You can help us here," Trevy said. "I think Lola would have liked that."

"*Si, si,*" the girls called out. "Join us."

Rosa stood and led Ceci to an empty desk. "This was Lola's desk. She'd want you to sit here. She was so proud of you. She used to brag about how you were going to go to college someday."

"I am," Ceci said, nodding her head as she sat in Lola's seat. "I promise. For me. And now for Lola too."

Trevy smiled at Ceci and walked over to stand by Cruz. "Let's give Agent Larsen a round of applause to thank him for stopping by tonight."

The patter of clapping filled the room until Cruz held up both hands. "I'm not quite finished yet. I need a minute alone with your teacher," he said, reaching for her.

Too surprised to resist, Trevy glanced over her shoulder at the girls as Cruz tugged her toward the door. "Read the next section of the handout. I'll be right back."

Out in the hallway, Cruz skimmed the tips of his fingers across her bruised cheek. "I wish I could have prevented this."

"I know." She cupped her hands around the strong contours of his face. His pale green eyes held a mixture of pain and longing. An echo of the same emotions she felt swirling in every cell of her body.

"The past few weeks have been crazy. We did this backward. All the hard stuff first. Will you give me shot at normal? You know, dinner and a movie, walks in the park, sappy cards, the works?"

He trailed a finger down the length of her neck and rested it against the hollow of her throat where her pulse beat in quick, fluttery strokes.

Then he lifted his gaze to her eyes. "I love you, Trevy."

His lips quirked up on one side, a crooked grin that shot straight into Trevy's heart. She held his gaze for a long moment without speaking. His eyes were hard to read, as always. But something there promised love and laughter. And probably a fair share of frustration and occasional disagreements. Life wouldn't always be peaceful with him, but it would be a happy sort of chaos.

"I love you, Cruz, just the way you are."

"Then how about dinner tonight, Doc? I know a great French restaurant."

"Yes."

"Yes?"

"Yes to everything," she said as she slid her bruised lips over his and inhaled his essence. "But what if I've developed a taste for crazy?"

He laughed against her mouth. "Then I'm definitely your man."

The girls stood in the doorway, cheering and clapping.

Cruz deepened the kiss, and for a moment, her world shrank down to this single point in time before expanding outward like an exploding star with more love than two hearts could contain.

Everything was going to be all right.

ACKNOWLEDGMENTS

Special thanks to my mom, Allana Deborah Sowinski, for sharing your love of reading with me, and encouraging me to keep on keeping on through the highs and lows on the way to publishing this book.

To my sisters Susan Atkins Yoo and Andréa Atkins Caldini, thank you for your support and willingness to read every version of *Broken Places*. I'm so lucky to have sisters who are also my best friends.

I owe Walter Sowinski a huge debt of gratitude for his brilliant eye for composition and the crash course in graphic design.

To my Kiss and Thrill blog sisters—Rachel Grant, Sarah Andre, Gwen Hernandez, Carey Baldwin, Diana Belchase, Manda Collins, Lena Diaz, and Sharon Wray—thank you for your friendship, generosity of spirit, and excellent good cheer. I'm in awe of your talents, creative minds, and fierce business smarts. I've learned so much from all of you.

Rachel Grant, thank you for contacting me off-loop back in 2011 to suggest trading manuscript pages. Saying yes was one of the smartest moves I've made in the new millennium. The reasons are too numerous to list here, except to say you are an extraordinary friend.

Sarah Andre, thank you for the insightful comments that helped me fine-tune this story. I couldn't have asked for a more stunning and poised representative last summer when you stood at the podium to accept the Golden Heart® Award for *Broken Places* on my behalf. I still owe you Champagne!

A grateful shout-out to Gwen Hernandez for sharing her oasis of calm and her mad Scrivener skills (which I used to format this book).

Many thanks to my editor Angela Polidoro for the nuanced and thoughtful editorial suggestions, and cover designer Naomi Ruth

Raine for giving my book a face.

To Macarena Carrasco and Thomas Bishop, thank you for checking over the Spanish dialogue. Holly van Schaick kindly shared the basics of what paramedics say and do when they are treating a gunshot wound at the scene. Any mistakes are mine.

To my husband David and kids M and C, you're my blue sky.

To my readers, thank you for taking a chance on a debut novel! I hope you loved reading *Broken Places* as much as I loved writing it! Please take a moment to write a review and let me know how you liked it. All honest reviews are welcome and appreciated.

ABOUT THE AUTHOR

Krista Hall won the 2013 Golden Heart® Award for *Broken Places*. She lives in the mid-Atlantic with her family. You can find her online at KristaHall.com and on the romantic suspense blog KissandThrill.com. You can follow her on Twitter @kristahall_ and Facebook.com/KristaHallWriter.

For news on upcoming books or sales, sign up for Krista's low volume newsletter by visiting her website at KristaHall.com. Thank you!